The Burke Foundation

The Burke Foundation

Anthony McCandless

MACMILLAN

ISBN 0 333 35899 6

First published 1985 by
MACMILLAN LONDON LIMITED
4 Little Essex Street London WC2R 3LF
and Basingstoke

Associated companies in Auckland, Delhi, Dublin,
Gaborone, Hamburg, Harare, Hong Kong, Johannesburg,
Kuala Lumpur, Lagos, Manzini, Melbourne, Mexico City,
Nairobi, New York, Singapore and Tokyo

Phototypeset by Wyvern Typesetting Limited, Bristol

Printed in Great Britain
at the Pitman Press, Bath

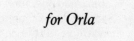

for Orla

Author's note

There was a major commando operation at Commachio in the spring of 1945. Some of it was fought in much the way described in this story. Some of it wasn't. None of it was fought by No. 49 Royal Marine Commando, which did not exist, or by its members mentioned, who did not exist, either.

They, like everyone else in the book other than a few public figures who appear briefly, are fictitious.

Some of the organisations mentioned did exist, among them 162 Turcoman Division of the German Army. For the account of the British insistence upon the repatriation from Italy to the Soviet Union of the survivors of this surrendered Division, of what happened to them when they got there, and of the connived-at evasions that saved some of them from extinction. I have drawn extensively from Nicholas Tolstoy's *Victims of Yalta* (Hodder & Stoughton, 1978). I gratefully acknowledge my debt to him.

The incident on page 165 is described in *Leap in the Dark* published by Collins in 1980. The briefcase Vlado Bilic is seen carrying on page 246 is presumably the one he placed in the cache at the Villa Ribar, also described there.

PROLOGUE

Commonwealth war graves commission cemetery, Stressio, Italy

AMONG the trimmed lawns and the blossoming oleanders the rows of
identical headstones were aligned as for a ceremonial parade, precisely
measured intervals between each, dressed by the right. It was unlike a
parade of the living in that placings in the ranks were haphazard.
Physical height or military seniority had not been a consideration when
the graves were filled. Order of burial had been determined by the
random chance of the date of death in battle.

The bodies of privates and gunners and marines lay side by side with
those of corporals and captains and colonels, intermingled in a posthu-
mous democracy emphasised by the uniform simplicity of the inscrip-
tions on the headstones: service number, rank, name, regiment or corps,
place of death, date of death.

At the end of the fifth row was HBL 1296. LIEUTENANT HUGO
SEPELOV BURKE. 49 ROYAL MARINE COMMANDO. COMMACHIO. 2 April
1945.

Ulick Burke, who had brought flowers to lay on the grave that he had
not before seen of the father whom he had never known, took them away
again and, later, threw them out of the window of his car. Unless the
inscription was inaccurate, which seemed unlikely, Hugo Burke had
been killed twelve months and eight days before his son Ulick was born.
This, too, seemed unlikely.

PART ONE

1944–5: Central Mediterranean. Yugoslavia, Italy

CHAPTER ONE

Montenegro, Autumn 1944

The Forward Observation Officer said, 'Up fifty,' seemingly aloud to himself, in fact into his throat microphone. He looked carefully through binoculars at the edge of a small olive-grove fifty yards ahead of where the first sighting shot had landed.

Laing said: 'Strongpoints in the sawmill, right front, and in the hospital, centre front, sir. They've a string of posts linking them, in those houses and gardens. There's a block on that ridge to the left, ten o'clock from the centre of the hospital roof, covering where the coast road comes into the town. The block's also used as their jumping-off place for replenishment parties for the hill-forts.'

The Force Commander, sitting like the others with his back to the rock-face, a map spread on his knees, took in what he was being told with professional speed. He stared appraisingly through his field-glasses at what he had been advised to look at. He glanced down from time to time to relate what he could see with what was marked on the map on his lap.

'Partisans?' he said at last.

'They're spread about around the sawmill and the hospital.'

Laing began to point out the Partisan positions one by one. He paused when a familiar sound obtruded. An echoing bang from the direction of the gun position hidden far behind the hills to the rear, a fluttering whisper in the air above, a protracted whistle growing to a shriek as the shell gathered momentum on its downward trajectory, and a second resonant bang, with flash and smoke accompaniment, from the olive-grove.

'Smack on,' said the Forward Observation Officer. His headset insulated him from Laing's briefing of the Brigadier, in which for the moment he was in any case uninterested. He was absorbed in a private little war of his own.

'Sixty-three. Two rounds gunfire. Over,' he said conversationally.

There was a further cluster of eight distant bangs, in two groups of four, from behind the hills. The Brigadier and Laing temporarily gave up their talk and focused their glasses on the olive-plantation, half a mile

3

ahead, two thousand feet below. The hissing, whistling, screeching noise from overhead was repeated, multiplied in volume. Eight closely grouped detonations erupted among the olives. Branches, clods of earth, dust and fragmented stone blew about, hovered, settled. Distant German soldiers, clutching weapons and entrenching-tools, scurried to the shelter of a nearby wrecked house. There was a lively crackle of small-arms fire from a hidden Partisan outpost.

'Sixty-three. Easy shot out. That's smartened up the bastards,' said the Observation Officer with satisfaction. He took off his headset, unclipped the throat microphone and lit a cigarette. Then he resumed his daily task of scrutinising systematically the town of Risan, its defences and its approaches, for suitable targets for the battery of eight 25-pounder gun-howitzers of the Royal Artillery, at present sited on a small upland plain behind the mountains and two miles to his rear. He and his signaller and the commando sub-section guarding them had been in their little eyrie for six days.

It was a visually enchanting eyrie. It was a tiny, protected rock-shelf set in a limestone outcrop high in a roughly crescent-shaped escarpment that loomed over a narrow alluvial plain. On the plain sat Risan, neat and compact, white-walled houses with red-tiled roofs, glimpses of gardens and casuarinas and shrubs, small fishing harbour and market-place, the hospital and the sawmill the only buildings of any size. Straight ahead to the south, lapping against a stone sea-wall, were the shimmering cobalt waters of the Gulf of Kotor, hemmed in by towering grey-white limestone cliffs. Along the southern shore of the Gulf wound a narrow coastal road, wedged between the tideless water and the steeply angled mountainsides, following the wriggling line of a multitude of inlets.

It was because of this road that the surroundings of Risan were temporarily inhabited by strangers of aggressive intent. The road was part of the westernmost negotiable route that led north from the southern Balkans. The departing German garrisons of Greece and Albania, with their 21st Mountain Corps at their head, were using the route to try to force their way home to the Reich, picking up their comrades at present in occupation of Yugoslavia as they went. There was urgency in their passage. The Russians, far to the north, had advanced into Serbia and Hungary. Unless the Germans moved fast their entire south-eastern European army would be trapped in a huge highland waste where they would be militarily useless and doomed to annihilation by initial atrophy and subsequent haemorrhage. The Partisans would see to the atrophy. The Russians would induce the haemorrhage.

Until a week previously the German withdrawal had gone well for them. They had brushed aside harassment by lightly armed and politically divided Greek and Albanian guerrillas. The communist-led

Yugoslav Partisans were resourceful and formidable opponents to be taken more seriously, but they, too, could be dealt with. They were an *ad hoc* body whose enthusiasm and courage outran their soldierly skills. They inflicted casualties and imposed irritating delays, but their road-blocks were invariably crashed through, outflanked, or both in concert. Their intentions were plain to read. Their tactics were as primitive as was their armament.

And then had come the present check at Risan. The fighting had suddenly taken on a character miserably familiar to German armies elsewhere but outside the Balkan experience of this one, which in terms of ramshackle equipment, soldiery hamstrung by physical disability, advancing age and soft living, and a command suffering from creeping debility and patriotic despair was probably the least effective German force currently in the field anywhere. But they were still German soldiers, people to be reckoned with. Their urge to leave these barbarous Balkan lands was stiffened by thoughts of the retribution awaiting them, if they failed, for three years of misdeeds committed when in occupation. But what, they wondered, did they do when local guerrillas, whom they were used to, suddenly produced support from modern, scientifically operated artillery, which they were not used to?

The Force Commander took a last look through his glasses at the suddenly depopulated olive-grove and turned his head towards Laing.

'Now that our young chum's finished his diversions,' he said, 'Let's get back to where we were. Partisan positions?'

'Two brigades, sir,' said Laing. 'At least, they call them brigades. By our reckoning weak battalions. Most of one in front of the hospital. Most of the other around the sawmill. A few odds and sods milling about in between. The hospital's more or less a stalemate. The sawmill crowd put in an attack every evening.'

'They getting anywhere?'

'No. They get wiped regularly.'

The Brigadier wasted no time in seeking unnecessary elaboration. The Partisan military virtues were iron discipline, exceptional stamina, an almost lunatic courage and a cheerful resilience in the teeth of setbacks and adversity. Their political virtues, if they had any, were beyond his understanding, and he had no intention of thinking about all that now, when he had practical matters to consider. Their military defects were natural products of their origins, which lay in popular resentment of a brutally conducted occupation of their country. The resentment was expressed in the recruitment and deployment of a mass force of enthusiasts, orchestrated by a communist leadership. It was inevitable that training should be inadequate and practices sometimes incomprehensible. Add a heterogeneous weaponry that ranged from pre-First

5

World War rifles to captured German Spandaus and Schmeissers, boots and clothing mostly stripped from German corpses, and commanders who learnt their trade by mistakes as they went along and it was hardly surprising that some odd things happened.

The Brigadier, who had had six months of co-operating with them in the Dalmatian islands earlier in the year, could imagine the sort of events that took place each dusk in the sawmill attacks. Brave, futile, unsupported charges over open ground against German professionals dug in with automatic weapons in prepared positions. The 25-pounders drenching the defenders with shellfire on a timed programme and the defence being given time to recover while the assault was delayed to finish off a late meal or for the delivery of a harangue by the Commissar on the joys of Marxism. . . .

'OK,' said the Brigadier, 'what's going to happen next?'

'Next?'

'Yes. Next. You've only had a fairly small Jerry advanced guard having a crack at this place so far. The main body are also trying to break out on the two inland roads. Do you think they'll now give up this one as a bad job and concentrate on the other two? Or put in something really big here and try to fight through?'

Laing, a commando troop commander whose task was to provide local protection for a battery of Field-artillery, not to crystal-gaze about Axis higher strategy, looked austere. It was an unfair question. He lacked essential information.

'All right,' said the Brigadier. 'Unfair question. I'll change it. *If* the Jerries have a major go here, will they, in your estimation, get through?'

'Depends on how major they make it, sir. I have no knowledge of how much stuff they have available. From what we've seen so far of this advanced guard it's a pretty job lot. They've a few armoured vehicles and trucks and a handful of 105s, but there's a tremendous collection of horsed transport and mules. Most of their troops are on foot. Even so, if the guns hadn't been here to stop them, they'd have been well away by now. If they bring up reinforcements and try a determined—'

'Well, they're bringing up reinforcements,' said the Brigadier. He had raised his glasses and was staring hard at a short stretch of coast road that curved around a low promontory half a mile beyond the hospital with the holes through the red cross painted on its roof. He pointed. A string of little black dots, travelling at a steady speed and at evenly spaced intervals, was moving towards Risan.

The Forward Observation Officer had seen them, too. He had replaced his headset and throat microphone, and was chatting away casually again. He had ranged on the road during his first day here. Like the hospital, the sawmill and several dozen similar fixtures likely to be in regular use by the enemy, it had been registered and given a coded designation, held by both the Observation Officer and the gun position, marked on maps. All he had to do was to quote the designation, specify the number of rounds he thought advisable, wait until the settings for range and bearing on the guns had been adjusted, and tell them when to fire.

He said something that sounded like 'D12'. Laing, his attentions immersed in the little black dots, missed the number of rounds called for. He heard: 'Fire.'

Drumming, echoing noises resumed from behind, followed by the overhead shriekings. The shells burst among the convoy vehicles, dirty puffs of smoke and rubbish. The crash of the explosions boomed up to the Observation Post some seconds later. The convoy motored steadily on, no direct hits, no amendments to speed or spacing.

The Observation Officer said, 'I suppose you buggers think it's your lucky day,' and gave range corrections to compensate for the movement of the target. There were further background drummings, further aerial sibilance and howlings, further detonations on and around the road, further delayed sound from these last. The vehicles trundled tranquilly along, unaffected, immune. There were eight in all. They disappeared into the lee of the waterfront buildings in the town.

Then, surprisingly, they re-emerged into view and one by one halted to form a neat, compact row along the stone jetty abutting the harbour.

Soldiers climbed down. They stood in loose groups, gossiping, stretching themselves. They were in shirt-sleeves. Some wore dark glasses, like bygone Adriatic tourists from a happier past. Down there, at sea-level, the autumn sun was warm. Up here, two thousand feet above, patches of morning mist drifted stubbornly in a dank chill, awaiting midday solar dispersal.

The Observation Officer said: 'You bastards really *are* pressing your luck. Parked in the open, for Christ's sake.' He added some terse technical mumbo-jumbo and sat up expectantly, like a dog poised for the throwing of a stick. Laing wondered how whoever it was at the gun position who was receiving the Observation Officer's signals separated the fire orders from the commentary. He assumed that the Observation Officer switched off his microphone when thinking aloud. He hoped so.

The Brigadier said: 'Do they always stand around in the open like that?'

Laing said: 'A lot of them do, sir, when they first arrive. Not for long, though.'

This time there was a savage fortissimo to the introductory noises. They came from behind like great rolling, prolonged peals of thunder. Invisible express trains seemed to be rushing into invisible tunnels in the upper air. All eight 25-pounders had been brought into action simultaneously. The jetty, the trucks, the German suntan *aficionados*, the blue inshore waters of the Gulf, and a segment of waterfront disappeared behind a billowing, spreading cloud of smoke and dust, thickened by palls of blackly burning oil, illuminated by continuous flashes. The booming reverberated around the hills, bounced back in disjointed echoes, merged with the protracted roar from the gun position.

The primary sounds of the discharges and the detonations were the first to stop. The echoes took more time over it. The smoke and the wafting dust from the debris took longer still to settle. When they had cleared enough for the jetty to come into sight again, things looked different down there. Three trucks, twisted and distorted, were ablaze. One had been blown into the sea, inverted, its wheels protruding from the shallows. Components of miscellaneous wreckage, strewn capriciously amidst a rubble of masonry and the bodies of shirt-sleeved dead soldiers, added up to two more trucks. Two others had vanished, taken from the carnage to concealment by quick-thinking and brave drivers. Some equally brave survivors, ignoring Partisan small-arms fire that could now be heard pop-pop-popping in the distance, were gathering their wounded, dragging away their dead.

The Observation Officer removed his headset and microphone, lit another cigarette, picked up his binoculars, and resumed his systematic study of Risan and its approaches.

The Brigadier took a last look at the destroyed convoy, lowered his own glasses and said: 'Good shooting.'

The Observation Officer, without letting his attention roam from whatever it was that he was examining at the moment, said: 'Thank you, sir.'

Sergeant Hankins, lying in the centre of the protection party in a scattering of rocks immediately above the Observation Post, and also following the progress of the morning's events through binoculars, said two things in quick succession.

The first was 'Fuck'.

The second, called out in controlled, urgent tones to the Observation Post below, was: 'Captain Laing, sir. Bottom right corner of hospital. Left, eight o'clock. Small house with hole in roof. Looks like Mr Burke.'

It was indeed Mr Burke.

From the time of his arrival with the Brigadier at the Observation Post an hour previously Laing, in between acting as a tourist guide, answering questions and being drawn into speculative discussion about politico-military philosophy, had been growing privately angrier by the moment. The object of his ire was not the Force Commander, who in Laing's view was no more and no less of a bloody nuisance than any other brigadier, but Hugo Burke.

8

Burke was the subaltern detailed by Laing to command the Observation Post protection party. The chances of the Germans being able to discover where the Observation Post was, let alone of their being capable of doing anything effective about it if they did, were slight. But the chances could not be discounted. The success of the whole operation depended upon the Observation Post's continued unimpeded existence. It followed that, although the strength of the protectors was no more than a commando sub-section of fourteen NCOs and marines led by a sergeant, it was an officer's job to supervise, co-ordinate and take responsibility for decisions that it would be unfair to expect a sergeant to take.

It also followed that when Hugo Burke was warned in advance that Laing would bring the Force Commander to the Observation Post at a specified time, it was not so much reasonable to assume that Burke would be there to meet him and brief him as unthinkable that Burke would not be. Burke had not been there.

Laing's preoccupations with the Brigadier had allowed him time only for a brief word with Sergeant Hankins. It seemed that bloody Burke, in defiance of common sense, operational efficiency, discipline and ordinary good manners, had buggered off on one of the solo expeditions that obsessed him. On occasions in the past, in the islands, the Burke penchant for these initiatives had been of great benefit. Put him on a German-occupied island with a signaller and a week's rations, and profitable consequences flowed. He was a natural loner, resourceful and self-contained. He wirelessed or brought back tactical information of exemplary detail and usefulness.

But this wasn't island raiding. This was a complicated semi-siege, of small proportions but wide strategic implications. In so far as anything to do with the Partisans could be described as formal, this was formal warfare. Locally there were gunner requirements to be met, Partisan allies to be wrangled with or placated, and a thrusting young Force Commander who knew what questions to ask and was famously unpleasant if he didn't get the right answers.

One of the more obvious questions had been hanging in the air with a doom-ridden inevitability all morning. Who, the Brigadier would ask, is in charge of your protection party? Where is he? I want to talk to him. He's where? You don't *know*? Christ above, what sort of . . . ?

Well, that question wouldn't be put now. Its rhetorical substitute was markedly worse. 'What in the name of God', the Brigadier was asking in exasperation, 'does that clown down there think he's doing?'

What that clown down there was doing was getting himself captured by a competent-looking operator dressed in Ustacha uniform and poking about with a Schmeisser. Burke, his hands in the air, was walking slowly towards the small house with the hole in its roof, the house indicated by

Hankins. Close in front of him, walking delicately backwards like a partner in a foxtrot, using Burke as a shield, was the Ustacha. Together they reached the house. Then with a final, concerted leap they disappeared inside.

'Jesus Christ,' said Hankins.

Nobody else said anything. They took Hankins's point. To be taken prisoner was a fair risk of war. It had happened to thousands – probably by now hundreds of thousands – of troops on both sides. To be captured by the Ustachi, Croat Nationalist auxiliaries of the Germans, was not a fair risk of anything. Their captives seldom lived long.

'I suppose', said the Brigadier two hours later, as he climbed into his jeep to drive to his headquarters at Niksic, far inland near the Albanian border, 'that that silly young bugger thought he could win the war singlehanded.'

There was a measure of sympathy and admiration mixed with his scorn.

Laing saluted and said: 'Goodbye, sir.'

CHAPTER TWO

AFTER SOME, not much, thought Laing listed Hugo Burke in his casualty-return as Missing, believed Prisoner of War.

Elaborate and efficient government machinery existed for the notification of casualties to next of kin. Three days after Hugo Burke had last been seen alive by friends, jumping into the little Montenegrin house with the hole in its roof, a telegram was delivered in Ottawa to his father and mother. Its opening phrase, 'The Admiralty regrets to inform you that Lieutenant Hugo Burke, Royal Marines . . .', brought them to immediate, sickening misery. They drew hope from 'has been reported Missing, believed Prisoner of War'.

Mrs Burke was one of the countless women of the era of many nationalities who on receipt of such messages broke into uncontrollable sobbing. Her husband comforted her, lying persuasively, trying to look more confident than he felt. He had fought in the Canadian Corps in France in the First World War, and the experience had made him apprehensive about the word 'missing'. He told his wife that life for Hugo as a prisoner would have its hardships and frustrations, but they should both thank God that at least their son would be spared from further danger in battle.

Later, when Mrs Burke was sufficiently composed, she drove to the nearest Catholic church. Her own religion was Russian Orthodox, but Hugo and her husband were Catholics and this visit was for Hugo. She lit candles in the chapel of Our Lady. As one mother to another she asked the Mother of God to intercede for her son Hugo, to guard him, and to bring him safely home. Then she had another little weep.

Hugo's father went to his office in the Burke Foundation building in Elgin Street. He told his secretary to cancel his day's appointments and to deflect all incoming telephone calls. He drank three large Martinis. Afterwards he did some telephoning of his own and wrote a number of personal letters.

At Bari, in the south of Italy, the news about Hugo Burke reached the girl who wanted to marry him through a chance part of a conversation in the

Imperiale hotel, which had been requisitioned as an officers' club.

A lieutenant in the Royal Navy Volunteer Reserve, anxious to impress Helen Grant, spoke fluently and mendaciously of the rough life he led. The Landing Craft (Infantry) that he commanded did a regular milk run across the Adriatic from Bari to Dubrovnik, he said, taking over stores and replacements, bringing back casualties. What with mines and Stukas and E-boats and other hazards that he invented, it was a pretty tricky way for anyone to earn his pay. But nothing that he'd been through, he explained modestly, began to compare with what the ground troops were having to put up with.

The gunners and commandos fighting alongside the Partisans were experiencing straight murder. Ordinary casualties, killed and wounded, were bad enough. It was the ones who disappeared without trace who made the whole thing so eerie. Last week, for example, a chap from 49 Commando named Burke—

'Hugo Burke?' she said sharply.

'Don't know his first name. Anyway, this character Burke—'

'What happened to him?' Sharper still.

'He was captured. Nothing more's been heard of him. There never is in these cases. Never will be. They. . . .'

He heard her begin to cry gently in the darkness. It occurred to him that he'd probably put his foot in it again. It kept happening. Maybe she knew the fellow, which was more than he did. There was only one reliable remedy when women like Helen became emotional. He stubbed out his cigarette in the ashtray on the bedside table and turned towards her.

At much the same time as Hugo Burke's parents opened their telegram from the Admiralty, Laing was visited by his Colonel. The Colonel, with the bulk of 49 Commando, the other two batteries of the Royal Artillery Field Regiment, and the Brigadier and his Force Headquarters, was based on Niksic. They were concerned in supporting Partisan operations designed to stop a German breakout along one of the inland roads from Albania.

To Laing, the Colonel was a welcome visitor. Unlike the Force Commander, who earned respect by competence and seniority but who was still a stranger from outside the family and a bloody nuisance, the Colonel earned respect because he was competent and was the senior member *of* the family.

Laing took him around the defensive posts set up to protect the gun position on the upland plain at Pod Han. This part of the Adriatic littoral was described in the guidebooks as having the highest rainfall in Europe. It was comprehensively demonstrating at the time that it had the highest rainfall in Europe.

They spoke to sodden sentries wearing dripping green berets and waterproof gas-capes that reached to below their knees, nursing Bren guns in flooded stone sangars. They went round crowded peasant cottages where damp off-duty marines were trying to dry steaming clothes in front of smoky wood-burning stoves on which others were cooking corned-beef fritters in mess-tins. The cooks were sharing the product with very old and very young Montenegrin hosts whose active relatives, men and women, were away fighting with the Partisans; or, not to be admitted openly, with the Chetniks; or, perish the thought, with the Ustachi. The food was indifferent and the weather appalling. A cheerful international accord prospered on a base of indiscriminate discomfort and about six mutually understood words of Serbo-Croat.

The Colonel had a few words with everyone in the cottages. He tasted a fritter or two and pronounced snap culinary judgements. He spent longer chatting to the drenched sentries in the sangars and inspected their weapons rigorously. He congratulated most of them on guns that in unpromising circumstances had been kept clean, bright and lightly oiled. He put one man on a charge for possession of a rifle that was filthy, tarnished and not oiled at all. With an affable grin he told all enquirers that things would undoubtedly get worse. This message generated pleasurable self-pity and rueful admiration at the same time.

'He may be a bastard,' they said when he was out of earshot, 'but at least he doesn't bullshit you.'

Later, after a disgusting lunch of Compo M and V (for tinned mutton and vegetable) stew, washed down with Compo pre-processed tea-sugar-and-dried-milk cubes boiled in water, Laing took him with an escort to the Observation Post. They marched climbing the rocky, winding track, through soggy clouds that changed unpredictably between uncompromising moisture and fluid, soaking discharges. The Observation Post was out of business. Visibility varied from about twenty yards to two, depending upon the consistency of the current squall.

'About the best you can say for it', said the Forward Observation Officer gloomily, 'is that this stuff flows downhill. It all ends up on those bastards below.'

He put up a superficially enticing idea. If the weather stayed as horrible as it was, and if the Colonel brought up all five fighting troops of his commando from Niksic or wherever they were, they could just walk down the hill and take the bloody town without firing a shot. The Germans wouldn't be able to see or hear them coming, and must be so browned off with baling out their positions that they probably wouldn't care, either.

The Colonel gave a homily that by now he knew off by heart. Talk of a commando assault was a political impossibility. The commando's present function had been specified unambiguously by the Partisan Supreme Staff in the agreement that had brought the Force to Montenegro. They were to provide local protection for British guns. The help of modern artillery was important to the achievement of the aims of the war of national liberation. The use of foreign infantry, when there was an abundance of Partisan infantry, would be an affront to national susceptibilities.

A communist internal revolution was being conducted in parallel to the anti-German war. If British troops started taking ground, instead of simply supporting Partisan troops taking ground, there would be blistering complaints about capitalist-imperialist attempts to subvert the progress of the proletarian revolution. It was in the interests of the Western Allies to keep the guns in Yugoslavia, because the longer the German withdrawal was delayed the fewer reinforcements would be available to the German armies fighting against the British and Americans in northwest Europe and in Italy, and against the Russians in the east. Therefore, the Partisan Supreme Staff, already paranoiacally suspicious of British motives, must be kept sweet. Therefore, no British ground assaults on Risan or anywhere else.

'I see, sir,' said the Observation Officer. 'We're all being buggered about, as usual.'

'That's about it,' said the Colonel.

The Observation Officer lit a cigarette under interlocking cupped hands, took a puff at it, watched it disintegrate in the rain into a squalid, squidgy pulp, and threw the remains away with distaste.

'Well, anyway,' he said reminiscently, 'old Hugo wanted a go. That's what he was doing down there when he was captured. Reconnoitring an approach for an assault. He was going to mark it up on his map and show it to the Force Commander.'

Laing stared at him.

'How do you know?' he snapped. 'Sergeant Hankins said nothing about that.'

'He wouldn't have told Hankins,' said the Observation Officer equably, 'Hugo didn't believe in baring his breast to NCOs. He told me, though. We talked about it the night before. I told him not to be a bloody fool. He wouldn't be shifted, though. Just said that unless someone took the bull by the horns we'd be mucking about here for ever.'

They skidded and squelched through the saturated gloom on the way downhill back to the gun position at Pod Han, picking their way around overflowing watercourses, dodging newly-created waterfalls. Laing led. The Colonel followed. The escort splashed about stoically in the rear, thinking of women, and of glowing coal-fires in public houses. Laing and the Colonel independently gave thought to Hugo Burke.

The Colonel's reflections were detached and professional. Burke was a particular loss because he had been a good young officer; where his island recces had been concerned, a very good young officer. He had got himself captured, and almost certainly killed, through what earlier reports had suggested was an act of inexplicable idiocy. The Observation Officer had now exposed the reason for the idiocy. Burke, like many a subaltern before him, including the Colonel himself when he'd been one, had thought that he could run a war better than the people who were actually running it. The difference with Burke was that, having reached this not unusual conclusion, he had done something practical about it. End of Burke. QED. And RIP.

The Colonel had been in this war for too long, had been shot at on and off for too long, had seen too many personal friends and impersonal colleagues killed for too long, to spare much time for sadness. He supposed that when he became an old man, if he lived long enough to be one, he might get sentimental over his whisky about the young dead he'd once known. Not yet. There were too many other things to do to preserve as many as possible of the young living for whom he was responsible.

Laing, too, regarded present mourning for dead friends as a luxury to be steered away from. You thought about them privately, of course, but carefully, with control.

In some respects he thought that he probably knew as much about Hugo as did anyone else alive, not excluding Hugo's mother and his lover, if he had one. Hugo had been one of Laing's subalterns for more than a year. They had landed at Anzio together, and fought on Mount Ornito above the River Garigliano, and lived together in a small tent of monastic frugality for six months in the middle of the troop position at Pod Selj on the Dalmatian island of Vis. From Vis they and their followers had sallied by landing-craft and schooner to other, German-held islands – Hvar and Korcula and Brac and Mljet and the rest – on small raids and big raids and complex joint operations with Partisans, supported by the Royal Navy, the Royal Artillery and sometimes, usually with unfortunate confusion about who was on which side when viewed from above, by the Royal Air Force.

Burke had been brave, imperturbable, companionable, intelligent, incisive when it was necessary, cheerfully relaxed when it wasn't. He had led from the front, stood no nonsense from his section, and cherished their well-being tirelessly. Et cetera. Full marks on all counts.

From professional to personal. When on Solta that bloody great coastal gun from Split was banging away, and you were sitting in a stone sangar with Hugo, and you'd done your count from the moment of the muzzle-flash, and you knew that the thing was ranged accurately, and you knew that the shell would land in twelve seconds' time, and you knew that in thirteen both Hugo and you might be dead, and you looked at Hugo and Hugo grinned, then you knew something about Hugo. Hugo doubtless knew something about you, too, for that matter, but that for the present was beside the point.

Now for the rub. Set aside the skills and attitudes of the soldiering Hugo and what did you really know about him? Remarkably little. After sharing that cramped tent with him on Vis for six months, after drinking with him often and getting drunk with him occasionally, after endless talk about troop training and morale and bright ideas and which corporal to promote in place of Sergeant Rolph who had been killed on Brac, and whether Marine Fraser was really going bomb-happy or was just trying it on, you knew all that you needed to know about Hugo the temporary warrior and next to nothing about Hugo the man.

He had been brought up largely in Canada and had spent two years at an Irish university. He was courteously reticent about his family and about his hopes, if any, about the future, if any. He spent countless off-duty hours immersed in paperback copies of *Das Kapital* (K. Marx), *Mein Kampf* (A. Hitler), *The Republic* (Plato) and something called *The Rights of Man* written by somebody whose name Laing had seen on the cover but couldn't remember. Hugo never said a word about any of them.

And that was all that Laing knew about Hugo Burke, whom he much missed.

It was a damp dusk when the party splashed into the troop position at Pod Han. The Colonel thanked the escort and went in search of dryness to the one-roomed cottage where he was to spend the night. It was Laing's home and Troop Headquarters, shared with its owner, a happy old veteran of the Balkan War of 1912 who had three teeth, insanitary habits, a pregnant granddaughter and a small great-grandson. These last two were in residence, which could have complicated communal domestic life but didn't.

Laing dismissed the escort and went to inspect his sentries. He had a critical look at the supper – tinned vegetable stew and unpopular – and watched the Troop Sergeant-Major supervise the distribution of the evening tot of rum from a one-gallon glass carboy. A spare tot, unclaimed by a Congregationalist teetotaller known as Holy Joe, was passed to Laing for his evening social-welfare project. Laing brought it to the three-toothed Balkan War old-timer who, in conformity with recently established custom, sank it in one gulp, belched and became obscurely reminiscent about bygone battles in a campaign of which neither the Colonel nor Laing had ever heard, in a language that neither of them understood.

After this monologue, listened to with grave appreciation and helped along this night by sympathetic audience participation from the Colonel

– 'Christ, they didn't!', 'God, that must have been something!' – Laing and the Colonel prepared for bed. They took off their boots, wrapped themselves each in his blanket on the beaten-earth floor, placed their webbing harnesses with their pistols and grenades on them by their heads, and said 'Laku noc' to the old-timer and his posterity. The old man hawked and spat a bit. The pregnant girl and her small son settled beside him on a low wooden platform in the corner. Everyone went to sleep. Peace or war, Montenegro was early-to-bed-and-early-to-rise country.

On the following morning, shortly after the Colonel had set off reluctantly through the still persistent rain to Niksic, a small convoy arrived at the gun position. It was led by a jeep, in which was the Battery Commander and an expressionless Royal Marine subaltern. Behind the jeep were two quads – broad, squat armoured vehicles used for towing guns. Behind the quads was a three-ton truck. The quads, and the limbers attached to them, bore a replenishment load of 25-pounder shells. The three-ton truck, driven by a marine who in civilian life had been a long-distance lorry-driver on the Great North Road between London and Edinburgh, carried small-arms ammunition, replacement boots and X Troop's NAAFI ration. These personal goodies, bottled beer (3 botts per man, max.), chocolate, cigarettes, toothpaste, razor blades and the like, ordered and paid for by individuals, were delivered at unpredictable intervals from Italy when there was available space on a landing-craft putting in to Dubrovnik. Laing was glad to see this small bonanza. It wasn't much but it would bring some cheer to hard-working troops living in miserable conditions.
    The replacement subaltern for Hugo Burke brought Laing satisfaction that his troop strength had been partially restored to its notional establishment and a personal reaction short of euphoria when he saw who the substitute was. His name was Mott, and Laing knew him of old. Mott was uninspiringly efficient and lived an impenetrable private life in profound silence. He was a beefily built enigma. He had been wounded in the leg in June on Brac with K Troop, and his recovery had been delayed by a series of weird surgical setbacks. He had passed the previous four months in Italy being chopped about, restitched and left to convalesce. During the year in which Laing had known him, Mott had made five identical concessions to animation. On each occasion he had drawn all his accumulated pay, gone to the nearest officers' club, put in some prolonged drinking in solitude, and had then made a public announcement. 'My father's left me a fortune,' Mott would cry hoarsely. 'Drinks on me.' This ritual completed, Mott would stumble away for a further period of wordless introspection, to break out again when he had built up enough capital to repeat the performance. It was comforting to

Laing to reflect that there were no officers' clubs in Yugoslavia. It was less comforting to contemplate a winter cooped up with Mott on a desolate Balkan massif.

Laing showed Mott his new home in the spartan cottage and took him to see those of Hugo Burke's old section who were available. First the two sub-section sergeants, then the troops. The introductions were carried out in a spirit of faultless discipline and correctitude, and with a conspicuous lack of overt enthusiasm on either side. Laing missed Hugo Burke.

That night in the cottage when the old man became fluent again with his rum-induced campaign recollections, Mott paid no attention to him at all. Mott paid no attention to anyone else, either. He gazed fixedly at a small photograph that he had inserted in the flap of his field-service pocket-book. Laing, without intent to pry, glanced over once and saw that the picture was of a girl. He recognised the symptoms immediately, with a mixture of sympathy and irritation. The poor miserable bastard was in love. It was a natural consequence of leaving a presentable-looking, strong, silent idiot hanging around nursing sisters and Red Cross girls for four months. It would do little for local social life.

CHAPTER THREE

TWO MILES to the north-east of the Observation Post, and at much the same height above sea-level, was a string of five stone forts. They had been sited and built in the latter half of the nineteenth century by a military engineer of the Imperial Austro-Hungarian Army. They had been designed to guard the inland approaches to the Gulf of Kotor, at that time a fleet anchorage for the Imperial Navy.

Their progenitor knew his job. The forts sat on hills with commanding views of the ground around them. They dominated the only road from the hinterland, a rough, narrow, winding thread that in 1944 followed the same line, and was in much the same undistinguished state, as in 1874.

The walls of the forts were twelve feet thick, their stone blocks mortared together with impressive workmanship. The one double door in each was of thick steel plate. Steel-lined loopholes gave a protected all-round field of fire. Given adequate food, water, ammunition and alertness the thirty-man garrisons were, so the engineer assured his superiors, invulnerable to attack by any known means available to any nineteenth-century army likely to make its way across the bleak highlands of Montenegro.

For many years no attempts were made to put this particular pudding to the proof. The first try was in the early winter of 1944. The forts were then occupied by a flank guard from the German 21st Mountain Corps.

The initial attempts were disasters, three in all, on a scale that fully justified the prospectus put up by the long-dead Austrian engineer. This was because, although he had carefully restricted his guarantee to the repulse of assaults by nineteenth-century armies, the tactics used in the twentieth century were approximately those of the fifteenth.

This anachronism was brought about by the intransigence of two people: a Partisan brigade commander inspired by a touchy Montenegrin pride, and his communist political commissar inspired by an ideological mirage. Between them they agreed optimistically that the forts could be reduced by the Partisan brigade unaided by foreign capitalist gunnery, thus demonstrating Montenegrin valour and proletarian invincibility at the same time.

Montenegrin valour was unquestionable. Laing and Chisholm, the Battery Commander, watched the three assaults, put in on three successive evenings, with appalled respect.

The first was mounted by an extended line of Partisans, in their ragged hotchpotch of old civilian clothing and captured German uniforms, their heterogeneous weaponry firing from the hip, jog-trotting over open ground, converging towards the steel gates of the first selected fort. There was no supporting fire, no diversion, no subtlety. The attackers were massacred by Spandaus and Schmeissers fired through the steel-lined loopholes. In the last stages a handful of brave and lucky men actually reached the gates. They were dispatched by grenades tossed over the walls. There may have been survivors. Laing saw none.

On the following evening, target the same fort, a battering-ram was used. It was made from a tree-trunk mounted on a farm-cart. It was pushed by a party whose members were shot down and replaced four times on its journey, and who were flanked by people in the same extended line formation that had been used on the previous attack. The final battering-ram team got it to within ten yards of the gates before they were slaughtered. It was left lying on its side, the uppermost wheel spinning slowly. Afterwards Laing saw wounded survivors from the line part of this attack. They had crawled back using the cover of rocks and scrub. There were few of them.

The next demonstration of incomparable courage and futility involved fire. Huge wooden wine-barrels, packed with straw soaked in kerosene, were rolled by a group at the centre of the advancing line. The group had to be replaced as frequently as had the battering-ram party on the previous evening. Miraculously, two of the barrels reached the gates. They were ignited, while showers of grenades fell among their handlers. The barrels emitted orange flame and thick, dark smoke, neither of which left an impression on steel plate and twelve-foot stone walls. The slaughter on this occasion was very slightly less than on others because the smoke masked the withdrawal of the few Partisans still on their feet.

Laing was drinking whisky in Chisholm's command vehicle, arguing desultorily about the correct Latin name for one of those medieval siege engines that fired large rocks at fortifications from wooden catapults, when visitors were announced by Chisholm's batman. The Partisan Brigadier, accompanied by his interpreter, a thirteen-year-old boy who'd studied English at school, had a suggestion to make. The Brigadier was a tough, volatile character with a broad weather-browned face, liked and admired by both Laing and Chisholm for his determination to concentrate upon matters of immediate concern; that is, winning the war. In this he differed from the Political Commissar, who seemed rather to have lost interest in the war and who was more preoccupied in planning the manipulation of the peace to Party advantage.

Chisholm gave the Brigadier a mug of whisky, and the interpreter a bar of NAAFI chocolate. The Brigadier came straight to the point. He'd made three attempts on a fort. All had been unsuccessful. New methods were necessary. Would the *Gospodin* Major now co-operate by demolishing the forts with his cannons?

The *Gospodin* Major, tactfully avoiding reference to earlier indifferent rejections of offers of help by his guns, expressed his admiration (genuinely felt) for the lion-hearted bravery with which the Brigadier's Montenegrins had pressed home their attacks. The *Gospodin* Major said that of course he'd co-operate with his cannons. He wanted no misunderstandings, though. He had never claimed that they were capable of demolishing forts. His earlier suggestions had been that he should provide supporting fire to keep down the heads of the defence, and blind them with dust and smoke, to cover Partisan attacks. The Brigadier smiled hugely, accepted another mug of whisky, and said that the *Gospodin* Major was making a traditional English modest understatement. As was widely known in military circles, the cannon was the Goddess of the Battlefield. The Brigadier had every confidence that the *Gospodin* Major's guns would flatten the forts like *Poo-oo-oof*.

'Christ,' said Chisholm, when the beaming Brigadier had departed. 'This is getting serious.'

That night, after some mathematics, he called a planning conference. The conference was followed by precise orders to gunners and commandos for an operation timed to begin shortly after dawn the next day. As a matter of courtesy, an emissary was sent to the Partisan Brigadier to let him know what was afoot. He was not invited to participate. It was taken for granted that if he saw something worth exploiting he would exploit it.

Under cover of a thick early-morning mist, a 25-pounder with its limber was towed by a quad to an outward-curving U-bend of the inland road, a thousand yards from the still invisible fort. The gun was unlimbered and pointed on a compass bearing towards its target. The Number One, the sergeant in charge of the gun, and the gun-layer, the loader, and the ammunition numbers took their stations around it. Distributed among the rocks in the spur that filled the U-bend were the fourteen members of Sergeant Hankins's sub-section, their firepower strengthened by the borrowing of all four Bren guns in the troop. Laing was with them.

On the road beside the gun stood Chisholm, peaked-capped and greatcoated, legs firmly astride, hands resting lightly on the binoculars slung around his neck. He was staring patiently ahead, waiting for the mist to shift.

A mile away, in the main gun position, the crews of the remaining seven 25-pounders stood to their guns.

Two miles away, in the Observation Post, the Forward Observation Officer sat alertly in the murk around him and hoped to God that it cleared at much the same time as the part of it that shrouded the fort. If there were some freak meteorological complications, there could be trouble for the isolated gun.

Signallers, squatting at their sets in the main gun position, beside Chisholm and in the Observation Post, checked that they were all on net.

At twenty minutes past eight the texture of the mist around Chisholm began to change from thick creamy to watered milky. It progressed to wispy. Then most of it went altogether, leaving a few obstinate pockets in hollows in the ground. The slanting light of the early sun fell upon the fort on its small up-turned pudding-basin hill, on the grey, eroded rock-strewn land in front of it, on the gun and its servers.

Chisholm raised his binoculars, studied the architectural intricacies above the fort's gates, and gave a detailed order to the sergeant. The sergeant repeated it to the Number One. The gun-layer peered through his telescopic sight and made unhurried, meticulous adjustments. He said that he was On. Chisholm gave the word to fire. The sergeant repeated it. A solid shot left the gun invisibly with a bang, startling in contrast to the post-dawn quiet that had so far prevailed. Almost simultaneously a cloudy puff of dirt and chippings developed three feet above the keystone in the arch that surmounted the gates. Sound-waves from discharge and impact echoed lingeringly among the mountains.

The dust in front of the arch dispersed. Chisholm spoke further to the sergeant. The gun-layer, one eye pressed to the rubber padding of his sight, made a delicate realignment, like a musician fine-tuning a violin. He took his time over it. At last he said that he was ready.

The next shot hit the keystone. So did the next three, fired blind from the firmly anchored gun through the dust stirred up by the first round. Chisholm switched to four rounds of high explosive. They blew away all the rubbish and left a clear view of the damage so far done. Chisholm saw through his glasses a slight but noticeable irregularity in the stonework. He ordered five rounds of solid shot, rapid.

The fort's occupiers, quiescent for longer than could have been hoped for, burst into violent life. They had been unsighted by the dust and chippings, but in the interval of clarity left between the explosions for Chisholm's damage-appraisal they had no difficulty in picking out an exposed large gun, firing at them over open sights at a range of less than a thousand metres. Their vision was immediately impeded once more, but they fired Spandaus through the dust-cloud in the general direction of the nuisance. This fire made ripping, tearing noises in the air above the gunners' heads and splintered chips of rock among the marine Bren party on the spur behind.

Laing, standing behind Sergeant Hankins, ordered an immediate response. The Brens blazed away into the dust-pall drifting about the gates. Laing thought it might cheer up the gun crew, who by now must be beginning to feel naked and lonely.

This nakedness and loneliness were at once underlined by a piece of German professional expertise reminiscent of the high days of the Wehrmacht's supremacy of a few years before. It became clear that the fort, after its brief view of the gun, had signalled a pinpoint map-reference of its position to the two remaining 105-millimetre guns in Risan.

The first shot nearly did for Laing. It came howling over the plateau and burst crashingly six yards from him, a moment after he had dived to the ground. Bits of it zinged over the Bren-gunners, one of whom said: 'Fuck this for a lark.' The second and third shells bracketed Chisholm and the gun team, without hitting anyone. The scream of the final approach of the fourth and fifth was drowned by a great booming roar from a mile to the rear of the fort-busting expedition.

The Forward Observation Officer, far away in the Observation Post, was the prime mover behind this sudden accretion of sound. During the past week he had located and caused to be destroyed all but two of the few German guns that had so far reached Risan. The two, 105s, had been moved by night, concealed in new positions, and left unused, presumably in an attempt to build up stocks of ammunition for the coming breakthrough to the north. They had now fired to meet the SOS call from the fort. Their muzzle-flashes disclosed where they were. The Observation Officer brought down a retributive hail of concentrated gunfire from the seven remaining 25-pounders in the main gun position. The 105s were blown off their mountings, turned into instant junk, and their crews destroyed. The crews didn't know it, but they took some opponents with them.

Their fourth round exploded on a high buttress of rock behind the marine Bren party. Shards of shell, mixed with sharp fragments of rock, spread laterally and downwards over the backs of people covered adequately from all directions except from above. The marine who had recently said 'Fuck this for a lark' died instantly. So did the number one on the left-hand Bren. Hankins's back was torn open from his right shoulderblade to the bottom of his ribcage. Laing ran to him. He was unconscious when Laing began to seal the wound with a field-dressing.

The fifth, and last, round hit the road twenty yards beyond the gun. It killed two of the ammunition numbers, sprayed the rest of the crew with chipped stones and dirt, wounded the driver of the quad, and destroyed an expensive watch on a bombardier's wrist.

Chisholm rose to his feet. He took a quick look around to see that his casualties were being attended to, dusted himself down, and returned his concentration to trying to dislodge the keystone above the gates of the fort.

The gun-layer reported that his sight was still focused upon where it should have been focused. Chisholm called for four more rounds of solid shot. Unpleasantly close bursts of machine-gun fire were churning the surface of the road.

Chisholm switched to high explosive. When this had done its dust-clearance duty there was a brief clear vision of sagging stone, disintegrating above the gates. Chisholm put in four more solid shot.

The dust-cloud grew. And then came a new sound – a heavy, tumbling rumble like that of a landslide. The pall of dust spread further, quadrupled untidily in size. The gun continued to fire, high explosive again. The Brens carried on, clattering away. The dust subsided, raggedly and gently.

The fort presented a new and satisfying prospect. Its near wall had collapsed into forward-falling rubble. The corners still held, but there was a huge central gap, a roughly shaped semi-circular breach. The steel gates in the middle of it were bent at the top and loose from their hinges.

Chisholm lit a cigarette. From above him he heard Laing roar 'Stop'. The gun-layer gave a thumbs-up sign. The throaty noise of Partisan cheering echoed from folds in the ground surrounding the ruined fort. At 9.20 on a by now clear and sunny morning distant figures could be seen running towards the obstacle that had cost too much blood and pain. The runners were not fired at. They surged unharmed up the scree of rubble.

Chisholm and Laing walked over. The bodies of six Germans killed by shelling and of one, badly wounded, left behind by his friends and clubbed to death by Partisan rifle-butts were sprawled among the wreckage. All seven bodies had been stripped of boots, clothing and usable equipment. The Partisans needed them badly. The survivors of the garrison had escaped to swell the ration strength of the old Austrian barracks in Ledenice, a mile away in the direction of Risan.

The second fort was reduced on the following day by identical means, although with no German artillery left to hamper the proceedings the operation was tidier and more clinical. The fort garrison again withdrew to Ledenice, leaving behind them four dead but no wounded.

The third was attended to on the next day with similar results.

The fourth fell with unexpected ease and sickening consequences. It was the only one of the five to lack a covered route to the Ledenice barracks. The second shot to hit its keystone revealed that its construction was defective. The sturdy-looking façade was a fake. It crumbled with the second shot and collapsed after the fourth.

The speed of this demolition left the occupants with no chance of outnumbered by fort refugees and an infantry company that in the last few days had come up. Such tenuous communication as had existed between Ledenice and Risan, a mile to the south and a thousand feet below, had been cut by marauding Partisans. Two of the captured forts directly overlooked the barracks. So did an almost complete ring of surrounding hills. The interior ground was too stony for the digging of adequate slit-trenches.

The defence, inspired by a high courage and a despairing knowledge of what was likely to happen to the occupants if they did not hold out, was tigerish. Eight 25-pounders drummed a continuous fire into the enclosure, blowing holes in the buildings and setting fire to the roofs of two of them. Investing Partisans rattled away with their miscellaneous weaponry. The four marine Brens thickened up the mixture with controlled and carefully aimed bursts.

Return fire, at first heavy, diminished inevitably, initially from the drain on limited ammunition, later from a shortage of soldiers to fire it. Laing, lying beside one of his Bren teams, began for the second time in a few days to feel sorry for Germans, whatever horrors they had been responsible for. His conviction that all Germans must be fought until they were crushed remained undented. But this was not fighting as he knew it. This was a mass public execution.

He ordered the Bren-gunner to put the contents of two full magazines through the windows of a barrack block from which the noisiest part of the resistance persisted.

The Bren-gunner was changing to his second magazine when an approximation to a white flag, a soiled dress-shirt attached to a rifle-muzzle, was poked out of the window that the Bren had been engaging. Laing bawled 'Stop'. His Brens did. Chisholm, standing on a low knoll a quarter of a mile away, saw the white flag and told his signaller to quieten the guns. The Partisans continued to bang away as heartily as ever, but then they, too, registered the overall change in the quality of the pervading noise. The volume of their shooting diminished slowly, resolved itself into an occasional crack, and ended altogether.

A bedraggled, bare-headed German officer with his right arm in a dirty sling stepped out on to the remains of what had once been a parade-ground. He was followed by an equally scruffy straight-backed soldie waving aloft the rifle with the dress-shirt flapping from its muzzle. Th moved with an impressive dignity.

Laing rose to his feet and walked towards them. He had no right t so. Strictly speaking, he shouldn't have been in the fight at all. I Partisan Brigadier had stuck to the book, and hadn't covertly welc the presence of any weapons that worked, Laing and the four Bren would have been back at the artillery gun position, sitting about defence. It was his sense of pity that impelled him to go to spe

26

evacuation, even if they had anywhere to go to, which
Scattered bunches of Partisans rose to their feet and ran fo
into the breach by covering fire from the 25-pounder and La
The fire was lifted at the latest possible moment, the Parti
through, and the sounds of a confused fight could be heard cl
gunners and marines: the hollow thumps of grenades, repe
from rifles, bursts of road-drill stammering from automati
intermittent savage shouting, and one high, thin scream. Th
acoustically amplified and distorted by the three walls of t
standing.

By the time that Chisholm and Laing went to view the me
dead had been laid in a line in the pallid sunshine at the foot of
further line of waxen-faced, blood-caked seriously wounded
of them. The unhurt and the walking wounded were moving
about, clutching captured German weapons, trying on Ger
and tunics, adjusting German leather equipment. A Partis
smiling broadly and wearing a newly acquired leather belt with
Uns' inscribed upon its buckle, led them over the rubble to i
inside. It was a shambles of half-naked German bodies. The
including the wounded, had been killed to the last man.

That evening Laing and Chisholm discussed ethics. The bu
wounded prisoners disgusted them both.

'But', said Chisholm, 'can you say with total honesty that if y
Yugoslav, and had had your own family and friends slaugh
Germans, and your own captured wounded run over by Germa
save German ammunition, can you swear that you would
German prisoners?'

Laing couldn't.

The fifth fort went down on the fifth day, in an exact replica of t
of forts 1, 2 and 3. Six killed were left behind. The balanc
defenders made their way to Ledenice.

The Ledenice barracks were on a flat area of ground in a shall
about the size of a football pitch. They lacked the defensive pr
of the forts. They were simply barracks, living-accommodat
administrative offices surrounding a small square. Walls and roc
designed to resist weather, not gunfire. It had been the concep
Austro-Hungarian engineer that any attack from inland woulc
against his impregnable forts and that the barracks would not
withstand violence.

They were by now overcrowded, their original occupants, supp
transport people who had been engaged in running mule-trains,

German officer. Laing wanted no more slaughter. He was doubtful if he could prevent it. He could at least postpone it.

The German clicked his heels together, bowed stiffly and said in passable English: 'Goertz. I wish to surrender my command to the British forces. I have many wounded.'

Laing, with similar formality, said bleakly that he had no authority to accept a surrender. His own commander, the Herr Major of Artillery, was the only man who could speak for the British. Since his guns had stopped firing, it could be assumed that he had seen the white flag. He was doubtless on his way over.

Goertz said that he must make one point clear. He would surrender to the British only. His offer did not extend to 'the terrorists'.

Laing repeated that Goertz must await the Herr Major. Partisans began to drift in through the wrecked perimeter. Goertz complained angrily about this intrusion. Laing said that there was nothing that he could do to stop it. More Partisans arrived and started roaming around, staring curiously and unselfconsciously at the damage. Chisholm appeared. So did the Partisan Brigadier and the Political Commissar. There was a convoluted discussion with no meeting of minds. Chisholm brought it to an end by telling Goertz unequivocally that there could be no question of his surrendering to the British. The matter was governed by a formal Anglo-Yugoslav agreement. All prisoners must go to the Partisans. The Commissar nodded venomously.

Laing had already developed a resentment of the unbending Goertz, a near-caricature of the archetypal stiff-necked Prussian of fiction and propaganda, which roughly speaking were the same thing. For the rest of his life Laing cherished the sheer bombastic gallantry of Goertz's reply to Chisholm.

'Very well,' snapped Goertz, gazing contemptuously at the growing number of Partisans swarming into the barracks, 'I withdraw my surrender offer. Get this rabble out of my position. We will resume hostilities.'

It was, of course, an impossible proposition. Triumphant Partisans and resigned-looking German wounded were by now inextricably mixed. German weapons, boots and wristwatches were being sequestrated, with no finesse evident in the transactions. Nervous batches of disarmed unwounded Germans had been herded into corners. An effective truce, unrelated to the negotiations of the commanders, had slid into being. More and more Germans, dazed, passive, were being winkled out, stripped of valuables, stood against walls.

Goertz accepted the inevitable with an undiluted disdain. He ignored the Commissar and the Partisan Brigadier and addressed himself coldly to Chisholm.

'Herr Major,' he said, 'I do not trust these barbarians. I rely on you to safeguard the lives of my men, surrendered honourably to you in battle.'

He clicked his heels, turned and strode away. The Commissar shot him in the back.

For a moment Laing feared that the killing of Goertz would precipitate a general massacre. Surprisingly, the Commissar prevented one by rapping out an instruction translated to Chisholm and Laing by the Brigadier's boy interpreter. The prisoners' lives were to be spared until their crimes could be considered by a properly constituted People's Court.

Almost simultaneously with this ukase a commotion broke out in a small, isolated building with barred windows. It had clearly been a guardroom. A bearded, untidy figure in a non-German uniform was booted out by two aggressive Partisans and was frog-marched towards the Commissar. The prisoner's non-conforming dress had seemingly provoked suspicions requiring political adjudication.

Before this process could begin the prisoner spoke.

'For Christ's sake, Johnny,' said Hugo Burke, 'tell these stupid bastards to let go, will you?'

CHAPTER FOUR

'HUGO,' said Johnny Laing, sipping from a tin mug of *rakija*, 'now that you're debearded, deloused and sobered up you'd better tell me what the hell you were doing when you were put in the bag.'

'I've told you. Recce for a commando attack on Risan.'

'Well, tell me again. This is official. The Colonel wants a written report from you.'

'OK. Recce for a commando attack on Risan.'

'Why? You knew it wouldn't get off the ground. Bloody awful embarrassment you caused me.'

'Answer to the first part is yes, I knew it wouldn't get off the ground. I thought it should. It seemed to me that if I recce'd and plotted a forming-up position and a start-line even that clown of a Force Commander might pay attention and do something about it. Answer to the second part is my renewed apologies.'

'The Colonel's also ordered me to give you a bollocking.'

'Bollock away.'

'Consider yourself bollocked.'

'I can't stand your militaristic brutality. It's unendurable.'

'Nor can I. Have the other half.'

'Are you becoming pissed, Johnny?'

'No.'

'I am,' said Hugo Burke.

'I've just read Burke's report,' said the Force Commander. 'There's not much of it.'

'I don't encourage my officers to be verbose, sir,' said the Colonel, with intent to irritate.

'Nor do I, dammit. But all this says is that he was captured by Ustachi, handed over to the Germans, was reasonably well treated and was released. With dates.'

'I told him that I didn't want his autobiography. Just facts.'

'There aren't enough facts in it. It doesn't explain why the Ustachi turned him over to the Germans.'

'I shouldn't think he knew why. They were hardly likely to consult him about it. My guess would be that the Germans grabbed him quick as a form of insurance in case they had to do some surrendering themselves. "We've treated your man well. Now you do the same for us."'

'Didn't do them much good at Ledenice.'

'They didn't have a chance at Ledenice.'

'Well, anyway,' said the Force Commander magnanimously, 'I'm glad he's been sprung.'

'Thank you, sir. So am I.'

'But the bloody fool shouldn't have got himself captured in the first place. It was a ridiculous performance. I watched the whole thing. It was like sitting in the Führer's box at the Berlin Olympics. Burke couldn't have made more of a public exhibition of himself if he'd—'

'I didn't know that you were at the Berlin Olympics.'

'I wasn't at the Berlin Olympics. I was simply saying that—'

'I'm sorry. I thought you said that you were with Hitler at the Berlin—'

'Bugger the Berlin Olympics. This report isn't good enough. I want a court of enquiry into the circumstances in which Burke was captured.'

'Sir, as you know, Johnny Laing's troop is detached. To divert him and Mott from their jobs, and to find a third officer for the court from here would involve—'

'I don't care what it involves. There'll be a court of enquiry. As soon as possible.'

'Sir!' said the Colonel. He saluted and left.

The Force Commander hadn't started by wanting a court of enquiry, but if the Colonel thought that he could get away with all that piss-taking about the Berlin Olympics he could think again.

When the telegram from the Admiralty was delivered in Ottawa, Hugo Burke's mother burst into tears again, this time of joy. Her husband hugged her speechlessly in a prolonged manifestation of delight and relief. Champagne and telephone calls followed.

A stream of congratulatory visitors started a spontaneous celebration punctuated by repeated toasts to Hugo and by Hugo's father saying 'Jesus Christ' benignly at intervals. Hugo's mother kept mopping her eyes with a handkerchief, explaining while all comers kissed her that she should be laughing and not crying, and that she was laughing really, but that the laughing and the crying seemed to have become mixed up somehow, and that's what came of being a Russian.

Afterwards, slightly tipsy, she went to the chapel of Our Lady in the Catholic church, lit enough candles to illuminate a fair-sized room and poured out her soul in a torrent of thanksgiving.

While she was at the chapel, her husband telephoned to everyone he had written and spoken to on the day when Hugo was reported as missing. He thanked them for their help, and cancelled earlier requests and instructions.

The Royal Naval Volunteer Reserve lieutenant took a long pull at his cigarette and said: 'Amazing thing about that chap Burke.'
   'What about him?' Cautious. Suddenly grave.
   'He's OK. He got out.'
   'He's *alive*?'
   'Yes.'
   Brief contemplative silence, followed by symptoms of deep, happy relief scrambled with illogical rage.
   'Get out of my bed, you bastard,' said Helen Grant, chuckling, sobbing, snarling. 'And don't come back.'

'Richard,' said the Colonel to his adjutant, 'the Force Commander has ordered me to convene a court of enquiry. About Hugo Burke's capture.'
   'Oh, yes, sir?'
   'Convene it.'
   'When?'
   'As soon as possible. That's what he said.'
   'Should be possible about six months after we get back to Italy.'
   The Colonel looked at him with affection. 'Richard,' he said, 'this unit would be in a shocking state without bloody-minded obstructionists like you to oil the wheels.'
   'Thank you, sir.'

The cryptographers and analysts in the misleadingly entitled Government Code and Cypher School at Bletchley Park in Bedfordshire, thirty-odd miles from London, gave a realistically low priority to intercepts dealing with the minor peccadilloes of individuals. Their prime attentions were focused upon more vital German signals traffic, harvested from the breaking of the secrets of the German Enigma encoding machine. The intelligence nuggets mined from this priceless vein provided planners and field-commanders with a detailed reading of enemy strengths, movements and intentions. The telegram to Berlin from the German embassy in Madrid was accordingly put to one side while more momentous matters were attended to. But the Bletchley organisation was thorough and tidy-minded. The telegram was dealt with in the course of a routine desk-clearance. A copy went to the counter-intelligence specialists in MI5.
   It was the second in a series. A Canadian citizen had been in contact with Germany through the agency of the Spanish ambassador in Ottawa. The ambassador had forwarded a message to his Foreign Office in Madrid, who had passed it to the German ambassador, who had sent it to

Berlin. The Canadian citizen, a man named Burke, was technically guilty of treating with an enemy in time of war. The evidence was unusable because to use it would risk the compromising of its interception origins. There was no sense in putting at hazard a treasure-house of invaluable information for the sake of prosecuting a minor sinner whose transgressions did no damage to the Allied war effort.

The crime, and only the unimaginative self-righteous could really call it a crime, was that of sending a personal plea to friends in high places in Germany for good treatment of Burke's son, a Royal Marine officer who had been reported Missing, believed Prisoner of War in Yugoslavia. The more recently logged in of the two telegrams expressed thanks for earlier help and explained that the son had now been freed. In both messages there was also some innocuous padding that suggested that they had been drafted under strain. Well, right enough, a direct approach of this sort was reprehensible. It was also understandable. What father who had the contacts wouldn't use them in the circumstances?

And Burke had the contacts all right. The MI5 file on the Burke Foundation dated back to the rise of Mussolini in Italy in the 1920s. It took in flirtations with the British Union of Fascists in the 1930s and held extensive entries about the Foundation's financial and Public Relations support for General Franco in the Spanish Civil War. The last was presumably where the connection with the Spanish Foreign Office originated. Burke himself was summed up succinctly in the file in the recorded words of a Royal Canadian Mounted Police intelligence officer: 'Burke is a rich, right-wing, Catholic kook, obsessed with a hatred of communism.'

Until the telegram episode Burke had broken no law, even if he had attracted considerable intelligence interest.

CHAPTER FIVE

THE ANNIVERSARY of the birth of the Son of God, messenger of universal Love and Peace, was celebrated by X Troop of No. 49 Royal Marine Commando in a stricken upland village called Viluse.

They had moved there, waiting for someone to find something useful for them to do, after the Germans had abandoned Risan in search of a less expensive way home. The seekers of something useful to do for the small British force in Yugoslavia had recently found the task unrewarding. The imperatives of Marxist polemics by now overrode considerations of co-operative military partnership. Suspicion and insult proliferated. Friendly acknowledgement of mutual sacrifices in past shared enterprises was no longer a feature of inter-Allied planning discussions, which were increasingly haunted by political harangues which the Force Commander found to be both irrelevant and incomprehensible.

'What does that sanctimonious little shit want now?' he had taken to asking the Colonel, when invited to attend some interminable summit meeting with the Party boss of Montenegro.

On Christmas Eve the marines of X Troop made cheerful inroads into an accumulated stock of vino and *rakija*. On Christmas morning they were awakened by their three officers, Laing, Burke and Mott, bearing steaming mugs of tea. Johnny Laing had decided on this piece of domestic cosseting as the best available variant of the tradition by which in more orthodox conditions officers acted as waiters at the men's Christmas dinner. Since a Christmas dinner of tinned mutton and vegetable stew, boiled sweets, and chewing gum was unlikely to be memorably festive Laing had concluded that a tea delivery to the lads in bed would better demonstrate seasonal goodwill.

The gesture was not an unqualified success. 'Bed' was a share of a stone or beaten-earth floor in one or other of the few houses still with intact roofs in the dismal village. There was snow on the ground and little glass in the windows. Viluse in the past three years had been pillaged and partially incinerated in instalments by successive Italian, Chetnik, Ustachi, German and Partisan visitors. Among what was left, the lads slept fully clothed, each under one blanket and a rubberised gas-cape, each with weapons and equipment to hand for emergency action.

Some did not take kindly to the interruption of *rakija*-induced slumbers by a shake of the shoulder and hearty cries of 'Happy Christmas'. Unchristian bleary exhortations to fuck off mingled with reciprocal Yuletide greetings. Laing laughed, and overlooked these aberrant disciplinary lapses. Almost anything, short of a really spectacular outrage, was overlooked on Christmas Day.

At ten o'clock Laing held a church service. He wasn't very good at church services but he improvised with the Lord's Prayer and six Christmas carols, the last interspersed with two one-minute silences. The first silence was for dead friends and comrades, alive the previous Christmas, since buried after actions at Anzio, on the Garigliano, in the islands. The second silence was for private thoughts of families and of those whom Laing, in mild embarrassment, could only describe as loved ones. The congregation, hardened and derisive in most matters, seemed to find no incongruity in this choice of words. They thought of their families and loved ones, leaving unexpressed a common sentiment. The arithmetic of war was random in its choice of victims, but it was inexorable. It was a statistical certainty that this was the last Christmas on earth for an unpredictable number of the little bareheaded group in the ruined Balkan schoolroom, sharing hymn-sheets written out in longhand by Lance-Corporal Smithwick, the troop clerk. The statistical certainty added a piquant intensity to reflections about homes and girls that some would never see again.

Laing took time off from a surprisingly tuneful rendering of 'Oh, Come, All Ye Faithful' to do some reflecting of his own. He was, he supposed, becoming too sentimental by half; but what the hell, this was Christmas, and he would be as sentimental as he bloody well liked. He looked at his carolling followers in their scuffed jerkins and their unpressed, threadbare battledress, with their well-shaved, weather-burnt faces and their temporarily serious expressions, and he felt an emotion that he could only define as Love, very apt at Christmas-time, probably magnified and crystallised at Christmas-time. It was a simple Love, uncomplicated by sex or possessiveness or jealousy.

For two years he had trained, encouraged, cajoled, disciplined, led in battle, shared discomforts and jokes and sorrows with these young men. He had been with them when some were wounded and when friends had been killed beside them. He had helped to bandage up the damaged, had told lies to dying ones, not here today, present last Christmas – 'Take it easy, chum. You'll be OK' – and had himself, when shot in the foot on the hilltop on Brac, been carried out of it on a sergeant's back. At differing times he had felt admiration, exasperation, trust, rage, confidence, amusement and enthusiasm in, for, with or about, as the case may be, *them*. Who had long since become *us*.

Judged by conventional Christian doctrinal standards they were a rather sinful crowd, with a bias towards lechery and strong drink. There were some talented thieves currently inviting the Faithful to come to Bethlehem, but they were thieves with a social conscience who only stole from strangers in other units and democratically shared the loot among their mates. There were inarticulate, sinister-looking toughs who had risked their lives repeatedly to get friends out of trouble in action. There were three hard cases whom Laing had seen with tears in their eyes, comforting children wounded in a German abomination, bandaging the kids with the field-dressings without which the vulnerability of the hard cases was enhanced, depriving themselves of their suppers to feed young victims of adult lunacy.

Hard and dangerous work was done efficiently with a collective cynicism and ribaldry. Language was appalling. There was little hate for the enemies they fought, except, as in the case of the injured children, when decency was violated. There was, indeed, a curious understanding sympathy for enemy front-line soldiers, sharers of dangers and discomforts and boredoms unknown to politicians, propagandists, and flag-waving Jingo journalists. There was— Better stop all this maudlin stuff. Coming up to the last-but-one 'Oh, come, let us adore him'. Just time to fit in a quick private prayer.

Laing had never been much bothered about whether Christmas was a survival of a northern European pagan rite to mark the turn of the year, or a commemoration of the birth of the Christ child sent by God to redeem humanity. His attitude to prayer was much the same as that behind his use of the Brens to reply to the Spandaus that had fired from the first fort: Might do some good. Can't do any harm.

'God,' he prayed, merging a realistic scepticism with a deeply felt hope, 'I don't know if You exist. If You do, please be kind to these men, the ones here. They deserve it.'

'Chri–i–ist the Lord,' thundered out finally, joyfully and triumphantly.

'The National Anthem,' said Laing quietly.

They came rigidly to attention, heels together, hands lightly clenched. He led them in 'God Save the King'. He supposed that afterwards a proper padre would have said something like 'God bless you all. Go in peace,' but it seemed too pretentious from an unqualified God-botherer in the sixth year of a war that would yet kill some of them.

Instead he said: 'Happy Christmas.' They said 'Happy Christmas' back and tramped to the snow-covered desolation outside, prior to setting about hair-of-the-dog self-administered remedial medicine.

Laing thanked Corporal Smithwick for his work on the hymn-sheets.

He looked at his watch. Two hours to go before midday drinks with the sergeants. Plenty of time for a small excursion that he had planned, with Smithwick enlisted as co-conspirator.

Hugo Burke was a practising Catholic in a pre-ecumenical era in which attendance at a non-Catholic religious ceremony was forbidden by the hierarchy. Burke stayed away from Laing's service. This annoyed Laing. Laing had no illusions of imitation clerical grandeur but regarded his amateur sky-pilotry as an important unifying device that would please the believers, cheer up the unbelievers, allow for the unobtrusive discharge of privately held heads of emotional steam, and generally do good to morale. Burke's absence did not vitiate these aims, but it diminished slightly their achievement. There was nothing that Laing could, or would, do about it. The sacred inviolability of a man's religious preferences had long been honoured in the Royal Marines, as in the rest of His Majesty's Forces. 'Church of England stand fast. Fall out the Catholics and other fancy religions' was a hallowed order that had preceded compulsory church-parades for generations.

Hugo went to the small dilapidated Serbian Orthodox chapel at the edge of the village. A berobed priest in a flat hat and with a luxuriant beard that reached to his waist intoned a Mass in Old Church Slavonic. The nostalgic smell of incense took Hugo back to his childhood. The Orthodox Church was classified by the Vatican as schismatic, but not heretic as were the Protestant Churches, a distinction that permitted Hugo to attend Orthodox services and would have driven Laing to blasphemous incredulity if he had either known of it or had been able to understand it.

Hugo's fellow-worshippers were five old women with hungry faces and arthritic knobs on the joints of their fingers. They were dressed in black and they looked frightened and defiant. The fright and defiance were because of two Partisans who stood in front of the chipped icons at the back of the chapel. Both had Schmeissers slung over their shoulders and one, clearly unused to handling a pencil, was recording in a notebook the names of those unwise and unenlightened enough to persist in religious practices discredited by the Revolution.

Hugo's mother had often taken him to Orthodox Masses. He knew the ritual. He stood and knelt at the right places. His concentration was elsewhere. He prayed for guidance on a problem of morality that bothered him deeply.

Three hundred miles to the west of Viluse across the Adriatic, at the 99th British General Hospital in Bari in Puglia, a Church of England padre of the Royal Army Chaplains' Department officiated at a service for the off-duty staff and for those patients sufficiently recovered to be allowed out of bed. It was a more polished affair than Laing's improvisation. In spirit it was similar.

The padre wore a surplice and a cassock. There was a crib and a Christmas-tree, with lights. Hymn-sheets were typed. A row of nursing sisters were in front of the congregation. Behind the nurses were two rows of officers, recovering wounded, recovering sick, doctors. About two hundred NCOs and soldiers, also recovering wounded and sick, mixed up with Royal Army Medical Corps orderlies, were behind the officers.

Towards the left end of the row of nurses was Helen Grant, her navy-blue Red Cross jacket and skirt standing out among the predominating khaki. She was singing her share of 'Once in Royal David's City', and was thinking confused thoughts. Kindly ones about Hugo and the impassioned letters that were now reaching her from him. Less kindly, but far from condemnatory, ones about herself. She was Hugo's. Totally, irrevocably, committedly Hugo's. But last night *had* been Christmas Eve, and the New Zealand Sapper captain with the limp *had* been a damned attractive man, and Hugo was God knew where, and. . . .

She had always been enchanted by carols. Their only uncomfortable present drawback was that the word 'virgin' kept cropping up. This made her giggle and feel pleasurably guilty.

'That the lot?' asked Laing, as Corporal Smithwick stowed two packs, small, on the floor of the jeep.

'Yes, sir. Plus the pouches,' said Smithwick. He patted the webbing Bren-gun magazine-pouches on either side of the buckle of his waistbelt. Laing did the same with his.

'OK. We're off. You look about seven months pregnant.'

'So do you, sir.'

They both grinned. Beneath their loose-fitting leather jerkins their battledress blouses bulged.

Laing drove. Smithwick, in the passenger-seat, held a tommy-gun in his right hand, finger along the trigger-guard, butt on his thigh, muzzle pointing vertically upwards. He methodically scanned the ground ahead and on either side of the narrow road, examining it right to left, left to right, looking for human tracks in the snow expanses, for non-geological oddities among protruding wayside rock formations. All hostile Germans had left this bleakness. There might be starving Ustachi, hunted by Partisans, desperate to get out. Or similarly starving Chetniks, equally on the run. Or Partisan roadside checkpoints manned by trigger-happy enthusiasts given to the deferment of attempts at identification until after a few satisfying bursts of small-arms fire.

There was no interference on their journey. Laing turned the jeep through the rocks and snow to a barbed-wire enclosure in which were damaged, derelict farm-buildings on a low ridge. Here were caged the survivors of the eighty-two German prisoners taken six weeks previously at Ledenice.

Passers-by on the road had a clear view of the prisoners. They were gaunt, grey-faced, half-starved, untidy figures standing listlessly with their hands deep in their greatcoat pockets, forage-caps pulled over their ears, faces stubbled, shoulders hunched against the cold.

There had been a steady depletion of their numbers. Their officers had been taken from them and shot. There had been further deaths from unhealed wounds, from disease aggravated by privation. That there would be more deaths, a final totality of deaths, was in their minds and in that of Laing a certainty. They believed that only the continued presence of the Tommis had kept them alive for so long. In the interim before what they regarded as inevitable execution they had preserved a cohesion, a discipline and a dignity that Laing on his three previous visits had admired. It was a reluctant admiration. Laing was not fond of Germans.

There was no reluctance in Laing's professional admiration for the remarkable Sergeant-Major Schneider who now commanded them. Schneider was the tall straight-backed soldier whom Laing had first seen at Ledenice, walking behind his commanding officer and waving that ludicrous white flag of a flapping dress-shirt. Schneider, with no enforceable disciplinary sanctions at his disposal, with no credible threats of the retrospective retribution that would reach the presently disaffected after release, held his doomed group together by pure leadership, example and personality.

Laing stopped the jeep in front of the Partisan sentries at the compound gate. He and Smithwick took their time over slinging their packs on to their backs and fastening the hooks to the buckles at the tops of their magazine-pouches. Laing walked to the sentries. Smithwick tucked the butt of his tommy-gun under his right armpit, pointed the muzzle at the ground, and followed him, three paces to his rear. Laing, in a shuffled-up mixture of Serbo-Croat, Italian, schoolboy German and mime, explained that he had come for another interrogation of the prisoners. The senior sentry, who was old and moustachio'd, and who had good family cause for wishing all Germans dead, admitted them after a short argument and an envious study of Smithwick's tommy-gun. He hoped, said the sentry, that there would be no unnecessary fussiness in the methods used by Laing in getting the information that he wanted.

Laing and Smithwick tramped through the snow towards the broken buildings. Schneider had watched the discussion at the gate and was ready and waiting. His tattered, weakened soldiers were drawn up in two precise ranks, standing to attention. Schneider saluted. Laing returned the salute. To Schneider an officer was an officer, whatever army he served in. Laing walked slowly, stony-faced, along each rank, inspecting them. Each man looked him in the eye, and each man turned his head in succession to gaze at Laing as he progressed. If this was how the bloody Krauts wanted it, thought Laing, then this was how they could bloody have it.

Laing finished his tour of the rear rank, marched to the front of the parade, and faced it.

'Stand the parade easy and keep them here,' said Laing to Schneider. 'Then you come with me.'

Schneider's English was adequate. He barked an order. The prisoners separated their feet in unison and relaxed. Schneider followed Laing and Smithwick into the building.

Inside, Laing and Smithwick removed their packs and opened their ammunition-pouches. On a rickety old farmhouse table they made a little pile of bars of chocolate, packets of raisins, biscuits, cigarettes, soap. The unclaimed NAAFI rations of Sergeant Hankins, of two sick marines with him in the 99th Military Hospital in Bari, and of the two members of the Bren team killed in the attack on the first fort had reached an unusual destination. Laing and Smithwick unbuttoned their battledress blouses and produced six bottles of *rakija* to add to the heap. Laing topped it with a bottle of Canadian rye whisky from his personal NAAFI ration. Schneider stood rigidly to attention.

'Sergeant-Major,' said Laing.

'Herr Hauptmann?'

'Don't let the guards see this stuff. No traces afterwards, either.'

'Sir!'

'And Sarnt-Major.'

'Sir?'

'Happy Christmas,' said Laing, holding out his hand.

'Happy Christmas, chum,' said Smithwick, holding out his.

Schneider, heels still together, made a half-bow, shook both hands with concentrated formality, and suddenly grinned hugely.

'Happy Christmas, sir. Happy Christmas, Tommi,' he said, 'and thank you.'

'I'll just wish the men a Happy Christmas, too,' said Laing, 'then we must go.'

Schneider led them out to the trampled snow, hurrying ahead to get his people standing upright, regimented, stiff-backed, staring to their front, before the arrival of an officer. Christ, thought Laing, if I were Sergeant-Major Schneider and he was me in this sort of set-up, I'd have done it rather differently. But this was the German bloody Army, and they had their pride and their own way of displaying it, and they were doing it very well, and you didn't muck about with the self-respect of starving men under a collective death-sentence.

He marched to the front of the prisoners, crashed his feet to a parade-ground halt, and turned smartly to face them. Smithwick, moving as if he were on the square at the depot at Deal, took up a position to the right and behind Laing. Schneider, his back to Laing, was tersely addressing his command. Laing needed no translation to work out what this was about. 'Don't move a muscle of your faces. The Tommis have brought us a Christmas present. I've thanked the Herr Hauptmann on your behalf. If any one of you gives away this secret, before or after he's seen what it is, *he'll wish he'd never been born.*'

No face muscles moved. Nor did any other muscles. Schneider turned. There was another exchange of salutes.

Laing said: 'Please stand them easy, Sarnt-Major. And wish them from me, and from the soldiers I command, a Happy Christmas.'

It was a trite, pompous message and, bearing in mind the predicament of its recipients, absurd; but it seemed to strike an appreciative note. There were weak smiles, and murmurings resolving themselves into 'Fröhliche Weihnachten, Herr Hauptmann'.

Laing felt suddenly that he couldn't stand any more of this. He said, 'Sarnt-Major. You carry on,' called to Smithwick to follow him, and walked briskly to the gate.

As they were getting into the jeep he looked up. Inside the wire, among the snow and the extruding chilled rocks, Schneider and his bedraggled companions had broken ranks. They were grouped in a loose half-circle, Schneider facing them. Schneider's right arm was pointed in the air, the palm of his hand open. *Christ. The bastard's giving them a Nazi salute*, thought Laing, in bitter, incredulous fury. Schneider's elbow bent, the hand jerked down, and the strains of 'Stille Nacht, Heilige Nacht' came sweetly towards the jeep in a hoarse, harmonious unison.

Laing started the engine. The Partisan sentry scowled at the prisoners. Schneider, his choir in full voice, turned, and provided the unprecedented sight of a sergeant-major of the Wehrmacht giving a military salute and smiling at the same time. Laing let in the clutch. He and Smithwick waved. As the jeep was driven fast around the first bend, with a diminuendo Germanic 'Sleep in heavenly peace' accompanying it, Smithwick made a remark.

'I'm glad we did that, sir,' he said gravely. 'After all, it is fucking Christmas.'

Laing was glad, too, but his gladness was attended by a nagging, irritating disappointment. For the second time on this day it was directed at Hugo Burke. Hugo's declining to come to the church service was at least explicable by his adherence to the rules laid down by the curious religion that he professed. His refusal to have anything to do with the delivery of the Christmas presents for the prisoners had no justification at all.

Dammit, he'd been a prisoner himself until a few weeks ago – of these very people who he'd said had treated him well and whose lives were not going to last for much longer. Laing had taken it for granted that Hugo would have been delighted to join in the little surprise that he'd dreamt up with Smithwick. Hugo had been adamant. 'I'm sorry, Johnny,' he'd said. 'It's not the kind of thing I want to get mixed up in. I just don't want to see those bastards again.'

It was a private decision on a private matter. Laing had no power to turn a suggestion into an order, and wouldn't have done so even if he had. Equally, he had no intention of arguing or pleading. He was simply perplexed, annoyed – and beginning to feel concerned about Hugo. Hugo, after the initial euphoria that followed his release, had lately been behaving strangely. Distinct traces of strain. Edginess, moodiness, drinking a bit too much. In this sort of racket it happened to quite a few people. To Laing, Hugo had always seemed one of the least likely to be affected.

Corporal Mingay, a tall, lugubrious-looking man with a lantern jaw and a deadpan sense of humour, was one of the two road sentries at the southern entry to Viluse. He and the other sentries were also by now probably among the few entirely sober people left in the place. Mingay waved the jeep to a halt.

'Happy Christmas again, sir,' he said gloomily. 'Mr Burke said to tell you he's got the Chetnik officer with him.'

'What Chetnik officer?'

'The one with Mr Burke. Big hairy bugger.'

There was no point in wasting time with Mingay when he was being funny. Laing thanked Mingay and parked the jeep. He controlled his third vexation with Hugo Burke of this day. What in Christ's name did Hugo think he was about? The British weren't fighting their ex-allies the Chetniks, but the Partisans were. In Partisan eyes Chetniks were fascists of a depravity almost as deep as that of the Ustachi, which put them politically far to the right of Genghis Khan. A Chetnik officer in a British position on a Christian feast day at a time when Anglo-Yugoslav relations were in shreds. Jesus.

'Major Milunovic,' said Hugo, doing the introductions courteously. 'Captain Laing, my Troop Commander.'

Hugo and Milunovic were drinking whisky from tin mugs in the gutted room where Hugo slept. Mingay's description of Milunovic was accurate. He *was* a big hairy bugger, with a black waterfall of a beard, its luxuriance untrimmed in accordance with Chetnik practice. Shaving for them would not be resumed until the Karageorgovics, represented by young King Peter, were restored to the Yugoslav throne. Milunovic was dressed up for the occasion by the addition of a light-blue cavalry cloak and a sword in a leather-bound scabbard to his workaday ensemble of a fur hat, a patched Royal Yugoslav Army tunic, stained German-issue trousers, and jackboots. He rose from the ammunition-box on which he had been seated, brought his heels together, and bowed to Laing. Laing shook him by the hand and said nothing. There were questions of protocol here that had him baffled.

'Sir,' said Burke, thereby indicating that everyone was on duty, 'the Major has offered his surrender to us. With forty-three men and eight women.'

Laing stared at them both. Bloody Hugo was making things impossibly difficult. This was worse than Goertz's trying to specify at Ledenice that he would only give up his Germans to the British. At least Goertz had been an enemy. Milunovic wasn't. He was a former ally, who through miscalculation, or ill luck, or stupidity, or unshifting loyalty to his king, or distaste for communism, or for whatever motive, creditable or ambivalent, had backed the wrong horse and was now on one of the losing sides in the closing stages of a lethal three-cornered civil war in which no quarter was given by any of the competitors. In the early days, in 1941 and 1942, a British military mission had gone in by parachute and submarine to the Chetniks, and had given them encouragement, moral support and such limited, very limited, warlike stores as could be spared from a beleaguered Britain. In 1943 the support had been withdrawn and transferred to the Partisans because the Chetniks had been doing less and less against the Germans, had intrigued and in some areas collaborated with them. The Partisans were 'killing more Germans', and were thus a more profitable ally.

At a high politico-strategic level the switch made sound sense. So did the argument that the post-war ordering of Yugoslav internal affairs could only be determined by Yugoslavs themselves and it was not for outsiders to interfere, however bloody the form of determination took. The logic of the thing was unassailable. The problem was that when neat, dispassionate solutions were devised in Whitehall and Washington and by the Combined Chiefs of Staff they became translated at several removes into what actually happened to people. And what was actually happening to one small set of people now, here, this minute, was that one of them – himself – would have to adopt an expression of spurious grimness and tell this poor bloody Milunovic to go back to his forty-three men and eight women and say 'Sorry, I've been told to bugger off. The Brits have left us to be carved up by the commies.'

And it was intolerable that he, Laing, should have been put by Hugo Burke into a position in which he, Laing, must put on his black cap and pronounce sentence of death. The deaths were inevitable. No purpose was served by giving even a hint that there might be a way out. Hugo should have refused flatly to speak to Milunovic.

'Let's all have a drink,' said Laing to Hugo and Milunovic. 'After all, it is fucking Christmas.'

'I suppose', said Milunovic cheerfully, 'that you're going to tell me to bugger off.'

'Yes. I am. Where did you learn your English?'

'I used to be the assistant military attaché in London – '36 to '38. Good place. Only thing I couldn't stand was the licensing laws.'

'They're bloody. Where's your *Cheta*?'

'Not too far. Not too near. You'll hardly expect me to spell it out if you're not going to accept my surrender. Not that I thought you would, mind you. But it was worth a try.'

'Didn't do any harm. Might have done some good.'

'That's about it. If I'd been you, I'd have given the same answer. If I'd been a Partisan and had heard that you'd been accepting Chetnik surrenders, I'd have been furious. And if the positions were reversed, and we were on your side and winning, and the Partisans were hanging around being a nuisance, I'd have chased and bumped off every Partisan in sight. No prisoners. You'll see I'm not complaining.'

'I can see that all right,' said Laing, grateful, admiring, touched, feeling a bastard. Milunovic, early death imminent, personal death and death for his fifty-one followers, men and women, making it easy for Laing, sank his whisky and stood up. So did Laing and Hugo.

'Time to go,' said Milunovic. The mask was slipping slightly. For a moment he looked defeated, hurt. Then back came the panache. 'Thanks for the drink,' he said, smiling. 'I'll sneak out the way I came in. No embarrassment. Sretan Bozic.'

He shook hands, saluted and went.

'For Christ's sake, Hugo, you should have refused to see him.'

'I know I should. I'm glad I didn't.'

'So am I. Pour me another bloody drink. Stiff as you can make it. Jesus.'

Good soldiers make themselves as comfortable as possible in any circumstances, however unpromising the available materials. Good Senior Non-Commissioned Officers make themselves more comfortable than anybody else. The senior NCOs of X Troop were good senior NCOs. There should have been five of them, but Sergeant Hankins was still in hospital in Bari.

Troop Sergeant-Major Mayne was waiting, hatless, at the door of the sergeants' mess when Laing led over Burke and Mott for pre-lunch Christmas drinks. Mayne was short and springy, with bushy, fair eyebrows and a nose like the beak of a hawk. He had a versatile voice that he used either to shrivel the slovenly and the backsliding or to charm with affable reasonableness those of whom he approved. He couldn't of course shrivel officers with scorn, but he could put more nuances into the word 'sir' than any man that Laing had ever met. Wise officers thought twice when Sergeant-Major Mayne combined disciplined acceptance of an order of which he disapproved with a devastatingly insulting '*Sir!*' that indicated that it would both be carried out at once and was in the Mayne view somewhere between half-witted and criminal.

This morning, as was to be expected, was a morning for affability and reasonableness.

Mayne brought both heels smartly together in attention, smiled and said: 'Sir. Gentlemen. Welcome. Come on in.'

Laing said: 'Thank you, Sarnt-Major. The outside's not up to much, but I've no doubt the inside looks good.'

Within the narrow limits available it did. A wood fire of scavenged house-timbering blazed in a stone grate, cut replenishments stacked tidily beside it. The floor had been swept spotless. Areas of damp and decrepitude on the walls were hidden by draped gas-capes. Gaps in the windows were boarded with neatly shaped wooden insets. All surfaces were dusted. The defects of a looted table were shrouded by a blanket upon which sat elegant translucent brown tumblers made from beer-bottle bottoms, severed cleanly from their tops by a process requiring dexterity with rifle oil, boiling water, and friction-induced heat from a pullthrough.

Sergeant Montague, promoted into dead man's shoes when his predecessor had been killed six months earlier on Brac, and a useful fellow with his hands, had pinned up a Star of Bethlehem cut from the waterproof lead-foil lining of an ammunition-box. Below it was 'Happy Xmas' fashioned from the white sides of cigarette-packets. Montague apologised with a grin for not having scattered a bit of artificial snow about. He'd been deterred, he explained, by comments about there being too much of the bloody stuff outside. The other two sub-section commanders, Rowley and Ingram, were brewing something horrible-looking in a large dixie balanced firmly on rocks and heated by two paraffin-wax tommy-cookers.

'Glass of punch, sir?' said Sergeant-Major Mayne.

'Thanks. What's in it?'

'Bags of vino. *Rakija* base. Rum. Sugar. Tea. Something called *travarica*, whatever that is. Then. . . .'

'Christ,' said Hugo Burke.

'I wanted to add Brasso and petrol,' said Rowley, 'but the buggers wouldn't let me.'

'You've made up for that since, mate. The *rakija* base has got the vino outnumbered. It's become a *rakija* bloody apex.'

They all clinked their glasses in a Christmas toast, chatted easily about nothing in particular. They were friends united by shared experience and hazard, separated by a formality that was artificial and regarded by all of them as necessary. The survival and success of their little itinerant community depended upon mutual trust and discipline. Not the unthinking, authoritarian, blind discipline imposed for doubtless sound national psychological reasons by the likes of Sergeant-Major Schneider, but a firm application of hierarchical principles to a society in which self-reliance and personal initiative were prized and encouraged within a framework of controlled endeavour.

They might be jointly drinking a murderously corrosive mixture of God knew what in a tarted-up hovel in a Balkan mountain slum, but the hovel was a sergeants' mess of the Royal Marines in which proprieties were honoured. There were things that couldn't be said, prejudices and resentments that couldn't be aired, conventions to be respected. The officer guests addressed Mayne as 'Sarnt-Major'. They called each sergeant 'Sarnt' followed by his surname. The hosts called each of their guests 'sir'. Conceivably there were other ways of doing it, but this one had worked adequately for three hundred years and nobody felt any inclination to change it.

It was after the fourth slug of Viluse Juice that the silent Mott showed evidence of life. It became immediately clear to Laing and Burke that the Mott metabolic time-clock was telling him that a new and enormous legacy from his father was due. If he had been in an officers' club and not in a sergeants' mess, he would have been proclaiming his prosperity and buying drinks all round. Faced with the lack of a suitable ambience, he compromised. He began to beam at everyone in a jovial and, because it was so unusual, disturbing fashion. He told a joke that no one but himself could understand and laughed at it extravagantly.

He asked for, and carefully wrote down in his brown-covered Field-service pocket-book, the formula for this superb drink, Viluse Juice. He was given a list of ingredients that was accurate and a list of proportions that was guesswork. Hugo went amiably to him to help get the record straight. This kindly piece of aid led to later trouble. Hugo, for the first time, saw the photograph of the girl fastened to the inside flap of the pocket-book. Hugo accepted another glass of the villainous Juice, maintained a surface cheerfulness and nourished an internal icy fury. So this great wordless moron had been sniffing around Helen, had he?

Afterwards, when they had left, with warm gratitude warmly expressed, and feeling slightly rocky in the fresh air, and were out of sight of the sergeants, and were out of sight but not out of sound of the troops who were becoming uproarious at the far end of the village, Hugo hit Mott. It was a hard blow, viciously and unexpectedly delivered, and it caught Mott on the side of his chin. He was large and strong, but he went down on the packed snow like a pole-axed ox. Hugo tried to pick him up to hit him a second time. Laing, ferocious, stopped him. Together they carried Mott to his room, stretched him out comfortably and tucked him up in a blanket. Laing took Hugo for a long talk.

On the following morning Hugo Burke was sent by jeep to Dubrovnik to catch the first available landing-craft to Bari. Laing had first offered him leave when Hugo had been released at Ledenice. Hugo had declined the offer. Laing had now turned the offer into an order. It was his assessment that a combination of capture by the Ustachi, imprisonment by the Germans, concentrated shelling by the Royal Artillery, release, compensatory steady drinking, whisky with Milunovic, Viluse Juice with the sergeants, and becoming besotted with Helen Grant was more than enough for a man to compress into a few short weeks. Hugo needed a rest. Laing valued Hugo, personally and professionally. He wanted him restored.

CHAPTER SIX

HUGO BURKE did not return from Bari to rejoin 49 Commando in Yugoslavia. The transaction was reversed. The Field Artillery Regiment, 49 Commando, the ancillary Sapper and Royal Army Service Corps detachments, the Force Commander and his Headquarters Staff travelled piecemeal to Dubrovnik. There they embarked in a shuttle service of Landing-Craft (Tank) and Landing-Craft (Infantry) and set course westwards to Bari, Barletta and Molfetta, ports in Puglia in southern Italy.

The British force departed unsung. There were no valedictory parades, no words of thanks, no farewells. There was some obstructionism, and much aggravation. All restaurants in Dubrovnik were declared to be out of bounds to British troops. There was little food available for civilians, and the requirement was not unreasonable. The offensiveness with which the order was enforced by the National Liberation Committee or some similarly named body was unreasonable. All bars were banned to British troops. There was plenty of liquor available, and the order was resented. Civilians were forbidden to talk to British troops. This edict was resented even more strongly. The treatment of local people out of favour or sympathy with the new rulers aroused disgust. Ustachi and Chetnik sympathisers, pre-war capitalists, royalists, Occupation collaborators, people who went to church, active critics, passive disapprovers of communism, Peasant Party members, anyone who was considered by an arbitrary yardstick to fail to measure up to the specifications of what a Marxist citizen should be, as defined by dogmatic zealots, was imperilled, intimidated, imprisoned, executed.

The weather during the passage across the Adriatic was as bleak as had been the goodbyes. A cold Force 6 wind stirred a white-horsed greasy grey swell that bucketed the flat-bottomed landing-craft all over the ocean. Squalls of driving rain rattled against the steel decks. Below, everything swayed and smelled nauseatingly of diesel oil. But it was warm and dry. The tubular-framed canvas bunks were the most comfortable beds that anyone had rested upon for months.

Laing went down to see that all was well. There was a spirit of muted contentment. The return to Italy was a well-liked move. Italy might be a dangerous place to fight in, but out-of-the-Line Italy was a home of relatively intact billets, passable food, plenty of vino, women who weren't festooned with weaponry, grenades and ammunition-belts, of occasional cinemas and concert parties, NAAFI canteens, mobile bath units, and an imaginatively conducted Eighth Army leave-centre.

Yugoslavia had, with the one exception of vino, lacked these simple amenities. Eight months on the Dalmatian islands and four in Montenegro had brought memorable moments of visual beauty, Slav singing that was a delight to hear, comradeship with allies of spirited quality. Living conditions had been austere. The whole thing had soured when the political leaders of people with whom you had once had a mutual respect began to treat you with an insulting disdain and to make it clear that you had once been useful to them, had been used, no longer needed to be used, and could get the hell out.

Most of the chit-chat on the troop decks was about the Italian future. Laing heard two comments about the Yugoslav past. One of the two self-proclaimed communists present was gloomily reconciling Party theory with recently observed Party practice. 'There's nothing wrong with the *system*,' he was explaining. 'It's just that the Jugs are too bloody dozy to understand how it works.'

Lance-Corporal Smithwick, Christmas-present distributor (retd), was more profound. Smithwick was arguing that he personally didn't give a damn about politics, British, Balkan, communist, conservative, anything else, or any combination of anything else. Smithwick's ambition was to get the war over, go home and become an ex-serviceman. The sooner the better. The central attraction in this programme was that it meant not being buggered about any longer. What he found hard to believe was that a naturally independent-minded, bloody-minded crowd like the Jugs, most of whom were good blokes who didn't like being buggered about any more than he did, would knuckle down for long to being buggered about by all those bloody commissars and their Russian bosses.

Laing had recently heard this identical point being made in more elegant phraseology by a senior officer of the British military mission accredited to Marshal Tito's headquarters. It had cheered him. So did Smithwick.

A naval rating said: 'Captain's compliments, sir. Would you and the other officer care to join him for a drink in his cabin?'

Laing, grateful for naval hospitality, roused Silent Mott from a catatonic trance on his bunk and took him up the swaying ladder.

The captain, a Royal Naval Volunteer Reserve lieutenant with discoloured skin on one cheekbone, mixed and distributed pink gins.

'Cheers,' he said. 'I suppose you'll be glad to get out of that lot.'

'Yes,' said Laing, 'I think so. I'll bore my grandchildren with it. But it's high time to go.'

'I think so, too,' said the lieutenant. 'I've been running up and down to Dubrovnik for three months now. The Jugs were more unpleasant every time I tied up. Bloody glad this is the last trip.'

He stared at the pinkness of the Angostura in his glass. It blended delicately with the mauve patch on his cheek.

'Mind you,' he added, 'when the war's over and things quieten down I'll be back like a shot. Lovely country for a holiday. Good people, too, if you count out those damned political *Gauleiters* or whatever they call themselves.'

'I agree,' said Laing.

'Took back one of your chaps about three weeks ago,' said the lieutenant. 'Burke. Hugo Burke. Off on a spot of leave. Nice chap. Gets a bit aggressive after a tot or two.' He chuckled.

'Really?'

'Yes. Had him up here for a bracer. We were getting on like a house on fire until I happened to mention a girl I knew. Red Cross girl. I'd heard her speak about him. Well, I'd just started telling him about the fun we'd had together – *you* know – when damn me if he doesn't put down his glass and hit me in the eye. Then he knocked me out cold. Woke up on the deck. By then he'd gone. Didn't even say goodbye in the morning.'

He chuckled again, ruefully admiring of these high-handed little eccentricities.

Laing looked at the bruising on the lieutenant's cheek and said: 'Is that right?' He couldn't think of anything else to say. Then he looked compulsively at Mott's chin. Silent Mott, uncharacteristically, was smiling a gentle smile. Perhaps he was pleased to discover that he was one of the co-founders of an unusual club that might achieve an extensive membership.

CHAPTER SEVEN

Italy

Two newspapers, both printed far from where the wedding took place, carried announcements about it.

The *Ottawa Citizen* reported that Randall H. and Tanya Burke of 900 Roxborough Avenue, Rockliffe Park, were glad to announce that their son, Hugo S. Burke, had married Helen Grant 'in the "Central Mediterranean Forces"'. It was Mrs Burke who insisted on the inclusion of 'Central Mediterranean Forces', and its being put in quotation marks. It was part of Hugo's postal address and gave some indication of where the ceremony had been solemnised. It indicated simultaneously that, unlike a horde of Canadian Zombie draft objectors, the parents of several of whom were known personally to Mrs Burke, Hugo S. Burke was away fighting for his country. It also eliminated tiresome enquiries about who Helen Grant was and why the enquirers had not been invited to the wedding.

The *Irish Times* described the event more formally:

The marriage recently took place quietly in the Central Mediterranean area between Mr Hugo Sepelov Burke, Royal Marines, only son of Mr and Mrs Randall Burke of Ottawa, Canada, and Miss Helen Eva O'G. Grant, younger daughter of Mrs Noelle O'G. Grant and the late Commander T. J. O'G. Grant, DSC, RN (retd), of Grantsbridge, Co. Monaghan.

In the context of the *Irish Times* announcement, 'quietly' meant explicitly no white gown, bridal veil, bridesmaids, flowered hats, morning coats, champagne, wedding cake, toasts and widespread affable insobriety. Its implicit message was that Mr H. S. Burke and Miss Helen Eva O'G. Grant were unable to enjoy this sort of traditional frivolity because both were engaged in a war for the defence of Christian civilisation, which was more than could be said for the elected government of the neutral Irish Free State and for most of its citizens. Mrs Noelle O'G. Grant knew a thing or two about how to combine Anglo-Irish social correctness with getting a dig in at people whose attitudes she disapproved of.

In the literal sense of 'quiet' the wedding wasn't all that quiet.

*

Johnny Laing was best man. He also acquired the responsibilities that normally fall to the bride's family on these occasions. He did both jobs very well. His task was simplified because factors of time and space imposed constrictions on when and where the event could be held.

Time dictated that it should be as soon as possible. This consideration had nothing to do with the one that has accelerated the date of many a wedding before and since, and had everything to do with the fact that, after a brief period of retraining, 49 Commando, and the groom with it, were due to go up the Line.

Space was similarly inflexible. The groom and most of the guests were on immediate call for a return to work. Their present place of work was a small, smelly mountain town named Putignano, twenty miles from Bari. The ceremony, the reception and the honeymoon could only be in Bari. Father Fahy, the Brigade Catholic Chaplain, had a choice of Italian churches that he could borrow. The reception could only be held in the Imperiale hotel, the officers' club. Food and drink were cheap and plentiful there and, in any case, Italian civilian hotels and restaurants were out of bounds to soldiers as part of an attempt to conserve foodstocks in a winter of shortages and tightening of belts. By extension, the same consideration governed the selection of the honeymoon location. All roads led to the Imperiale hotel.

The Colonel took a benign interest in the arrangements. They had first come to his notice on a semi-official basis, through a question put to him by the Adjutant.

'Sir, Hugo Burke's marrying this girl Helen. He wants to do everything a hundred per cent right. He's asked Johnny Laing whether he needs your official permission. Johnny didn't know and asked me. I don't know, either, so I said I'd ask you. Does he?'

'Buggered if I know,' said the Colonel. 'Isn't it all written down in one of those Handy Hints for the Adjutant leaflets that you cart around wherever we go?'

'We must have left the Marriage Guidance bit at home.'

'Damned slack. It's the sort of thing that crops up almost daily in this place. Well, if it cheers him up, tell him to come and argue his case and I'll say yes. Make it just before lunch. I'll buy him a drink.'

'Johnny,' asked the Colonel, 'anything I can do to grease the axle of the nuptials? Unfortunate metaphor, but you know what I mean.'

'Don't think so, sir, thank you. It's all tied up.'

'Good. What's your view of this girl Helen?'

It was not the sort of question that the Colonel would normally ask. Laing stared at him.

'If I didn't think much of her, I wouldn't tell you so, sir. As it is, I think she's a sweetie. She's also damned amusing company.'

Yes, thought the Colonel, she's those. And more. He'd found out for himself when he had met her for the first time during a short leave in Naples, and after two hours of her damned amusing company had with no regrets whatsoever found himself engaged in astonishing feats of athleticism in a bedroom in the mess of a transit camp. She was handsomely generous about whom she was a sweetie and amusing with. The Colonel was one among many who had had cause to be grateful. Marriage would doubtless settle her, and she would leave all that behind her. What worried the Colonel was that, if young Hugo ever got to hear of what his new wife had once been up to almost indiscriminately, he would be hurt beyond remedy. Hugo could be as light-hearted as the next man, but there was an inflexible narrowness about some of his attitudes that in a curious way added to his moral strength. One of those attitudes would undoubtedly be a traditional Catholic notion of bringing a virgin to his bridal bed. The Colonel hoped to God that all the beneficiaries of Helen's pre-marital largesse would have the wit and the good manners to keep their mouths shut. He himself certainly would.

It was a happy wedding day. The bride wore navy-blue beret, jacket and skirt, with accessories of a white shirt, a black tie, black stockings, black shoes, 'British Red Cross Society' stitched in red on the shoulder of each sleeve, and small red crosses beneath the lettering.

The groom wore khaki battledress, khaki shirt and tie, brown shoes, with accessories of a green beret with a Globe and Laurel cap-badge (beret tucked under his left shoulder-strap for the ceremony), a white-blanco'd waistbelt with highly polished brass fittings, and at the shoulder of each sleeve, embroidered in red on a navy-blue background, reading from top to bottom, *49, Royal Marines, Commando*, and a triangular shield with an upthrust fighting-knife in its centre, the symbol of Commando Group.

The bride, who had silky fair hair, high cheekbones, blue eyes, and was of lithe construction, was serene, composed and smiling throughout. The groom, who was dark, weather-burnt, broad-shouldered, and as lithe as the bride, was in what was later described as cracking good form throughout.

Throughout began at five o'clock in the evening in an over-ornamented Italian church, full of extravagantly bleeding Sacred Hearts and sad Madonnas. Since the process of Helen's instruction in the Catholic Faith was incomplete there was no Nuptial Mass. Father Fahy was crisp and kindly during the short service. Bride and groom made the responses in glad, clear voices. Father Fahy pronounced them man and wife. They kissed chastely and signed the register on an army form. Then bride, groom, priest, best man and a delightful nursing sister named Gert, who was supporting the bride and about whom the best man was already making provisional private plans, packed themselves into Father Fahy's jeep and headed for the reception in the bar of the Imperiale hotel.

By the unusual nature of things the reception was well under way before its principals put in an appearance. All twenty-eight officers of 49 Commando, less Silent Mott who had prudently answered the call for a volunteer to mind the shop, had arrived in convoy in good time, dressed as was the groom in best battledress and white-blanco'd belts. They joined five nursing sisters and a Royal Army Medical Corps doctor, friends of Helen, all who could take time off from hospital duty. The bar was already thronged with officers on leave from the Line, and with recuperating hospital patients allowed out on ticket-of-leave, British, Indian, Canadian, South African, New Zealand, Polish, representatives of all the international fighting community of Eighth Army. They were young and fit and in the high good-humour that comes to men who have recently been shot at and missed or, if they haven't been missed, haven't been hit too badly and, whether they have been hit or missed, will shortly be shot at again.

The drink was at floodtide, and the guests awaiting the bridal pair made no attempt to leave the beach. They mingled cheerfully with what at a conventional wedding reception would have been gatecrashers, here legitimately in possession of the premises before the proceedings began. A certain unpredictable *élan* superimposed itself upon planned events.

When Laing brought Hugo and Helen into the bar the invited guests, glasses in hands, formed a queue. Led by the Colonel they advanced in turn, kissed Helen on the cheek, shook Hugo by the hand, and made appropriate references to felicitations and congratulations. Genial strangers in exotic uniforms attached themselves to the queue, kissed the bride with affectionate enthusiasm, wrung Hugo's hand, and pressed drinks upon both. A spontaneous urge to mark a rare occasion began to flower.

An Irish–Polish extempore choir sang a harmonious and improper version of 'I'll Cherish Thee'. Canadians, tipped off about Hugo's origins, orchestrated a stylish version of 'Alouette'. A group of South African fighter pilots choreographed 'Hold Him Down, That Zulu Warrior'. The New Zealanders, led by a Maori major, danced a Haka. The 49 Commando officers did their party-piece of 'Hej Kommandie, Zdravo Kommissar', the rousing, hauntingly melodious marching song of the Partisan First Dalmatian Brigade. Helen and Hugo stood side by side, inner hands entwined, outer hands holding glasses of Asti Spumanti, smiling, happy, murmuring to one another at times, joining in the singing at times. It was not the sort of wedding reception that would necessarily have appealed to Mrs Noelle O'G. Grant of Grants-bridge, County Monaghan, Irish Free State.

Laing, the controller of the revels, looked at his watch. Time for dinner. He took Helen by one hand, Hugo held the other, and they led the invited guests towards the dining-room, to a choral accompaniment of 'We're the D Day Dodgers, Out in Ital-ee', the Italian Campaign adaptation of Lilli Marlene.

The dining-room was quieter, but not much more so. The invited guests, in prime celebratory condition, made most of the noise themselves. Courtly, bald, pear-shaped majors and colonels, Rear Area functionaries employed in routine staff jobs, dining at adjacent tables, gazed benevolently at the young and healthy enjoying themselves, wondered how soon how many would be dead and gone, became sentimental about the calm beauty of the bride. When they could catch her eye, the old gentlemen raised their glasses and called 'Good luck'. Helen and Hugo raised theirs in a series of return salutes, with Helen smiling devastatingly and Hugo saying 'Thank you, sir'. The older generation of uninvited attenders were as warm-hearted as were their juniors in the bar across the foyer.

Laing rapped on the table with a knife-handle and said: 'Charge your glasses.' Waiters bustled. The Colonel stood up. Everybody else at the table except Hugo and Helen stood up. It had been agreed that there would be no speeches. The Colonel examined the bubbles in his Spumanti, grinned, looked Helen in the eye, looked Hugo in the eye, wondered whether he should propose a toast to 'The Bride and Groom' or to 'Helen and Hugo', and compromised on a merger of the two.

'The Bride and Groom. Helen and Hugo,' he said.

'The Bride and Groom. Helen and Hugo,' said the guests.

They drank. Young Peter Sims, a subaltern in Y Troop, drained his glass and threw it over his shoulder. It hit one of the pear-shaped colonels, who didn't seem to mind very much.

'Sorry, sir,' said Sims. 'Old naval custom.'

No other Royal Marine officer present honoured this old naval custom of ten seconds' seniority. They all sat down again to coffee and liqueurs.

The bride and groom left for their honeymoon. The first part of their journey took them to the lift, just outside the dining-room door. They were escorted thus far by the entire wedding party, to a background accompaniment of sustained clapping and oral messages of goodwill from the old gentlemen in the dining-room. Helen blew them a kiss, which caused an intensification in the volume of the clapping.

At the lift gates they were joined by representative choristers of the fighting forces of the British Commonwealth of Nations, supplemented by a cluster of Poles and two officers from the newly formed Jewish Brigade. The lift gates opened, Hugo and Helen entered, and the choir gave them 'Roll Me Over in the Clover'. Hugo held the lift button at Open with one hand and Helen's hand with the other. When the choir boomed into 'This Is Number Five, and It's Good to Be Alive', Hugo whispered to Helen and kissed her. There was an outbreak of cheering. The bride and groom waved, the lift gates closed, and the guests, invited and uninvited, returned to the bar.

Johnny Laing, who was noted for the skill with which he always allowed for an element of flexibility in his operational planning, had left a wide margin of time for the final phase of the wedding celebrations. To ensure that there were no mistakes he had arranged with the Signals Officer for the doubling up of the Imperiale's rickety internal communications system by a field-telephone installed at Hugo's bedside and connected by land-line to another at the reception desk. Laing had bribed the receptionist to listen for its buzz and to pass a message to him immediately it did so.

The good tidings were brought to him personally in the bar.

'It has buzzed, Signor Capitano,' said the receptionist dramatically.

Laing called for silence. He invited the guests to charge their glasses yet again, and he urged them to follow him into the street. It was bitterly cold outside, and no one but Laing knew what they were to do when they got there, but they followed him without question. He was running this caper. He knew what he was about.

He stood well back from the entrance, and in the light of a full moon stared upwards at the front wall of the hotel. They stared with him. A third-floor window opened and a hand emerged, clutching something brassy with a bell-shaped mouth. There was a click, a hissing noise. A red Very light soared parabolically into the night sky. A green light followed. A last red.

The audience cheered. Hugo had fired the unit's Success Signal of red over green over red. Objective taken. He had the rest of the night to consolidate his position.

'Darling,' said Helen Burke, recently Grant, 'what a perfect, lovely day.'

'Not too noisy for you?'

'Perfect was what I said.'

'You didn't mind the uninvited song-and-dance team?'

'They were lovely.'

'Or even "Roll Me Over"?'

'That was lovely, too.'

'Not even the Very pistol?'

'That was the loveliest of all. Well, next to loveliest of all.'

They consolidated.

CHAPTER EIGHT

TROOP re-equipment and retraining was resumed early on the following morning. Hugo Burke missed four days of it. He had been posted to Special Duties. The Colonel, who didn't need a Liaison Officer, had appointed Hugo as his Liaison Officer, with orders to base himself on the Imperiale hotel and there to await instructions about whom to liaise with. Richard, the Adjutant, spelt out the degree of commitment expected of Hugo in the discharge of this task.

'If you feel that you *must* leave the hotel for a little while,' he said threateningly, 'make sure that you're not out of reach of a telephone for more than fourteen hours at any one time. But, then, I don't suppose that you *will* want to go out for long.'

Hugo was a dutiful Liaison Officer. He hardly left the hotel at all.

The re-equipment and retraining of 49 Commando was part of a programme designed to prepare them, and the other three commandos in the brigade, for a changed role. For the past year all four – two of them Royal Marine, two drawn from army volunteers – had been racketing around semi-independently in the Balkans, in Yugoslavia, in Albania and Greece on interesting but militarily unsophisticated operations. They were now to fight as a brigade of assault infantry in the technically seasoned and mature Eighth Army, two years and four countries on in their advance that had started at Alamein in Egypt, now building up for a final spring offensive in the eastern half of northern Italy.

To old Balkan hands used to making do with what could be spared from more stylish embroilments, the re-equipment seemed comfortingly lavish. New battledress replaced the threadbare, decaying things that had doubled as working-clothes and pyjamas in a Montenegro of damp marches by day and lice-infested cottage accommodation by night. Comfortably broken-in ammunition-boots, worn down almost to the uppers, were discarded in favour of footwear of a vaguely mountaineering cast known as 'SV boots'. They had crenellated soles of hard rubber, and no one ever discovered, or minded, what 'SV' stood for. Sleeveless leather jerkins, similar to those worn by the soldiers of Henry V during the run-up to Agincourt, and by now looking as if they had indeed been reissued by the reincarnation of some Plantagenet quartermaster, accompanied the old battledress and the ammunition-boots to the bonfire; or, in the suspicious opinion of some critics of the Administrative Officer and his staff, to the Italian black market. In place of the jerkins came the most practical garments yet to have reached the soldiery: sturdy thigh-length camouflaged Airborne smocks, loose-fitting, four usefully large pockets secured by press-studs, a flap like a tail that was fastened under the crotch and prevented the jumping-jacket from riding up.

There was a considerable sentimental resistance to parting with worn-out green berets, travelled tokens of bygone strife, old and familiar, bleached by sun and salt, leather headbands beginning to rot. They went. The Colonel was inexorable. Substitutes of pristine verdancy, with an almost luminous nap, came compulsorily into vogue, were despised, were accepted with resignation.

There was no controversy about the abandonment of webbing big packs, date of birth *circa* 1910, secured by webbing straps that dragged at the shoulders towards the end of a long march. The Bergen rucksacks that replaced them were mounted on a light tubular frame that distributed efficiently the weight to be carried. If, prevailing opinion had it, you were stupid enough to get yourself involved in all this tramping about carrying heavy loads while unfriendly people took shots at you, you might as well do the carrying with something that mitigated the exertion.

Weapons were given attention. All rifles and Brens were re-zero'd, the armourers spending days over adjusting individual sights. Worn Bren-gun barrels were replaced. So, in the Heavy Weapon Troop, was a defective base-plate of one of the four 3-inch mortars and a suspect cooling-jacket of one of the four Vickers medium machine-guns.

Grenades (No. 36, Fragmentation; No. 77, Phosphorus smoke) were checked and cleaned. The PIATs (Projectors, Infantry, Anti-Tank) were serviced meticulously and with scepticism. They were primitive and unpopular rocket-launchers that looked like plump lengths of drainpipe with protuberances. There was one to each troop. Corporal Smithwick, the X Troop clerk when out of action, the X Troop PIAT-operator when in it, had spent a year in the carriage, discharge and maintenance of this gadget. His dealings with it had been interrupted at intervals by periods of recuperation from injuries that it inflicted upon him. He regarded it without love.

Universally looked upon without love were the new Lifebuoy flame-throwers, two to each troop. Silent Mott was put in overall charge of these, it being tacitly agreed between the Colonel and Laing that the Mott reluctance to speak made him a suitable choice for the job. The less said about the bloody things the better. Criticisms of the technique of

57

carrying a back-pack load of inflammable fluid to within its maximum range of twenty-five yards of its target, pointing a nozzle like that of a hose in the right direction, and burning to a cinder whatever or whoever the nozzle was aimed at were part-ethical, part-practical. The idea of frying people was disliked. The mechanics of carrying the thing to within twenty-five yards of whoever had been selected for frying, when he could be more comfortably, more humanely, and less dangerously shot from several hundred yards away, were ridiculous.

Hugo lost his job as Liaison Officer when the issue of new equipment was complete. Sergeant Hankins, released from hospital, his back carrying jagged puckered scars but otherwise in excellent shape, had supervised the distribution of the new wardrobes and the checking of the weapons of Hugo's section in his absence. Hugo concurred with the Laing view that Hankins had probably done a more thorough job than Hugo could have done.

'Training starts in earnest tomorrow. Feeling fit?' asked Laing unkindly.

'As well as can be expected.'

'Where's Helen?'

'Back at work. Welfaring away with the sick, lame and lazy.'

'According to Richard, the best man always buys the groom a present. I've bought you a present.'

'Johnny, you're a decent old bastard at heart. I'll forgive that crack about feeling fit. What's the present?'

'Pair of boots.'

'That's a bloody insulting present. I withdraw my forgiveness.'

'Special sort of boots. Those Canadian lumberjack things they have in the officers' shop. You've probably forgotten but you once told me that you'd like a pair.'

'Thanks, Johnny. I really have had my eye on those. Forgiveness restored.'

They were handsome boots, calf-length, with a leather flap fastened by two small buckles at each top. Laing had had them inscribed by the Congregationalist teetotaller Holy Joe, who had been a cobbler in civilian life. Holy Joe had done the job by knocking small brass nails neatly into the instep. The nailheads read: 'H.S.B. FROM J.R.L. 15.2.45.' Hugo was genuinely touched.

Training began with a speed-march, seven miles in one hour, twelve miles in two, Light Fighting Order worn, full complement of weapons and ammunition carried, never mind keeping the step, double down all slopes, stride out up all slopes and on the flat. Nobody in Laing's troop fell out, although two hard tickets who had consistently punished the bars of Putignano were violently sick by the roadside and Hugo covered the last three miles by willpower rather than by stamina.

For two weeks there were practice section attacks, troop attacks, commando attacks of all five fighting troops supported by the mortars and medium machine-guns of the Heavy Weapon Troop, live ammunition used in all. There were patrol exercises in the valleys and hills, and signals exercises, and practical training in co-operation with tanks. There was a daily dose of close-order drill for everybody because the commandos, Royal Marine and Army, had satisfied themselves from experience that the highest possible standard of turnout and parade-ground drill was reflected in a high performance in action.

A general feeling grew that all this bullshit had lasted long enough.

The Colonel was well content.

The journey was by rail, in cattle-trucks. For many years afterwards survivors of the trip bored and discomfited their wives and families by comparisons of the joys of this form of travel with the rigours peddled by package-tour promoters. Blankets or sleeping-bags were spread on the floors. There was plenty of room to hang kit and to move about. The train moved slowly and stopped frequently. An endless supply of boiling water for brewing tea or shaving could be drawn from the boiler of the engine, in the teeth of the driver's anguish at the repeated sight of this drain on his power unit. There was ample time for sleeping, reading, watching the changing scenery; and at the longer halts, and for those so inclined, for going for short walks in the country. At most of the rural stations Italian women sold fruit, wine, cheese, and in some cases, regrettably, themselves. It was a memorably pleasing four days of near-Hedonism for most. For some it was their last rail journey.

It came to an end at what was known in military administrative jargon as a railhead. Here, also to cite the jargon, they de-trained. When the train stopped at the station, they got off. A convoy of Royal Army Service Corps three-tonner trucks was waiting to carry them onward. The Colonel cast a relaxed, approving eye over the transfer of four hundred men and their belongings from train to trucks. It could be done in confusion and, at its worst, in chaos.

When, as now, it was done by the experienced it was an orderly, disciplined, simple process with a pleasing symmetry to it. The troops, shaved, clean, berets adjusted to the regulation one inch above the eyebrows and battledress collars buttoned up under the new Airborne smocks, boots polished, equipment uniformly adjusted, rifles and tommy-guns slung, Brens and PIATs at the trail, fell in by troops. Within the troops they stood in their sections and sub-sections. Senior NCO's led their files to allocated trucks. Tailboards were unbolted, rucksacks were passed from man to man and loaded, everyone clambered aboard, tailboards were rebolted, officers and troop sergeant-majors climbed into cabs. The Adjutant reported formally that he had inspected the train and that all cattle-trucks had been tidied up and left as if they had never suffered human occupation.

The convoy set out through the flat countryside of the Romagna, towards Ravenna, once dignified by the presence of the Byzantine Imperial Court, now dominated by the influence of V Corps of the Eighth Army.

To Balkan primitives it was a new, strange world. This set-up was *organised*. Red-capped military policemen controlled and directed the traffic. One-way routes were clearly marked with placarded symbols: Sun Up, Sun Down, Moon Up, Moon Down. Dumps of stores and ammunition were laid out under guard behind barbed wire in roadside vineyards, access-tracks bulldozed to each. The way to Corps, Divisional, Brigade and Unit Headquarters was indicated by arrowed signposts, decorated with the sub-heraldic stencilled devices of each formation – Galleon in full sail, Black Cat, Kiwi, Battleaxe. There was a multitude of vehicle-parks, maintenance-workshops, field-hospitals, transport-pools, dispersed clusters of tanks and artillery, low-loaders to carry the tanks over roads towards battle.

In the ancient ochre city itself mysteriously acronymic entities like DADOS and BRASCO had established themselves among the more easily identifiable NAAFI canteens, the theatre requisitioned for troops' entertainment, the chapels for separate religious denominations, the VD prophylactic centres, the bank that had become an officers' club. Infantry on rest from the Line, fifteen miles to the north, roamed the streets – British, Indian, Gurkha, New Zealand, Polish. A few scattered tourists from the American Fifth Army that covered the west side of northern Italy were among them – Americans, French, some Brazilians. All movement was unconcealed and casual. The Luftwaffe, who a few short years previously would have modified notably life in a city of that size, in that location, put to that use, had been forced out of serious business.

The commando settled in in civvy billets. Three days later they resumed warfare.

CHAPTER NINE

THE GERMAN TASK in northern Italy was essentially the protection of the southern marches of the Reich. They were masterly at the exploitation of the defensive potential of river obstacles. They contested the ones of their choice until a rigidly calculated operational profit-and-loss sheet demonstrated that the price of holding on was an unacceptable drain on resources of men and material. Then they pulled back to prepared positions at the next suitable river, harassing the pursuit with skilled rearguards and by a wholesale sowing of mines and booby-traps throughout the area that they had abandoned.

By now there were only two sizeable rivers, the Po and the Adige, left between the Germans and Austria, the southern bulwark of metropolitan Germany itself.

The Allied task, expressed at its simplest, was to break the German Army in northern Italy. The achievement of this aim would threaten the southern flank of the German national fastness and, should events elsewhere not make the final phase unnecessary, implement the threat. There was, of course, a vital interplay between force exerted in Italy and force exerted simultaneously on the western and eastern frontiers of Germany.

For the Eighth Army there were some encouraging local elements in the jigsaw. The Allied air forces dominated the skies. Both sides were poor relations when it came to the allocation of weaponry and ammunition, the bulk of which went to meet the prior claims of the rival armies on the Rhine, but in Italy the Germans were the worst off. The ground ahead was the broad north Italian plain which had to be given time to dry out sufficiently to carry the weight of a vast mass of tracked and wheeled vehicles. It would be firm enough by early spring. In the meantime, while preparations went ahead and resources accumulated, the Line had to be held.

The part of it given to the Commando Brigade was the extreme right. The easternmost soldier had the waters of the Adriatic Sea at his right shoulder. It was a curious development in that troops who for years had rehearsed and executed assault landings on beaches were now on yet another beach, but one that was askew. Instead of coming into it at a right angle to the shoreline they were facing laterally along it.

Inland, separated from the sea by a sandy, scrubby spit of land about a mile wide and seven miles from bottom to top, was a large, shallow, marshy, brackish lake, the shape of an apple squashed in on all sides. Each side matched in length the spit side, roughly seven miles. This was Lake Commachio. The name became applied generically to the operational area of the Brigade. Later, it was to be written on the headstone of Hugo Burke in the Commonwealth War Graves Commission cemetery at Stressio. Other headstones were to bear a similar inscription.

The Line was not a continuous Line, like the one that stretched as an attenuated trench system from the Swiss frontier to the English Channel between 1914 and 1918. This Italian version was, rather, a series of interdependent lumps, defended stone farm-building complexes, slit-trenches dug on river flood-banks, in woods, each position in view of its neighbour, sited so as to be covered by the fire from its neighbour. Its German opposite counterpart was laid out in much the same pattern. To the west the two opposing lines were close, separated by the width of the narrow, sluggish-flowing River Reno, antagonists living in holes scooped in the earth of high flood-banks on either side. The intervening distance widened towards the sea, until the British in a pine-wood at the base of the spit were nearly a mile across low sand dunes from the nearest opposition.

The most advanced localities were manned by people like Johnny Laing's X Troop, self-sufficient infantry armed and equipped with what they could carry personally – rifles, Brens, PIATs; the German equivalents with rifles, Spandaus, Schmeissers, Panzerfausts. Close up, but farther back, a few hundred yards back, were the support weapons, the mortars, the medium machine-guns. Farther back still, tucked out of sight in places unknown to and uncared about by the forward soldiers, were the artillery, the batteries of 25-pounders nearest, the heavier mediums the furthermost.

In the same way as the calibre of the guns increased in direct proportion to their distance from up front, so did the weight of the overall responsibilities carried by commanders, a function of the exercise of proper control, not of Privilege seeking safer havens.

Laing's Troop Headquarters was in a small clearing in the pine-wood, a hundred yards behind the forward edge of the wood held by Burke's section and Mott's section, deployed side by side in well dug-in and concealed clusters. The Colonel's Headquarters was in a farmhouse half a mile more to the rear, from where he could co-ordinate the activities of his five fighting troops, also side by side, between them looking after a stretch of about a mile. Brigade Headquarters was sited over a mile behind that of the Colonel in another farm, from which the Brigadier could control the doings of his four commandos. There were plenty of others as the command pyramid narrowed and the headquarters establishments broadened. Field-Marshal Alexander's Allied Force Headquarters was in a palace at Caserta near Naples, 250 miles away, although the Field-Marshal always left it and came well forward to his Tactical Field Headquarters when major battle was planned or joined.

The Colonel's driver put the jeep into four-wheel drive and eased it slowly along the sand track through the pine-wood. He had two grounds for caution. The surface of the track held an ankle-deep coating of dry dust and sand. Too much speed would generate a dust-plume, which would attract a shower of German 81-millimetre mortar-bombs, which would annoy the Colonel. And it would be unpardonable to attract through carelessness a mortar-stonk on to the permanent residents, scattered in functional groups among the trees on either side of the track.

The second incentive to prudence was underlined by the sight of the heavy white tape, slung from tree to tree, that fenced off large areas of the wood. The Sappers had not yet had time to clear mines from these enclosures. If the jeep strayed from a path certified as mine-free, Errors and Omissions Excepted, the Colonel would have even greater cause for complaint, although its expression would be unlikely to be either transmitted or received.

The jeep stopped. The Colonel headed for the track and turned left, called to his driver to follow him on foot, and padded along the loose sand through the tape-bedecked trees. The tapes branched away right and left after fifty yards. The front quarter of the wood had been given priority in mine-clearance. Constrictions on movement there were potentially more dangerous than they were farther back.

As he approached the rear of Laing's position the Colonel glanced approvingly at Laing's hospitable provision for travellers. Slit-trenches had been dug at ten-yard intervals along one side of the track. Replenishment parties bringing up food and ammunition, messengers or walking wounded going back, visitors like the Colonel had somewhere solacing to jump into if caught in the open by a stonk of mortar-bombs or shells.

Laing was waiting outside the clearing that accommodated his Troop Headquarters. He saluted.

'Morning, sir.'

'Morning, Johnny. You still hiding in that underground brothel?'

Laing grinned. The previous holders of this sector had been the Garibaldi Partisani, Italian communist-led guerrillas with an idiosyncratic approach to soldiering that would have appalled their austere Yugoslav opposite numbers and that had captivated X Troop. 'Dead stylish, these buggers,' said the marines. 'If only old Laingy'd get things organised like this, we'd all sign on for ever.'

The Garibaldi Partisani military system seemingly centred around the fulfilment of three desiderata, safety, comfort and entertainment, none of them listed in Napoleon's Principles of War. The local application of these had led to the digging of four large, deep pits roofed over by logs, the logs buried below a thick layer of sand. These bomb-proof, shell-proof refuges faced the rear. To while away the *longueurs* of their occupancy they had been stocked amply with barrels of wine, musical instruments, and women. The more charitable of the marines insisted that a duty sentry must have peered over the top from time to time, but there was much speculative controversy about what he would have done if he had noticed anyone unpleasant approaching. The Partisani had never got around to the preparation of any defences at all.

Their relief by X Troop had been like a parody of one of the noisier operas. Chattering drunks waving firearms about dangerously and muscular, dishevelled ladies shouting warlike cries streamed dramatically from their foul-smelling shelters. They weaved their way rearwards in a straggling column that marched to an accordion accompaniment. It was the simple frankness of the motto on their cap-badges that really dissolved any tendency to be critical: 'Momma, Io Ritorno Presto', translated loosely as 'Mummy, I'm Coming Home Quick'.

'Dead fucking right,' said the marines admiringly.

'No, sir,' said Laing. 'Brothel-free. One's now an ammunition-store. We've taken the logs from the others for revetting. Lots of other home improvements since you were last up.'

'I liked your transit-passenger holes. Very consoling.'

'I'll take you round, sir. I'll tell you when to duck.'

And, thought Laing, one of the many reasons why I like serving under this man, this professional, is that I can tell him when to duck and he'll duck. He'll duck not to preserve himself, but because to him it would be unthinkable to demonstrate his personal bravery by a showy disregard for danger that would attract enemy fire upon a position occupied by troops who, unlike him, would stay on it. A recent visitor from Brigade Headquarters had provided a lesson in how these things should not be done. He had proved his indifference to anything the Germans could do to him by disregarding contemptuously local advice, walking about openly, and standing up with icy courage to study the ground through binoculars. He had left insouciantly after five minutes, presumably to repeat the performance on somebody else's doorstep. Two marines had been wounded in the artillery concentration that accompanied his departure. Hugo Burke had since detailed off a party to stand by to fill in all the visitors' slit-trenches beside the approach track should this hero come calling again.

Laing led the Colonel along a short winding path to the front edge of the wood. Beyond it was a broad expanse of sand, flat in places, wind-blown into dunes in places, scattered with sparse coarse grass and scrubby bushes. To the right, glimpsed through the bare lower boles of the pines, was the Adriatic, glittering in the slanting sunshine, minuscule waves lapping softly on the sand.

Hugo's home was in a little hollow, shielded from view from the front and sides, near enough to his carefully sited slit-trenches to allow him to keep in touch with each of them by raising his voice in proportion to his distance from them. Hugo, dressed like everyone else present in a woollen cap-comforter, camouflaged jumping-jacket, and battledress trousers, had one distinctive sartorial curiosity to his ensemble. On his feet was his wedding present from Laing, the Canadian lumberjack-type boots, the brass buckles on their calf-flaps now painted over to eliminate shine that might draw attention to where he was at a wrong moment, the former high polish of the leather dulled by dubbin for the same reason.

The Colonel, an avid researcher into any piece of kit that could contribute to operational comfort, and thus operational efficiency, at once began a cross-examination about the properties of boots.

'Morning, Hugo,' he said. 'Before I take a look around, tell me all about your boots.'

'Very comfortable, sir.'

'More so than SV boots?'

'I think so. Don't have to mess about with strapping on anklets. Just put 'em on, tuck in your trousers and do up the buckles. Once they're broken in they're as good as any for marching. The flaps support your ankles better than the anklets with the other things. The—'

'OK. They're OK boots. Suppose we got them for the whole unit? That be an improvement?'

'Certainly, sir. If you can get them.'

'That's Part Two of the problem. Mine. There'll be loud cries of pain from all over the place, but I'll have a go. Any other contributions to the case? For or against. Johnny? Sergeant Hankins?'

'I can think of one, sir. Against,' said Hankins.

'Yes?'

'When we're on patrols, sir, Mr Burke keeps leaving us nice and neat and goes wandering off on his own. He always comes back, mind. Well, so far. But I've spent a lot of time working out what to do if one night he doesn't. One easy way to find where he went is to follow his footprints in the sand. His are different from everyone else's. If we all had the same, we'd never find the – er – Mr Burke.'

Hugo grinned and said nothing. The Colonel said that he'd never really thought about this footprint business before, because they'd never patrolled sand continuously before. Identifiable footprints had never been an issue on Dalmatian and Montenegrin rocks. But if Senior NCOs felt a compulsive urge to track down wanderlusting junior officers the appropriate aid for their trackings would be a minor addition of something artificial to bootsoles, not an embargo on the provision of a new type of boot which probably wouldn't be provided anyway. Still, it was an interesting insight into an aspect of patrolling that hadn't perhaps had the attention that it deserved, and he was grateful to Sergeant Hankins for raising the matter.

Laing reflected briefly, silently and admiringly, on the deadpan subtlety with which old soldiering hands like the Colonel and Hankins found out what they wanted to find out or, in Hankins's case, lodged a complaint discernible as such only to an experienced initiate by the oblique raising and earnest discussion of irrelevancies. The Colonel hadn't a hope in hell of equipping his entire unit with expensive Canadian lumberjack-model boots, available only in limited numbers on private sale in NAAFI officers' shops. The Colonel knew it. Hankins couldn't care less about the patterns left in the sand by Hugo's bootsoles.

The Colonel's excursion into comparative footwear utility was an introductory device to enable him to satisfy himself that the constructive individualism of Hugo Burke remained unaffected by recent marriage to an absorbingly attractive wife, who unlike the wives of the few other married people in the unit was fresh in her husband's mind, was physically in Italy and, given fair luck over his survival and their joint entitlement to leave, was in a position to renew conjugal joy in not long from now. Hankins's talk of differential footprints was high-flown balderdash that concealed two points, one of information, one that was bothering him. The information that he was contributing was that Hugo Burke as a patrol commander was as unpredictable, resourceful and, as Hankins saw it, nutty as he had ever been. The bothersome question rested upon the continued exercise by Hugo of these qualities upon the constricting environment of an Italian beach, which geographically and tactically was dissimilar to sparsely guarded islands with room to move and plenty of cover.

What Hankins was really saying was this: If Burke chooses to go roaming around on his own, that's OK by me and is his affair. If he runs into trouble, it immediately becomes *my* affair. I must pick the correctly balanced course of action between doing whatever I can to help him to get out of it, and not wasting lives and prejudicing success in a futile histrionic gesture provoked by the personal eccentricities of one man. If I settle for the second course, assume from available evidence that Burke is irrecoverable, and bugger off home with the rest of the patrol, there is a danger that I might be accused of – or, at any rate, suspected of – failure of nerve and determination, cowardice, or Christ knows what. I am putting down a marker that if this choice is forced upon me, and if I do decide to bugger off, I will do so for sound reasons and not to save my own skin.

'What you do', said the Colonel, 'is hang on for as long as you can. Then, if necessary, beat it.'

Hugo took the Colonel on a guided tour of his section position. Dug in among the scrubby bushes were a collection of two-man slit-trenches, six feet long, three feet wide, four feet deep. The sandy soil was built into a low parapet around each, with a scattering of pine-branches placed to give concealment but not to impede view. The pits had been sited so that each one was supported by at least two others, and so that every visible patch of ground ahead could be shot up from most or all. Two slits, one with a Bren in it, the other with rifles, were permanently manned. A working party was busy digging a complex of narrow, shallow crawl-trenches, zig-zagged to minimise the effects of a direct hit by mortars or shelling, designed to provide a covered approach to any threatened part of the position. The diggers worked with impressive enthusiasm.

Until three days previously, Hugo explained, digging had been as unpopular an activity as it had always been, even though sand was eminently diggable. The Germans had then brought a sudden social respectability to manual labour by giving the whole area a thorough evening pasting by mortars, and following up with a regularly delivered 6 p.m. hate of mixed shelling and mortaring that lasted for precisely seven minutes. To the normal and familiar unpleasantness of all this had been added two new phenomena: air-burst and tree-burst. Air-burst did what its name suggested that it did. A time-activated fuse detonated the shell twenty feet or so above ground level. The fragments sprayed downwards and could be destructive unless some form of head-cover was provided for slit-trenches. Tree-burst had a similar effect to air-burst but was more random, the chance result of a shell or mortar-bomb on its way down impacting against a tree and going off bang up there instead of down here.

Until the communication-trench network was completed there were four areas in partial view of German spotters away out to the north-west. Would the Colonel kindly duck when traversing these exposed parts of the layout? The Colonel kindly did.

Later, as he walked back to the jeep parked under the trees, the Colonel reflected upon his morning's findings. Laing's troop, as assumed, were in good condition and quietly and effectively getting on with things. Hugo Burke, considered in a narrowly professional perspective, was as good as ever. Sensibly enforced, and voluntarily reinforced, precautions were keeping the erosion of the strengths of the fighting troops holding the Line to as low a level as could be hoped for. Laing, as an example, had taken in a total of fifty-two men. In ten days he had lost two badly and three lightly wounded. It didn't sound much. But do some simple arithmetic, and convert an inconstant trend into something close to a rough average, and you came up with some disconcerting results. The cost of holding an acre or so of scrubby sand and spiky pine-trees would reduce Laing's command to a total of nothing after not much more than three months.

It wouldn't, of course, work out like that. They wouldn't be left in the Line without periodic reliefs for anything like three months. And, in any case, the Line wouldn't stay where it was for much longer. The purpose of its present occupation was an acclimatisation, a familiarisation with its topographical peculiarities. Defending it was part of the process. Patrolling the ground in front of it was a more tactically profitable part. Planning for a Brigade attack over it was well under way.

Sergeant Hankins allowed himself three seconds of silent, fluent obscenity. Then he shifted his left foot until it was touching the right foot of the marine to his left rear. Until half a minute previously Hankins had been one of a star-shaped formation of four people, all lying on their stomachs in the sand, facing in different directions, peering carefully outwards, with three tommy-guns and a Bren ready for immediate use against strangers. Their legs were spread wide apart, each foot resting against the nearest foot of the neighbouring man. If any saw or heard suspicious movement, he would signal his discovery by a pressure of his foot. Hugo had brought them too close to the outer wire of the German position for whispering or subdued talking to be chanced.

Now the four had become three. Bloody Burke had lapsed into his customary bad habits, and had buggered off into the night, Christ knew where, leaving Hankins to make whatever he could of whatever developed while Burke was away. Tricky but not as bad as it once was. There was now a cast-iron authorisation to bugger off, if buggering off was the right thing to do.

CHAPTER TEN

HAPPENINGS during the mid-March of 1945 were in essence not substantially different from those of the springs of the previous five years. There were some significant shifts of emphasis. The chief of these was that it was now clear beyond doubt that the side that was going to win the war was not the one that had looked as if it would win it a few years previously.

March 17th, 1945 is as good a day as any to pick as broadly indicative of what some people did, or had done to them, during this period in the Italian segment of what it was fashionable at the time to call 'the Big Picture'.

Shortly after dawn 49 Commando, who had been out of the Line for five days and were living in tents in the grounds of an old farmhouse, started upon their second day of intensive training in the use of Buffalos, Fantails and Weasels. These were tracked armoured vehicles that could swim.

These sophisticated amphibians were a far cry from the primitive trappings of bygone rehearsed landings from dories, longboats and cutters. These new things were reasonably bullet-proof, splinter-proof and mobile. They were not proof against anti-tank weapons – but nor, for that matter, were tanks. To the users, the charm of the new technology was that of being moved with comparative speed and safety to the jumping-off place for an attack on foot instead of having to walk there after disembarkation whilst being shot at. The training consisted largely of getting in and out, fast and in the right order.

Some of the Buffalos were also loaded with collapsible canvas assault-boats. Competitions were held, prize a case of beer, to establish the best speed and accuracy with which these could be unloaded, assembled, carried to the bank of a nearby canal, launched, and paddled across. A component of this exercise was the securing of thick ropes to heavy wooden stakes hammered into the ground on either bank. When the ropes were in position, one to each boat, the boats could be pulled backwards and forwards by hand. This was quicker than paddling.

*

In Switzerland further hands were played with deadpan expressions in a continuing diplomatic poker game between emissaries of General Kurt Wolff, the German SS commander in northern Italy, and negotiators under the local control of Mr Allen Dulles, the political representative of a young United States organisation, the Office of Strategic Services.

These convoluted discussions on neutral soil arose from General Wolff's floating of the idea of a unilateral surrender to the Allies in Italy of the German armies in Italy. But the Wolff proposal carried conditions. These were difficult both because of their intrinsic nature and because conditions, any conditions, cut right across agreed and proclaimed American–British–Soviet policy, which was Unconditional Surrender.

What Wolff was really talking about was not a surrender but a truce. The truce would be presentational. It would last until suitable arrangements had been made between what he saw as two truly civilised élites, his and the Western Allies', who would then coalesce to crush the only real menace to European traditional values, the incursion of Godless, atheistic, Bolshevik barbarians. Wolff's concept was of an unlikely team of SS men, the cream of the Wehrmacht, and the British and American armies going off to destroy the Russians. It was the product of a logical, isolated mind fenced off from reality in a Nazi Cloud-cuckoo-land. Negotiations were abandoned and Wolff, to his lasting puzzlement, was later found guilty of war crimes in Poland and Italy. He was imprisoned.

Before the talking ceased, however, the Dulles side of them, instructed by Washington, had brought in for consultation and assessment senior officers from the Intelligence Staff of Allied Forces Headquarters at Caserta. One of these officers was a Canadian lieutenant-colonel named Andrei Sepelov, a White Russian refugee with a remarkable fighting record that took in Dieppe, Sicily, the Sangro, three decorations for gallantry and the loss of his right hand and his left eye. At the end of the Dulles–Wolff encounter Sepelov was a very disappointed man. He thought that Wolff was right. Sepelov was the brother of Hugo Burke's mother. He was in regular touch, through a Croatian monsignor in the Vatican Secretariat, with Hugo Burke's father in Ottawa. Colonel Sepelov's intelligence job caused him to make frequent liaison visits to V Corps Headquarters in Ravenna. He was thus able to see something of his nephew Hugo, although less than he would have liked.

Helen Burke, lying chaste and alone between the sheets in the aseptic little room in the hospital in Bari, awoke thinking happily of Hugo. She worried about him, as what woman wouldn't about a husband in the Line, but her worry was paradoxically eased because she knew that she was the victim of a conspiracy. It was a kindly conspiracy. She had been much cheered by the lies of a marine named Bungy Williams, the latest liar in a short but distinguished tradition.

Williams had two days previously been carried on a stretcher into Surgical Ward 4 with mortar-bomb fragments in his right thigh. Williams was in X Troop, Johnny Laing's troop, Hugo's troop. Williams, according to himself, was the victim of an astonishing piece of bad luck. He had been standing in the wrong place when the only German weapon to have landed anything near 49 Commando since they had moved to northern Italy had lobbed over the bomb that had hit him. She wasn't to worry about her husband, Williams said. He was a good bloke. The lads would look after him.

There was a cosily familiar ring to all this. Corporals Skinner and Rankin, marines Wood and Birch, all admitted to the 99th General Hospital within the past two weeks, all wounded in the Line, had suffered remarkably similar misfortunes. Just hanging about they'd been, minding their own business in some idyllic peaceful backwater, when *Wham*, some stray piece of accidentally directed shell or mortar-bomb had fortuitously found its way towards them, at them, in them. Their messages for her had been identical. Don't bother your head about your husband. Good bloke he is. The lads'll look after. . . .

It was all nonsense, but sustaining nonsense. You could, in good moments, actually persuade yourself that no harm *could* come to Hugo. The lads *would* look after him. In slightly less good moments you began to hope that Hugo would be removed from the board by much the same sort of wound that had brought Williams to his comfortable hospital bed, nice clean severance of muscle and tendon in a fleshy part of the body, no bones gone, no long-term problems, Hugo safe for at least as long as it would take to put him on his feet again. And then you thought Well, he wouldn't like that, so you mustn't think it too hard, but you thought it all the same, and now there was this other sweet thing to think about.

Helen had news for Hugo. She would not phrase it thus, because she was lovingly sensitive to his feelings, but Hugo in four days of honeymoon had to her delight achieved something that nobody else to her relief had ever achieved. The doctor had said that it was too early to tell, but she knew better. From puberty onwards she'd been as regular as the phases of the moon. She was twelve days late. She hugged herself with content.

After breakfast she closed the zip of the small travelling-bag that she had been told was all the luggage that she could bring with her, and walked to the jeep. Seven days' leave ahead, one and a half each way wasted on travel, four complete days and complete nights with Hugo in Ravenna. Hugo had written to say that he had the use of a flat. An elegant and pleasing flat, ownership unspecified. The flat sounded nice but of no burning relevance. In her present condition – well, in the light of recent biological developments, perhaps 'mood' was a better word – she'd have welcomed with delight the chance of four days and nights with Hugo in a hayloft.

Her driver and travelling companion, a Royal Army Medical Corps doctor named Joe something-or-other, greeted her with bitter reticence and, limping slightly, placed her bag in the back of the jeep. He was a specialist in stomach wounds on temporary transfer to a hospital in Forlì, to which, for reasons that she did not care to think about, a larger than usual number of patients in need of his special surgical skills was expected to be delivered shortly. He was embittered and limping because in the early part of the previous night she had kicked him in the testicles.

This radical expression of displeasure had followed upon a knock on her bedroom door and the putting forward of a suggestion by Joe. Since, he had said in his best debonair seducer voice, he had put himself to some inconvenience to make room for her in the jeep the least she could do in return was to pay for her ticket. In her case it wouldn't exactly be the first time she would have raised the morale of the troops in this manner.

The kick had been fierce, accurate and with plenty of follow-through, product of much boring tuition during a country childhood spent largely in the company of her elder brother Oliver, who had ambitions to play full-back on the Irish Rugby team. Joe had retired hurt, physically and emotionally.

The conversation, on a drive that started on a lovely, clear Italian spring morning, did not flow smoothly. The drive itself had its impediments. Every bridge over every river crossed in the 350 miles between Bari and Ravenna had been blown by the retreating Germans. Their temporary substitutes, wooden-decked Bailey bridges pieced together by sappers from steel framework that looked like a grown-up's version of a child's construction kit, carried single-line traffic only. Military policemen presided at these frustrating bottlenecks, controlling the flow with competence and enforcing road discipline.

Helen was prepared in case Joe's motoring frustrations were deflected to channels unconnected with the free flow of vehicles along a disrupted highway. Neatly inserted into the outer seam of her slacks was a long Edwardian hatpin, presented to her for use in this very contingency, along with some valedictory woman-to-woman advice, by Mrs Noelle O'G. Grant, of Grantsbridge, Co. Monaghan, on the occasion of her daughter Helen's departure for the wars.

Helen used the hatpin once, when they stopped for a haversack-ration lunch of corned-beef sandwiches beside a bombed vineyard south of Foggia, and had to threaten to use it again after a halt for fuel at a petrol-point near Termoli. Joe drove for the rest of the journey with the indecisive look of a man unable to decide what irritated him more: the defensive hatpin, or the expression of near-imbecilic happiness that lights up the faces of young glad-to-be-pregnant women about to be reunited with fertile men that they love.

The Colonel spent most of the morning watching over and supervising the exercises with the big Buffalos and the big Fantails and the small Weasels. His reiterated message, sometimes abusively uttered, was consistent. These new gadgets could go where landing-craft couldn't but the principles governing their use were identical. Once a landing-craft had grounded and the ramps were down you got off the beach as quick as Christ would let you. The same applied to these things. Once you were out of them you didn't hang around. They'd attract every kind of enemy fire. Move, move, move and keep moving. The lesson, like all lessons compounded of common sense and self-preservation, was quickly absorbed.

Later he umpired an assault-boat race, the crate of beer he had donated as the prize for the fastest crew nestling beside him in his Weasel. It was a mercilessly competitive, no-holds-barred event, conducted in a spirit that would have led to wholesale disqualifications and suspensions at the Henley Regatta. Boring, ramming, sabotage, piracy, cutting out, and maritime hand-to-hand fighting with paddles used as weapons marked its cheerfully chaotic progress. The Colonel enjoyed it as hugely as did the competitors. It combined the merits of practical exposure to the problems of handling clumsy flat-bottomed boats in conditions of sudden, unpredictable interference with a necessary opportunity to let off collective steam.

In mid-morning the Colonel went to join his *ad hoc* Planning Staff of the second-in-command, Richard the Adjutant, the Intelligence Officer and a subaltern recovering from jaundice and on light duties. They were sequestered in a locked and closely guarded room in the farmhouse headquarters, working intently among maps. He studied the talc trace superimposed upon the map-sheets that portrayed the spit of ground between Lake Commachio and the sea. The spit had now for planning purposes become the Spit, capital S. A tongue-shaped section of it, on the eastward, seaward side, separated from the main bulk by the narrow, slow-flowing River Reno, had become the Tongue, capital T. The Spit, and the Tongue with it, seven miles of sandy, scrubby nothing very much, made up the objective for the coming Brigade attack, designed to launch Eighth Army's spring offensive, draw German reserves from where the real big punch would be. The Colonel had thirteen days left in which to refine and revise his share of the plan.

The two army commandos would paddle across the lake by night and come ashore about halfway up the western side of the Spit. Once they had signalled that they were across, 49 Commando would set out from the base of the Spit to join them, destroying or capturing all Germans on, or

73

in, the way. Junction on the first day. Advance of all three commandos three miles further north to the top of the Spit on the second. All good, tidy, copy-book, Staff College stuff that years later would be summarised in textbooks, illustrated by diagrams carrying neat arrows.

The present trick was to try to make sure that the arrows came to rest where they should, a process requiring a careful, realistic assessment of the possible, some astute crystal-gazing about what the opposition was likely to get up to do its best to bend the arrows back upon themselves, and a complex initial deployment of all the various available resources so that they could be used to their best interacting advantage and could react with reasonable chances of success to the unexpected. And one thing that could confidently be expected was the unexpected. After all, the unknown factor in the equation was German – professional, military German.

He went through it all again with an infinite capacity for taking pains and neither illusion nor ambition about being a genius. He just wanted to get it right. Do the job properly, at minimum cost. There would be casualties, and he disliked that, accepted it as inevitable. There would not, if he had anything to do with it, be avoidable casualties, people lost through carelessness, lack of forethought, lack of attention to detail.

Then he left them to it and went to brief Laing on this damned patrol that Brigade had suddenly called for. The patrol would have to start out from old X Troop territory, the front edge of the pine-wood on the shore of the Adriatic. It would have to cover more old X Troop territory, the beach on the eastward side of the Tongue. It was a clear X Troop job. The Colonel didn't like giving it to X Troop because he was a kindly man and there was a fifty per cent chance that Johnny Laing, whose responsibility it was to choose its leader, would choose Hugo. Laing would not choose Hugo for the sake of choosing Hugo. He would choose him because it was Hugo's turn and not Mott's. And Laing, too, was a kindly man and would dislike choosing Hugo, but nothing on earth would induce him to send out Mott if it wasn't Mott's turn, because Laing like the Colonel was a slave to duty or whatever the bloody silly expression was and they both knew that duty came first *tra-la-la*. Just as they both knew that Helen Burke was due to arrive in Ravenna on the following day – to stay, what was more, in the Colonel's own flat, lent by him to Hugo in a cloud of fraudulent disclaimers about its otherwise lying empty and Hugo might as well have it as leave it so. . . . Which led on to the wholly horrible possibility that if something went wrong and Hugo ran into trouble on this bloody patrol, then both the Colonel and Laing might find themselves with some personal widow-consoling to do, which was away and beyond the sort of thing that normally had to be attended to on occasions when things, as they often did, went wrong.

74

'Johnny,' said the Colonel, 'I want you to send out a patrol tonight.'

'Right, sir.'

'Officer patrol. Who'll you send?'

'Hugo Burke.'

Neither the Colonel nor Laing showed external traces of emotion of any description. They discussed details.

The necessity for this unexpected patrolling commitment had been identified, almost casually, by the Brigade Major. On the previous afternoon he had gone up to the wooded area behind the old X Troop position to mark in on a large-scale map the precise boundaries of the Forming-Up Position and the Start Line selected for 49 Commando's part of the Brigade attack. The extremities of both had already been picked out by wooden stakes driven into the sandy topsoil. Nearer the time the stakes would be linked by tautened white tape that would limn the edges beyond risk of error. Pinpoint accuracy in mapping was wanted so that the artillery support programme could be calculated to the nearest yard. The Brigadier and his staff, like the Colonel and his, thrived on a philosophy of Bash On Regardless once the shit began to fly. To fail to take every possible opportunity of minimising its potential effects while the stuff was still quiescent was in their view despicable and inexcusable negligence.

His cartography completed, the Brigade Major had a chat with the colonel in command of the infantry battalion currently manning that section of the Line. Most of the talk was about confirmatory detail of arrangements for the return of 49 Commando prior to the assault, an enterprise about which the infantry colonel held reservations. He was a young, experienced cynic, gloomily accustomed to being set imaginative objectives that as often as not were achieved bloodily some weeks or months after the timings optimistically laid down for them. Inured to disappointment, he forecast more, this time for the commandos.

'Seven miles in two days,' he said sardonically. 'Christ.'

The Brigade Major saw no point in starting an argument but felt that courtesy demanded that he say something. He said something.

'Ah well,' he remarked inconsequentially, 'at least the beach isn't mined.'

'Who says it isn't mined? You people have been buggering about in the Balkans for too long. I've never put in an attack yet in this bloody country when there weren't mines all over the—'

'But your night patrols must have prevented any—'

'My night patrols don't go out more than two hundred yards. We gave up all that Cowboys and Indians stuff after the Sangro. All you get is unnecessary casualties for no gain.'

'Sir, we handed over to you on the clear understanding—'

'I don't give a bugger what your clear understanding was. *My* clear understanding was that I was asked to patrol the Tongue nightly. I do just that. My patrolling policy is that no patrol goes out more than two hundred yards ahead of my forward positions.'

'I see, sir. Thank you.'

The Commando Brigadier, told by his right-hand man that there might be a bit of a hiccup in his carefully worked out Brigade plan, brought about by 49 Commando's being sent in over a mined beach in the belief that it was mine-free, smiled gently, said, 'Another illusion destroyed,' and telephoned the Infantry Brigade Commander, who was tetchily uncontrite. The burden of his riposte was that if the Commando Brigade wanted permanent night domination of the beach they could permanently and nightly dominate it themselves. He would gladly offer them every facility. The Commando Brigadier said, 'OK, Dick. You're on,' and rang off.

'Somebody should shoot that bugger,' said the Brigade Major.

'Somebody already has. Three times. Once in Tunisia. Twice in Italy. Fix up a patrolling programme with 49, will you?'

The Brigade Major went off to do so. Before returning to yet another look at his planning the Commando Brigadier put in some brief, and on the whole sympathetic, thinking about the attitude of his old Sandhurst chum Dick and of the young colonel of the infantry battalion in the Line. He concluded that, had he been them, his reactions would have been similar. The battalion had landed at Salerno eighteen months previously. It had worked its way north, by one river crossing after another. In the course of its journey it had suffered 300-per-cent officer casualties and 200-per-cent Other Rank casualties. Aside from a few surviving old sweats it now consisted of replacements of replacements of replacements. Its immediate corporate prospects were of further loss and further replacements. A defensive scepticism was inevitable in the circumstances. Commando soldiering was expensive in casualties, too. But they had not been incurred in the muddy, bloody erosion of a slow, bitter progress, river by river, the length of the Italian peninsula. And thank Christ for that.

The mechanics of establishing whether or not about three square miles of Italian beach were mined was less complex than at first glance might have seemed to have been the case. The Mediterranean and its Adriatic offshoot are tideless. There had been some light breezes but no strong winds in that Italian early spring. The sand of the beach had lain undisturbed by nature for weeks. The only disturbance had been from human feet and, when the humans had prostrated themselves, human bodies. The feet and the bodies had left uneradicated traces of who had been moving where. To those familiar with earlier tracks, some contributed by themselves, some by friends, some by enemies, it was easy enough on a moonlit night to deduce from the patterns what had been happening since the last visit. The answer was: remarkably little. The commander of the German position near the tip of the Tongue, doubtless a veteran of the other end of all those bloodstained river crossings, seemed to have developed much the same jaundiced view of the value of a forward patrolling policy as had his British infantry opponent dug in near the Tongue's root. This sensible reticence embraced the laying of fresh mines. There were none.

The mine-check aside, there was a second leg to Hugo's orders. He was to dominate the beach until one hour before first light. The manner in which he discharged this task led to an unexpected bonus in the form of useful tactical information, and also to some non-stop blasphemy from Sergeant Hankins and the infantry Company Commander through whose defences the patrol went out and came back.

It went out appropriately dressed, armed and briefed. Dress was woollen cap-comforters, camouflaged jumping-jackets, and webbing equipment stripped down to two ammunition-pouches on waistbelts, all brass fittings dulled with black paint. Weapons, for a total party of ten, carried a high firepower – there were three Brens, four tommy-guns, three rifles and grenades for all. The briefing by Hugo, listened to in approving silence by Laing, had been comprehensive, unambiguous, and economical of words, a verbal shorthand almost meaningless to outsiders and instantly understood by experienced initiates.

They set out silently in the moonlight through the forward infantry slit-trenches on the beach, spaced out in a single file with five paces between each man, Hugo in the lead, each man with a segment of their moving periphery to keep an eye on. Navigation on a clear night on a beach running north to south was Boy Scout training stuff.

Initial progress was fast, but prudent. The moon-splashed expanse of sand looked to be flat, but there were bumps and folds and, inland a little, low dunes. At intervals of a hundred yards Hugo lowered himself to the ground, and his followers did likewise. Pause for the careful scanning of the newly foreshortened skyline all round. Any Germans on the move would be silhouetted. So would the patrol when they were up if there were Germans down, but you couldn't have jam on it all the time, must take some chances, etc.

After five hundred yards and five of these lowerings, Lance-Corporal O'Driscoll's flank-protection Bren-group slipped away into the dunes to the left and set themselves up to wait, watch, protect and be ready to offer whatever help might be necessary if things became lively later on in the proceedings. Hugo took the remaining seven on again, now increasing the frequency of sinkings to the ground to every seventy-five yards, then fifty yards. He measured the distance covered by counting paces. So did Sergeant Hankins, behind him. Brief, occasional whispered comparisons never exposed a discrepancy of more than five or six paces.

At one thousand yards from the start Hugo dropped off the three-man back-up group, one Bren, one tommy-gun and the getaway man. If any rough stuff started, the Bren and the tommy would join in as opportunity offered and wisdom suggested. The getaway man would beat it for home, fast. His job was to provide material for a reconstruction of what had happened and where, so that if nobody else got out there would be sufficient available information to prevent a recurrence or engineer a reprisal. The back-up team established themselves in a shallow hollow near the edge of the dunes, taking it in turns to scoop out with their hands enough sand to allow for the rudimentary protection of the trunk of a prone man. In the diffused light they looked like strangely shaped dogs burying bones.

Hugo, Hankins and the two marines moved forward again, this time with all caution. They were within 150 yards of the German outposts. At first they crouched, moving slowly and noiselessly, going to ground and skyline-scanning every few paces. Finally, they crawled. Hugo gestured, they stopped and formed themselves into a flat-on-their-stomachs starfish shape, legs wide astride, feet touching, Hugo staring to the front, the north, the others covering east, south and west. They lay in attentive silence, guns with safety-catches eased forward, a round up the spout. They heard, above the gentle slap-slap of the waves, a murmur of voices, a cough. Alerting feet immediately pressed against Hugo's own outstretched ones. He ignored them. The pressure abated. Decisions were for him to take, and a decision to do nothing about a catarrhal enemy entrenched in a prepared position was, by unspoken consensus, a good decision.

Hugo's next decision, taken twenty minutes later, had less popular appeal. He gave Hankins a light kick on the ankle, waited until Hankins had turned his head to look at him, jerked his own head, rose to a crouch like a sprinter on his starting-blocks, and disappeared into the night on all fours.

It was at this point that Hankins began a mental conversation with himself in a mood of rancorous self-pity. Jesus Christ, said one half of Hankins to the other half of Hankins, the bastard's done it *again*. He's done it often enough before, but usually there's been a bit more room to move in than there is now with Jerry fucking nicotine addicts coughing up their bloody lungs about eighty yards off and not the slightest bloody indication of when bloody Burke would. . . . Hankins reassembled his fragmented personality, indicated by further ankle-tapping that the four-man starfish should rearrange itself into a three-man starfish with each pair of eyes covering 120° instead of ninety, and went back to a total vigilance complemented by a simultaneously independent woefulness. If, for Christ's sake, Burke wasn't back by. . . .

A kick on his left heel drew his attention to something that his own senses picked up a minuscule fraction of a second later. A small German excursion was on its way. There were low voices, the swish of boots in sand. Against the skyline, becoming progressively larger and clearer, could be seen first the head, then head and shoulders, then trunk, then body complete down to feet, of a man holding a Schmeisser in a casual manner. Behind him, in a spaced single file, came another and another and another, six in all. They were moving less cautiously than was sensible, presumably confident that nothing upsetting was likely to happen so close to the Off.

It happened when the outline shape of their leader, taking his patrol on a route twenty yards across the front of a Bren and two tommy-guns, was beginning to diminish in size. He was now visible from the knees up only.

This was no occasion for fire orders. The three-man starfish disengaged its feet, crawled into a short line, took first pressure on triggers, and selected personal targets. Two of them, as it happened, picked the same one. Hankins chose the patrol leader and before he squeezed the trigger in a brisk, noisy, lethal burst reflected sardonically that bloody Burke was just about due for some interested speculations about what was going on.

Hankins fired, tommy-gun muzzle pointed low to allow for upward kick. The other tommy-gunner, also aiming low, and the Bren-gunner, unworried by kick and distributing a complete magazine like a gardener spraying vegetables with a hose, opened up almost at once. The sound, contrasting hideously with the previous peaceful quiet, was shockingly, brutally, overwhelming. The guns vibrated, streams of empty brass cartridge-cases were ejected on to the sand, muzzle-flashes flickered rhythmically, released cordite gases smelled acrid. The six Germans went down. Two were certainties – the leader, felled by Hankins, and number three who couldn't have survived four bursts of .45 tommy-gun ammunition and half a magazine of .303 Bren fired into him from twenty yards away. It was impossible to tell which of the other four had been hit, which had dived for cover.

Somebody certainly hadn't been hit. He demonstrated it. Something was lobbed slowly through the air and exploded flashily a few feet from the Bren-gunner, identifying itself by doing so as a stick grenade. A stream of Schmeisser bullets cut a channel in the sand six inches from Hankins's left shoulder. The Bren-gunner, unhit, slightly stunned, unsighted by the brief glare from the grenade, stopped firing and with trained reflexes changed magazines. Hankins rolled to his right, also changed magazines on his tommy-gun, and had another crack at where the Schmeisser's muzzle-flash had been. A new tommy-gun, firing from over to the left front, joined in. Ah, thought Hankins, hosing away to his right, the Burke boy's back. With this bloody row going on he could hardly lose the way.

There was some hoarse shouting, shadowy movement, and shuffling noises diminishing into the darkness. Then silence, a very temporary silence.

Burke underlined it by calling 'Stop' in a low, authoritative voice, and loomed out of the night, gun tucked comfortably under his arm. Hankins, finding his thoughts forming with clarity, registered two in immediate succession: Why not shoot this bastard Burke and end all this sort of nonsense once and for all? and Thank Christ he's OK, back, and responsible for sorting out what to do next.

Burke sorted out what to do next.

'Everyone OK?' he asked briskly.

Three yesses.

'Right. Twenty seconds for identification. Then beat it for the back-up group. Then, when I say Go, run like buggery to the sea.'

Burke and Hankins went rapidly to the fallen Germans, weapons at the ready in case some dying hero tried to take a foe with him in a last defiant gesture. There were no gestures. Three dead, one wounded, the last pressing a hand to a shattered shoulder, blood seeping through his spread fingers. He looked terrified when Hankins drew a knife, and less terrified when Hankins used it to cut away the identifying regimental badges on his collar and shoulder-straps. Hankins quickly emptied the man's pockets of his paybook, two private letters and some photographs. Hankins clucked censoriously at this slack security. He himself was a scrupulous routine checker of pockets before a patrol started out. None of *his* people brought exploitable snippets of information with them.

Hankins said, 'Hard luck, matey,' considered whether to apply his field-dressing to the man's wound, and decided against it. It might be needed by his own side. There was a long way to go yet. He picked up a Schmeisser with blood on its stock and turned to Burke. Burke, a freshly acquired rifle slung over his left shoulder, was stuffing some papers into his jumping-jacket pocket and fastening the press-stud.

'Right?' said Burke.

'Right.'

'OK. We're off.'

Burke led them at a trot towards the back-up party's hollow, called to them to join on. He did not lower his voice. Concealment was no longer relevant. Speed was. The back-up party, who had been impressed, puzzled and apprehensive about all the noise, wasted no time. All seven lined up, Burke snapped 'Go,' and they ran for the sea. They waded out until the water was above the knees of the shortest man. The sea-floor fell at a gentle angle. When Burke said 'Stop' they were forty yards out, paddling in the moonlight like holidaymakers having a bit of a lark after the pubs had shut.

'We'll wade home,' said Burke conversationally. 'Safer out here.'

The thing about this bastard Burke, thought Hankins admiringly, is that he uses his loaf. He's a bloody nuisance when he goes roaming off on his own, and he was luckier than he knew not to have been shot as a humane measure by Hankins a few minutes previously, but it's when he pulls little tricks like this that you realise that he's not such a bad bugger after all. Hand it to him, judging from what was going on on the beach it certainly *was* safer out here. The Burke timing, calculated upon an accurate reading of the turn that events would take, had been faultless.

The sequence, as Hankins reconstructed it, and as Burke had predicted it, was logically straightforward. German patrol gets bounced eighty yards in front of its own home position. Germans in that position can't shoot into the confusion in case they hit their own people. Brief silence when the immediate excitement's over, but static Germans still hold their fire because they don't know who won or what has happened. They'll find out and react when their survivors get back, but that will take time, short. Burke takes advantage of short time to make identifications, collect his back-up team and bugger off into the sea. German survivors report developments, probably with some emotion and in exaggerated terms. Germans open up on the beach with everything they have locally got. German commander ponders. He *thinks* that it was probably a minor patrol action, but he can't be sure. The Tommis haven't patrolled with much ostentation recently. It might be an attack, probing or full-scale. German commander gets on the air to his battalion headquarters, describes situation, recommends that no chances be taken, and calls for Defensive Fire tasks.

The Defensive Fire tasks were now being put down upon the beach in a magnificent pyrotechnic uproar. They had been preceded by pretty coloured lights that soared into the night sky, hovered like some celebratory firework display, and bathed the sandscape in a pale, phosphorescent luminosity that accentuated edges and shadows. Spandaus, firing on fixed lines pre-set by day, stitched an angled criss-cross pattern of tracer two feet or so above ground-level. That part of it had been the immediate, local reaction.

The Defensive Fire task element in the piece, now developing fortissimo, was more spectacular. From a distance to the right rear of the departing waders came a ripple of flashes, the merging roar of the discharge of guns and mortars. There came growing whisperings, howlings, neatly grouped screeching, crashing eruptions placed methodically on pre-selected and registered bits of beach, picked skilfully as the best areas to break up any attack. The concentrations worked by phased lifts down to the base of the Tongue, settled there for a time, were lifted, worked their way back, repeated the process.

'I suppose we're better off out of that lot,' said one of the wading marines, 'but my mother did warn me *never* to get my feet wet.'

Corporal O'Driscoll, in charge of the flank-protection group, was not confident that he'd worked out correctly all that was happening. The first part, signified by a lot of flashing and banging from small-arms fire about six hundred yards ahead of him, was easy enough to interpret. Burke had bumped Germans, and both parties were busily shooting at each other. There was then a silence, which presumably meant that one side or the other had won but God alone knew which. It could also, of course, mean that some sort of stalemate had evolved. Whatever it was, it was clearly up to O'Driscoll to hang around and cover in Burke's crowd, or whoever was left of Burke's crowd, when they came home. If they came home. O'Driscoll settled down to watch.

Things had then taken a turn for the worse. Star shell and Spandau tracer in extravagant quantities had been followed by an altogether unhealthy stonk of mixed shelling and mortar-fire that roamed disconcertingly all over the beach, pausing at repetitive intervals to land all around O'Driscoll. O'Driscoll and his team burrowed deeper into the sand with zeal, commenting fluently about fucking officers who wouldn't let well alone. Marine Viall, who had the furthest to burrow because he was larger than most, wasn't fast enough and was sliced across both buttocks by a hot, jagged fragment of mortar-bomb. Viall complained about this. O'Driscoll told him unsympathetically that fat-arsed comics could expect to get what they asked for.

O'Driscoll held on until he calculated that further waiting was pointless. If Burke was coming back, which now seemed improbable, he wasn't coming this way. O'Driscoll rose to his feet, lay down again as a cluster of 105s exploded around him, got up again, and gave the order to withdraw in terms unlisted in the manual of infantry training.

'Let's fuck off out of this,' said O'Driscoll.

Back where he'd started he was glad to see Burke, Hankins and the rest, looking smugly pleased with themselves and unaccountably all saturated from the waists down.

The infantry Company Commander was less glad to see Burke than was O'Driscoll.

'This was a quiet spot until you bloody people started mucking about with it,' he said morosely. 'You've stirred up more shit in one night than we've had in ten days.'

Hugo apologised, without sincerity.

'That bloody stonk went on for five minutes until they lifted it back a bit. All of it on my forward platoon position. It. . . .'

Hugo was staring past him, rearwards, southwards.

'More trouble coming your way,' he said. 'Seems to be a German seaborne landing or something.'

The Company Commander gazed back wearily at a distant, continuously rekindled illumination of the night sky, coloured flares, Very lights, arcs of tracer, charming, sinister, some miles behind the Line.

'Oh, that,' he said with indifference. 'It's been going on for hours. I rang up Battalion HQ when it started. It's the Irish Brigade. Pissed again. It seems it's Saint Patrick's Day. They're firing off about a year's supply of flares and every other bloody thing. No one's been able to stop 'em so far.'

CHAPTER ELEVEN

'WELL, GOODBYE,' said Helen Burke. She stood with her zip-bag at the door of what had once been a bank. It had been taken over as an officers' club and renamed, without much originality, the Club Ravenna.

'Goodbye,' said Joe, looking disappointed.

'And thank you. You didn't *have* to bring me all the way, you know. I could have hitched a lift from Forlì.'

'I said I would and I have,' said Joe, commissioned medical lecher (failed), partially penitent and wholly defeated.

'I hope we meet again,' he added wistfully.

'The hospital world's a small world.'

'You won't have to bother with that damned pin or whatever it was. Felt like a bayonet.'

'Next time I'll use a syringe. With a lethal dose.'

'Ah. It's nice to know there'll be a next time.'

'Not will. If. Conditional.'

'Better than nothing. There's some fellow waving at you.'

'It's Hugo. *Hugo!*'

Joe saluted with quick nervous courtesy, sprang into his jeep, and did a racing start with whining tyres and no further comment. Once, on routine casualty duty in Bari, he had applied cold compresses to the badly bruised cheekbone of a newly disembarked Royal Naval Volunteer Reserve lieutenant.

Marine Viall, lying face downwards on a stretcher, awaiting the ambulance that would take him to the Casevac Dakota that would fly him to Bari and the 99th General Hospital, was given in person a farewell message from Troop Sergeant-Major Mayne. It came in two parts, one reflective, one cautionary.

The reflective part was short. The Germans, said Mayne appreciatively, had achieved in less than two seconds what he, Mayne, had been unable to accomplish in two years. They had prevented Viall from sitting around on his arse.

The cautionary part was concerned with Viall's comportment in Bari.

If, said Mayne, Viall in hospital were to be questioned by a good-looking bird dressed up as a Red Cross welfare officer about the events surrounding the sacrifice that he had made for Democracy, Viall should leave Mr Burke out of whatever load of bullshit he chose to use to describe his terrible ordeal. Otherwise, added Mayne, there would be a few more terrible ordeals awaiting Viall when he finally got out of bed and came back to do some work. Mayne would devise these personally.

The Planning Staff showed signs of good cheer when the Colonel went to see them. No mines on the beach, and Hugo had accidentally triggered off a demonstration of what must have been most of the German Defensive Fire task programme. He'd also had the good sense to try to memorise where most of the stuff had landed.

Observations made in the moonlight by a man with other things on his mind while wading through sea-water could hardly be classed as of diamond-studded accuracy, but he'd turned in enough to enable a useful trace to be plotted. Two recordings on the trace were precise: the place where Corporal O'Driscoll's flank-protection group had endured their sorrows, and the place where the forward infantry platoon had endured theirs.

Some approach routes in the attack plan had been altered accordingly. Some, including the infantry position that was just in front of the Start Line, were geographical bottlenecks incapable of modification. Those would have to be got through or out of as quickly as possible.

The Colonel said yes, he agreed. Young Hugo had put in a good night's work. The Colonel did not add that he had stayed awake until he was told by telephone that Hugo was back. Or that what had kept him from sleep was not a professional avidity for information of use to the attack. He accused himself of becoming soft. He had been thinking of the hurt to Helen, a hurt that he personally would have had to transmit, if word came in that Hugo was missing or dead. God damn and blast all war, and specifically the presence of women anywhere near it.

'Young Hugo Burke put in a good night's work,' said the Commando Brigadier with satisfaction.

'He did indeed, sir,' said the Brigade Major.

'Where is he now? I'd like to see him.'

'Putting in a good night's work.'

'At three o'clock in the afternoon?'

'His wife arrived at lunchtime.'

'Oh. I see. Make it tomorrow morning.'

'Yes, sir.'

'Darling Hugo, you look tired.'

'Hardly surprising.'

'Don't be crude. I mean you looked tired when you met me. As if you'd been out with the lads all night.'

'Well, not all night. Fairly late, though.'

'Anything special? Or just spontaneous combustion?'

'It was Patrick's Night, dammit. You Monaghan Protestants—'

'Good heavens. So it was. And listen to me, Hugo Burke, you needn't start all that Canadian-Irish papist paddy-whackery on me. What sort of party was it?'

'Quite lively at times. Fireworks and all. The Irish Brigade put on a turn. I was damned glad when it was over, mind you. Kept thinking of you coming up today. Wanted to get some sleep in.'

Pause.

'Hugo, you're a love. You're also thoroughly unconvincing as a liar.'

'Liar? *Me?*'

'Oh, Hugo.'

'Helen.'

'Yes. Please.'

Johnny Laing started to walk across the dance-floor of the Club Ravenna and then changed his mind. The All Blacks, represented by 2 New Zealand Division, had taken over the floor as the arena for their match against the Rest of the World at a modified form of Rugby, played without a ball by two twenty-strong packs with five-man front rows. Victory went to the side that scrummaged the opposition off the floor. The All Blacks were doing well at the moment. The destruction of several ringside tables seemed imminent.

An alternative and equally high-decibelled spectacle was available for non-sporting spectators. An unfortunate poor bastard of an Italian entertainer, dressed in an angular dinner-jacket, stood in front of the band giving his impersonation of a train. It was a familiar and well-loved performance that attracted audience participation of a sort that the entertainer accepted philosophically but without relish. The purity of his art, his expression suggested, was being sullied by vulgar over-enthusiasm. The crucial moment was approaching. Patrons at the tables and at the bar were unbuttoning their left breast pockets, taking out whistles attached to shoulder lanyards.

'*Chuff*, chuff chuff chuff, *chuff* chuff chuff chuff, *whee-eee-eeee-eeee*,' went the entertainer gallantly.

'*Cheee-eee-eeeep*,' went about forty unsynchronised, discordant customers' whistles.

'*Wheee-ee-eeee*,' whistled the entertainer, through long-rehearsed pursed lips and cupped hands.

'*Cheee-eeeee-eeep*,' whistled forty whistlers through whistles.

'*Wheeee-eee. . . .*'

'*Cheee-eee. . . .*'

Laing picked his roundabout way through the tables and the noise. He saw Helen, looking lovely, sitting with Hugo and a one-eyed, eye-patched, one-armed Canadian colonel with a bald head. Laing walked towards them, grinning.

'Hallo, Helen. Good to see you. Christ, what a row,' he said, kissing her on the cheek.

'Hallo, Johnny. This is getting like Old Home Week. How are you? You're looking well.' She squeezed his hand.

'Can't be looking as well as you're looking. Civilising feminine oasis in a desert of rowdy male Yahoos.'

'Are you a male yahoo? And Hugo?'

'It's been known to happen. Not tonight, though. With you here.'

She said fiercely: 'Don't give *me* that Yahoo talk. It's the type of patronising guff that keeps coming up from fat rear-area slobs in Bari. If they ever got their precious carcasses and finely tuned intellects into the Line, they might feel like letting off a bit of steam while they're still alive to. . . .'

She was still holding his hand. He squeezed it tighter.

'Helen. Take it easy. You don't have to. . . .'

'I'm sorry. I'm a bit upset. I've no right to be. You haven't met Hugo's Uncle Andy. . . .'

The entertainer gave a last resigned *Wheeee-eeee* and bowed with relief. The whistle-blowing part of the audience whistled him off the stage and clapped thunderously. The All Blacks beat the Rest of the World in a welter of splintering furniture and crashing glass. The band struck up powerfully a brassy rendering of something that seemed to be called 'Arriba La Banda' or something Italianately similar.

'Johnny,' bawled Hugo. 'My Uncle Andy.'

'How d'you do, sir,' roared Laing.

'Hi,' shouted Colonel Sepelov economically.

'Bit noisy tonight,' bellowed Laing courteously to Uncle Andy.

'What?'

'Bit noisy.'

'Can't hear a bloody word you're saying.'

Hugo mouthed something to Helen and Laing.

'What?'

Hugo's uncle poked him in the ribs with his one surviving forefinger and displayed impatience. Hugo repeated his mouthings.

'What?' bellowed Laing again.

'Arriba La Banda', if that was what it was called, stopped abruptly. Conversational volume shrank with equal suddenness and inconsequentiality. Hugo was late in identifying the trend. He found himself addressing the equivalent of a public meeting.

'Look after her for a moment, Johnny. My uncle wants a quiet. . .,' bawled Hugo into the silence.

There was a roar of laughter, a hearty cheer, and some proffered encouragement. Amidst cries of 'Lucky Johnny', 'Bob's your uncle' and 'Johnny, I hardly knew ye', Hugo, grinning, left the table. So did Uncle Andy, not grinning. Very much not grinning. Scowling.

An alcoholic Highland major said clearly and with wonderment: 'I had an Uncle Bob once. He was imprisoned for buggery.'

There was renewed cheering.

It then became possible to talk.

Helen held Laing's hand again and began to cry, softly, unobtrusively. She blew her nose, looked about to see if anyone were watching her, found that they weren't, and dabbed at her eyes decisively.

'Sorry,' she said.

'Don't be,' said Laing.

'I am. I swore to myself that I'd stop myself from doing anything silly. You – all of you – have enough on your plates without stupid weeping women complicating the issue. It's that damned Uncle Andy,' she said. 'He gives me the creeps. He upsets Hugo. He just turns up here out of the blue and takes over. First time I've seen Hugo for weeks. It's the second half of our honeymoon, really. And then this creature Andy appears and keeps popping up when he's not wanted and dragging Hugo away for quiet little chats. From which I'm excluded,' she added savagely.

She sipped at her wine. Laing felt embarrassed, an intruder. Disturbed, as the friends of both partners of a new marriage always feel disturbed, at the first symptoms of anything short of absolute harmony. This was none of his business and he didn't want to hear about it.

She stared at her glass reflectively. There was more on her mind. Hugo's nightmares, the sweating, the thrashing about, the rasped mutterings. Should she mention those to Hugo's friend Johnny? By God, she wanted to. But Hugo's friend Johnny was also Hugo's boss Johnny, 'sir' on formal occasions, and it would be a betrayal of Hugo and an imposition of an appallingly unfair weight of irrelevant worry upon Johnny, who in the interests of the task he was called upon to perform could only ignore it and who probably had to assume that a high proportion of the men for whom he was responsible also had gibbering nightmares. And Hard Luck. Perhaps he was a night-time howler himself. Perhaps, if pressed, he would say that he and Hugo, and that other strange person, Silent Mott, whom she'd once bedded out of curiosity and had found it very curious indeed, had slept side by side in all manner of uncomfortable accommodation and not a whisper of psycho-neurotic disturbances had been broadcast. And if he did, and it was all hypothetical because she wouldn't raise the subject and aside from the wine there were the metabolic adjustments brought about by that tiny little foetus that was manoeuvring about in her womb in a small way, and the wine and That One were clouding her judgement. . . .

'Sorry,' she said again.

'Don't say sorry,' said Johnny Laing.

'Well, what should I say?'

'Just shut up.'

'About everything?'

'No. Talk about the weather. Not about the weather. About you. Not about Hugo's horrible uncle. Or you say he's horrible. Hardly seen him, but he seems OK to me.'

'Johnny,' said Helen. 'I'm pregnant. There's a little Hugo on the way. Or a little Helen.'

'I thought there might be,' said Laing, thinking of an emotional sister of his. 'Congratulations.'

'Johnny Laing,' said Helen with formality, 'you're a kind man. And understanding. You can see through a girl's defences.'

'I am actually. Very kind. But try that on the troops,' said Laing, grinning.

They laughed together and squeezed hands again.

Helen, who had liked Laing from the time that she had first met him, decided that she liked Laing. Laing had no reconsideration to do. He liked Helen. And thought that Hugo was lucky.

Hugo came back with Uncle Andy. Uncle Andy looked grim. So did Hugo. Helen said venomously: 'Had a nice chat, darling?' Hugo said: 'Yes.' Laing ordered another bottle of wine. Uncle Andy glowered silently. The band played 'God Save the King'. They all stood up, to attention. When they went to collect their coats from the cloakroom they had to protect Helen from the edgings of a fight between the Scottish major whose uncle had been convicted of buggery and a New Zealand gunner who maintained that anyone who wore a kilt was asking to be buggered. Laing and Hugo held both contestants off with firmness and geniality.

They said goodnight. Uncle Andy looked surly. Helen and Hugo, arms around each other's waist, looked radiant. Laing, with a lot to think about, walked pensively back to his billet. He still had to decide whether Mott's section or Hugo's section should go in first in the attack.

The MI5 Liaison Officer, who didn't like his job, and only did it because he had a strong streak of responsibility and a foot lost at Tobruk that limited his choice of useful employment, went argumentatively to talk to his contact man at the radio-intercept establishment at Bletchley Park.

'Burke,' said the MI5 representative succinctly, 'Canadian.'

'What about him?'

'You've given us a lot. Not enough.'

'Haven't unbuttoned it yet.'

'Could be serious.'

'The war's serious. More pressing priorities.'

'The war won't last for ever.'

'Nor will Burke.'

'He'll last longer than the war.'

'Your crowd are becoming obsessive.'

'We're looking ahead.'

'Sorry, Jock. There's so much tactical information coming in, we're swamped. We'll give you what you want when we can. Not yet.'

'He's still in touch with the Germans. Through the Spaniards.'

'We're more concerned with people directly in touch with the Germans. Not *through* anyone.'

'All right,' said Jock resignedly. The missing nerves in his missing foot were painful. He returned to London to report failure. It had been expected.

Richard, the Adjutant, began to wonder if the Colonel was pissed. He was.

'Richard,' he said, swirling his whisky, Canadian rye whisky which he disliked, in his glass, 'you've been in this unit longer than most.'

'Man and boy,' said Richard cautiously. 'I seen 'em come and I seen 'em go.'

'That infantry battalion. They're no bloody good.'

'No. They used to be. The Brigadier says so. He was with them at Salerno. He says they were bloody good then.'

'They went wrong.'

'They hang on. You can't ask for much more than that. They don't seem to like it very much, but they still do it.'

'But no zest.'

'No. If we'd been grinding through the manure for eighteen months getting thumped over and over again, we'd have run out of zest, too.'

'Zest is best. How's our zest at the moment?'

Richard looked at his boss man with careful, affectionate appraisal. It did no harm for the man with the responsibilities to let his hair down occasionally, so long as he did it with discretion and in the right company. Richard was the right company. Discreet, too. Part of his role when this sort of thing came up was to make sure that things weren't said that might subsequently cause repentance or resentment.

'To coin a cliché,' he said precisely, a diplomat committing himself to nothing, 'and to misuse a metaphor, I imagine that your finger is firmly on the pulse of our collective zest.'

The Colonel chuckled and topped up both glasses extravagantly.

'Prudent old Richard,' he said. 'Treading delicately. On eggs. Yes, my finger's on the pulse all right. It's also well out. *And*, after having been licked, is held vertically in the air to test the direction of the wind. It's all over the bloody place. What I want is some confirmatory findings of where my finger is pointing. From another qualified source.'

Richard pondered. 'OK,' he said at last, 'our zest is adequate. Not what it was when we started. Better than that infantry crowd. By far. But casualties and the sheer length of the performance have taken some of the stuffing out of us. Not all. Most of the stuffing out of a few. A little of the stuffing out of more. None of the stuffing out of some. It's the some that keep us going.'

'Yeah. Go on. Interesting stuff, this. What's your definition of the some?'

'Hard to classify them. Easier to identify them. More among the officers and the sergeants than the rest. Particularly the sergeants. Understandably. Aside altogether from selection processes they've decisions to take, responsibilities to fulfil, moves to work out, plenty of action to keep their minds occupied. It's worse for the troops. They get taken to where they're led, hope to God that the choice has been good, and can't get on with their part of the job until they get there. What amazes me is that some of the best among the some are junior NCOs and marines.'

'We're doing well so far. That's my reading, too. Why did you say that you found it easier to identify than classify?'

'Well, we all have our limits and we all vary. And the variations aren't constant. You get balls of fire who suddenly burn out. Or stolid plodders who suddenly rise to an occasion. Or perfectly normal-looking people who all at once go to pieces over some seeming triviality – a breakfast that disagrees with them, a lukewarm letter from a girlfriend. Or toughs with fearsome appearances who're as weak as water, and tiny little unobtrusive chaps who go on for ever. Or—'

'OK. You're still with me. Do some identifying.'

'Sergeant-Major Mayne. Complete professional. Stands no nonsense, but an intuitive understanding of what makes men tick and adjusts the winding mechanism accordingly. He'll go on for ever, because it's why he joined and what he's trained for. Johnny Laing because he has a conscience and an overpowering feeling of responsibility to his troop. He hates war but he gets on with it. To him it's a detestable but necessary job that calls for a full personal commitment and should be got over as quickly as possible. Ken Kershaw in Y Troop. He actually likes war. He's something of a psychopath. He's good at killing people and knows it. Gives him work satisfaction. He'll be lost when it's all over and he has to settle down to some boring nine-to-five humdrummery. Then there's

Hugo Burke. He's a crusader. Possibly the only one we have left. He regards—'

'Ah. Hugo. Tell me more about this crusading. It hadn't occurred to me before.'

'A lot of us were crusaders when we started. Diffident ones. We'd have been embarrassed out of our socks if anyone had said we were, but that was us. You're a professional. Like Mayne. You chose soldiering as a career, presumably because you thought that it would be interesting, satisfying, possibly exciting. And honourable. We were different. With a few exceptions we cursed when the thing started. It disrupted our private lives. We got stuck in because we thought that Hitler, Nazism and all the rest of it were evil. Had to be stopped. We didn't use the word "evil" much because it sounded too stagey. Politicians and flag-wagging journalists had debased it. But it's what we meant. So we volunteered, trying to look cynical. Volunteering wasn't all that much of a self-sacrifice because sooner or later we'd have been called up anyway, but at least we *felt* that we were on the side of the angels.'

'Felt? Not feel?'

'The angels have acquired some pretty crummy friends. The practical arguments for lining up with anyone who's prepared to fight Germans are unassailable. But there's a pretty messy moral fringe to the whole enterprise. Idealism takes a bit of a knock when we find ourselves the warm allies of people who practise most of the things that we originally set out to fight against. God alone knows what the Russians get up to. All we get from the propaganda is that they're fighting like hell and taking enormous casualties, which is undoubtedly true. They're also supposed to be dedicated to Freedom, Democracy, Justice and all those other abstractions beginning with capital letters that sounded so good in 1939. If the Jug example is anything to go by, that's all largely bullshit. I, for one, among the initial enthusiastic suckers, didn't expect what I saw naïvely as a straight contest between Right and Wrong to deteriorate into a morally fuzzy dust-up with means justifying ends and the acceptability of the pernicious as the only available alternative to the even more pernicious. I'm glad that we helped the Jugs to throw the Germans out of Yugoslavia. I'm less glad that we played a small part in leaving the place in the hands of a communist set-up that is as ruthless with its political and ideological opponents as the Germans ever were.'

'OK. Point taken. Let's get back to Hugo. The last of the crusaders, you say. Why's he not disillusioned or making moral compromises or whatever it is that the rest of you Galahads are doing?'

'I don't think Galahad was on the crusades.'

'I don't give a bugger whether he was or not. Try Lionhearts if you prefer them. Only I'd always understood that Lionheart was a rather unpleasant brown-hatter. Anyhow, you started this crusader stuff. Call 'em whatever you like.'

'The first thing to bear in mind about Hugo is that he's the only genuine volunteer among us. Volunteer to the war. Not just volunteer to the commandos. I said earlier that we'd have been conscripted to something or other whatever had happened. Hugo was born in Canada, which has no conscription for overseas service, and educated later in Ireland, which is neutral. So his involvement comes from a purely personal decision. He didn't join because he needed the money. He's rich. Nor for the adventure or whatever you like to call it. I think he enjoys at least some of that side of it, but it's not his prime motive. He puts on a cheerful, indifferent sort of surface, but fundamentally he's a committed Christian of high moral purpose and standards who refuses to be lured into any easy-seeming accommodation with what he sees as the Wrong. At the moment he's in a dilemma. He knows Nazism is wrong and must be beaten. He also thinks – or, if you prefer, *knows* – that communism is wrong and must be fought. But since he's also highly intelligent and sees no prospect of taking on both at the same time singlehanded he's dedicated himself to doing what he can to deal with them one after the other, recognising of course that one man can't do much but seeing it as his duty to do the utmost whatever he can. So, if we're talking about zest, Hugo has it.'

The Colonel refilled their glasses thoughtfully. He drank a powerful draught of his own, in silence. Then he said: 'With that lot to contend with he's about three-quarters of the way further up the creek than I thought he was.'

'Yes.'

'Where d'you pick up all this, Richard?'

'Keep my ears open. And eyes. And I've been around longer than most.'

'What are you going to do when the war's over? Psychiatry or something bogus like that?'

'Something bogus like that. Take up where I left off when I joined up. I was training for the Church.'

'Oh Christ,' said the Colonel.

Before he slipped into a disordered sleep the Colonel brooded disconsolately on war and life and ethics and faith and love and the effect that they, or a combination of some of them, had on people that he knew and liked. Amazing and confusing lot, people. Of basically similar construction, with a few modified protuberances for purposes of identification, you'd think that they'd have roughly the same sensible ideas about things. Or things that mattered, like doing your job to the best of your ability, taking life as you found it, survival, helping your neighbour, and hitting your enemies where it hurt. And then, without warning, you discovered all sorts of high life in progress beneath smooth surfaces. Bland, suave Richard revealing himself to be a percipient amateur psychologist, observer of mortal men, principled philosopher, and interrupted servant of God. A tough, resourceful and carefree subaltern, Hugo Burke, marrier of a beautiful wife and this week's Brigade choice as most popular patrol commander, turns out to be a zealous moralist with a personal mission to smite the forces of sin in the world. Johnny Laing, the best Troop Commander in the unit, a hater of war. Who else had been on Richard's list? Sergeant-Major Mayne. Well, thank Christ for Mayne. He at least was uncomplicated and comprehensible. The Colonel fell asleep dreaming of a simple, happy world, full of simple, happy people like Mayne and himself, just getting quietly on with things, not trying to change too much and never complaining.

CHAPTER TWELVE

THE STARS had a hard, diamond glitter against an opaque, blue-black sky, clusters and pendants masked intermittently by pine-branches ruffling in gentle shifts of the night air. From nearby, to the east, came the interminable, repetitive, rhythmic, muted smack of extended low waves breaking on the sand. Cigarettes glowed here and there under the trees.

Laing, neck and shoulders propped up by his Bergen rucksack, legs outstretched on the sand, looked at his watch, decided that he was looking at it too often, and felt irritable. Around him in the Forming-Up Position everyone was precisely where he should be: with his mates in his rifle-group or his Bren-group, which was part of his sub-section, which was part of his section, which was half of the troop, the fractions commanded by an ascending hierarchy of corporals and sergeants and subalterns, the whole commanded by Laing with his Troop Head-quarters of Sergeant-Major Mayne, the signaller, and the PIAT and two-inch mortar teams, and the medical orderly.

All the neat, clinical, well-thought-out, rigorously rehearsed preliminaries to the Brigade attack had been implemented without a hitch. And already the bloody thing had been postponed by one hour. Unless the subdued rasping coming from the headset of the signaller sitting with his back against a pine-tree beside Laing meant something really original, like, say, the mass overnight conversion of the German army to Quakerism, it was about to be postponed again. Pre-attack wireless silence, said the orders, would be broken only exceptionally.

The signaller said, 'Roger. Out,' pulled his right earphone away from his head, turned to Laing, and said: 'Tarsus plus one, sir.' Laing said, 'Fuck it,' to himself, 'Thank you,' to the signaller, and 'Stand by for one more hour, Sergeant-Major,' to the Sergeant-Major. Sergeant-Major Mayne, as irritated as Laing, impassive, passed the word around. Laing wondered who chose these bloody silly biblical code-words. Probably Richard, the Adjutant, scenting himself to be on the home stretch of his return run to his seminary.

Delays were common and unavoidable because any reasonably sophisticated plan was dependent for success upon the interaction of mutually supporting component parts. A delay to one part led inevitably to delay in some or all of the others. To let individual parts go ahead regardless of related developments elsewhere would be to ask for trouble, defined in blood.

Laing disliked delayed attacks. This one could only have been held up because its opening gambit, the silent crossing of Lake Comacchio by the two army commandos in flat-bottomed assault-boats, had run into difficulties. Since there was neither sight nor sound of flashings or bangings from the direction of the lake, and the selected landing-area of the crossers was five miles in a straight line to the north-north-west from where Laing was, it could be assumed that the delay had been caused by nature, not Germans. Either the expedition had lost itself in the night, which given the professional skill of its leaders was improbable, or low water-levels in what wasn't much more than a flooded marsh had caused the voyageurs to stick in mud, which was more probable. Whatever the reason, something had better happen soon. The sky was paling, the stars were dulling, the pre-dawn mist-cover central to the planning was assembling. If the whole thing had to wait until the sun had eaten away the mist, a lively bloody day lay ahead.

Laing dozed off.

'Sir,' said the signaller, deadpan. 'It's on.'

Laing, instantly awake, alert, rose to his feet, buckled his waistbelt, shrugged his rucksack into a comfortable position, and straightened his woollen cap-comforter. He nodded to Mayne and said: 'Right, Sergeant-Major.'

Mayne said, 'Right, sir,' and sent off his waiting runners into the milky mist (thank Christ) of the early dawn. Rustling movement developed among the trees, some low-pitched authoritative voices were heard, there was no fuss. The four sub-sections fell in and were led by their sergeants along the sandy track through the pines to the clearing where the three Buffalos were parked. The vehicles stood, hard and impersonal, high-sided, steel-plated, tracked, wide-mouthed exhausts like ships' ventilators sticking up from their rear ends and curved forward, protection against water swamping their engines. Lashed to the vehicles' sides were the untidy flat shapes of the assault-boats, black canvas sides collapsed. Wooden paddles, coiled ropes, sledgehammers and sharpened four-foot stakes were stowed securely on the Buffalos' floors.

The troops clambered aboard. They swung themselves down into the metal interiors and fidgeted their bodies into the least uncomfortable positions available in overcrowded mobile steel boxes. It had all been practised, repractised. Everyone knew where to go, and went there. Laing stood outside on the sand with the sergeant in charge of the

Buffalos, a hard-faced functionary from an armoured cavalry regiment. The sergeant seemed to regard his transition from the command of a tank to the operation of a small flotilla of shot-proof taxis for thick-headed foot soldiers as a degradation of status. Laing felt no urge to be sociable with him.

Hugo Burke, who with most of his section was to travel in the leading vehicle with Laing, and who had been peering from a position on its engine cowl into the crowded insides to check that his people were properly accommodated, jumped down grinning in enjoyment of a laconic wisecrack of Corporal Smithwick's. Hugo joined Laing and the Armoured sergeant. So did Silent Mott, after conducting a check similar to that of Hugo on the second and third vehicles.

Nobody said much. The sergeant, precluded from warming up his engines because the noise would alert the Germans, hoped grimly that they would start first time. The indignity of possibly having to explain to his clodhopping passengers that they must get out and walk distressed him. Laing, for reasons not to do with dignity, was hoping that the engines would start first time. Hugo, looking cheerful and unconcerned, was examining appreciatively his wedding-present Canadian lumberjack-style boots. Silent Mott, huge in his loose-fitting jumping-jacket, strung about like everyone else with pouches, webbing equipment, rucksack, was silent. For Christ's sake, thought Laing, let's get going.

The signal to go came with a massive, deafening, sudden intensity. The murmurous tranquillity of the wood was riven to shreds by an arc of dappled flashings in the sky to the rear, followed within seconds by the vast, thundering, palpitating roar of every field and medium battery of the Royal Artillery whose guns could be brought to bear upon the Tongue. The German position at its tip was drenched by a prolonged lethal concentration. Selected targets across the River Reno, identified from air photographs, were battered similarly. Half of the guns firing at the Tongue target lifted their attentions, shortened the range, and put down a devastating curtain in front of the advancing two forward troops of marines, travelling in Fantails.

As the first instalment of the barrage shrieked overhead, Laing gave the thumbs-up sign, pointed to the Buffalos. Speech would be inaudible, was purposeless. He climbed aboard.

He stood in the left front of the bowl of the vehicle, body exposed from the waist up. He wanted a clear view of where they went, of what was happening. The Armoured sergeant relaxed theatrically in the right front, leaning against the rim or whatever the specialists called it, holding lightly to the semi-circular mounting of a belt-fed machine-gun poking over the front. Hugo was hanging over the side at the left rear looking

97

interested, like a day tripper at the rail of a cross-Channel steamer. The driver, sunk deep in the entrails, tinkered with knobs, made fussy adjustments.

A newborn vibration, noiseless in the overwhelming uproar, indicated that the engine, or perhaps engines, had fired. Laing tapped the sergeant on the shoulder and pointed ahead towards where the track debouched from the wood on to the beach. The sergeant nodded. By some imperceptible witchdoctory he passed the instruction to the driver. The vehicle jerked and settled down to a cumbrous trundle. Laing looked behind and saw that the other two Buffalos, Silent Mott prominent in the second, Sergeant-Major Mayne peering smartly over the bows of the third, were lumbering along behind. Well, thought Laing, what about that? The first three minutes of this battle had gone entirely according to the script. They often did. The next item on the programme was to watch for the first cock-up, analyse it, and do something sensible to put it right. Meanwhile stick to the plan until it was manifestly unstickable-to.

It became unstickable-to within three minutes of the emergence of the three X Troop Buffalos from the pine-wood. The two leading troops, carried in the lighter, more vulnerable Fantails, should by now be well away behind the barrage that was creeping by timed lifts methodically up the Tongue. The barrage crashed destructively ahead. The Fantails were not with it. Two of them, hit, were ditched in the sea. Their passengers were prone on the sand, some of them in a bad way. Fountains of sand, dirty orange puffs of smoke, and something unfamiliar, eerie, high-pitched whooping-cough noises, demonstrated that not all of the hideous pervading cacophony derived from the supporters of the attack. The Germans had thickened up the content of their Defensive Fire since Hugo's recent patrol had triggered off a display of their selected targets. They had also altered the range of the forwardmost one. It now fell two hundred yards ahead of where it had been previously directed. They had also added the new, whining, coughing things, which left behind them on the sand unfurled cardboard cylinders like the ones used by artists to hold paintings. Laing had no previous experience of these, but he identified them at once. They had been much talked about. *Nebelwerfer*, Moaning Minnie rockets fired in clusters. They had made a contribution to cock-up number one.

Laing signalled to the sergeant to halt the little column of Buffalos. He had a decision to make. Before he made it he needed some accurate information. How badly stuck were the forward two troops? The best way to find out was to ask. Go himself? Send Hugo? Or send Mott? Or. . . .

Hugo Burke, individualist, astute reader of fights, instinctive knower of what was wanted, made his move before Laing had time to tell him to make it. Hugo swung himself over the side of the Buffalo, jumped, waved to Laing, ducked when one of those bloody whooping things split the air above him, and stepped out into the confusion, his shoulders hunched like those of a walker in a gale-force headwind. He was back within four minutes. He climbed up on to the Buffalo's track, cupped his hands, and bawled into Laing's ear: 'They're stuck for the moment.'

Four howling 105s bracketed the vehicle in a welter of zinging fragments, gouts of sand, and the sort of noise made by berserk blacksmiths. Hugo, unhurt, continued to shout something. Laing missed most of it but picked up '. . . killed . . . casualties. . . .' 'Stuck' came into it again.

Laing wasted no more time. He hoisted Hugo over the side of the vehicle and dropped him on to the heads of offended marines whose complaints could be heard above the pervasive racket. Laing tapped the sergeant on the shoulder, pointed straight ahead, and moved his right forearm up and down vigorously from the elbow in the infantry signal for Double March. He hoped that a mechanised horseman could understand infantry signals. The sergeant raised his eyebrows, indicated dour approval, and communicated his wishes by osmosis to the driver. The vehicle lurched forward into the shit and shot and gathered speed. The other two followed.

They clanked through the uproar of the German Defensive Fire shoot, slid past the two forward troops without running anyone over, and emerged into a trouble-free stretch of sand. Nothing was bursting here, but above it was a screeching turmoil of shells going in both directions. The mist, clearing fast, was still thick enough to be helpful. There were charming glimpses of shimmering blue sea.

'How far?' roared the sergeant.

'The whole bloody way.'

The sergeant sucked his teeth and nodded. The misuse of his troop-carriers seemed to be bringing out the nostalgic best in him. Laing began to develop a mild liking for the fellow. Manners a bit crude but heart in the right place.

Laing felt unreasonably elated. It sometimes happened in action to him and to others with lucky metabolisms, but it shouldn't happen so early. Must control it. This damned battle had barely started. He stared ahead at the sand and scrub, now being crossed at what the sergeant would doubtless call a canter. He chuckled unexpectedly and stared down into the insides of this admirable travelling tin fortification to see how the lads were getting on. Fine form they seemed to be in. Some of them were grinning rather mindlessly. Two were actually asleep. It looked almost like the near-halfway stage of a troop party. Hugo, upright at the stern, hand against that towering exhaust-vent, smiled and waved. Laing waved back. By God, this was exhilarating. The troop really were a bloody good. . . .

For Christ's sake shift your mind, now, from all this philosophical gibberish and concentrate on what has to be done next. Trouble is, it's getting a bit difficult to concentrate. Feeling almost drunk. Haven't touched a tot for days and drunk in charge of a troop. Come to think of it, they look a bit plastered, too. This should not be possible at this time of the morning. . . .

The sergeant prodded him on his upper arm, pointed ahead, and raised his eyebrows. Expressive eyebrows he had, like two question-marks. He presumably wanted to know when to stop, so that they could get out of these comfortable mobile tin boxes and go in on foot to fight the fucking foe. Well, why the hell should they get out? They were fine where they were.

'Charge,' roared Laing.

The sergeant nodded. The driver accelerated. A complex of slit-trenches, fronted by barbed wire, came into view. Streams of Spandau tracer whistled by. There were pinging noises on the steel plating. The Buffalos crashed through the wire. The sergeant was noisily firing his belt-fed machine-gun. Laing drew his pistol and banged off a few rounds like a ham actor in a Hollywood gangster movie. The Buffalo slewed to a halt. A grenade, a 36 grenade, one of *our* bloody grenades, dropped into the patch of sand at which Laing was gazing, lay there innocently for a moment, and exploded with a flash followed by buzzing noises about Laing's ears. Hugo must have thrown it. Very careless of him. German soldiers, hands high in the air, climbed out of the slit-trenches looking apprehensive.

Laing bawled, 'Out,' jumped down pistol in hand, and fell over. He climbed to his feet at once, feeling shakily light-headed. The others were on the ground now, staggering about, the last out more noticeably so than the first. They rounded up the prisoners efficiently, but with a strange mixture of hilarity and deliberation. What the hell was going on?

A white Very light suddenly soared into the air from behind a sand dune. There was an immediate burst of tommy-gun fire followed by the entry into view of Sergeant Montague. Well, Montague's reflexes were still sharp enough. He'd clearly fixed some suicidal Kraut who had been trying to call down a mortar-stonk on his surrendered position with a view to a massacre of both captives and captors. Good for Montague. Another resolute German made a break across the sand, sprinted for the river, narrow still at its mouth, waded in and started to swim across. There were some half-hearted shots at him, all of which missed. Laing was glad. Good luck to the brave bastard.

Better get a grip on all this, mental muzziness or not. The orders came out all right, crisp, sensible, incisive. Prisoners to be formed up in batches of twelve. Captured weapons to be piled in a heap. Vehicles to be deployed as hull-down as the hulls could be downed. Signal to be sent to say that the Tongue had been taken. Hugo could do that.

'Hugo, get on the air and say we've captured the Tongue.'

'What's its code-name?'

'Buggered if I know. It wasn't one of our objectives. I've forgotten.'

'Fudge it.'

'OK.'

Casualties to be checked. The Germans had about twelve, mostly from the shelling, now assembled lying or sitting in a loose line, being attended to by a squarehead with a Red Cross armband and a metal medical box. Own casualties? Should be nil. Laing's glance settled upon Lance-Corporal Jones, the medical orderly, crouched on his hunkers beside two prostrate marines. Five others were standing groggily nearby. Christ. How did that happen?

Laing walked over. Jones looked up.

'Nobody hit, sir,' said Jones. 'Carbon monoxide poisoning.'

'Carbon what?'

'Carbon monoxide. It's the waterproofing on those exhausts. The gases were discharging into the carriers. We're all half bloody intoxicated. The lads in the middle got it worst. You and Mr Burke standing up only got some of it.'

'Is that why everyone looks pissed?'

'Feel it, too,' said Jones. 'It'll wear off. Like a hangover. Except for these two. They're out for the count. They'll have to go back.'

So. That explained a thing or two. Item for entry under Lessons Learnt in the post-battle summary. Always check that the Royal Armoured Corps aren't trying to poison you. Alternatively, why not get everyone hopped up on controlled doses of this stuff before going into action? Very high-class aid to martial ardour. Laing went to where Hugo, standing beside a signaller deeply affronted by the temporary confiscation of his apparatus, was demonstrating that a mildly toxic dose of carbon monoxide had its military drawbacks.

'Sunray Minor Xray here,' Hugo was saying impatiently. 'Xray has swallowed his Tongue. I say again, for about the twentieth damned time, Xray has swallowed his Tongue. Over.'

There were vaguely annoyed crackling noises, and a silence. Hugo switched back to Send.

'All right, you bastard,' he roared to Commando Headquarters, the Eighth Army signal-monitoring section, the German army tactical wireless-intercept organisation, and anybody else accidentally tuned to the frequency. 'If you can't understand what I'm talking about, I'll fucking tell you. Loud and clear. This is Hugo Burke, broadcasting. Johnny Laing's troop, I say again Johnny Laing's troop, have captured the bloody Tongue. I'll give you the fucking map reference if you don't know where that is. Have I made myself clear? Over.'

An agitated squawking suggested that Hugo had. He handed the headset and the throat microphone back to the aggrieved signaller, and reported to Laing.

'I've passed your message on OK,' said Hugo. 'Had to dress it up a bit. That fellow Richard's a nice guy but there are times when he's not very bright.'

There was no point in lingering at this place. While held by the enemy it had been a threat to the flank of the next phase of the advance, the crossing of the River Reno. Now that it had been eliminated it could not be reconstituted in a strength sufficient to make it once again a serious nuisance. There was brief tidying-up. German weapons and ammunition were made useless by an explosive charge detonated rather too light-heartedly by Silent Mott, inhibitions gassed out of him, laughing away to himself as he set off a dangerously spectacular bang which was followed by other irregular sub-bangs as the flames reached new batches of ammunition in the heap. Souvenir binoculars, watches and wallets were distributed around necks, on wrists, in pockets. Disarmed prisoners were sent back on foot down the beach in groups, each group escorted by one of the gas cases. Laing led his armoured cohorts back to the site of their proper job, the bank of the Reno half a mile to the rear.

The morning mist had by now cleared. The sun was well up. The sea twinkled beguilingly all the way to its semi-circular horizon. The tawny sand near the tip of the Tongue, scarred only by the track marks of the Buffalos, deteriorated in appearance the farther back they went. In the neighbourhood of the crossing-point it was disturbed and soiled by more vehicle tracks, footprints, jettisoned equipment, blast marks, and people. The people were spread in clusters, some around vehicles, some lying down warily. The Tongue had been overrun, but there were some last-ditchers left of its original defenders. Lonely Spandau teams, bypassed in the advance, still being heroically troublesome.

Laing, head and shoulders protruding above the steel plate of his Buffalo, signalled a halt and gazed around him. He ducked as a rending burst of Spandau missed his head by a few inches. Hugo laughed, and then also ducked as the gunner had a go at him. Laing lowered himself cautiously over the side away from the Spandau and trudged through the sand towards a group of vehicles from which wireless antennae waved.

'Morning, Johnny,' said the Colonel. 'Come round on the shady side. That damned fellow's too obstreperous by half.'

Laing stepped into the lee of the command vehicle just in time. The sand that he had crossed spurted with little dirty puffs, prolonged. The Colonel glanced disapprovingly at the puffs and said that Richard was dealing with it. Trying something clever with a mortar.

The Colonel listened carefully to Laing's account of the doings at the top of the Tongue, said 'Good', and told Laing to get on with the river crossing as soon as Richard had disposed of that damned Spandau. If, that is, Richard didn't first dispose of everybody else as well. There were interesting possibilities attached to the firing of a three-inch mortar at fifty yards' range.

An argumentative voice from behind one of the Heavy Weapons Troop Fantails asked if Richard seriously meant range fifty yards because if so they'd have to unship the bloody mortar from its bipod, point it more or less straight up in the air, guess the correct angle and hope for the best. God alone knew where the bombs would land. Richard called back patiently that he seriously meant fifty yards and how the mortar crew chose to meet the instruction was their affair, not his. Just do it, fast. There were sounds of procedural unorthodoxy – 'Cock her up a bit more, Jock' – and five successive bangs. The spectators stared upwards. At the top of their trajectory the bombs could be seen clearly, little black ten-pound blobs high in the sky. Then they turned themselves over and came howling downwards. The Colonel, Richard, Laing and everyone else in the vicinity hit the ground shortly before the bombs did. They burst crashingly in a pattern among some scrubby bushes beyond the command vehicle. Fragments clanged against its side and whined overhead. Two Brens from somewhere towards the sea opened up in sustained bursts into the cloud of blown sand. When it subsided a German soldier stood up, hands raised, bleeding from his forehead. He jerked his head to point out two others, motionless beside him.

'Richard,' said the Colonel, 'that was bloody dangerous. There's a limit to all this Faith in God and Keep Your Powder Dry stuff.'

'Yes, sir,' said Richard.

'OK, Johnny,' said the Colonel, 'you're off. Good luck.'

The Reno, here about forty yards wide, had banks as flat and devoid of cover as an athletics stadium. The water moved sluggishly towards the sea. The far, hostile side stretched levelly and inhospitably to a low transverse bank a quarter of a mile away. Laing and Hugo studied the far shore through binoculars and took an intense dislike to it. Silent Mott, the ferrymaster, still grinning and yammering obscurely to himself, stood by with his section ready to go. Laing wondered briefly if Mott had gone mad, the process helped along by exhaust fumes, and decided that it didn't much matter whether Mott had or not. His behaviour was odd, but he still seemed capable of doing his job.

The artillery smoke, thickened up by a supplement from the three-inch mortars, came down exactly on time. A creamy white billowing cloud obscured the low bank and any view from it of the crossing-point. The cloud hung in a gentle light breeze, was nourished by a lazy stream of further smoke-shells.

Laing turned to Mott and said: 'Go.' Mott gave a manic guffaw, unexpectedly shouted 'Fuck the Pope', and led his boat-carrying party at a slow jog-trot to the river bank. The four clumsy canvas assault-boats, already put together behind the vehicles, were carried by six-man teams, three to a side, moving in a co-ordinated step called by the junior NCO in charge of each. Mott sprinted ahead with the stake and rope group. The stakes were thumped securely into the sand with sledgehammers. Rope ends were clove-hitched around the stakes. The boat-carriers overtook, splashed the flat bottoms over the bank into the water, clambered aboard, picked up Mott, and paddled, paying out rope as they went. The smoke continued to drift benignly in the background. So far no interference.

The four boats bumped against the far bank in a close finish. Mott and the stakers sprang ashore, ran a few yards, bashed in the stakes, pulled the ropes taut, and fastened them. The two men left with each boat hauled hand over hand to return to the near side. Mott and the others ran farther forward and spread out in a defensive arc. Laing brought the next lift over, the boats rocking, all free hands heaving on the ropes, low bubbling bow-waves developing. They scrambled ashore and ran to reinforce Mott, enlarge his holding. The boats went back for Hugo's section. Still no interference.

Hugo's people came quickly over. Laing's troop was complete. Sergeant Montague, now running the ferry, could set about bringing over the rest of the commando, strung behind on the Tongue, waiting to move through Laing and northwards up the Spit.

All so far so good, so much better than it had any right to be. Real life wasn't like this. This was a training exercise without umpires to interfere and criticise. Any self-respecting German with half an eye, knowledge of the ground or a map could work out from the smoke what was happening and where. Some German did. The leading lift of the next troop over bullocked ashore amidst a protracted concentration of shelling and mortaring. Noise-levels rose. Huge high plumes of water lifted and collapsed in the river. Both banks repeatedly were masked by a flashing, smoking mess of eruptions, rolling in spasms. Montague and his ferry-men stuck to it, heaving on their ropes, crouching as a new load of stuff came screaming down, cursing the slow and inept among their passengers, helping the hit, getting hit themselves.

Laing, lying with the bridgehead perimeter party clear of the uproar, rolled over on his back and watched it with concern. Sergeant-Major Mayne drew his attention back to a local, immediately pressing problem.

'I don't know who these buggers are,' Mayne was saying, 'but there's hordes of 'em.'

Laing rolled over again to face his front. From the flat, featureless ground ahead, very close ahead, small bunches of small uniformed men, each man preceded by open-palmed hands stretched high in the air, were climbing awkwardly to their feet. They had sallow, blunt faces and narrow eyes, and some of them were calling out what sounded like carefully memorised phrases of placation and goodwill. 'Churchill OK. Roosevelt OK. Democracy good.'

Laing identified them at once: 162 Turcoman Division, summarised in the intelligence brief as 'Russian deserters and ex-POWs enlisted in German Army, morale assessed as doubtful', were giving an illustration of the doubtfulness of their morale. Laing gave short contemplation to what these people could have done to his river crossing if their hearts had been in their work, decided that he'd rather not think about it, and ordered their rounding-up and assembly in batches of reasonable size. They co-operated thankfully, chattering away about Churchill and Democracy. Laing started them off towards the river. He stopped them again. It was too unhealthy down there for the time being. They were instructed by gesture to lie flat in the open and advised in the vernacular by Sergeant-Major Mayne to pray for Peace.

The bridgehead was becoming crowded. More reinforcements thrust through the curtain of shellfire and mortar-fire around the ferry. Wounded were accumulating. The Mongolian prisoners were taking up room. Laing made more space by advancing his protective screen by a hundred yards. The two troops preparing to pass through to attack the low bank ahead shook themselves out into an extended line. The smoke-shells inexplicably ceased to thicken the smokescreen, which slowly diminished, fragmented, dispersed altogether. A series of detonations resounded from the objective, accompanied by sudden mushrooming fountains of earth and muck along the stretch of low bank. Who did that? There had been none of the familiar preliminary aerial whistlings of approaching shells before the bangs, and anyhow the explosions looked different from—

'Demolitions,' said Sergeant-Major Mayne with satisfaction. 'They're blowing up their doodles and buggering off.'

The two assault troops set out over the flat, alert and dispersed, weapons at the ready, walking steadily at the bank. The supporting artillery-shoot screeched overhead, shells bursting spectacularly and noisily in neat clusters, fired on range settings unchanged since the smokescreen. Laing saw three little sharp flashes at ground-level, three of the attackers going down. *Schu* mines. Three poor buggers with missing feet. The attackers reached the bank, put up the Very-light flares of the Success Signal. The defection of the Turcomans had helped more than the river crossing. The follow-up troops, plodding along under their weight of weaponry, rucksacks, pouches, water-bottles, body outlines blurred by shapeless camouflaged smocks, moved through in a long single file, their turn to leapfrog the attackers of the bank, take over the lead, head for the next objective. Laing, temporarily out of work, saw them on their way, enjoying as he did so some of the more inspired exhortations from X Troop's registered comedians. Then he walked back to the river bank to see Sergeant Montague's ferry party. Laing was not optimistic about them.

Montague was dead. So were three marines – two of them, hit by a phosphorus shell, with bodies roasting slowly like gruesome parodies of a Sunday joint. Jones, the medical orderly, was with three of the others, each wounded, none fatally. Jones had applied temporary dressings and was supervising their departure to the Regimental Aid Post, now well forward on the east bank: 'That's it, Reg. Arms round their shoulders and grab a couple of handfuls of smock. They're idle sods pretending to be worse than they are, but they'll get you there.'

Laing said, 'Thanks, lads. Good luck,' as they started off, an awkward fusion of three humans with five working legs, four and a half working arms, and sundry patched abrasions. They grinned. One said: 'Roll on, hospital. Sheets on the bleeding beds.'

The one unhurt survivor was Corporal Smithwick, troop clerk and PIAT-operator, slipped in at the last moment to replace one of the more badly afflicted carbon monoxide victims. Laing returned to the main body of the troop marvelling at Smithwick's resilience and trying not to mourn losses. Montague, kindly, neat, dexterous Montague, the quick thinker who'd shot that Very-firing Kraut at the top of the Tongue a couple of hours ago, the deviser of a lead-foil Star of Bethlehem and a Happy Christmas sign made from cigarette-packets to decorate a scrupulously cleaned hovel of a sergeants' mess in another country in a different life. Or a different compartment of a similar life. An age ago, but not really. Christ, it was three months. Williams, Bungy, one of the phosphorus-shell casualties, had been a good one, too. Back only a few days from hospital in which with fair success he'd tried to bullshit Helen Burke into believing that Hugo passed his days padding peacefully about in some rural backwater, bored but unthreatened. Ruxton, whose repetitive renderings of a Bing Crosby song about swinging on a star had driven everyone to blasphemous distraction. . . . Switch this line of thought off. Save it for later when there's time for it. More urgent demands on your current thinking. What was this? Corporal O'Driscoll was saying something.

'Is it Bungy Williams, or Wilkins?'

O'Driscoll repeated it. Word of casualties travelled fast, was sometimes corrupted in transit. O'Driscoll had been a close friend of Williams.

'Both,' said Laing shortly. 'Williams dead. Wilkins wounded, but OK.'

'Bugger,' said O'Driscoll. 'I'd hoped it was Wilkins who'd copped it.'

O'Driscoll turned away. Laing understood, was sympathetic, had on a couple of occasions in the past felt the same way himself. O'Driscoll bore no animosity to Wilkins. It was just that someone was certain to be killed on these jobs. O'Driscoll had been hoping desperately that the haphazardly inevitable had not overtaken his chum.

Sentries were out as a precaution, but the battle had for the time being passed on. Rumblings and bangings and *brrrmmms* echoed back from about a mile away. The sun became pleasantly hot. Wounded drifted back from the direction of the noise, walking, limping, helping each other along, some on stretchers, all patched with the pale-brown bandaging of field-dressings. There was much talk of *Schu* mines. Fucking *Schu* mines were all over the fucking place. A few of the less badly hit escorted bunches of listless Turcoman prisoners. Laing spoke to a tall subaltern from B Troop, holding a gauze pad to where his right eye had been, a mass of blood on his face and soaking into the shoulder of his smock. Hit by a piece of boot, he said. Man in front trod on one of those bloody mines. Foot was blown off. Chunk of his boot took out the subaltern's eye.

Laing's troop gave help and consolation, asked questions, cleaned weapons, ate corned-beef sandwiches, replenished ammunition and water, gossiped, and dozed in the sun. Hugo talked in Russian with the Turcomans. They weren't much good at Russian, he explained afterwards. Their proper language was some strange Mongolian dialect. But a few of them knew enough Russian to make themselves understood. They'd had a bloody terrible time. They were mostly illiterate Asiatic nomads who didn't know much about anything except that they wanted to be left alone. The Russians had conscripted them to fight in a war that meant nothing to them. They'd been given little training, lousy equipment and elderly weapons. They'd been thrown in to fight German Panzer divisions. It had been a massacre. The ones who'd lived, this lot among them, had surrendered in droves. Then some Red Army general who had changed sides had enlisted them in the German Army, where at least they'd been decently fed and equipped; and here they were, stuck in a country they'd never heard of, fighting for God knew what against God knew whom, getting—

'Ah, for Christ's sake, Hugo,' said Laing irritably. 'My heart bleeds for the unfortunate poor sods. Let's take one war at a time.'

'Look, Johnny, we're supposed to be fighting this war to—'

'Captain Laing, sir,' called the signaller, stretched on the sand five yards away, propped up on one elbow, headset on. 'Message from Sunray Major.'

Laing took the earphones and the throat microphone. The forward troops had bypassed a position, held in about platoon strength, overlooking a track junction, map reference given. X Troop to clear it. Watch out for mines on the first part of the way up. Stick to ground with fresh footprints on it. Laing to go ahead for detailed orders from the Colonel. Troop to follow at once. Ack.

Laing acked. He gave the signaller his gadgetry back and sent for Mott and Mayne to join Hugo. They stood together in the sunshine among the sad litter of a successful river crossing, looking at folded maps, listening to Laing's terse orders. Laing took his runner and set out for the Colonel. Sergeant-Major Mayne called out: 'Get rigged.' The troops rose to their feet and got rigged. When Laing was almost out of earshot he caught faintly an inconclusive exchange between Hugo and Mott. Hugo was saying: 'These luckless Turcoman prisoners have. . . .' Mott, unveiling another of his surprises of the day, was using an excellent imitation of a strong Northern Ireland accent. 'Hugo, you papist bastard,' he roared, cackling happily. 'You can tell your fine frands up there in the Free State that. . . .'

Laing missed the rest of it, and wasn't sorry. God Almighty. Hugo getting all worked up about the Turcomans. Mott trying out the opening rounds of religious warfare. And they weren't through the first half of the first day of the operation yet. What were subalterns coming to nowadays?

CHAPTER THIRTEEN

BY NOON on that day Helen Burke, in Bari, had written three letters to mothers dictated by sons too badly wounded to write themselves, had done a fourth from a blinded sergeant to somebody else's wife, and had distributed eight small drawstring linen bags, each holding a razor, shaving-brush, toothbrush, toothpaste, soap, air-letter cards and a small bar of chocolate, to eight newly arrived patients. She had run an occupational-therapy class in the making of stuffed toys for those among the recovering who wanted to make stuffed toys. She had exchanged paperback books from her small library, and had organised a gramophone concert, a film show and a whist drive to be held during the evening for the convalescent.

In between times a fevered patient had told her that he loved her, a bellicose Glasgow revolutionary who held himself to be a pawn in the Class Struggle had insulted her, and an agile hedonist with his leg in traction had pinched her bottom.

Broadly speaking, it had been a representative morning. Less run-of-the-mill, but entirely satisfying, had been a personal medical examination that had confirmed that her pregnancy was making a healthy and natural progress. She left the check-up happy. The first of the Commando Brigade's Commachio casualties had yet to reach Bari. She did not know that Hugo was in action. She thought of him incessantly.

First reports of how the battle was developing were summarised by V Corps and signalled to Allied Force Headquarters in Caserta. Colonel Sepelov of the Intelligence Staff studied them carefully. He was especially interested to read that a high proportion of the prisoners so far taken were from 162 Turcoman Division, part of General Vlassov's force of what the purists described as Quislings, traitors, defectors. Sepelov himself privately called them nothing of the sort. Sepelov regarded General Vlassov as a good guy.

General Vlassov had been one of the most able of the Red Army generals, promoted while young to fill one of the countless vacancies left by the 1930s mass slaughter of Soviet senior commanders during the

Stalinist purge of the General Staff. Vlassov had fought well against the Germans in the early phase of the invasion. He had been captured and, disillusioned, had changed sides. Stalin's incompetence, brutality and megalomaniac cynicism had, in the proclaimed Vlassov view, destroyed every value that the Revolution stood for.

Vlassov recruited from Soviet prisoners of war. They volunteered by the thousand. Some were idealists. Some were opportunists. Many were incapacitated by upbringing and illiteracy from understanding the politico-patriotic implications of their choice. Personal motives aside, service with Vlassov was preferable to death by disease or starvation in the casually barbarous prison-compounds reserved by German captors for ethnically contemptible Slav *untermenschen*. In some of these camps only a resort to cannibalism could influence survival.

Colonel Sepelov pondered deeply on the possibilities inherent in this sudden accretion to Allied custody of citizens of Soviet nationality. He wondered how his nephew Hugo was getting on.

On her way back from her gynaecological testing Helen called at the post-room. The circulation of mail was not among her responsibilities, but a failure or delay in delivery of the greatest morale-sustainer of all had upsetting consequences for her Welfare charges. Her friend and admirer, the post corporal, gave her a cup of tea and an assurance that all was well. Today, better than well. The bags of lightweight aerograms flown in daily by the RAF had been supplemented by several sacks of sea-mail, slow-travelling packages and letters of more solid content than could come in by air. The sea-mail was still being sorted but the trawl had so far turned up two letters for Mrs Burke. The corporal would give them to her when she had finished her tea.

The first was an outdated circular, written in a jocularly finger-wagging style, threatening displeasure if she failed to attend the annual reunion of her old school. She threw it away. The second, from a girl named Anne whom Helen had known all her life, was a delayed message of love and congratulations upon her marriage to Hugo. There were printed enclosures stapled to the letter.

Anne was a very nice, very kindly girl, with a tendency to gush, emphasised by her use with the written word of a generous sprinkling of exclamation marks. The letter carried a long apology and explanation of her lateness in writing, brought about by the Women's Royal Naval Service posting her to somewhere new about once every three weeks. Her mail was all over the country!! It was only when she had been home to County Fermanagh on a short leave that her mother had told her of Helen's marriage, producing as supporting evidence the notice put into the *Irish Times* by Helen's mother. Anne had read the notice twice before it had dawned upon her that she was pretty certain that she knew the groom!!!! Not all that well, mind you, and it mightn't even be the same Hugo Burke, but there couldn't be all that many Hugo Burkes from Ottawa who were commissioned in the Royal Marines and if Helen's Hugo Burke had been at Trinity College, Dublin, in the early days of the war, then that was the absolute clincher!!!!

And if it *was* that Hugo, then Helen was a very lucky girl. Hugo had been two years ahead of Anne at Trinity and as an immature girl fresh from school she had worshipped (Ha, Ha!!!!) from afar, but he had been by far the most accomplished and *attractive* man in the place. . . . To show that she had not been the only one to have held this view she had searched out some old copies of *TCD* she had kept. Here were the cuttings attached! Also one from the *Irish Times*. Anne hoped that Hugo wouldn't find them too embarrassing but, after all, a new bride had a right to know what her man had once been up to (Ha, Ha!!!!) particularly when it all did him credit!!!!

There were several pages more of this sort of stuff. Helen smiled in affectionate exasperation and turned to the enclosures. She would finish Anne's letter at leisure.

The first clipping, from *TCD*, confirmed in a pleasing manner something that she had known already. Hugo, without much elaboration, had told her vaguely that he had once enjoyed playing Rugby. She had not realised, because he had not told her, that he was good at it. The *TCD* extract suggested that he had been very good at it. '*Dublin University 13. Bective Rangers 12.*' Possibly the decisive, certainly the outstanding, contribution to Trinity's win over a powerful Bective side that fielded three Internationals in an absorbing Leinster Senior Cup Match was the defensive covering and aggressive support in attack of H. S. Burke at wing forward . . . superb tactical sense . . . speed, strength and cool, anticipatory intelligence . . . right place at the right time . . . destructive zest . . . cheerful grace.' The blow-by-blow account that followed was largely unintelligible to Helen. She skipped through it until towards its end 'the phantasmagoric Burke materialised from some unidentifiable point of origin, took Craig's inside pass, and crashed over in the corner'. She liked that bit. The phantasmagoric Burke indeed. She chuckled, feeling proud. She'd try that one on him sometime. Preferably in bed.

On to clipping number two. This was more of a surprise. H. S. Burke, the phantasmagoric try-scorer, gave way to Mr Hugo Burke, the gifted political orator. He had never mentioned either politics or oratory to her, but, then, they'd had so little time together that there were any number of things that neither he nor she had had the chance to discuss. Anyway, here was Mr H. Burke in full voice at the Historical Society, skilfully shifting the emphasis of a debate upon the proposition that Self-Rule was preferable to Good Rule.

The supporters of the motion may have been disappointed that Mr Burke's target was different from their chosen bogey-man of British Imperialism, but they can only have been impressed by his devastating analysis of the threat posed to Christian civilisation by international Communism. Nazi Germany and Fascist Italy, Mr Burke told us, did many evil deeds but the evil was peripheral to their central philosophies. They should be persuaded, by force if necessary, to abandon the foulness of some of their practices. Remove those practices and there remained a central core of respectable aspiration – love of country, hard work fairly rewarded, orderly development of national resources, encouragement of the arts, respect for the family, religious tolerance.

Communism, the protagonists of which made no attempt to conceal their intention of trying to dominate the whole of mankind, embraced all the totalitarian evils of Fascism without touching the virtues that mitigated the evils. Communism was inherently evil. It compounded this disability by being plain silly. The lessons drawn from the particular circumstances of the English Industrial Revolution by a German-speaking refugee living in London in the nineteenth century had been applied as if they were Holy Writ to a fundamentally different backward rural society living in the Russian Empire in the twentieth. The application had been accompanied domestically by a sickening brutality and by a calculated scorning and rejection of concepts of love, honour, trust and spiritual concern that had evolved throughout centuries of Christendom. The horrors of the Soviet domestic revolution would become inexorably the horrors of the international revolution unless all men of goodwill identified and recognised the threat, and then, simply, fought it. If ever the conditions existed for the involvement of Christian manhood in that theologically endorsed regrettable necessity, the Just War, surely the Marxist enslavement of. . . .'

Well, well, thought Helen. So this was what went on beneath the surface. The cheerful, considerate, amusing young commando officer, dedicated seemingly to their mutual love and to his warlike responsibilities, took life more seriously than he had so far revealed to her. Not only thought deeply about it, but was also prepared to stand up publicly and express his thoughts in terms described by the recorder in *TCD* of the Historical Society debate as 'in the elegant and articulate tradition of his namesake, our distinguished founder, Edmund Burke. (Applause.)'

The bringing of Edmund Burke into it was doubtless student hyperbole, and some of Hugo's youthful sentiments about the Russians sounded pretty strange when you considered the fact that he was now a fighting soldier allied to them, but none the less this was evidence of Hugo's unsuspected mastery of – to her – a totally new kettle of fish. All right, mastering kettles of fish was beyond the versatility of even Hugo, but she knew what she meant. What she meant was that she felt more pride. And wasn't ashamed of it. And, Anne, your exclamation marks are an appalling irritant, but you're a sweet, kind friend to have taken the trouble to send me all this printed evidence of Hugo's bygone minor triumphs and I'm grateful, truly grateful. Or, as an earnest of my gratitude, grateful!!! Truly grateful!!! Helen giggled.

The piece from the *Irish Times* was from 'An Irishman's Diary', a column from the centre page and one that she knew of old. It was signed Pro Quidnunc, which indicated that Quidnunc, the regular contributor, had taken the day off and had left his column in the hands of some ambitious aspirant who had yet to make his journalistic name but was working at it.

Pro Quidnunc's affably described personal obsession with strong drink suggested that he was unlikely to last the course. He had, he wrote, been caught in Dame Street in a sudden heavy shower of rain. Had his wits been more about him he would have paused for thought and then run for shelter to O'Neill's, or the International, or the Wicklow, or the bar of Jury's Hotel. Instead he had stupidly put his head down and sprinted to the front gate of Trinity, which was rainproof, architecturally distinguished, and flawed beyond redemption by its lack of a barman. The rain came down interminably. Pro Quidnunc, bored and thirsty to near-desperation, had whiled away the time by reading the notices displayed within the arch. Most dealt with unappetising physical activities; one, put up by the Dublin University Players, advertised a theatrical performance, in progress at that very moment, accessible with minimum exposure to the rain.

Pro Quidnunc, one of Nature's non-theatregoers, went straight to it. There might, he calculated, be a bar. There wasn't. What there was was a production of impenetrable obscurity, performed by noisy actors whose voices grated janglingly on his alcoholically undernourished nervous system. To the summary rough justice of this critique he made one shining exception. An altogether arresting contribution to Thespis, whatever that was and if he had spelt it right, was made by a talented young man named Hugo Burke. Pro Quidnunc was technically unqualified to assess Mr Burke's command of stagecraft, and was unable to work out how he fitted in with whatever had been going on previously. All that need be said was that Mr Burke, by some subtle process of facial adjustment and bodily rearrangement, had made himself look successively charming, persuasive, pathetic, threatening and downright alarming. It was a piece of acting that deserved the highest accolade that Pro Quidnunc could give. Anyone thinking of holding a party at which some of the guests might be likely to become difficult would be well advised to invite Mr Burke. He could be guaranteed to keep things under control with the least possible fuss. Pro Quidnunc was no judge of whether, in the stage context, Mr Burke had the makings of a great actor. He could say with authority that Mr Burke had all the qualities of a great chucker-out.

Helen was less impressed by Hugo-on-the-boards than she had been by Hugo the sportsman and by Hugo the political philosopher, but she was still impressed. Pro Quidnunc was clearly heading fast for the ministrations provided for the embottled by the Brothers of Saint John of God, but even if his drivellings were discounted as a quickly scribbled page-filler contrived to leave his evening clear for his favoured relaxation he had left her with one scrap of pleasurable information. Hugo patron of the Arts. Well, not patron. Practitioner!!!! as Anne would have put it.

Contented, pregnant, glowing Helen went back to work. Her watch showed the time agreed with Hugo, telepathic love-sending time. All Love, Hugo. Is my message getting through to you, wherever you are, whatever you're doing at this moment? My whole Love, and God keep you safe.

By this late stage of the war the treatment and processing of battle casualties had been refined by practice and experiment to an almost mechanical sequence, adjustable to meet unusual requirements, its cold efficiency modified by considerable sensitivity and devotion. As in all major attacks in Italy, the arrangements made for tending the Commachio wounded were as good as forethought and ingenuity could make them, given the rider that the succouring of the injured was necessarily secondary to the prime task of winning the fight.

Troop medical orderlies, Royal Army Medical Corps lance-corporals equipped with a first-aid small pack and a Colt .45 pistol, the latter in contravention of the Geneva agreements because Hitler had already breached the Geneva agreements by ordaining that commando prisoners should be shot, and the orderlies deserved a chance to defend themselves, were the first link in an attenuated chain. The orderlies, working in the heat of battle, examined, disinfected, bandaged, strapped up, injected, sometimes splinted. Sufferers who would walk or limp then walked or limped back. Those who could do neither were helped by those who could or, if sufficiently bad, were removed by stretcher.

The destination aimed for by all, walkers, limpers and stretcher cases, was the Regimental Aid Post; supervised by a doctor with more sophisticated surgical paraphernalia at his disposal than could be carried by the troop orderlies, it was placed as far forward as was possible. In this haven of skill and care priority went to the patently urgent cases. The doctor attended to these personally, changing his schedule arbitrarily in the light of his medical sergeant's assessment of who looked worst at any one time, an assessment complicated by an inability to forecast who would turn up next in what state. If he had the time and opportunity, the doctor dealt personally with everyone. If the pressure was intense, the less badly damaged were looked after by the sergeant and his team of orderlies. Earlier dressings, hurriedly applied usually under fire, were checked and if necessary replaced. Labels listing diagnosis, treatment given, injections made were pinned to patients. The more mobile were encouraged to get out as soon as possible, to make room for successors. The less mobile were helped or carried.

A pool of motor-ambulances was based in the pine-wood at the base of the Tongue. These, each with an attendant orderly, shuttled between the tail end of the battle and the military hospital in Forlì, twenty miles behind the Line. The Forlì hospital, normally civilian, was modern, manned by teams of Royal Army Medical Corps doctors and Queen Alexandra's Imperial Nursing Service sisters, and was provided elaborately with everything necessary for major surgery. Serious cases, in need of uninterrupted attention, stayed in Forlì until they were fit to be moved. Early recoverers were driven to Forlì airstrip by ambulance and evacuated by Dakota to Bari for further treatment.

The first ambulance-loads of these evacuees were assembling as Helen Burke was transmitting her telepathic message of love to her husband Hugo.

CHAPTER FOURTEEN

THE TAKING of the bypassed German platoon position near the track junction was an elaborately organised affair, mounted with high professional skill and an unthinking indifference to the expenditure of the taxpayers' money. A battery of 25-pounders, fire directed by a nonchalant young Forward Observation Officer who sat with his signaller on the sand beside Laing and confused Sergeant-Major Mayne by quoting Shelley in between shoots, softened up the target with a concentration from all eight guns. Two Vickers from the Heavy Weapon Troop, out to one side, loosed off belt after belt of medium machine-gun tracer. The artillery-fire lifted from the objective, a scrubby low knoll, and dropped its shells in a line fifty yards ahead of X Troop. Laing rose to his feet, X Troop to theirs, and they advanced in extended order behind a barrage that preceded them in a precisely timed series of searching, devastating, symmetrical hops.

Laing kept X Troop close up behind the barrage. Better to risk a casualty or two from a short-falling shell than to invite more than a casualty or two by giving the defence time to collect themselves, get their heads up, and fire aimed bursts.

The defence fired no bursts at all. Whether the shelling had ruined their resolution, or provided them with grounds to persuade themselves that they could opt out of the war with their honour untarnished, Laing didn't know. He didn't care, either. What mattered was that they were coming out, hands on high, proper Germans this time, not Turcomans or Aztecs or whatever that other crowd were, the ones that Hugo kept going on about. This lot had five killed and seven wounded, all from shells.

This tidying-up routine was becoming repetitive. Prisoners sent back. Loot looted. German medical orderly and helpers to see to German wounded, to carry them to the Regimental Aid Post when the orderly said that he was ready. Consolidate position, post people to cover all its sides. Report by wireless to the Colonel. Hugo could do that. No, he couldn't. Don't want another comic-turn cross-talk act with Richard. . . .

'Sunray Major from Sunray Xray. Ecclesiasticus taken, I say again, Ecclesiasticus taken. Track junction clear and open for traffic. Own cas Nil. Out.'

That bit about 'Own cas Nil' was nice. We could do with a little more 'Own cas Nil'. But Ecclesiasticus? Theologian Richard and his biblical bloody code-names would do for us all if this went on. Next signal would be something like 'Woman in Adultery taken'. Hugo could send.

The Intelligence Officer drew a red ring with a chinagraph pencil on the transparent talc cover of his map, wrote Eccl. for Ecclesiasticus beside the ring and handed the map to the Colonel. The Colonel looked at the red ring and studied it in relation to four others that marked the present locations of his other four fighting troops. All were more or less where the plan had said they should be. All had got there more or less on time. None had got there in exactly the way that they had originally meant to, which didn't matter. Much resourcefulness, improvisation and blood had gone into the getting. More of all three would be necessary tomorrow. The Colonel hoped and intended that a lavish use of the first two would save on the third.

While pondering upon the best way to send who to where, and when, he glanced from time to time around Commando Headquarters. Fine, grand-sounding name for a bunch of disciplined scruffs in need of a wash, grouped with maps, wireless sets and weapons in a cluster of bushes on a God-forsaken sandspit in northern Italy.

'No Surrender,' roared Mott on the following morning. 'Home Rule is Rome Rule. Not an Inch.'

'Sir,' said Sergeant-Major Mayne primly, firmly, 'Mr Mott, I think, has gone round the bend.'

Laing said: 'Thank you, Sergeant-Major.'

Neither of them said anything else. There was nothing more to say. They – in the hierarchy, specifically Laing – were for the time being stuck with Mott. If Laing ordered him to go back when there was more fighting ahead, the troops would rightly resent the departure to safety of an officer. If Laing overrode that consideration and Mott went unaccompanied, he could get into all sorts of trouble, blunder into a minefield, say, have to be rescued at the risk of other people's limbs or lives. The sending of a guide was impossible. Nobody could be spared. The troop had started the operation fifty strong, less than there should have been because casualties from the time in the Line and from sickness had not been replaced. They were now down to forty-one. Losses so far nine, the two carbon monoxide cases from the Tongue, the four killed and three wounded from the river crossing.

So no guide. Mott would have to stay. He was, at least, still doing his job with acceptable competence. It could even be argued that in one sense the new Mott was a military improvement on the old. He gave the lads something to think about other than where the next stonk would land. Pity Montague wasn't still alive to keep an eye on him. Montague had been more adaptable than Mott's surviving sergeant, Ingram. Ingram just kept looking embarrassed. Montague would have— Also there was Hugo. Hugo was too good a soldier to show resentment publicly at the halfway stage of a battle, but he was a devout Catholic, which to Laing was a mysterious thing to be, and he might be becoming so riled that there could be a perhaps subconscious hiccup in co-operation at a time when hesitation. . . .

'Hugo.'

'Johnny?'

'How badly is that crackpot bothering you?'

Hugo laughed. 'Not in the least. Makes me feel nostalgic for the good, dear days gone by.'

'What on earth started him off on all this? Any idea?'

'I don't know what started it. I can tell you when it first came my way. The night before we left Ravenna. When I got back to my billet there was old Silent, propped in the corner with an almost-empty bottle of grappa. Said that he and the grappa had spent the evening in meditation on the proposition that whom the Gods love died young. After thinking the thing out carefully he'd decided against it. But since I was a Catholic and went to Mass when I could, and had what he called a direct wireless link with God, maybe I disagreed with him.'

Laing stared. How many hidden Motts made up the external, silent Mott?

'I said that I had no credentials to speak on behalf of God or of the Gods but, so far as dying young was concerned, I was against it, too. Just what he'd thought I'd say, he said. Typical papist answer. Spend all your lives praying for a happy death and, when death gives an encouraging knock on the door, duck. Well, the Motts were made of sterner stuff. Because he spoke with a plummy public-school accent we all probably thought he was English. This was balls. He'd been to school in England but he came from Ballymena and Ulster would fight and Ulster would be right and have a slug of this grappa. Made by some Wop papist, but none the worse for that.' Hugo laughed again. 'So I helped him out with what was left of the grappa. After which he produced a hip-flask of whisky and said that he wanted to ask some serious questions. He fell asleep in the middle of them, but he was fairly lucid in the preliminary build-up. He'd mentioned in a letter to his father that he was hobnobbing with a chap named Burke. Kept his distance, mind you, but there was Burke daily, had to be talked to, on official business. His father, some sort of historian, wrote back to say Watch out. The Burkes used to be Earls of Ulster. Decent Norman Paddy-bashers, but they went wrong. Kept mating with Fenians, and spoke Irish, and were officially classed as degenerate. Degenerate at the time meant literally an abandonment of prudence about inter-racial breeding, but in the opinion of Silent's father the whole bloody lot of De Burgoes, De Burghs, Burkes were as degenerate in the modern sense as were the entire crummy, papist population of the Irish Free State.'

'All right,' said Laing, 'he's nuts.'

'Not entirely,' said Hugo.

'How not entirely is not entirely?'

'Grappa followed by carbon monoxide followed by all this shit that's been flying around recently has made him turn private thoughts into open expression, probably for the first time in his life. He was brought up to believe that life was a simple business of frugal, hard-working Protestant Motts being responsible and doing things, under constant threat from idle, feckless Micks who mucked everything up and bred like rabbits and were a bunch of rebels who—'

'Bugger the Virgin Birth,' bawled the distant voice of Mott.

'You see what I mean,' said Hugo.

'No,' said Laing.

'Captain Laing, sir,' called the signaller, 'O Group at 0900 hours.'

Before he left for Commando HQ, five hundred yards behind, Laing walked around and chatted to his troop. Since they had done a night march through 2 Commando's position at Amos they had had three hours' sleep, which was good. They were now scattered about in sand and scrub, indistinguishable from earlier sand and scrub, and, forward Bren-group sentries excepted, were brewing tea in mess-tins over tommy-cookers, rearranging rucksack loads, cleaning weapons with four-by-two and oil-bottles, and shaving. They were in much the mood that he had expected. Tiredness and danger accentuated individual characteristics. The cheerful were more cheerful. The morose were more morose. Two about whom he was worried, post-Yugoslavia reinforcements from a draft of Fleet marines, were very quiet and looking as if they would rather be somewhere else, anywhere else, but what the hell, here they were and they'd better make the most of it. Corporal Smithwick, the only representative present of the hard-hit ferry party, contributed comment.

'You OK, Corporal Smithwick?'

'OK, sir? Every time I *fart* I take cover.'

It was good to have Smithwick around.

'All here?' asked the Colonel.

'Yes, sir,' said Richard.

'Right. Detailed orders in a couple of minutes. First, take a good look at your maps. We're going to bum on to Porto Garibaldi and the Valetta Canal.'

Laing had already taken a good look at his. The map study was for the benefit of two subalterns, now commanding their troops, substitutes for their former bosses, one killed, one wounded on the previous day. The subalterns concentrated on their work, picking out and memorising the track layout on the flat top end of the Spit, bisected laterally at its northern extremity by a narrow artificial water-channel, the Valetta Canal. On the far bank of the canal was marked a large, scattered village, Porto Garibaldi.

Laing glanced around at the O for Orders Group. The five Fighting Troop commanders and the Heavy Weapon Troop commander sat comfortably on the sand in a loose half-circle, with their backs to a chest-high sand-hump. The Colonel, his Intelligence Officer, and Richard the Adjutant stood, relaxed, in front of them. Smocks and trousers had the creases and crumples and stains to be expected of clothes that had been fought in and slept in for thirty-six hours. Boots were scuffed and had impacted sand in the welts. Faces were shaved because the Colonel held firm views about the therapeutic and disciplinary value of shaving in action. Hands and fingers were grubby because there was insufficient water to clean them. All but young Peter Sims, now elevated to the running of Y Troop, wore their woollen cap-comforters at an identical angle. Sims's cap-comforter had been torn to tatters on the Tongue by a mortar-bomb fragment that had also sliced away the apex of his left ear. The ear was now taped to the side of his head by a broad band of dirty pink sticking plaster from which protruded a blood-stained gauze pad, giving Sims a vaguely dramatic appearance like someone in an advertisement for a film.

Sims looked as casually unconcerned as did all the others. One of the products of youth, fitness and training was a resilient ability to look casually unconcerned, sometimes because you were exactly that, sometimes because when you were feeling far from casual and very concerned it did no good to you or to anyone else to show it.

The Colonel began his orders, incisive, no ambiguity. Porto Garibaldi and some strongpoints in front of it held by the enemy, morale unknown but probably dented by the previous day's happenings. Commando intention to go for the canal. Cross it into Garibaldi if the Germans showed signs of cracking. Start-time 1400 hours. Approach area heavily mined. Minefields fenced off in barbed-wire enclosures. Advance would have to be channelled along narrow track between these fences. Single file and no room to deploy if it bumped trouble (Oh Christ, thought Laing expressionlessly, and was pretty sure that everyone else, equally expressionless, thought it, too). Order of advance. X Troop to lead . . . (Oh Christ, again). Artillery support barrage moving forward by fifty-yard lifts at half-minute intervals. Wireless frequencies same as yesterday. Call-signs unchanged. Troops to dump rucksacks and move in light fighting order. Synchronise watches. Coming up to twelve minutes past nine. Five, four, three, two, one, *now*. . . .

At twelve minutes past nine in Bari, Helen was feeling markedly less sanguine than she had when she went to bed the night before. She had, as was her daily custom, checked the overnight admissions-list prior to starting her day's work. It was a longer list than had become usual in the recent winter slackening of fighting. Most of the names on it, unit given after each name, were from the Commando Brigade. Ten were from 49. Not – O God, thank you – Hugo. Not yet.

She went to see them, bar two who had suffered a relapse on the air journey and were unseeable, and gave them their little linen bags of goodies, and books, and a warm smile and kindly chatter. She did not, could not, ask them about where the fight had been, was it still continuing, how long was it expected to last – all the things she wanted to know, was terrified of knowing. She did hear some of them talking among themselves about what was referred to as a 'duffy'. There were enquiries about whether mutual friends had yet arrived in Bari or were still in Forlì, and mention of old Jock and Chalky who got knocked off on the Spit. But when the talkers noticed that she was listening they stopped, with a clannish reticence to discuss their experiences before strangers.

She was used to that. Fighting soldiers seldom did. She had once asked Hugo about it. He had tried his best to explain, but conceded eventually that he couldn't. It was nothing to do with an order, or a convention, or a snobbery of initiates, he had said. It was a personal, intimate thing. He himself would talk for hours with Johnny about who had done what, and why, and how, and whether they could have done it better, or worse, who was still good and who had had enough and was beginning to show it. But let an outsider appear and they both would clam up instinctively. The nearest parallel that Hugo could suggest – and it was, he said, far from exact – was sex between happily matched partners. The partners might make it plain that it prevailed. To discuss the details publicly would be unthinkable. And, he had added, in case she misunderstood him he wasn't suggesting that there was a sexual dimension to infantry fighting, which was essentially a messy, unpleasant affair illuminated from time to time by acts of selflessness and comradeship. What he was saying was that the pressures of the fighting uncovered so many facets of people's characters that it would be obscene to disclose them to anyone who hadn't been there at the time.

Then he had laughed and said that the years would doubtless erode the inhibitions. He would become a terrible war bore in his old age.

Please, God, give Hugo an old age.

She looked at her list and took her collection of little linen bags to the next ward.

CHAPTER FIFTEEN

HUGO, map in left hand, standing at the head of the long single-file snake of the column, pushed back the sleeve of his camouflage smock and glanced at his watch. He stepped to his right and turned towards Laing, a hundred yards behind. Laing was also examining his watch.

Between Hugo and Laing, spread at five-pace intervals, each in his familiar place, were the marines of Hugo's section. They looked workmanlike and mentally alert. Equipment had been stripped down to ammunition-pouches and water-bottles. Weapons were carried as each man found to be personally comfortable, at the trail or points of balance on shoulders. Nobody much liked that stuff about narrow tracks channelled through wired-off minefields.

Sergeant Hankins's sub-section was in front, Hankins ahead, the butt of his tommy-gun tucked neatly under his right armpit. Behind Hankins were three three-man rifle-groups, each led by a corporal. The last Hankins responsibility was Corporal O'Driscoll's Bren-group, O'Driscoll stolidly in front of them, the pouches of the gunner and his mate burdened with the heavy spare magazines. Ten yards behind O'Driscoll's Bren-team was Sergeant Rowley's sub-section, distributed in the same sequence as was that of Hankins. Rowley, who detested errors made through oversight, was moving slowly along his line-up, rechecking that the press-studs on all ammunition-pouches were fastened securely.

Ten yards behind the last of Rowley's people stood Laing, his Troop Headquarters dispersed behind him: Laing's runner; the signaller, antenna waving whippily above his back pack; Sergeant-Major Mayne looking disdainful about the inferior standard of turnout acceptable in action; Jones the medical orderly; Smithwick's PIAT group toting their temperamental weapon and its bombs in cylinders fastened together in clusters of three, the two-inch-mortar team similarly encumbered. Mott's section was strung out behind Troop Headquarters. The track bent behind Mott. Out of sight the rest of the commando waited, each troop identically disposed.

The sun shone from a clear blue sky on to the ochre sand and on to the darker untidiness of clumps of scrub. There was an unnatural, peaceable silence. Laing, still staring at his watch, raised his right arm in the air. Laing's head came up, he gazed towards Hugo, grinned, and jerked down his hand. Hugo grinned back, waved an acknowledgement, stepped back to his position in front of the column and said: 'Right, lads. We're off.' There was a ripple of movement from the front to the rear, the muffled swishing of forty-one pairs of boots trudging through loose sand, occasional creakings from equipment.

Hugo led them the quarter of a mile to their first point of reference, a track junction where the sand was disturbed by a plenitude of footprints, all leading northwards. Here he halted, checked his watch again, and ordered everyone to lie down. The artillery barrage would precede them. Its initial salvoes, range calculated from maps that might hold minor inaccuracies, by Gun Position Officers who might be weak on arithmetic, aimed by gun-layers who might be absentminded or have a twitch, would not necessarily land where they were intended to land. They *probably* would. The virtuosity demonstrated during earlier shoots suggested that they *would*. But no point in taking unnecessary chances on an afternoon when plenty of necessary chances remained to be taken.

Nothing fell short. The concentration of shells made its usual hideous, lazy shriek as it passed overhead, and its usual hideous, eardrum-twanging bangings as the shells burst comfortingly in a dispersed line fifty yards ahead. Unspoken apologies all round to those meticulous perfectionists, the cartographers, those talented, numerate Gun Position Officers, those steady-handed, clear-headed gun-layers, excellent chaps all, won't hear a word against them.

Hugo stood up. So did the rest. Hugo led them on again, as close to the barrage as he could reasonably get, just short of straying into the effective radius of its explosions. The first wire fence came into sight behind the curtain of raggedly bursting shells, a neat, agricultural-looking contrivance of parallel tautened strands stapled to wooden posts, the barbs the long, vicious German ones, bigger and spikier than British ones, Stations of the Cross, Crown of Thorns, model barbs. The track led to a gap in the centre of the fence, continued through the gap, wound out of sight at a gentle curve eighty yards ahead. Laing, watching carefully from his controlling position further back, saw Hugo head unhesitatingly for the gap, walk through it, his section after him now looking more alert than ever, players of Follow My Leader with unusually stiff penalties built into the rules of the game. Each of them examined intently the arc that he had been given to observe. The last one went through. As Laing reached the gap, Hugo was disappearing round the curve.

Within the minefield the track was bordered on either side by two more wire fences, same tidy construction, same wooden uprights, same barbs. The cleared channel was about four yards wide. Signposts were planted at intervals behind the wire, stencilled skulls and crossbones surmounting *Achtung Minen* notices. This was unpleasant time, neck-stuck-out time, hope-the-bastards-have-buggered-off time, Hugo-for-Christ's-sake-keep-going-fast time. Serious opposition here would be a killer. Not a hope in hell of putting into practice all those rehearsed drills of leading section pinned down and shoots back, Laing controls things from there on, decides whether to take the rear section round by the right or round by the left depending upon the configuration of the ground. In this constricted bloody corridor you couldn't take anyone round anywhere.

Well, anyway, so far so good, Hugo's stepping out fine, nothing's happened yet, just give your well-known impersonation of stylish confidence and hope to God that the whole thing doesn't deteriorate into a pig-shoot with you and your trusting followers the pigs. How deep *is* this bloody minefield? Hugo in sight again, Hugo out of sight again round another gentle curve, the lads striding out in good order, vanishing one by one after him, no noise other than our own shelling and some distorted snatches of song from behind, presumably that nutcase Mott. Christ, suppose old Mott really goes berserk while we're still stuck between these fences? Ah, this looks better. Parallel fences coming to an end, Hugo out there ahead in the fresh air, still plugging on unemotion-ally across a wide expanse of gently rolling sand scattered about with a handsome spread of those scruffy-looking bushes.

Oh dear, another damned fence coming up behind the shellbursts. Gap in the middle, Hugo going for it, procession following, two more parallel wire fences, same old *Achtung Minen* signs. Why aren't these minefields covered by fire? Very uncharacteristic piece of German slackness. Christ, a *horse*. Odd sort of afternoon this is turning into. Frightened grey cob, protuberant, swivelling eyes, indifferently groomed, cantering briskly down the track with a wise determination to get the hell out from whatever complicated nastiness the squalid humans have devised this time.

Hugo in sight again, Hugo out of sight again, last man of Hugo's section out of sight again, still the only bangings those from our own stuff dropping down in front, carry on looking spuriously phlegmatic. Round this curve, straight stretch ahead, fences funnelling outwards, end of minefield number two, forty yards in front. Thank Christ for that. If this map's right, which it must be because if it wasn't the gunners would have made a thoroughgoing cock-up of things by now, Porto Garibaldi is about to come up on the other side of that high scrubby clump of bushes, the name of which stays a mystery.

Porto Garibaldi duly came up, smack where it should have been, its layout modified artificially since the map had been made. The few buildings that had once stood on the near, southern side of the canal had been razed to give a cleared field of fire that was part of an elaborate defensive system of which the minefields had been a component. The flattened area was uneven, spread about with the concrete bases of destroyed houses, rubble, rubbish and undergrowth. About a hundred yards from the clearing's near edge, and on the far bank of the canal, was a backdrop of an irregular line of low houses. Within the confines of this roughly defined arena a great deal of noisy confusion was developing at speed.

Soldiers in German uniform were milling about all over the place. Some, small groups and individuals, were on their feet, arms raised in surrender. Others showed signs of being about to join them. Others were scurrying about like distracted sheep. A few, still lying down in cover, were firing desultory rifle-shots. Towards this disorderly indecision Hugo's leading sub-section, Hankins's, was running spread out in an extended line, Hugo at their centre and slightly in front. Rowley's sub-section, with less time to deploy from the funnel of the track exit, were following in blobs of twos and threes, trying to catch up, shaking themselves out into line as they went.

Hugo, pistol in hand, reached the first of the hands-in-the-air people, judged by Laing from their short size to be Turcomans. Laing made an instant decision, retained Corporal Smithwick and his PIAT group, and sent Mott's section to hurry to the open ground at Hugo's right rear. They, too, were hampered by the bottleneck of the track exit, but Mott, mercifully abjuring sectarianism for the occasion, brought them through at a spanking rate. Laing paused to see half of them on their way, and then, with Smithwick's team, moved in pursuit of Hugo.

Hugo's advancing line, impeded by a growing mass of aspirant prisoners, swelled by new candidates popping up from unexpected places, began to lose its symmetry. Hugo, by now well out in front, was heading for a low bridge over the canal. Hankins and a bunched group were chasing him. So far the thing had the appearance of a slightly chaotic replica of the prisoner-gathering, watch-and-wallet-collecting walkover ('Own cas Nil') of the previous day. Spandaus that suddenly opened up from the houses on the far bank of the canal transformed it.

The range was negligible. The Spandau-operators – too early to work out how many but certainly too many – were untroubled by inhibitions about the destruction of comrades trying to surrender to, inextricably mixed with, the attackers. Streams of Spandau bullets ripped into the mêlée. Most of the prisoners, candidate prisoners, and marines not hit in the initial savage bursts dived to the ground, searched for somewhere safe to crawl to, if lucky crawled to it. Some of the better-placed marines, suitable cover of rubble or fold in the ground chanced upon, fired sporadic bursts and single rifle-shots at the houses. Hugo, already on the little bridge, continued to run across it, reached the far bank. Laing saw him jerk violently and then fall crashingly face down to the ground, his body skidding to a stop in puffs of dust and dried sand.

Hankins was thrown on his back by shots that took him in the shoulder. Smithwick set up his PIAT on top of a pile of rubble, got off two bombs that exploded satisfyingly on the fronts of two of the left-hand houses, and collapsed over the butt of the weapon. From the right, one of the Brens of Mott's section, partially clear of the carnage and hidden from view in scrub, began to chatter away in controlled bursts, its tracer bouncing off the houses, correcting, going through the windows. Sergeant-Major Mayne ran out to pull in Hankins, went down with a shattered leg. Laing, who had stayed on his feet because it was his job to assess and to try to contol, made a quick assessment, concluded that matters for the moment were out of control, and with two streams of machine-gun bullets buzzing about his head reached the shelter of Smithwick's heap of rubble in a jinking run of eight steps and a dive.

Marine Hart was already there. Between them they pulled down Smithwick by the ankles, in a shower of ricochets and stone chippings. He had been shot through the forehead. He was still breathing, bubblingly, stertorously. Laing rolled over on his back, took out the field-dressing from its pocket in his battledress trousers, unwrapped it, and pressed the gauze pad to the massive, messy exit wound in the back of Smithwick's head. Smithwick couldn't last. Laing was careful to fasten the bandage with considerate precision. He had liked and admired Smithwick.

He had liked and admired quite a few other people, too. How many of them couldn't last or hadn't lasted? There were bodies, mixed marine and prisoner bodies, lying temporarily irretrievable out in the open to the right front. Some would certainly be dead. Some unconscious. Some pretending to be dead because they had nowhere to go to and, if they moved, one of those bloody Spandaus would have another crack at them. Mayne and Hankins were closer to the canal and had looked alive when Laing had last seen them, just before his dive for Smithwick's rubble. Hugo? Not a chance. He'd gone down like an axed tree or whatever the appropriate simile was. And hadn't flickered afterwards. Dead Hugo. Sad Helen. Major, ghastly, overriding responsibility to be honoured, but not yet to be thought about. Too many other responsibilities to think about.

The immediate thing to think about was that his troop had been carved up, that its survivors were, like him, stuck behind bits and pieces of low cover, and that there was absolutely nothing that he or they could do about it unless some unimaginably successful intervention came from friends behind or until dusk fell and they could all quietly bugger off with their tails between their legs.

'What's your view on all this, Hart?' asked Laing affably.

'Fuck it,' said Hart.

'I agree,' said Laing.

It was three o'clock in the afternoon. Nightfall would be at six.

Four more ambulance-loads of commando Commachio wounded were delivered from Bari airstrip to the hospital by noon. More came in after lunch. Among these was a tall young subaltern named Dick something, last seen by Helen behaving with elegant exuberance at her wedding reception. Dick something had lost an eye. He was pale and bandaged, and had been sedated for the air journey, but the first thing that he did on partially coming to in his hospital bed was to ask the nursing sister to send for Mrs Burke. He smiled at her when she arrived and said: 'Hugo was OK when I left. There was quite a lot happening at the time but he was still going.'

Then he fell asleep again. Helen thanked God for the likes of Dick something.

Later, on her rounds, smiling, smiling, looking sympathetic and serene, the sympathy genuine, damn the serenity, she said her standard piece to three marines who had been saying something about a river crossing when she came in, but who had then stopped. One looked at her closely.

'You're Mrs Burke, aren't you?'

'Yes, I am.'

'I thought so. Took a message from Captain Laing to the Imperiale. Just after you were married.'

'Are you in X Troop?'

God, I hope he is. God, no, I don't. God, I don't know what I hope. God. . . .

'Yes. Good one, old Burkey. Mad as a hatter, mind you. Drives old Busty Hankins round the twist. Don't worry about Burkey. That's if you *are* worrying about him. Born lucky. Take more than a few Tedeschi to sort *him* out. He's fireproof.'

'Thank you. I. . . .'

'Here, Mrs Burke. You're not looking too good. Have some of this Eyetie surgical brandy they dish out in this place. Can't stand the stuff. *Look*, Mrs Burke, your husband was *fine* when we last saw him. Don't worry.'

'Thank you,' said Helen, and walked out of the ward. She wiped her eyes in the corridor and went to the small room that had been converted to a temporary chapel. There she knelt and thanked God again for the likes of Dick something, and thanked God for the first time for the likes of the consoling injured river-crosser, and thanked God for the uncounted time for the gift of pregnancy, and asked God for another uncounted time to keep Hugo safe. She didn't ask God to make her less emotional because that was a product of pregnancy, and natural. Then she made up her face and returned to the wards, smiling, and looking sympathetic and serene. Pro Quidnunc, she felt, the *Irish Times*'s reluctant theatre critic, would have been proud of her.

An edgy, deceptive quiet fell upon the southern approach to Porto Garibaldi. The sound of shooting petered out, stopped. The subdued humming insect noises of a Mediterranean spring afternoon became obtrusive. The sun shone down, warm and benign. Secondary sounds, which a few minutes before would have been lost in the overall hullebal-loo of concentrated gunfire, were now sharply defined, accentuated. A displacement of stones by an invisible German moving behind the houses. An occasional groan from one of the wounded lying in the open. A cough. A snatch of song. A snatch of . . .? God. Mott was at it again.
    'Sleughter, Slaughter,
    Holy Water,
    Kill all the Cath-o-lics, one by one. . . .'
There was a short burst of Spandau fire, a pause, and a bellow of 'Bollocks' from Mott, over to the right where the bushes were thickest.
Mott the vocalist continued from where he'd left off.
    'Tear 'em asunder,
    Grind 'em under,
    The Protestant boys who—'
This time two Spandaus interrupted with about half a belt of ammuni-tion each. They stopped. A peal of lunatic laughter echoed from the bushes, followed by a happy cry of 'Missed'. The Spandaus started up again.
    'Music critics,' said Hart to Laing.

At twenty to four Smithwick gave a gasping gurgle and died. Laing took the PIAT, loaded and cocked by Smithwick in his last conscious moment, eased it round the end of the rubble, and banged off a hasty shot that hit one of the houses with a pleasing crash. That one for Smithwick. Laing withdrew his head smartly. A retributive volume of Spandau agitated the surface of the rubble for the best part of a minute.
    Hart said: 'Fuck.'
    At five past four Laing heard movement among the ruined, flattened masonry of what had once been a farm-building, immediately behind him. He turned cautiously. The top of a German steel helmet peeped out. It moved farther. A face and shoulders came into view. Ten yards away. Laing raised his pistol, rested the barrel on his left forearm, and aimed. More of the man appeared. He was wearing a Red Cross armband. Laing, bitter about Smithwick, decided to shoot him anyway. He began to squeeze the trigger. Hart said: 'I wouldn't, sir. Medical orderly.'

Laing lowered the pistol and said: 'Thank you, Hart.'

Shortly after half-past four, three Hurricanes with South African Air Force markings, a 500-pound bomb slung below each, streaked in deafeningly at low level from the direction of the sea. They skimmed over the German-held houses, zoomed away in a circling climb to starboard, and vanished momentarily. While they were away, two 25-pounder shells screeched from behind over the heads of Laing and his diminished following and landed with a plop, one at each end of the Garibaldi row of houses. Both shells were smoke. There was not enough of it to obscure the houses. There was enough, in the right two places, to make an efficient target-indicator.

The Hurricanes, in line ahead, came in from the east again. This second time around they were serious. Hart said, 'Fuck,' and burrowed deeper behind the rubble. Laing took Hart's point and said nothing. The pilots made successive perfectly timed runs, dumped their bombs among the houses and disappeared, this time for good. There was a ten-second delay on the fuses. Then there were three shattering eruptions, the earth vibrated, most of three houses disintegrated, a shower of fractured masonry and timber fell indiscriminately all over the area, and the sound of shouting and of tumbling brickwork came from beyond the canal.

Laing said: 'Somebody loves us.'

Hart, who had had a near-miss from what looked like an Italian version of a Welsh dresser, said: 'Yes. But I hope he doesn't smother us with it. Overpossessiveness has a traumatic effect on human relationships.'

Immediately afterwards most of the Spandaus opened up again. Whoever was manning them wasn't going to be intimidated. Hart said: 'Fuck.'

The accuracy with which the smoke-shell indicators had been placed, and with which the Hurribombers had bombed, was a clear demonstration that the Colonel now had reliable and precise information about exactly where X Troop was stuck, and about who was who and where. Somebody sensible, presumably from Mott's section, must have managed to get back. Further encouraging evidence of efforts to help extrication came within a few minutes of the departure of the Hurricanes. Salvo after salvo of high-explosive shells thumped down on to the German-manned houses of Porto Garibaldi.

The shoot brought a message in many parts. We're with you. If you think it right, get out under cover of what we are providing. If you don't think it right, stay until dusk. But we can't keep up this squandering of shells until dusk. If you decide to hang on, for your own good reasons which we respect, that's for you to decide. Whatever your decision, we'll help.

Nice piece of verbal shorthand, expressed in a stonk, by two leaders with experience of how each other's mind worked.

Laing decided to stay. He had wounded to recover.

A bonus, expected by Laing, was that the Spandaus stopped firing. They, too, were bothered about conserving ammunition. A silent stalemate ensued during the remaining daylight. Hart said that he was beginning to reach the conclusion that contemporary western democratic society was decadent. Laing said that he didn't give a fuck whether it was or not.

Laing allowed ten additional minutes after the short southern twilight, rose stiffly to his feet, stretched, and led Hart carefully to where Sergeant-Major Mayne had been lying. They trod softly. Mayne had bled freely but was conscious. He said that Hankins had begun to crawl back to bring help as soon as the light started to fail, but God knew how far he'd got. Hankins had lost a lot of blood, too.

They crouched one on either side of Mayne. He bent back his good leg to get purchase from his foot and put an arm around each of their shoulders. Laing said: 'Now.' They straightened up in slow unison. Mayne made no sound to betray the severe pain that he must be in. They hobbled clumsily back to where the whole recent shambles had started – the track exit from the minefield.

There were muted noises. Low-voiced challenges and responses, rustling movement, terse questions and answers. Sergeant Ingram of Mott's section had eight fit men with him and four walking wounded, three of whom could travel under their own steam, one, semi-delirious with a heavily bandaged head-wound, who had to be led.

'Where's Mr Mott?'

'Dead, sir,' said Ingram.

'How many others?'

'Five. Walker, Murray, Crowe, Stewart and Viall.'

'Viall? He's in hospital in Bari.'

'He was sprung a few days back. Reached Ravenna yesterday. Could have stayed there but said he wanted to be with the lads. Hitched a lift in a ration-truck. Joined on behind just when this caper started off this afternoon.'

Viall. Shot in the arse three weeks ago on that very good patrol of Hugo's. Now shot again, this time finally, while with Mott. Who was also, and finally, shot. As Hugo, also finally, was shot. As was. . . .

This was neither the time nor the place to go into all that. Sorrow could wait. Badly wounded could not. This lot must be got out of here, and properly.

'Sarnt Ingram.'

'Sir?'

'Form 'em up, one fit man in front, walking wounded behind him, other fit men spread as necessary to help. Two fit men at the rear. I'll take two more to scratch around to see if we can find anyone else. If I'm not back in ten minutes, start off. Be bloody careful how you approach our forward people.'

'Sir.'

Laing found two more among the bushes. One concussed, deranged or bomb-happy – impossible to tell. One, Corporal O'Driscoll, unhurt, sleeping peaceably and snoringly at the base of a stunted tree. Laing kicked O'Driscoll awake, guided the other one by the arm and rejoined Ingram within eight minutes. The moon had risen. Laing led his decrepit little column out of battle.

Peter Sims of Y Troop and Richard, the Adjutant, were waiting for them at a bend in the track four hundred yards back. Richard, who had been about to bring out a search party, had with him a medical orderly and stretcher-bearers. Mayne, Hankins and two of the others were given morphine injections and placed on the stretchers. There were mugs of strong tea for everyone. The welcomers were undemonstrative, practical, kindly, unfussy. Laing gave Richard a brief run-down on the events of the afternoon. They set off down the narrow fenced track again, weary, feeling detached, aware of background intermittent rumblings and booms and chattering bursts of distant automatic fire that seemed no longer to be of relevance to them.

There was a last cruelty at the rearmost track junction, the one at which Hugo some hours (days? weeks? years?) earlier had paused while awaiting the opening of the supporting barrage. German 105s, ranged on all nodal points, were ranged on this one. They put down randomly timed shoots of random intensity on each. Their random selection coincided with the random timing of the arrival of Laing's party. There was one casualty. Sergeant-Major Mayne, drowsy from morphine, lying on a stretcher lowered quickly to the ground as the shells whined down, was killed by a splinter in his head.

On the following day 49 Commando, relieved by a battalion of the Coldstream Guards, returned in a convoy of trucks to Ravenna. Laing's transport requirements were meagre. He had nineteen men, alive and unwounded, of the fifty with whom he had started two and a half days before.

CHAPTER SIXTEEN

THE GREY-HAIRED full colonel in charge of the hospital had always taken a friendly, if rather remote, interest in Helen's work. He considered it to be a useful auxiliary to the hospital's function of giving medical treatment and care of high quality, and he had made it his business to satisfy himself that the Welfare component of the whole was conducted with efficiency and dedication. Once convinced on this point, he stood back from it, told Helen to ask for any additional help or advice she might need, and left her to it. He visited her regularly when on his formal rounds, was scrupulous in having a courteous word with her when they happened to be in the mess at the same time, had sent her a wedding present, and usually remembered to ask after Hugo.

She had never before been sent a summons, dressed up as an invitation, to his office. She forced herself into a surface composure and went. She could guess.

He was calm and grave. He stood up when she entered. He stepped from behind his desk and told her to sit down in the chair in front of it. In his experience, he said, it was always best to get these things done quickly, without preliminaries. He had very bad news for her. Her husband was dead.

Laing slept for fourteen hours in his billet in Ravenna and awoke physically renewed, mentally alert and in spiritual suspension. There was much of importance to do today. He composed a list in his mind while he shaved, and jotted it down after he had dried his face and hands. Item 1, in no need of a jot, of top, automatic priority, was to go to the lads, all nineteen of them, talk to them, listen to them, compare notes with them, thank them, tell them that they had the rest of the day to do whatever the hell they liked. Most of them would probably end up fairly drunk, which would do them good, help to clear their systems. Then, early on the following morning, there would be a parade in best battledress with Laing looking grim, Ingram, now acting as Troop Sergeant-Major, looking grimmer, a rigorous formal inspection with names taken of delinquents with dirty brasses, inadequately blanco'd belts, underpolished boots and faulty shaves, followed by a session of close-order drill. The parade would do them good, too. They would complain to each other about it, would expect it, would understand it, and would feel that something had gone badly wrong if they didn't get it.

The written list read:

1. Reorganisation. Two under-strength sub-sections. Expand as wounded return, reinforcements come in. Persuade CO not to redistribute us to other troops.
2. Check which hospitals casualties in. Messages through Padre.
3. Auction dead men's kit.
4. Replace damaged weapons, equipment, clothing. (Ingram)
5. Replenish ammunition. (Ingram)
6. Recommendations for awards. (Discuss Ingram)
7. Promotions. Temporary until wounded back.
8. Demotions + 2 disciplinary. 2 RTU.
9. Soccer.
10. H.

Aside from '10. H.', they were not in order of priority. He wrote them down as they came into his head. '10. H.', Helen, was at the foot of the list because she was professionally of least interest, was personally of most moment to him, and because he wanted time to think about her, what to do about her. Whatever it would be, it couldn't be done immediately. He had a pressing job to do here, in Ravenna, with people for whom he held responsibility. He would write, and consider whether to telephone, and would go to see her as soon as he could get a couple of days' leave. . . .

'I'm a bit bothered by one thing,' said the Colonel.

'Sir?'

'Technicality, I know, but you reported Hugo Burke as Killed. I listed him as Killed. Richard's now looked up those damned pamphlets of his and tells me we're wrong. Hugo's body wasn't recovered. Until it is, or until his grave's been identified, he should have been down as Missing, believed Killed.'

'I thought of that. He's dead. I saw it. Nobody could have survived the amount of Spandau that was put into him at close range. I think, though, that I'd have clutched at a straw if it hadn't been for Mayne. Mayne and Hankins were lying within about thirty yards of the canal and could see Hugo's body clearly. After that Hurricane airstrike the Jerries sorted out their casualties in view of Mayne. They were pretty unceremonious about it. They took off their wounded and dumped the dead in a pile. They put Hugo with the dead. Mayne told me all this on the way back. Before he was doped with morphine.'

'I entirely accept all that. But we're still technically at fault.'

'Look, sir, if we said that he was Missing, believed Killed, when we knew he was dead all that would have happened was that Helen and his people in Canada would think that there was a chance. They'd grab at it, hold on to it, hope. And then, when we confirmed what we already knew, there'd be a corresponding, horrible—'

'OK. You're right. We'll let it lie. Johnny, what have you done about Helen?'

'I wrote. Bloody difficult letter. I thought of telephoning, but the lines are so bad I was afraid that they'd fade at the wrong moment. Or be cut off. I didn't want her to be left with the idea that I might – just – have good news. So eventually I spoke to her friend Gert – the matron of honour, or whatever she was called, at the wedding.'

'How's Helen taking it?'

'Very silent. Numb. The CO of the hospital did things as well as these things can be done. Told her himself, and had Gert waiting round the corner with brandy. Helen cried a little and had a couple of slugs of brandy, and then Gert took her off to comfort her. Helen had another short weep and then insisted on returning to work. Said that there were people to be looked after, and the looking-after would take her mind off her own troubles.'

'Can she do that? I mean, if she's numb and silent, won't she upset the people she's trying to look after?'

'Apparently not. Gert said that she puts on a very good act on duty. Smiles a lot. Very thoughtful. She spends most of her off-duty time with two dying patients. Holds their hands. One of them's a blinded Jerry. Gert thinks she cries a lot at night. But she won't talk about it.'

Pause.

'Fuck this fucking war,' said the Colonel savagely.

Hugo's mother was all but destroyed when the Admiralty telegram was delivered in Ottawa. The especial bitterness lay in the previous despair of October and its subsequent joyful release. This time there was no prospect, no hope of release. The increasingly good news from Europe, the slaughter nearly ended after five and a half years, was further gall. She had been quietly planning for Hugo's return, telling herself carefully that he was married now, had his own life to live, would be a visiting son, not a resident son, and that she must be sure not to trespass on this status, but why not get his old room redecorated, refurbished to accommodate his bride as well, think happy thoughts and dream happy dreams of grandchildren, and weekends at the cottage on Lake Mahon, and fishing and barbecues and sailing and . . .?

Her husband hugged her wordlessly, mopped her eyes repeatedly with his handkerchief, said little because there was little to say and he, too, was hard hit. He forced her to drink a stiff measure of vodka. He telephoned their doctor, who drove over immediately and gave her a sedative. Hugo's father helped her to her room and put her to bed. He sat beside her until she fell into a tortured, tossing, sweating sleep.

Once he tip-toed away to telephone his friend the Spanish ambassador. The ambassador expressed deep and genuine sympathy.

Afterwards Hugo's father took the vodka-bottle and a glass and returned to his chair by his wife's bedside. In between thoughts of misery and defeat he dried the sweat on her forehead with a towel, kissed her, and retucked in bedclothes displaced in her jerking nightmares.

In the morning, pale and taut, he drove her to the Catholic church and knelt beside her as she prayed, sobbing, in the chapel of Our Lady.

'There's a Canadian officer to see you, sir,' said Richard, the Adjutant.

'What sort of Canadian officer?' asked the Colonel warily.

'He's a half-colonel with one eye and a damaged hand. Name of Sepelov. Says he's Hugo Burke's uncle.'

'OK. Show him in.'

Richard showed him in. The Colonel stood up, shook him by the hand, asked him to sit down, offered him tea and said how sorry he was about Hugo.

Colonel Sepelov didn't sit down, ignored the offer of tea, made no comment on the condolences and said bleakly: 'That's what I came about.'

'Of course.'

'I want to know how he died and where he's buried.'

'I'll give you a short run-down on how he was killed. Then you can have a word with his troop commander if you like. He was with him at the time. There are a few others around who were there. I'll line them up, too. As for where he's buried we don't know. We didn't recover his body.'

Sepelov looked incredulous.

'Haven't recovered his body? Then, why did you report him dead?'

'Because there's no doubt. Several witnesses saw him go down. Short-range Spandau-fire. Later his body was put with German—'

'What witnesses? Apart from his troop commander. Laing, isn't it?'

'The Troop Sergeant-Major. Since killed. His Section Sergeant. Now in hospital. Laing—'

'I met Laing once. I wasn't impressed. What was he doing when Hugo was hit? Hiding?'

The Colonel drew a deep breath and held it for a moment. Bereaved relatives deserved sympathy and courtesy. By the nature of his past operational service, invariably abroad, he had had few dealings with them. He took it for granted that some at least would translate grief into suspicion and insult. He found it impossible to believe that an experienced fighting soldier would do so. This man's DSO and MC ribbons, his eye-patch, his missing hand labelled him as an experienced fighting soldier. Furthermore, he wasn't the father or a brother. He was an uncle. He might have been a very close uncle, but he wasn't going to get away with this sort of thing in the Colonel's own office, or anywhere else for that matter.

'I renew my sympathies about Hugo,' said the Colonel levelly. 'And I renew my offer of getting in the people who were with him to talk to you. That's so long as you behave yourself. But unless you first apologise for that remark about Laing, and unless you undertake not to behave like a bloody fool, you can go. Now. And if you don't get out I'll have you thrown out.'

Sepelov stared with his one unblinking eye, touched a vein that was pulsating in his temple, seemed to think things over, and said expressionlessly: 'OK. I apologise. I promise to be a good boy. Now tell me about it.'

The Colonel did. So, later, did Laing. So, later still, did some of the survivors of Hugo's section. None of them found it rewarding. It was hard to maintain sympathy when the object of the sympathy made no response to kind words and no comment upon answers to questions.

That evening, over a drink, the Colonel said: 'Johnny, I hope that that Canadian Neanderthal doesn't go calling on Helen.'

'I don't think he will. She told me when I last saw her with him that she loathed his guts. I think she told *him* so, too.'

'Good for Helen,' said the Colonel wistfully.

'Message from Brigade, sir,' said Richard. 'Stand by to move at 0900 hours tomorrow to Conselice.'

'Where the hell is Conselice?'

'Near Argenta.'

'Oh, yes?' said the Colonel. 'I'd heard that there's quite a lot going on up there. O Group here in half an hour.'

At nine o'clock on the next morning the commando, each man rigged for action, ammunitioned, rationed, left Ravenna in a convoy of Royal Army Service Corps three-ton trucks. The Colonel was not altogether clear about what they would be asked to do. They were to support, which could mean any of a number of things, a major attack at the Argenta Gap mounted by the New Zealanders and 78 Division, backed by armour. The fight had been in progress for two days. German resistance was fierce. If Argenta went, so did most of northern Italy.

The commando's role, when defined with more accuracy, turned out to be a modest one. They were to mop up areas already bypassed in the assault and to round up German strays.

The first day's work was undemanding, and at times entertaining. Each troop was given a sector to clear. Laing, with the fewest men, had the smallest sector. He took all precautions, but they weren't really necessary. Surrenders had become a matter of routine, delayed only because the surrenderers had been unable to find anyone to surrender to. X Troop plodded about the flat, flood-banked, dreary land of the Romagna, collecting dispirited groups of abandoned Germans and a few even more listless Turcomans. Wrinkled old farmers appeared from time to time and proffered jugs of wine. Drinking in action? Could this seriously be described as action? Let the lads have it so long as they didn't overdo it. They deserved it. Same blind eye to the pretty girls who mucked up neat tactical formations by walking into the middle of them and distributing fruit and blowing kisses. Why not? The war was as good as over. Must still keep things under control, though. Ingram was so far seeing to that. 'O'Driscoll, return kisses in action may be blown but not delivered personally. Save your baser bloody nature for your next leave in Naples.'

This was war as it should be fought, including knocking off at dusk and a return to warm, dry billets in Conselice, where the mayor had organised a *dance*.

Shortly before noon on the second day Laing, sitting at a crossroads, studying a map and drinking tea with his signaller and Ingram, heard a shout from Corporal O'Driscoll. O'Driscoll and two marines were escorting a bedraggled line of about twenty lethargic Turcomans. The front Turcoman looked alarmed. O'Driscoll, who was unnecessarily covering him with a rifle, looked alarming. O'Driscoll halted them and explained.

'This bastard, sir,' he said, 'is wearing Mr Burke's boots.'

He was. Laing gestured to him to take them off, and examined his wedding present to Hugo. Canadian lumberjack type, calf-high, flaps secured by straps. Laing scraped the mud from the sole. There it was, marked in brass nailheads, skilfully driven in by Holy Joe, now in hospital in Bari. H.S.B. FROM J.R.L. 15.2.45.

'Parlari Italiano?' asked Laing.

The prisoner shrugged, negative.

'Sprechensie Deutsch?'

'Nein.'

'Well, neither do I,' said Laing. 'Sarnt Ingram.'

'Sir?'

'Take this fellow to the Brigade Interrogation Section. Take the boots with you. Say I want to know how he got 'em.'

'Sir.'

'And don't do anything silly like shooting him. They were probably given to the poor bugger when the loot was dished out.'

★

Laing saw the Russian-speaking member of the interrogation team in Lugo that night. The prisoner, said the interrogator, spoke just about enough Russian to be intelligible. He had said that the boots had been given to him by a sergeant in an SS machine-gun company after a fight a few days previously at Porto Garibaldi. The prisoner had tried to surrender at the start of the fight, but had ducked down again when the SS Spandaus had suddenly opened up. There had been a lot of British casualties. The British had withdrawn at nightfall.

There had been German casualties, too, most of them from an airstrike. On the following morning the dead, including one British in a camouflage jacket, had been taken to the village square. Their boots and equipment had been removed from them, and were stacked up to one side. When the prisoner had walked through the square there was an SS sergeant standing at the equipment-heap. He looked at the prisoner's boots, which were falling apart and tied up with cord, laughed, and tossed him a pair from the heap. He did it contemptuously, as if he were throwing a scrap of meat to a dog. The prisoner did not like the SS.

'I think he's telling the truth,' said the interrogation officer.

'It fits in. Garibaldi was the way he said it was.'

'Can I send him back now with the others? This place is getting overcrowded.'

'I want nothing more from him, thanks.'

'Do you want his name? In case you feel like a further word when he's in a POW cage?'

Laing didn't, but he said OK, thank you, it might come in useful. The interrogator had been helpful, and Laing had no wish to dampen his keenness. The interrogator wrote it down on the back of a message-form. Laing glanced at it – '5947918, Achmet Rashidov, 162nd Turcoman Div.' – and tucked it into the pocket of his battledress. On his way back to Conselice in the jeep he pondered on whether to pass this latest information to Helen. Probably not yet. Later, when she would be more ready for it.

An irritating severance of the ordered domesticity of life in Conselice came with the calling by the Colonel of an O Group at four o'clock on the following morning. The troop commanders, bulky in their smocks behind small desks in an Italian schoolroom, took notes by the light of two hissing pressure-lamps. The Colonel pointed as necessary to a map pinned to the blackboard.

'More mopping. . . . Farther forward this time. . . . The Irish Brigade have taken Argenta. . . . Few odds and sods of German infantry still holding out. . . . Co-ordinated sweep, two troops up. . . . E Troop left, X Troop right. . . . Start Line this floodbank here, map reference. . . .'

CHAPTER SEVENTEEN

HEADACHE, severe gusting to splitting, predominated when Laing awoke. There was also a dull, throbbing pain in his left arm and a numbness in his left thigh. He was lying on a spread blanket on a stone floor. Somebody had modified his clothing. The left leg of his trousers and the left sleeve of his smock, of the battledress blouse beneath it, and of the shirt below that had been cut off. The top of his bare thigh and the middle of his arm were wrapped in padded dressings held in place by bands of sticking plaster. His left arm was too sore to move. With his right hand he could feel the texture of thick bandaging around his head. What in the name of God . . .? Ah. He remembered vaguely. Something to do with mopping up in the Argenta Gap.

He moved his head cautiously. There was a brief, blurred delay until his eyeballs caught up with the movement, focused. He saw that he had plenty of company. His blanket was one of a line of occupied blankets laid at the bottom of a long farmhouse wall. At the far side of the room were stretchers, men reclining on them, most unconscious, one groaning spasmodically, a couple looking as if they hadn't long to go. Barefaced class distinction in this place, and quite right, too. The aristocracy of the bad cases got the stretchers. The lower classes of the lightly hurt got the blankets and less deference and attention. The doctor was bent over some unfortunate poor bugger with a pale-green complexion whose stretcher had been placed on a kitchen table. His arm was connected to off-white translucent tubing through which blood was being fed to him, and the doctor was prodding about inside him with – what were those things called? – forceps or something similar. No doubt about it. The position to be in at the Regimental Aid Post was as near as possible to the bottom layer of the social strata.

Medical orderlies were moving about, quietly, efficiently, cleaning wounds, bandaging, labelling, giving anti-tetanus injections. There was a steady two-way traffic through the open farmhouse door. Patched-up walking wounded went out, helping each other when necessary, clearing space for new arrivals. Some of the new ones walked in, some limped with their arms around somebody else's shoulders. A few were carried. All were briskly checked, categorised, told where to go or sent to where

139

they had to go by the medical sergeant. The bodies of two patients whom the doctor had been unable to save were taken without fuss through the back door, presumably to join others.

'Tea, sir?' said one of the Royal Army Medical Corps lance-corporals.

'Thanks.' The tin mug had clearly seen hard service. The tea was hot, strong and sweet. Ambrosia.

'How are you feeling?'

'Fine.'

'You don't *have* to say that,' said the corporal censoriously. 'The leg and the arm shouldn't bother you much at the moment. The crease in your head *must*. Sort of like migraine. Like being banged over the head with a hammer. That's more or less what seems to have happened. Chunk of shell or something knocked you cold. No fracture, mind. But a bloody great bump, and a lot of skin and hair missing.'

'I see. Yes. I've a bit of a headache.'

'Haven't we all? Mine's that bleeding nutcase over there from Y Troop. Won't stop talking. I've heard his life-story three times already this morning. It's concussion. . . . Sorry, sir. Must go. Bloke on the stretcher's waking up.'

'You do that, Corporal. Thanks for the tea.'

Bang on the head? He couldn't remember being banged on the head. Which was presumably one of the distinguishing symptoms of being banged on the head. But the rest of it was now coming back. The Start Line. That lateral floodbank.

The floodbank, about twenty feet high with a wide, flat top and angled sides, was built of earth surfaced with sparse grass. Laing, his depleted troop strung out behind him in single file, waited until the second-hand of his watch touched six o'clock. Then, in a pearl-grey dawn with visibility improving by the minute, he said, 'OK. We're off,' and clambered up the bank. At the top he turned around to check that his followers were in motion, turned around to study where he was going, and as near as dammit got shot. The earth at his feet ripped and bubbled as a Spandau firing from somewhere close by put a protracted burst along the top of the floodbank.

Laing jumped forward and skidded down the far side of the bank on his buttocks. The Spandau continued to drill away. The troop came over in a series of hop, skip and jump manoeuvres, and arrived intact and resentful. This was not the class of mopping-up to which they had grown accustomed.

The first checkpoint was a square concrete pump-house, four hundred yards ahead on top of another floodbank at right angles to the first and on the right-hand side of the advance. Laing headed for the pump-house. The Spandau rattled behind them, firing at nothing. After two hundred yards a commotion broke out behind the bank. Laing halted the column and climbed up to see what was happening. There was little to see but much to hear. Two neighbouring parties of Germans, seemingly confused by unfolding events, were shooting at each other from cover with Schmeissers and rifles. One side in this civil war had just brought a small mortar into play. Laing threw two grenades to stir things up further and slid back down the bank. That lot could carry on cancelling each other out for the time being. On to the pump-house.

Corporal O'Driscoll said: 'I thought the Irish Brigade had captured Argenta.'

Somebody else said: 'So did I. The thing I'm not sure of is whose fucking side they're on.'

Laing led them forward again. A tremendous noise, compounded of Brens, Spandaus, grenades and raised voices, broke out suddenly to their left. E Troop's mopping was also developing on unsavoury lines.

Laing was just short of the pump-house when from directly in front of him came a flash, followed instantaneously by the crashing explosion of a shell. It burst a hundred yards ahead, at the foot of the bank. It was followed by another, seventy-five yards ahead. The next was fifty yards ahead. No warning screeches from them. They were from an 88 firing over open sights at short range, time-lag between discharge and impact indiscernible. The fourth shell drove into the ground twenty-five yards in front, splattering Laing, Ingram and the marines close behind them with earth and stones. The bloody gun was simply banging off along the bank at mathematically spaced intervals. The time between the intervals was too short to allow for getting out of the way. Laing roared: 'Down.'

Sergeant Ingram said chattily: 'I reckon the next one will just about land on you, sir.'

It landed three yards from him. Fragments hit his arm and thigh. Other fragments, dispersed capriciously at high speed, killed the signaller, broke Corporal O'Driscoll's leg, cut away most of Hart's calf-muscle, and destroyed the PIAT without harming its new operator.

The shooting stopped suddenly. Laing rose shakily to his feet, staggered, righted. He limped back to see his casualties. Jones, the medical orderly, was already attending to O'Driscoll. Jones pointed to a marine lying still behind O'Driscoll.

'Dead,' said Jones laconically. 'Not a mark on him. It's blast.'

Friends were applying a field-dressing to Hart's leg.

Ingram said: 'Are you OK, sir?'

Laing said yes, he was, and no thanks to Ingram's tote forecasting about the fall of shot. Jones to stay here with the wounded. Since the dead signaller's set was u/s, Ingram to send someone back for stretcher-bearers. Rest to move on aga—

Then that bloody 88 must have opened up once more. He remembered nothing more until he woke up on this blanket.

Laing, lying there, head painful, brain muddled, became increasingly anxious about what had happened to the troop, X Troop, *his* troop. The medical people were too busy to be asked and, anyhow, they wouldn't know. O'Driscoll and Hart should be here somewhere. They must have been taken away at much the same time as himself. Unless they, too, had been hit a second time they'd at least been conscious. They could tell him. Laing called to the corporal who had given him tea.

'Is Corporal O'Driscoll, X Troop, here?'

'Over there, sir. Third stretcher.'

'I want to speak to him.'

'You can't. One, you're not to move. Two, he's out for the count. He'll be OK, but he's still under the anaesthetic.'

'Look, is there anyone else in my troop? What about Hart? I must—'

'Talk of the devil,' said the orderly. 'Look who's coming through the door.'

Sergeant Ingram was coming through the door. He was holding a field-dressing to his throat and he looked annoyed. He saw Laing and walked over to him.

'How's it going, sir?' he whispered.

'What?'

'How's it going?'

'No need to whisper in here.'

Ingram removed the dressing.

'Can't do anything else,' he hissed, offended. 'Shot through the fucking adam's apple.'

'Serves you bloody well right. Next time you're in action leave out all that prophecy stuff. Particularly with me.'

Ingram grinned.

'What happened to the troop?'

'Not much,' whispered Ingram. 'That 88 fired a couple more rounds at us and then had a big blast at somewhere farther back. Then it buggered off. So did almost everyone else. The mob rioting over the bank packed it in. Or most of them did. I went over to round them up and some bastard shot me in the adam's apple. Rifle, it was. Then a message came up from the Colonel to hang on where we were. So we did. Everything's quietened down now. Perhaps the Irish Brigade *have* taken Argenta after all.'

'Any other casualties?'

'No. Only my fucking adam's apple.'

Laing felt a deep, happy relief. He dozed.

*

142

Subdued voices broke into his slumber. He opened his eyes. The Colonel was chatting to the man on the next blanket. It was a conversation that seemed to amuse both parties. The Colonel did this sort of thing very well. Critics could dismiss it as an act, a contrived, calculated element of 'leadership', but it wouldn't have worked if the Colonel's feelings hadn't been genuine. He moved on to Laing.

'Hallo, Johnny. How are you feeling?'

'Hallo, sir. OK, thank you.'

'Well, a lively old morning that turned out to be.'

'You're telling me.'

'The butcher says you'll be as right as rain. You do rather well out of this. About a month in dock in Bari, comfortable bed, cool hands of nurses on your fevered brow. Or any other bits of you that feel fevered.'

Bari. Helen. Hugo's boots.

'We picked up a prisoner yesterday wearing Hugo Burke's boots. The interrogation people say that he confirms that Hugo's dead. I suppose we'd better tell the records people. And Colonel Sepelov.'

'I heard about the boots. Not the interrogation.'

'I'll pass it on to Richard. He'll be looking in later?'

The Colonel, genial, concerned, paused fractionally before his reply.

'Richard won't be looking in later,' he said. 'He was killed two hours ago. That 88 that hit you put a stonk in among my headquarters.'

The doctor, all that he could do for his patients done, came over, said, 'You're doing fine, Johnny,' and led the Colonel away. The two of them stopped at each blanket and stretcher. The doctor gave terse diagnoses. The Colonel talked easily, encouragingly, adjusting the tone and content of his remarks to conform to the severity of the injuries. The man first seen by Laing lying on the kitchen table, green-faced and fastened to the blood-drip, seemed close to death.

'I'm afraid this one's had it,' said the doctor.

The patient's eyes opened. He moved his trunk spastically until he was propped upon his elbows. He stared angrily at the doctor.

'Has he *fuck*,' he said loudly.

The doctor looked delighted. The Colonel laughed. Those patients who were conscious cheered.

'He'll live,' said the orderly who had brought Laing the tea. 'Too bloody-minded to die.'

A feeling of unreasonable benevolence settled upon the afflicted.

CHAPTER EIGHTEEN

HELEN read the latest list of admissions, saw under Officers' Ward, Surgical, B, that Capt. J. D. Laing, 49 R.M.Cdo, was among them, and thought: God, please, God, not Johnny, too. *Please* don't let it be a stomach wound, or eyes, or genitals. . . .

'Someone you know?'

'Johnny Laing. You remember. From the wedding. Hugo's best man.'

'Of course I remember,' said Gert. 'And I should have remembered that you didn't know that he was here. He came in last night. And you needn't worry about him. Bump on the head and two flesh wounds. Be on his feet in a couple of weeks.

She put her arm around Helen's shoulders and squeezed. For a brief, hopeful moment she thought that Helen was about to cry, which in Gert's view would have been the best possible thing to happen to her. Helen didn't cry. She put on the smile that was unmatched by the lifeless eyes and went away to begin her day's work.

'Hallo, Johnny.'

Brittle wide smile, artificial composure, hurt disciplined by what? Courage? Despair? Compassion for those damaged in body as she was in spirit?

'Hallo, Helen. You're looking lovely. We'll all be cured in half the time just from gazing at you.'

'I'm not here to have passes made at me, Captain Laing. I'm a working girl. I'm from the British Red Cross Society. May I present you with this little bag here? It contains razor, shaving-brush, toothbrush, comb—'

'Helen.'

'Yes, Johnny. I wish you wouldn't interrupt. Soap, air-letter cards, chocolate. Et cetera. Library books will be brought round on a trolley every morning at—'

'Helen.'

'Johnny. There you go again. Interrupting. I know this damned spiel off by heart. I thought I'd impress you by letting you know the full range of the services provided by—'

'Helen. Don't. Listen.'

'All right, I won't. I'm listening.'

'You know what I want to say. This ward's too public to say it properly.'

'Yes. I know what you want to say. You're sorry about Hugo. You're not as sorry as I am. I'm a very sorry person nowadays. But you're sorry, and I know it, and I'm grateful. And if we talk about it now I'll break down and make a bloody fool of myself in front of these other patients who are watching our little get-together with interest. So thanks, Johnny. Deep, deep thanks. We'll talk later when you're up and about and we can find somewhere to go in private and you can tell me all about it. I want to know *everything*. I'll cross-examine you inside out. And then I'll give in and wail like a bloody banshee and sob all over you. Excuse me now. I've left something outside in the corridor and. . . .'

She ran towards the door, shoulders hunched, shoulders beginning to move in spasms. She was reaching in the pocket of her white overall as she disappeared from sight.

Gert came in later and said: 'You made her cry.'

'I know I did. I'm sorry. I should have had more—'

'Why are men such idiots?' said Gert cheerfully. 'It's the most helpful development since she first heard the news. She had me to cry on. Until now she's been doing it alone, at night.'

Helen was back within half an hour, eyes dry, smile readjusted. She nodded pleasantly to Laing and turned briskly to an infantry subaltern in the bed opposite, his leg in traction poking out from under the sheets, the toes pointing disconcertingly at Laing's face. Her voice was steady, reassuring, kindly.

'I'm from the Red Cross. You might find one of these useful. There's a razor and a toothbrush and. . . .'

Within the next two weeks:

The German armies in Italy laid down their arms.

Mussolini and his mistress, Clara Petacci, were butchered by Italian Partisans while trying to run away to Switzerland. Their naked bodies were hung up disgustingly in public display.

The Russians overran eastern Germany.

American armour raced through Bavaria into Austria.

The British and Canadian armies cut across the north German plain.

Hitler was reported to have committed suicide in his Berlin bunker.

Admiral Doenitz surrendered Germany unconditionally to the Allies.

The war in Europe ended.

Towards the close of this period an Italian smallholder, digging in his vegetable patch near Porto Garibaldi, uncovered a shallow grave. In it was the unshod body of a man wearing a riddled camouflage smock and battledress trousers. The body was disfigured by extensive gunshot wounds. The smallholder knelt down to say a little prayer. Then he bicycled to Porto Garibaldi to tell the mayor of his find. The mayor added to his list of several similar unsurprising but still distressing discoveries in his much fought-over mayoral district, and sent the consolidated list to the Allied Military Government office in Ravenna. Soldiers from a Graves Registration Unit collected the body for reinterment in the Stressio war cemetery. Before the burial the NCO in charge of the party cut away one of the two fireproof identity-discs that were looped to the body's neck by a leather cord. The sergeant wrote 'HBL 1296 Lieutenant H. S. Burke' in his register.

On the same day that the body was reburied, but before word of its finding reached Bari, Laing, now allowed up and convalescent, had his private talk with Helen. The grey-haired Royal Army Medical Corps colonel collaborated sympathetically by bending the rules and lending Laing a jeep for the occasion. Laing drove her along the coast to Torre a Mare and pulled in to an isolated grove of trees. She had chatted tensely, inconsequentially, on the journey. When he switched off the engine she was silent for a minute, staring in front of her. Then she said firmly: 'Now, Johnny. I want to hear all of it. Every single bit of it. From the time that that damned battle started. Till Hugo was killed. And I've already warned you that I'll sob. And keen. And make a fool of myself. Just so that there's no misunderstanding I'm warning you again.'

He told her. And she sobbed and keened and he hugged her and said that she *wasn't* making a fool of herself, and when she could speak she said that he was a kind man and brought her much comfort, and then she sobbed again.

Early on the following morning, after a grief-haunted night, she miscarried.

*

Several years later, a middle-aged Laing gave serious consideration to taking a holiday in Italy. The Italian State Tourist Office was very helpful in the provision of maps and brochures. He read the pamphlet on Emilia Romagna, Adria, with nostalgic interest. One short paragraph was particularly arresting.

'In order to participate in the life of the locality,' it read, 'one must be active. Sport, practised with modern and amusing equipment, is the most restful training.'

Well. They could say that again.

PART TWO

1980s: Italy, Ireland, England, Canada

CHAPTER NINETEEN

ULICK BURKE'S return to his hotel in Ravenna from the Commonwealth War Graves Commission cemetery at Stressio provoked criticism among the reception staff and concern to his wife.

'He's plastered,' whispered the receptionist to the cashier. He whispered because Signor Burke was very large and looked dangerous, and was very rich and thus deserved the tolerance of hoteliers.

'You've been on the bottle,' said Alice Burke, when he blundered into their suite. She did not whisper.

'Yes. Still am,' said Ulick. 'Join me?'

She considered it and said yes. She mixed two gin and tonics and gave him one. She raised her glass and said: 'Good luck.'

'Good luck.'

'Look,' she said, 'I can see that going to your father's grave might be a little upsetting. But since you never knew him, and he died all those years ago, surely not all *that* upsetting.'

Ulick grunted.

She thought of saying more and decided against it. What she would have said was that Ulick would never have gone to the cemetery at all if she hadn't suggested it. Ulick, for that matter, wouldn't have been in Italy if she hadn't suggested it. She was here to gather material for a book that she was working on. He had agreed to come only when she had shown him a piece in the tourist literature about sport, practised with modern and amusing equipment. Ulick would go anywhere where there was sport, practised with any sort of equipment. It was she who had searched for Stressio on the map, had checked with the hotel reception-desk how to get there, had bought flowers. She began to wish that she had gone with him. It had been his idea that he should go alone for the first time, take her along later in the week when he was familiar with the way. She had had a backlog of notes to put in order and hadn't insisted.

'I should have gone with you,' she said.

'Wouldn't have made any difference.'

'Oh, Ulick. . . .'

'He's not my father,' said Ulick Burke. 'He was killed over a year before I was born. Date on the headstone. Clear as day.'

She stared at him.

'Are you sure that you saw the right grave?' she said at last. Not a particularly sensible question, she knew the moment that she had put it.

'Yes. I'm sure. I know nothing about how the military were organised, but I do know that a commando wasn't all that big. There can't have been two Hugo Burkes, both lieutenants in 49 Royal Marine Commando, killed at the same place and buried in the same cemetery. Not only can't. There weren't. I got the grave-number from the caretaker's register. The names were in alphabetical order. There was only one Burke in it. My father. I mean not my father.'

'Oh, Ulick,' she said again.

'Oh, Ulick is right,' he said. 'Or perhaps it's not. The Oh is OK, but I'll need notice of the Ulick. I don't know who I am.'

Much later, in bed, after she had given him comfort and had told him that she loved him for who *he* was, and what *he* was, and not who his father had or hadn't been, he said suddenly: 'Have you thought about the money?'

'No. What money?'

'My money. Our money. The Burke Foundation Trust Fund money. If I'm not the son of Hugo Burke, I'm not entitled to it. Never have been.'

She pondered.

'Ulick,' she said, 'are you trying to tell me that we're broke?'

'Looks like it to me.'

She thought of the large house in Ballsbridge, and of the cottage on Lough Corrib, and of the unthinking ordering of expensive meals in expensive restaurants, and of the clothes and the travel and the hotels and the girls' school fees and. . . .

She turned towards him and hugged him.

'Well, get this into your thick skull,' she said. 'I don't care who your father was and I don't care about the money. I don't care who you are. Except that you're you.'

Ulick Burke, lucky in love, hugged her back.

At breakfast she said: 'I've been thinking. About the money.'

'I thought you loved me for myself.'

'I do. I'm not talking about money as money. I mean that Trust Fund. There must have been some monkey business going on.'

'There certainly has been some monkey business going on.'

'How does the Trust work – the terms of it? You've never really said much to me about it. I just know it's there.'

'I don't know a great deal about the terms. Only the mechanics. It's administered by solicitors in Bachelor's Walk. All I know is that as the only son of the late Hugo Burke – or, if you prefer, the chap who's been passed off as the only son of the late Hugo Burke – I've inherited a large slice of this massive Canadian family outfit. I can't touch the capital or flog any shares. I just get the dividends, paid through the lawyers. Since the dividends are enough to keep you in the style to which you're accustomed, and I can't understand a word of the ghastly jargon these legal eagles speak, I sign where they tell me to sign and cash the cheques they send me.'

'There must be some legal piece of paper. A deed or whatever they call it.'

'Yes. With the solicitors. They showed it to me once. Insisted that I read it.'

'Can you remember what it said?'

'Remember? It was meaningless to me. Gibberish. I looked interested and courteous and said thank you and gazed at it long enough to seem spellbound with enthusiasm. I was thinking of something else at the time.'

Alice poured herself more coffee and imagined Ulick looking interested and courteous and thinking of something else. It was a recurrent habit of his. The something else would have been the eighth green at Portmarnock, or his backhand follow-through, or the three-thirty at Leopardstown. The list once included line-out tactics, but he had hung up his Rugby boots the previous season. Ulick was an uncomplicated man. It was one of the reasons why she had married him.

'We'd better start by looking at the deed thing,' she said.

'Start what? There's nothing to start. Whoever benefits under the deed it isn't me. I've taken what I've so far taken in good faith. I can't reasonably take any more. In fact I suppose I should pay back what I've already had. God knows what with.'

'Ulick, you're being uncomplicated and scrupulously honest.'

'Correct. That's me.'

'For uncomplicated and scrupulously honest read simple-minded.'

'Add it if you like. Don't substitute it.'

'Listen. Let's start at the beginning. That Trust Fund was set up for Hugo Burke's heir. You're your mother's son. I mean of course you're your mother's son, but for the purposes of this discussion you're the son of the woman who was married to Hugo Burke.'

'*Was* married. Not when little Ulick was started, though. Unless there was some sort of gynaecological miracle. Hugo Burke was dead.'

'Did your mother ever talk about another man? I mean a possible mating man? Someone who could have been your father?'

Ulick snorted. 'You bet your sweet life she didn't. You know my mother. Mating man indeed! She never even talked about mating. I always had the impression that she regarded it as an unsavoury biological requirement, necessary for the continuation of the human race.

151

Otherwise disgusting. If she'd lived a bit earlier, she'd have been one of those women who went about covering table-legs with cloth in case they stimulated impure thoughts.'

'All right, then. Did she talk much about your father? I mean H. Burke. That father.'

'A little. Not much. There was always a photograph of him in the sitting-room. In his uniform, looking dashing. You've seen it. The one she has in Ottawa now. But she hated talking about the war. It used to distress her. She did tell me that he was kind and good and intelligent and brave. All the things a boy likes to hear about his father. As I grew older he just didn't seem to crop up very often. When I see her now in Canada – sorry, when *we* see her now in Canada – there's always something else to talk about.'

Alice filled his coffee-cup.

'What I'm getting at is this. The Trust money comes from the Burke Foundation for Hugo Burke's son. You're not his son. The only person who could have pretended that you were is your mother. Either they accepted what she told them without thinking to question it or she tinkered with the date on the birth certificate.'

'The date on my birth certificate is my right birthday.'

'How do you know? You've taken her word for it. The same as everyone else takes their parents' word for it.'

'I don't know what sort of bog you were delivered in, but me, I'm a product of Holles Street Maternity Hospital, Ireland's premier baby-factory. The register gets filled in by nurses or midwives or that class of operator. I repeat. The date on my ticket is correct.'

'OK. It's correct. But it must be different from the one she gave the Foundation. Whether or not she forged a phoney certificate.'

'So what?'

'So there's a very large sum of money involved. Collected under false pretences.'

'That's why I want to put a stop to it.'

Alice curbed her exasperation, just. 'I know you do, you dummy. But before you give your conscience an airing you'd better think a bit about your mother. Whether or not she was careful to spend all the loot on you when you were young, she's a clear case for a charge of fraud. The Foundation might not press it, mind you, but if you come clean you'll leave her wide open. I suppose it depends on who the Foundation boss-man is.'

Ulick looked appalled. 'I hadn't thought of that,' he said. 'They'd press it right enough. The boss-man's a horrible old bastard named Andrei Sepelov. He's a great-uncle of mine. Well, I thought he was and so did he. My mother hates his guts.'

*

The sub-title of the book that Alice was writing was 'An Analysis of Politico-Military Interaction in the Central Mediterranean, 1941–6'. It described the subject-matter succinctly and would appeal to fellow academic historians. It wasn't the punchy, intriguing handle that would rivet the attention of a wider reading public who browsed in bookshops or were seeking something to pass the time with on a train or on an aeroplane, or who occasionally read the reviewers in the press.

Sellotaped to the inner cover of the folder in which she assembled her notes was a sheet of paper upon which she wrote possible publication names as they occurred to her. There were 'Tangled Web' and 'Lethal Dilemma' and 'Tarnished Victory' and 'Winners Took All' and 'The Triumph of Opportunism'. Collectively they sounded like the list of runners in the Grand National. Individually they were unsatisfactory. 'Balkan Balls-Up', contributed by Ulick when he had asked about what he called the plot and she had described it to him, wasn't much help, either, but came closer to the mark than anything she herself had been able to come up with.

After breakfast, when Ulick had left to play five sets of tennis with the hotel professional, Alice was restless. She looked with distaste at her list of titles and could think of nothing to add to them. She flicked through her scribbled notes and felt no urge to put the latest batch into typed orderliness. She went to the balcony, leant over, watched the glittering parabolas of spray from the fountain making little rainbows in the sunshine, and gazed half-seeing at the trimmed well-watered green of the lawns, the clipped poinsettia hedges, the oleanders, the geometric pattern of coarse palms, the strident reds and yellows of landscaped flowerbeds. She thought about her husband Ulick.

That he was hurt and troubled she had no doubt. She was not misled by the five sets of tennis. They were partly a clinging to normality amidst an unexpected instability, partly a manifestation of the operating mechanics of Ulick. He had taken hard physical exercise all his life. If he missed a day of it, he became sluggish and mentally blunted. The mental bluntness had to be considered with an affectionate realism. Even at a peak of fitness the sharpness of his brainpower was less than honed to a cutting edge – a characteristic about which he was cheerfully unworried. In this partnership, he said, he left all that to her.

He did not say, because he wouldn't, and didn't have to, that in this partnership he also gave her love and fun and tolerant affection and considerateness and security and was a marvellous father to the two daughters that she had borne him. The security, of course, had been financial as well as personal. But, although she enjoyed unashamedly the fruits of his riches and made the most of them, they had never meant more to her than icing on the cake, gilt on the lily. She could get by without them. She would shortly *have* to get by without them. She could not get by without Ulick.

She thought briefly about what life would be like on her university pay, supplemented by meagre book-royalties and whatever Ulick could earn. Ulick would enjoy himself as a sports coach or a farm labourer, at anything energetic in the fresh air. He might indeed find life even more enjoyable than he had until now, and that had been highly enjoyable. It would probably do the girls good to come down a notch, to be faced with the realisation that there was more to—

She had better apply her mind to the point, which was beginning to be drifted from. The point was that unless in this new situation rational consideration were to be given to the consequences of either action or inaction, and unless some control and direction were imposed upon developments, there could be a casual slide into the undesirable or the unnecessary. Ulick, if she didn't keep a close eye on him, would do something silly, like the something silly that she had had to talk him out of that would have left him confused about why the price of burnishing his honour was a stretch in gaol for his mother.

Alice recognised dispassionately that one of her uses to him was an ability to isolate the essentials of a problem, discard irrelevancies, and predict with fair accuracy that if A would inevitably cause B, and if B of itself were good, B might lead to C, D or E, which could range from the less good to the pernicious. And C, D or E might or might not generate F, G or H, which could be capable of recovery but one of which at its worst could be disastrous. Ulick's thinking stopped at B. Ulick the Action Man needed Alice, the forward-looking, scheming Director of Plans.

The scheming Director of Plans left the balcony, helped herself to a glass of chilled orange juice from the refrigerator, took a pad and a ballpoint pen from the desk, and returned to the balcony to sit at a table in the shade of a striped blue and white sun-umbrella. She thought intently, jotted notes, crossed pieces out, added insertions and amendments in balloons to other pieces, reread the fragmented, unexpurgated residue, and went inside to her portable typewriter.

Her typed preliminary assessment read:

1. Ulick is a bastard. He found out yesterday. It's not the bastardy that bothers him (Why should it? The old stigma, unfair and cruel, has long since gone) but:

    (a) He's been living well all his life on money that's not rightly his.

    (b) (I think.) He has been sustained more strongly than I believe he realises by the legend of a father whom he never knew, but whose reputation and memory he revered. He's hurt by finding out that that man was not his father.

    (c) (I think.) He feels betrayed by his mother, whom he loves and respects. Had she told him when he was old enough to understand, he would have accepted the position without distress. She deceived him, which is painful to him. The pain is the stronger because her persistent prudery about sex was despite her bearing him out of wedlock after a consummation with a man whose identity he doesn't know within a short time of the death of his 'father' in battle.

(d) (I know, because I told him.) If, as he wants to, he follows his instincts and tells the Burke Foundation that he's not the son of Hugo Burke, the Foundation can (will?) take reprisals against his mother. He can't reconcile these two. (Nor can I at the moment. Search for a way round.)

NOTE: '(I think)' at (b) and (c) to be translated into either '(I know)' or eliminated.

2. We can't proceed without more information. If we can find out who the father is, and the circumstances in which Ulick's mother persuaded, or conned, the Foundation into accepting Ulick as Hugo Burke's heir, we'll have at least a basis upon which to think about what to do next.

3. The one wholly knowledgeable holder of the information needed is, of course, Ulick's mother. Once she knows that Ulick knows she might be induced to talk. But since

(a) she's kept her counsel, successfully, for so long;
(b) her prudery would be a constraint, adding sexual shame to financial – almost certainly criminal – guilt;
(c) Ulick can/will certainly ask her but is too good-hearted/dutiful/ generous/conventional/unsubtle to press if she evades, obstructs or refuses;
(d) I certainly won't ask her (I like her and get on with her well, but it's not the sort of question a woman can put to her husband's mother)

we mightn't get far, or might get nowhere, or might stir up much sorrow with no useful result.

4. In conjunction with an approach to Ulick's mother, which is likely to be unsuccessful or only partially successful, it would make sense to try to find out more about Hugo Burke, particularly the last year or so of his life. That would involve identifying and questioning the people he soldiered with. We would have to be discreet and devious. I think that I could put up a plausible cover-story myself. Writer/historian, claiming to be doing research for a book on 'Aspects of the Closing Phase of the Italian Campaign, 1944–5', or some such. (Might even write it.)

5. Therefore:
   (i) Work on Ulick generally to get some system into all this;
   (ii) Work on Ulick to go to Ottawa to pump his mother;
   (iii) Work out how myself to track down old soldiering colleagues of Hugo Burke;
   (iv) Arrange timings so that either Ulick or I am in Dublin at any one time with the girls after the school term starts. University term will limit my movements.

Alice read it through, thought it a reasonable enough start, tore up the original arrow-and-balloon-stricken draft and threw it into the

155

wastepaper-basket. She was putting the typed analysis into the top of her research file when Ulick came in. He was in a dark-blue towelling jacket, sweating.

'Who won?'

'I did. Three sets to two: 6–4, 4–6, 12–10, 7–9. . . .'

'Attaboy,' she said hastily. 'Well done.' She kissed him lightly on his damp brow.

'Get much work done?'

'I did. Very productive morning.'

'What bit are you on now?'

Kindly, encouraging Ulick. He wouldn't have understood what bit of the book she was on if she had illustrated it with colour slides. Poor, hurt Ulick, trying to hide his hurt to avoid saddening her. She smiled and reinforced the peck to his forehead with a warm, thorough hug, sweat and all.

'The first sentence of what I was working on', she said in his ear, 'is "Ulick is a bastard". I typed it out to see if it looks any starker in print. It doesn't. It doesn't make a damn bit of difference. To anything.'

He hugged her in return, hard.

'Of course *one* of the reasons it makes no difference', she said, 'is that I've always said that you weren't a bad old bastard.'

Ulick laughed comfortably, released her and went to the shower.

Ulick sipped at the sample of wine poured by the waiter, rolled it round his tongue, adopted the concentrated expression of a vinophile connoisseur and told the waiter that the wine was excellent. The waiter, gratified, filled both their glasses.

'What I'd like', said Ulick to Alice, 'is a decent pint.'

She chuckled. They were dining on the terrace, elegantly, crystal and silver and damask, muted rhythmic music under the stars and a golden half-moon.

'Be brave,' she said. 'Courage. Only five days to hold out.'

Over the minestrone she said: 'Can you recall any more of what your mother told you about your fa – I mean *him*, Hugo Burke – when you were young? You said that she didn't say much except that he was good and gallant and so on. And she didn't like talking about the war.'

'That's about it. But I've been thinking since I said that. I don't want to give you the wrong impression. She didn't try to conceal anything. Looking back on it, I think she did it just right. She didn't overdo it. That would have underlined that both she and I were missing something. She said exactly enough to give me a sense of a father to be proud of.'

Alice put down her spoon, reached over the table and squeezed his free hand.

'Ah, Ulick,' she said.

'No, it's all right. That's all long behind me now. Aside from the talk, there was one thing she left handy for me to look at at any time I wanted to. There was a folder with old papers about him. Letters from people after he was killed. Old press cuttings. The cuttings were about his being a hotshot sportsman at Trinity, and an actor, and making speeches. The letters seemed very impressive to me when I was a boy, but I suppose that they were the sort of letters that were written when anybody was killed. 'Great loss', 'fine young officer', that sort of stuff. The bit I liked to boast about was that he'd been captured once and got away. It tied in with a television serial that was running at the time. None of the other kids I went around with had a father who'd escaped.'

'Do you remember who the letters were from?'

'No. They were just names. I think there was one from his Colonel. Padre perhaps. Several friends. One simple, very nice one, a bit stilted, signed The Lads from His Company, or Troop, or whatever it was. Said he was a good bloke and would be much missed. They all signed it.'

'He must have been a good bloke if they went to that sort of trouble.'

'I suppose he was.'

'Where's the folder now?'

'Haven't seen it for years. Must be with my mother in Ottawa.'

Alice broke the crust of her roll, chewed a bit of it, sipped at her wine, and looked gravely at Ulick prior to saying something very serious. He stared back at her innocently. Suddenly her lips began an uncontrollable twitching. Ulick laughed. So did she.

'Damn you, Ulick,' she said, 'you've done it again.'

'Well, if you will keep telegraphing your punches. . . .'

'I can never understand your sweaty sporting metaphors but, if that one means what I think it does, you're taking an unfair advantage.'

'Unfair nothing. I can read you like a book.'

'You've never finished a book in your life.'

'OK. Better than a book. You've worked it all out and you want me –'

'– to do something that you might not necessarily want to do.'

'*Yes,*' they both said in unison, and clinked glasses, and drank to each other.

Ulick was never a pushover on these occasions. His resistance always satisfied Alice because, although it was in one sense irritating, it was also a stimulus to clarity of thought and to the expression without ambiguity of what needed to be said. Yes, he'd go to Ottawa. It would be nice to see his mother again. No, he could foresee few difficulties about borrowing the folder with the material in it about Hugo Burke. Yes, if she briefed him with a list of questions to be answered, he'd ask them as opportunity offered, but would not guarantee to ask them all. And, Dear God Above, yes, he fully understood that the prime purpose of the enterprise was to find out who his father was, and why and how his mother had conned both the Burke Foundation and himself into believing that it was Hugo Burke, but did Alice really appreciate what she was asking of him? Had she thought about what it would be like to cross-examine *her* own mother about who *she'd* been to bed with when she was young? How did anyone set about asking their mothers about their early sex lives? Did you engineer a solemn sort of interview: 'Please sit down. Let's have this out in the open. You've been a very good mother, and I'm grateful, but I happen to know that I'm a bastard and you've been fleecing this Foundation crowd for thirty-odd years . . .'? Or did you try a throwaway approach over lunch: 'Delicious soufflé, Ma. By the way, as you know, I've always been a bit slow on the uptake, but I've finally caught on to this leg-pull of yours. You know the one. You having a roll in the hay with this guy whoever he was, and spreading it about that he was Hugo Burke so that you and me could scoop the jackpot. God, what a *laugh*. . . .' Or would a better way to go about it be to—

'Ulick,' said Alice.

'A further complication', went on Ulick, ignoring her, 'is that I wouldn't be addressing any old mother. Not one of these tolerant modern ones, mellowed by the relaxed moral standards of the Permissive Society. None of this To hell with hypocrisy stuff. No such luck. I've drawn something like the Mother Prioress of a Dominican convent in the closing years of the nineteenth century. In Mullingar.' He stared bitterly at her.

'Ulick. I know it'll be difficult, but unless it's done, somehow—'

'*Difficult*. You can say that again.'

'Well, just do your best,' said Alice.

'OK. I'll do my best. But don't be too surprised if it's not much of a best,' said Ulick gloomily.

Alice told him that she accepted that it mightn't be much of a best. Privately, she acknowledged that it was more likely to be not much of nothing at all.

Depressed by the prospect of having to conduct what he called the Spanish Fly Inquisition, Ulick was obstructive when she put forward her ideas about the second leg of the search, the attempt to trace friends of Hugo who had known him at the end of his life. Too many things could go wrong, he said. It was a small world. For all that Alice and he knew, his mother might still be in touch with some of these people. Suppose they wrote to her and said: 'Some pretty odd goings on here recently. Your daughter-in-law's been sniffing around asking which of us put you in the family way. I've warned the rest of the boys to play it cool, but you should know. . . .'

'It won't be like that,' said Alice, 'and you know it. What I'll say is

"I'm Hugo Burke's daughter-in-law. I write books. I'm doing one on the Italian campaign. I'm looking for eye-witness accounts. Can we meet?" And whilst I'm gathering genuine information I'll probe about, very gently, very tactfully. And when I've seen enough of them I'll put all the stuff together and see if there are any leads. If there are, and there may not be, I'll not follow any of them up until you and I have talked it over thoroughly. Not at all if you don't want me to.'

Ulick said 'All right', grudgingly. He thought of another obstacle.

'How are you going to find this lot?' he asked with scepticism.

'That's my problem. I'll start with the British military records people.'

Ulick suddenly cheered up. 'This is all bloody terrible,' he said, 'but it is interesting, isn't it?' He ordered an extra glass of brandy each with their coffee. Alice looked at him fondly. Game and set to Alice, she reckoned. Stiffer opposition than most. About 6–3.

The girls said that they'd had a lovely time in Galway and Orla had caught three sea-trout and Brigid had fallen off a pony and they'd watched the currach-racing at Spiddal and Aunt Eva had driven them around Connemara and that was lovely and Uncle Michael had got a bit drunk one Sunday and thank you again for the presents they're lovely and. . . .

The girls were eating scrambled eggs and drinking milk at the kitchen table in Ballsbridge. Ulick sat with them, smiling hugely in absorbed enjoyment, asking questions when he could get a word in, laughing with them in their pleasure. Alice, placid with contentment, stirred a spoon in a pan and watched a replenishment load of thick yellowish liquid transforming itself into a second helping. She was glad to be home.

CHAPTER TWENTY

ULICK'S appointments-diary was nearly as crowded as was Alice's. They sat side by side on a sofa in the sitting-room, seeking the best times for each of them to be away.

'The girls go back to school on the first of September,' said Alice. 'The university term starts on the fifteenth of October. I'll have to fit in a trip to England between those two.'

She began to turn pages over.

'Symposium at UCD during the first week of September. Poetry reading at the Goethe Institute on the ninth. The Theatre Festival in the week after that. Exhibition of landscapes opening at the Hackett Gallery on the sixteenth. The Youth Orchestra at the National Concert Hall on. . . .'

Ulick was turning his pages over, too.

'Boxing at the Stadium on the twenty-eighth of August,' he read. 'Regional tie of the Davis Cup at the RDS on the twelfth. Golf at Baltray on the twentieth, and at Delgany – I can postpone that if you like – on the twenty-fifth. Leinster and Ulster at Lansdowne Road on the fifth of October. The Dublin Marathon on the thirty-first. Can't miss that. Put too much into training for it. . . .'

'OK,' said Alice. 'You needn't go on and on.'

'Why shouldn't I go on and on? You were.'

'Your diary sounds like the recreational programme of the Hitler Youth Movement.'

'I could probably work out a crack about yours if I could understand what most of it meant. What the hell is the Gert Institute?'

'Goethe. G-O-E-T-H-E. It's in Merrion Square. There's a reading of Irish poetry that's been translated into German.'

'G-O-E-T-H-E spells Goath. Like Goes, with a lithp. And, if you want to listen to a bunch of Krauts reading Irish rhymes out loud, that's your—'

'Ulick.'

'Yes.'

'How long do you think you *need* to be in Canada?'

'Not *that* long, I suppose.'

'Right. Let's take it from there. It might be slightly better if you started with your mother before I went to England but I doubt if it matters much which way we do it. What about between the tennis and the golf?'

They took it from there. It was agreed that Ulick would go to Canada in the second week of September. Alice would go to England as soon as she had made the necessary contacts.

After three days of selective reading of every book about the Italian campaign that she could find in the Trinity library, Alice wrote identical letters to the Ministry of Defence in Whitehall, the Public Record Office in Kew, the Imperial War Museum and the National Army Museum in London. She began by introducing herself as the person to whom they had all been so helpful over her research for the book on the wartime Mediterranean that she was presently working on. She was considering doing a new one, in some ways a byproduct of the first. It would be about the closing days of the fighting in Italy. To give it a focus she would like to pay special attention to a commando operation that had been mounted at Lake Commachio in northern Italy in the spring of 1945. Until recently she had known nothing of this beyond the fact that a connection of hers by marriage had been killed in the course of it. She had now done some preliminary homework, but could find little in published sources other than brief mentions of what was described as a successful curtain-raiser to the final Allied assault.

Would they tell her what material they held on the battle, and what it was referenced under? A more difficult question, but one that she hoped that they might be able to help her on, even if the help were no more than a steer towards the right direction, was about how she could get in touch with surviving participants. Her relative who had been killed had been serving in No. 49 Royal Marine Commando. That seemed a good starting-point. She would be most grateful for any advice that they could think of on whom she might approach.

On the morning after she had posted the letters she was telephoned by Ulick's Uncle Oliver. He invited her to lunch.

Ulick was jealous.

'Just you? Not me as well?'

'Just me. He's not in love with you.'

'You're being boastful. You want to keep clear of that old goat. He's dangerous.'

'He's one of Nature's gentlemen.'

'He's one of Nietzsche's gentlemen.'

'Ulick, where did you pick that up? And you thought Goethe was Goath.'

'Saw it in a book,' said Ulick proudly, 'while I was waiting at the airport. Paperback I was browsing through. I didn't buy it, mind you. But I couldn't understand the joke so I rang up the German embassy. They couldn't understand it, either, but they coached me on the pronunciation.'

'What was the book about?'

'The SAS.'

'I see,' said Alice.

'What was the joke about?'

'I'll try to explain it for you later,' said Alice, putting on her coat and taking her car keys from her handbag. 'Must get on to Oliver.'

He kissed her goodbye and went to the lawn with a handful of golf balls and his putter.

Oliver Grant's club was a Georgian building of beautiful symmetry, one of a terrace in St Stephen's Green, an Anglo-Irish legacy from the days when Dublin was the second city of the British Empire, built before the Union in 1801 diverted much of Anglo-Irish talent and rapacity to London. Nearly two centuries of national impoverishment had preserved it and its elegant counterparts in neighbouring squares from demolition and replacement by something more functional and profitable. The property developers and commercially calculating bandits who were thickening their bank accounts by destroying the architecture of the city with Yahoo assiduity had yet to lay their hands on it.

Oliver Grant, like his club a tolerated anachronism in a tolerant Republic, was waiting in the front hall, his back to a glowing gas-fire, when Alice arrived. A courteously cheerful porter held open the glass-panelled front door for her. Oliver, stockily built, still light on his feet, the healthy russet complexion of an enjoyer of fresh air in all weathers, wearing a tweed coat with leather elbow-patches and a faded pair of corduroy trousers, grinned pleasurably when he saw her. He kissed her on the cheek and helped her off with her coat. He escorted her up the broad, red-carpeted staircase to the drawing-room, a high-ceilinged apartment with a marble fireplace and comfortably distinguished furniture. Ulick, after examining its proportions appraisingly, had once described it as having the makings of a bloody good squash-court.

A genial barman in a white jacket like a Victorian soldier's tropical tunic brought them drinks on a silver tray, campari for Alice, pink gin for Oliver. Oliver raised his glass to her.

'God, it's good to see you,' he said.

'It's good to see you, too.'

'How was Italy? How are you?'

'Both in excellent condition, thank you.'

'How's that muscle-bound halfwit you married?' asked Oliver chattily.

Alice put her glass carefully on the occasional table.

'Now, look, Oliver,' she said, 'don't start that again. I'll not put up with it.'

'I'm talking about my own nephew, dammit. I've known him all his life. Which is more than you have.'

'He's my husband and I love him, and you watch out what you say about him to me.'

'All right,' said Oliver affably. 'Just trying to seduce you.'

At lunch in the Ladies' Dining-Room ('Old standards of good, reliable sexist prejudice still maintained in this place. Anyone who's ever kept hounds knows that you always keep the bitch pack separated from the dog pack') they talked of politics and of religion and of music and of growing vegetables in County Monaghan, Oliver's current obsession. He lived in a gate-lodge of what had once been the Grant family home, bequeathed capriciously in her will by his mother to the Irish Arts Council. The main house was now a haven for poets, playwrights, musicians and painters, who holed up there for intervals of work unimpeded by domestic distraction. Oliver found the inmates an interesting subject for sardonic anthropological study. Their shenanigans, he said, were an eye-opener to a man whose working life had been circumscribed by the colonial austerities of the Malayan Civil Service.

'How are the artists?' asked Alice. Oliver always liked to be asked about the artists.

'There's a bit of trouble broken out with the present crowd. They clubbed together to send the only one who has a car over the Border to buy cheap whiskey. He came back with the whiskey full of tales about how he'd braved British army checkpoints and the RUC and the IRA and everything else and it wasn't worth it. Northern Bushmills was the same price as Southern Bushmills, according to him. They said it wasn't. He produced receipts to prove that it was. They as good as called him a crook. I was walking by the lake so they called me in as an adjudicator. The receipts were OK. I know the pub well. What the eejit had done was to take an unapproved wriggly road, cross the Border about four times, and end up in the South again.' Oliver laughed.

'How did the adjudicator adjudicate?'

'I recommended a peace celebration, and the sinking of differences. Sink the hooch along with the differences, I said, buy him a map and send him back for another go the next day.'

'Did they?'

'Oh, yes. It was a very good night. Lots of singing and that. The only thing was that when I went back the following morning to speed him on his way he was holding his head and saying: "These bastards keep telling me to read the map. I can't even *see* the bloody map."'

'I still can't get used to the idea of your going up to your own old house as a visitor. Don't you ever feel bitter? Wish your mother had left it to you?'

'Never a bit. Far too big for me. I've no family. Helen didn't want it, either. She only had Ulick. And her husband left her so well off that she had no cause to worry about money.'

'I'm thinking of doing a book about him.'

'About Ulick? What'll you call it? "Muscle over Matter"?'

'Now, *Oliver*. You'll not talk to me like that about Ulick.'

'Well, I suppose that if they clean his cage out occasionally he's a reasonably presentable. . . .'

'*Oliver*! No. Not about Ulick. About Hugo Burke.'

Oliver munched a cutting of steak, washed it down with a swallow of Beaujolais, and said that he'd never met Hugo but had heard only good of him.

Alice was surprised. 'Never met him? I've never really thought about it, but I'd always assumed that. . . .'

'They were married in Italy. During the war. I was locked up by the Japs at the time. Helen was a widow before I even knew that she'd been married. Pregnant widow. Sad sight she was when I got home, I can tell you.'

Alice, assembling a mouthful of spinach on her fork, registered an item of significance. One outside chance could be dismissed. Helen *had* been pregnant. Ulick had not been adopted, and accepted as a beneficiary of Burke Foundation wealth as a memorial gesture to the dead Hugo. She could, she knew, exploit the unexpected turn the conversation had taken. She wouldn't. It would be unforgivable. Oliver would forgive her anything that she ever did; but she would never be able to forgive herself, if what she did was to abuse his kindness, manoeuvre him into saying things without forewarning him that she was hunting something that he might for honourable reasons be otherwise reluctant to talk about. Alice took a cynical mental look at her Christian conscience and found that she rather liked it.

There was another, complementary inhibitor. Once, when Oliver had got very drunk, and it would have been dangerous to let him drive himself home, she had taken him in her car back to his Monaghan gate-lodge. He had insisted that they stop for what he called a quick tot at a large selection of pubs along the route. In one in Ardee he had spoken seriously and without self-pity of his own return after the dropping of the atom bombs on Hiroshima and Nagasaki had forced the Japanese to surrender.

He must have been as sad a sight as he had just said that his sister Helen had been at the time. He had weighed five and a half stone. He had been a slave-labourer on the Burma–Siam railway, where sixteen thousand of the sixty-one thousand prisoners of war put to work by the Japanese had died of disease, malnutrition and ill-treatment. He had been sustained throughout this experience by thoughts of his new wife, like Helen a pregnant new wife, whom he had last seen when he put her on a Dutch cargo-ship at Singapore from a jetty shadowed by a huge, oily smoke-cloud derived from Japanese bombing of the city in January 1942. He had hugged her a relieved goodbye before she steamed towards peace and safety.

He had not heard from her for three and a half years. He heard *of* her within a few days of the Japanese laying down their arms. The Dutch ship, destroyed by Japanese aerial bombing, had gone down in the Straits of Malacca. There had been no survivors.

Could anyone risk the stirring up of memories about that harrowing reunion in 1945 between brother and sister – debilitated childless widower, distraught pregnant widow? Some might. Alice couldn't. Oliver was saying something.

'Sorry, Oliver. My mind was drifting.'

'Well, don't let it. Aside from your teeth and your eyes, your mind's the best bit of you.'

'Is that your idea of a pass?'

'One of them. Plenty more in the locker. But put it aside for the moment. I said that a book about Hugo Burke would be a pretty short book. There wasn't enough of his life to make a long one.'

'I wasn't as clear as I should have been. The book would really be about the final stages of the war in Italy. Not only the chessboard moves and the feints and the strategic tie-up with other operations elsewhere and arrows on maps. This one would go fairly deeply into what it was like for the people actually doing it. But I've never met anyone who actually did it and there'd be a lot of hard work in trying to find them. Ulick's father's an obvious card of entry. If I can trace one or two of the men who were with him and say that I'm his daughter-in-law and tell them what I'm looking for, they might be more responsive than if I were a total outsider. So I've written around to Whitehall and the Public Record Office and a couple of museums to ask for advice on how to start things off.'

Oliver leant back as the waiter brought them their pudding, thanked him, and said to her: 'Do you know Paddy Madden?'

'No,' said Alice. 'Should I?'

'You may remember reading about him, or seeing him on the telly. He lives in County Wicklow. About eighteen months ago there was a complicated shoot-up at his house with the IRA and God knows who else.'

'That Madden? I recall it happening. I don't know him.'

'He's an OK chap,' said Oliver, using a term that she recognised as one that in his vocabulary signified extravagant praise. 'He was in Malaya in my district during the Emergency. We still keep in vague touch. He should be able to cut a few corners for you. He was in the same unit as Hugo in Yugoslavia during the war.'

'Yugoslavia? I thought Hugo was in Italy.'

'Both. In Malaya I used to spend hours pumping Paddy Madden for dope on the brother-in-law I'd never met. Hugo came out of it very well. Madden must know how to get in touch with at least some of his old chums. Why don't you telephone him?'

Oliver didn't know the number. It would be in the book under D. J. O'C. Madden, Kilmacanogue. She took her address-book from her handbag and wrote the name down. She thanked him for lunch. He collected her coat and helped her on with it. He accompanied her to her car and held the door open for her. He kissed her on the cheek and blew her another kiss as she drove away. She blew one back. She wished that one of his valedictory contributions to conventional courtesy, a message of goodwill to Ulick, had been expressed differently. 'Give my warmest compliments to the Missing Link', indeed.

Her telephone call to Madden prompted an invitation to herself and Ulick to a drink before lunch on the following Sunday, and the immediate provision of a helpful name, English address and telephone number.

'The man you want to start with', said Madden, 'is called Johnny Laing.'

CHAPTER TWENTY-ONE

ALICE'S long-dead grandfather had been a wise old man who once gave her advice that she had never forgotten. He was by unprosperous profession a riding instructor. The young Alice, invited by him to put her horse over a high hurdle, had rushed it with an undiscriminating enthusiasm and had ended on her back in the mud. As she picked herself up, suffering from mild concussion and a deflated self-regard, he said: 'Remember. If you're ever in a hurry, take your time.'

Alice applied this principle to her present concerns and restrained herself from making an immediate telephone call to Laing. She placed herself mentally in his position. Man, presumably in his late fifties, presumably doing a job of some sort, presumably with a wife and by now grown-up children, presumably whatever else within a realistic range of human probabilities you presumed about a name, address and telephone number, gets rung up by a woman whom he's never heard of. She says that she's married to the son of an old associate of his, that she writes books, and that she wants to come to see him to discuss events that occurred over thirty years ago. When would be convenient?

How does man react? Well, he might say: 'Fine. What about next Wednesday afternoon? Greatly look forward to it.' But, then, he might not. He mightn't wish to be reminded of a past of death and suffering, let alone to talk about it with a stranger. He might be in a bad patch of overwork, or have had a row with his wife, or be overhung, or simply be irritated by some domestic inconvenience or the mechanical inadequacies of his car. He might be anything. So, decided Alice, don't rush it. Give him time to reflect in privacy.

She wrote him a carefully worded letter. She explained that she was a serious historian, and listed her credentials to confirm it. She told him what she had in mind for the book. She said that her interest had first been drawn to the subject because she was married to Hugo Burke's son. And she described how she had been put in touch with him through the agency of Brigadier Madden. At this early stage she had no fixed ideas about how to proceed, but if he could spare the time to talk to her she hoped to be able to get a clearer view of the best way to set about the task.

Aside from whatever material, oral or written, that he might himself offer, perhaps he would suggest the names of some others with information that could be of help?

The good sense of this cautious approach became evident on the following Sunday at Kilmacanogue when Paddy Madden was dispensing gin and geniality. He asked her if she'd had a reply to her letter to Johnny Laing.

'Not yet. How did you guess that I wrote instead of telephoning?'

'He told me. Rang up and asked about you. Wanted to know if you were straight. Like a personnel manager checking on a character reference.'

Alice was amused. 'What did you say? Or, rather, how did you know what to say?'

'I knew what to say because I'd checked up on you, too. With Oliver Grant. He said that you were OK. Rather more than OK, the way he was going on about you. I told Johnny that what was good enough for Oliver Grant was good enough for me, and good enough for him. He'll be delighted to see you. You should hear from him within the next day or so.'

Alice laughed. 'I've fallen among the Thoroughs,' she said. 'Good old Oliver. I hadn't thought of him as a referee before.'

'He never was a referee,' said Ulick. 'He once had an Irish trial as a full-back, though.'

'Tell me more about Johnny Laing,' Alice asked Madden. 'What's he like? What does he do? Has he a wife? Will he be easy to talk to?'

'Taking your questions backwards, you'll find him very easy to talk to; he's a very nice wife, whom I first met when she was a nursing sister in Italy; he's some sort of civil servant; and, as for what he's like, you'll have to make your own mind up. But since I seem to have become the central clearing-point for the exchange of references I'll give you the same one about him that I gave him about you. Or that Oliver gave him through me about you. He's what Oliver would call an OK chap, and let me top up your glass.'

They talked about Hugo Burke. Madden spoke of him with liking and admiration. Very cheerful, very brave, very tough, highly intelligent character. Older and more mature than most subalterns. Took his religion seriously. Didn't make a fuss about it, and didn't let it affect his work, but he was one of the few among any of the British force in Yugoslavia whom Madden had heard expressing troubled reservations about the moral ambiguity of Christian soldiers furthering the aims of a communist ally. He'd only done it once, mind you, and that had been in rather special circumstances. Madden and he, the only two Catholic officers in the unit ('He was a much better one than me'), had come out of Mass together in a beautiful old Venetian church in Vis town. They'd

168

gone off for a drink and, since nothing much was happening at the time, the drink had developed into several drinks. The conversation had burgeoned from soldiering trivia into earnest reflections on the meaning of life, the nature of the universe, God's purpose in creating the world, and similar concepts that seldom exercised the minds of people usually more preoccupied with the earthly realities of raiding German-held islands and how best to maintain standards of training and morale. It must have been first the incense and then about a bottle and a half of shared *rakija* that got them on to it, said Madden.

It was then that Hugo had raised his doubts. Madden had forgotten how, if at all, they had been resolved. Madden mentioned the matter now, in the presence of Hugo's son and daughter-in-law, solely to illustrate that Hugo had been no run-of-the-mill, mindless subaltern who got on with the job without bothering about its implications in a wider context. He had been a thinking soldier. The *rakija*-inspired philosophising had been of no consequence in itself but it had stayed in Madden's mind because it had shown that there was at least one man about the place whose horizons weren't limited to those of the next operation.

Alice decided that she liked Madden. Anyone who took the trouble to dredge his memory for kind things to say to a son – well, an assumed son – about his dead father was, in that damned phrase that had kept cropping up in the past few days, an OK chap. She put a question.

'He must have been relieved to get to Italy? No ideological complications.'

'I suppose he was. I never had the chance to ask him. I was transferred to France when we left Yugoslavia. I didn't see him again.'

'Oh. Pity. I was hoping to manoeuvre you into talking about what went on around Commachio. For this book of mine.'

'I thought that you might. But that's really why I put you on to Johnny. I wasn't there. I heard about it, of course, and later talked about it and read about it, but anything I gave you would be secondhand hearsay. It would only confuse you. You'll do much better with Laing the horse's mouth. Particularly about Hugo. Johnny was with him when he was killed.'

Alice felt a slight shiver. Were all the people that she would be seeing going to be so matter-of-fact about friends of theirs who had been killed? She supposed that they would be, would have to be. Their occupational hazards had been different from any that she and her generation had experienced.

'Even in Yugoslavia I didn't see all that much of Hugo,' went on Madden.

'We were in different troops, most of the time in different places. I remember seeing him a couple of times near a place named Risan when we went there for a short job. But, again, ask Johnny. They were together all the time. Except for a short stretch when Hugo was a prisoner.'

Alice looked surprised. So did Ulick.

'That was in Yugoslavia, was it? Ulick said that his father had been captured by the Germans and had escaped, but I'd somehow thought that that was in Italy.'

'Slightly wrong on all three counts. It was in Montenegro, he was captured by the Ustachi and not the Germans, and he was released when some Germans the Ustachi had passed him on to surrendered. He didn't escape. Sorry, does "Ustachi" mean anything to you? They were Croat nationalists who supported the Germans.'

'Let me be pompous and say yes,' said Alice. 'I know quite a lot about the Ustachi. They keep making a sinister appearance in a book I'm finishing off at the moment. From what I've read of them it must have been pretty rare for one of their prisoners to survive.'

'Well, Hugo did,' said Madden. 'But, then, Hugo was pretty rare himself. Real hard ticket. Have the other half.'

They had the other half. Madden, already mentally awarded high marks for thoughtfulness by Alice, rose to greater esteem yet by chatting easily to Ulick about Rugby and golf and boxing, restoring to his depth a guest who had clearly recently been out of it. Madden's appointments-diary seemed to have much in common with Ulick's.

'I liked him,' said Alice, when Ulick was driving them home.

'He's an OK chap,' said Ulick.

Orla and Brigid, clear-eyed, hair-brushed, school-uniformed, complexions the flawless, enchanting bloom of healthy young girlhood, sat at the circular wooden table in the kitchen eating their cereal and admiring the way in which their father disposed of the morning mail. He had interrupted his breakfast to collect it from the hall when the rattle of the letter-box had been heard. He handed three letters, two of them bills, to Alice, glanced briskly at a large rectangular manila envelope addressed to himself, sat down again in front of his rashers and eggs, and skimmed the envelope with an adept backhand flick to the far corner of the room. It dropped neatly into the wastepaper-basket.

'Good shot, Daddy,' said the girls.

'What was it?' asked Alice.

'Some bumf from the lawyers.'

'About what?'

'I don't know. They shower me with the stuff. God knows what it costs them in stamps. If there's anything important, they telephone me and I go to see them. If the envelopes are small, I open them to see if there's a cheque. Otherwise I throw them away.'

'So I've noticed. But do you not think that now that things have changed it mightn't be a bad idea at least to look at what they send you? We might pick up something useful.'

'How? It'll only be some company report or an illustrated advertising brochure or—'

'Of the Burke Foundation?'

'Yes. Ah. I see what you're getting at.'

'Yes,' said Alice.

He went to retrieve the envelope and sat down at the table again.

'Bet you can't get it in the basket a second time,' said Orla.

Ulick scored a bull for the second time. He did it for a third time for Brigid. Then he opened the envelope. It was the Annual Report, glossy, garnished with colour photographs, of the Burke Foundation. He buttered a slice of toast sheepishly.

'What's yours?' he asked.

'Signed John Laing. Very nice letter. Why don't I telephone him to fix up a meeting? First give him a few days to look out some old papers and records and maps he has. Then he'll be at my disposal for as many evenings as I like after he finishes work. Or a whole weekend if I prefer it.'

Ulick stared suspiciously.

'I'd be careful of a weekend with a man you don't know. He might turn out to be someone like Oliver. The terror of the massage parlours.'

'Pas devant les enfants,' said Alice primly.

'Il faut partir pour l'école,' said Brigid. 'Nous sommes en retard.'

Orla laughed.

After Ulick left to drop the girls off at school Alice put the breakfast things in the dishwasher, wondered how much longer they could afford a dishwasher, and decided that it didn't matter very much. She took the Burke Foundation brochure to the room that she used for writing and research. She had never been able to bring herself to call it a study. It was a disordered, comfortable retreat that had started its career as a sewing-room and a haphazard repository for children's gumboots and wind-cheaters during summers, and tennis rackets and croquet equipment in winters. It had progressively acquired wooden bookshelves run up by a neighbouring pocket-money-earning do-it-yourself carpenter, and an elderly desk, rugs and armchairs bought at local auctions. The book-shelves, filled, by now reached the ceiling on all four walls. Papers were stacked in asymmetric heaps on side-tables. Alice's portable typewriter, surrounded by more, seemingly dropped-at-random clipped-together bundles of paper, sat on the aged desk. Alice had always maintained that it might look untidy, but that she knew precisely where everything was. Ulick and the girls were sceptical, but left everything where it was. Alice was famously sweet-natured. Good-hearted attempts to smarten up this room stimulated a grittily expressed resentment that preserved the well-functioning chaos from interference.

Autumn was setting in. She lit the portable Calor-gas heater and left it with one panel glowing. She took a notepad, a ballpoint pen and the Burke Foundation Report, relaxed in an armchair and got down to work.

The Report covered in detail the history, aims, current activities and funding of the Foundation since its inception in 1921. The Foundation was the child of the Burke Corporation, formed in 1886 to exploit and safeguard the wealth accumulated by the first Canadian Burke, Richard Manus (1850–1911). That much was explained on the cover. Alice glanced through the index, dipped into odd sections, baulked at pages of, to her, intimidatingly obscure financial statements, and began at 'The Burke Family Story: A Canadian Dream Come True'.

Richard Manus Burke had migrated from Crossmolina in County Mayo when he was in his very early twenties, and was known to his contemporaries, for some reason, as Black Dick. Penniless when he had disembarked at Quebec, Black Dick had found work with one of the gangs that were laying the track of the Canadian Pacific Railway. Dedicated hard work, physical strength, determination, natural powers of leadership and a shining faith in God (the writer did not go in for faintly praising benefactors) had soon caused Black Dick to become a foreman ganger. The foreman ganger, in turn, had become a contractor controlling a growing number of gangs of his own.

The area of operations of the Burke construction gangs had been the forests of British Columbia, which with the exception of the epic blasting of a route through the Rockies had provided the track-layers with the most formidably difficult engineering problems of the whole line. Led by the forceful Black Dick, his gangs had hacked, dug and dynamited their way through all obstacles.

Where lesser men saw handicaps, Richard Burke identified opportunities. As they advanced he staked out one enormous land claim after another. The completion of the line in 1885, its linking of Montreal to Vancouver, of the Atlantic to the Pacific, made the far-sighted Richard a wealthy man. There was access to his trees, transport to take out his timber, and markets to take it to.

During the following few years Richard presided with energetic shrewdness over a steady expansion of his business empire. He acquired more forest. He built his own wharfs and bought his own ships. He branched out into banking and insurance. By his fortieth birthday he employed several thousand people, directing their activities from a giant headquarters building in Montreal (Pix P43).

So, noted Alice, we know now where the original money came from. We also know that there seemed to have been – in the early days, at any rate – remarkably more of it than she, for one, had imagined. She read on. The next sub-heading was 'Christian Philanthropist'.

Black Dick had found Mammon to be less than totally satisfying. He endowed orphanages, contributed to the cost of churches, subsidised nuns, and nourished missionary orders with reliably regular infusions of hard cash. The scale and scope of these already generous benefices had been enlarged and systematised after 1887, a year in which on a triumphal return visit to Ireland he met, wooed and won Katherine (Kay) Doyle. The new Mrs Richard Burke was of exemplary piety and of profound efficiency. She largely took over the ordering of the charitable side of the Burke enterprise. The formally posed Victorian lithograph (Pix P77) showed a beautiful and determined-looking young woman of a cast unlikely to be intimidated by any level of opposition extant in nineteenth-century Canada.

The only child of Richard Manus Burke and of Kay Doyle Burke, a son, was born in 1888. His baptismal name was Randall Hugh Burke, and a handily inserted genealogical table showed him to be Hugo Burke's father.

What had until then been a huge, privately owned family business was in 1890 turned into a corporation, with a share issue floated for public purchase on the Montreal and Toronto Stock Exchanges. Sixty per cent of the holding was retained by Black Dick, to be passed by irrevocable deed to his heirs.

Black Dick died in 1911. His son Randall, who inherited, had the advantages of a Jesuit schooling and a university education that his father had lacked. These assets, and a genetically contributed full share of Black Dick's addiction to hard work, his physical strength, faith in God, etc., had generated a sophisticated commercial dynamism that, if anything, outdid that of his father. The lumber, the shipping, the banking and the insurance prospered. Randall's revolutionary innovation was to apply the resources of the Corporation to investment and development projects beyond the confines of North America.

In an era in which other pioneering merchant tycoons were opening up Malayan rubber, Katangese copper, Assamese tea or Caribbean bananas, Randall Burke, an economic analyst of flair tempered by conservatism, picked for the site of his expansionism the territory with the fastest and most consistent economic growth rate of the times. His selection was Imperial Russia.

Characteristically, he took personal charge of the operation. He was too restlessly energetic to stay behind in Canada while subordinates engaged upon the adventurous and profitable task of applying Burke capital and skilled technique to potentially rich, previously untapped tracts of a land as climatically inhospitable and as geographically vast as the British Columbia that had once challenged his father.

Randall Burke placed the domestic Canadian concerns of the Burke Corporation in the safe care of 'The Three Wise Men', a talented and experienced group of operatives whose Pix, lugubrious and hirsute, were featured over Scottish names on P85. Aside from continuing to make money, they were charged by Randall with the supervision of the transfer of the Corporation's headquarters from the riotously decorative palace in Montreal to a modern, more staid and equally hideous building in Elgin Street in Ottawa, within walking distance of the railway station and the Château Laurier hotel, both institutions of contemporary commercial significance. The prime purpose of the move was not, however, commercial. Now that the Corporation was acquiring a large-scale international dimension Randall wanted an intimate liaison with the centre of Canadian government.

As in its treatment of the rise to success of Black Dick, the Report was adulatory, almost reverential, in its description of Randall Burke's triumphs of negotiation in St Petersburg and of practical administration of a growing complex of timber, fur, Caucasian oil, transport, and mining concessions in the Tsarist provinces. It was clear that, even when the cloud of sycophancy had been dispersed, there had been an enormously impressive range of achievement.

Commercial profitability was supplemented by a romantic cement. Randall married Tanya Grigorievna Sepelov, the eldest of the four daughters and one son of Count Alexander Sepelov. The Count emerged from the prose as urbane, multilingual, rich, ambitious, and experienced in silviculture, geology and mineralogy, a patron of the ballet and the visual arts, and, as Alice read it between the lines, something of a chancer. Whether or not Alice was right made, as it happened, little difference to anything.

Count Sepelov was the spokesman and possibly (Alice's reading again) manipulator of a shifting consortium of Russian noblemen and landowners who lacked the ability or self-confidence to treat with Randall Burke on their own. The Burke–Sepelov alliance was a roaring success.

The First World War broke out in August 1914 and Randall went to it as soon as he had handed over the safeguarding of the Burke Corporation's Russian interests to his Canadian number two. The successor was enjoined to continue to co-operate fully with Sepelov. Patriotic duty in the face of the common German enemy was now intertwined with commercial self-interest. What was good for Sepelov and the Russian Empire was good for Burke, Canada and the British Empire. And vice versa. Randall Burke, taking Tanya with him, travelled to Vladivostok by the Trans-Siberian Railway, embarked for Vancouver and enlisted in Princess Patricia's Canadian Light Infantry.

By the close of 1918, when Randall Burke was demobilised as a lieutenant-colonel with two wounds, the Military Cross and two mentions in dispatches, the Burke commercial Russian empire, the associated Sepelov commercial Russian empire, the Sepelov family, and much else Russian including the Tsar, his political empire and *his* family were no more. The Bolsheviks had destroyed most of the destructible assets and were on their way to sequestrate without compensation whatever residue was indestructible. Count Sepelov, his countess and Tanya's three sisters had been slaughtered when the train in which they and likeminded others had been trying to escape from Petrograd to the Crimea had been attacked and pillaged by Red cavalry. Of the family, only Tanya's young brother, Andrei, providentially staying with a distant aunt at the time of the massacre, was known to have survived. And how long he had survived for, and whether the survival had been maintained, was unknown in Ottawa at the end of 1918.

Randall Burke, home from the wars, faced with a distraught wife worried almost out of her senses by the absence of news of her only living sibling, had put the question to the Three Wise Men not of where the boy was but of why they hadn't found out where he was and done something about it. They had the resources and influence of a hugely wealthy corporation at their disposal. Why hadn't they used them? Russia was in a turmoil, but there were still personal, diplomatic and military strings there for the pulling. What about the British? Max Aitken, Andrew Bonar Law, Hamar Greenwood, all fellow-Canadians, were in positions of power in London. What approaches had been made to them? What . . .?

The Three Wise Men, unwise enough to fail to realise that making money for their boss was good but that looking after the interests of his closely devoted family was better, were dispatched with alacrity to obscurity, no longer to appear in the narrative either in word or Pix. The narrator wrote simply that Colonel Randall H. Burke, decorated returned veteran, at once resumed full control of the affairs of the Corporation after thanking the Three Wise Men for their services in a brief ceremony prior to their retirement.

Alice decided that for this deed at least she rather liked Randall H. Burke. And what of the boy Andrei? Well, obviously he got out of Russia somehow, because he could only be Ulick's assumed uncle, the 'horrible old bastard' who now ran the Foundation and was detested by Ulick's mother Helen.

CHAPTER TWENTY-TWO

THERE WAS a tap on the door, the honouring of Alice's only rigorously enforced household disciplinary measure: No unsanctioned interruptions when she was working. She called to Ulick to come in, and he did, athletically fitted out in a blue tracksuit and transatlantic-looking running-shoes with deep rubber soles. Training for the Dublin Marathon was well under way. There were twelve thousand entries. Ulick was aiming to finish among the leading five hundred. He probably would. He took his preparations for these matters seriously. Occasionally she wished that he would take a few other matters as seriously, but more often she was glad that he didn't. There was less fun in being a power behind the throne if the throne took too active an interest in its responsibilities.

'This Burkery's fascinating stuff,' said Alice. 'Did you ever hear anything of it? The Canadian Pacific Railway, and millions of dollars, and an alarming-looking Irish beauty, and the Russian Revolution, and a family massacre by the Bolsheviks, and your Uncle Andrei the only survivor—'

'How did they miss him?'

'He was staying with an aunt.'

'That's life,' said Ulick. 'All the wrong people get bumped off while the only worthwhile target's staying with an aunt. I suppose the aunt saved him by prostituting herself to the Cossacks and you want me to ask him about *her* sex life as well when I go to Ottawa.'

'I don't know yet. Haven't got that far. Hugo's father Randall's sacking people for not getting the young Andrei out of Russia.'

'He'd have done better by giving them a bonus for keeping the bastard there for ever.'

'I didn't know that you felt as strongly as that about him.'

'I hardly know him. But he made my mother cry. I'd never seen her cry before. I've not forgiven him.'

No, thought Alice suddenly, I don't imagine that you have. She had only twice seen Ulick, tolerant, easy-going Ulick, genuinely angry. The first occasion had been when an unusually objectionable drunk at a party had pestered her to the point of reaching his hand down the front of her

176

dress. The second had been when a neighbour's small daughter, the same age as Brigid, had been molested when coming home from school on a dark winter's evening by a man who was never identified. Ulick had half-killed the drunk at the party and would doubtless have finished the job had not she and about six of his friends pulled him and held him away from a bloodied wreck. Ulick had gone hunting for the child molester, and had he found him, she was convinced, would certainly have killed him, however many people tried to stop him. Both experiences had terrified her – for Ulick, not for herself. All restraint left him when his womenfolk were under threat or insult. A feminist confidante of hers had described it as the reaction of a male chauvinist outraged by a violation of his personal feminine property. She didn't see it like that. To her it was the blind exercise of some uncontrollable primeval protective urge. There was much to be said for being included within the ambit of the protected, and she was unsurprised that Ulick's mother Helen was counted among those to be cherished. But she hoped, for all of their sakes – Helen's, the girls', her own, and Ulick's – that a protective requirement would never become really serious.

'How far are you doing this morning?'

'Fifteen miles. I'll run up and down Killiney Hill a couple of times to tone things up a bit more.'

'OK. Good luck. When you're back I'll give you the full dramatic story of the boy Andrei's rescue from the heathen Rooshians and a run-down on where all this Burke wealth came from.'

'I'm not sure that I'm much interested in either,' said Ulick, 'but you can always try.'

Alice returned to her reading.

The Andrei getaway was covered in a few bland sentences. His aunt had entrusted him to the care of an English governess, a lady of resource and dedication who had set her sights on the simple, overriding objective of getting the boy to safety through the chaos of a mercilessly fought civil war, and had achieved it. After more than two years of itinerant hardship she brought him to the White Russian army of Admiral Wrangel in the Crimea. The White Russians were in contentious disorder at the time, and Wrangel's haven lacked permanence, but among the names listed for priority evacuation on the books of the British military mission attached to the Admiral was that of Andrei Sepelov. The instruction had come directly from the British War Office, who had had it from the Foreign Office. Burke Corporation influence in London in high places held by Canadians had seen to that. The boy and his governess were taken with other evacuees by a Royal Navy cruiser to Constantinople, where they were met personally by Randall Burke and taken by him first to London, and then by Cunarder to New York and Canada.

The Burkes made handsome provision for the governess, who thereafter did not reappear in the account. Andrei, adopted by Randall and his wife, Andrei's eldest sister Tanya, was brought up as a Canadian.

Before she turned from the tribulations of the early Andrei, Alice gave them brief supplementary thought. The Report had glossed over the horrors and terrors and sights and hungers and fevers and hatreds to which a small child had been exposed for two years of wandering amidst the bloodshed in a country destroyed by civil war. It was hardly surprising that he had grown into a horrible old bastard who had made Helen Burke cry. And, since he had been adopted by Randall and Tanya Burke, he had been more than just an uncle to Hugo Burke. He had effectively been a much older brother, and presumably a pretty formidable older brother at that.

Significant? She didn't yet know. But worth making a note about. She made a note.

Alice applied a professionally experienced eye to the task of isolating the meat of the tale of the genesis of the Burke Foundation from the rolling verbiage that surrounded it. The essentials, when she returned for a closer look at them, started with: 'Capitalism: The Christian Responsibility'.

Its philosophical message was that those rare beings gifted by God with the intellect, enterprise and initiative to accumulate great personal wealth carried a corresponding social obligation to succour less fortunate beings. Black Dick had honoured this commitment. His son Randall had, if anything, surpassed him with his range of supported charities, clergy, churches and good works. As with commerce, however, so with social and moral responsibility. Black Dick had been a domestic entrepreneur, Randall an international one. Black Dick's benefices had been Canadian. Randall had pushed his beyond the national borders, at first in their traditional form, later in a refinement of much greater sophistication. Randall had recognised a threat to the whole fabric of Christian civilisation and had taken constructive steps to fight it. Only governments held the resources to withstand and overthrow the insidious menace of international communism. Randall, in 1922, set up the Burke Foundation to acquire and disseminate information and to stiffen the wills of those governments that needed stiffening and had the capacity to do something practical if they were stiffened.

The Foundation's charter was succinctly worded:

1. To provide facilities for study and research into all aspects of the international communist conspiracy, overt and covert.
2. To organise and develop propaganda machinery to expose all instances of communist subversion, from attempts to undermine lawfully constituted governments to the infiltration of small groups and individuals into industrial, educational and opinion-forming institutions.

3. To offer support to, and enlist the co-operation of, all bodies, governmental, religious, corporate, commercial and cultural, that are pledged to resist communist expansionism and aggression wherever it may show itself.

Randall Burke demonstrated simultaneously his Christian devotion to the cause of Righteousness and his brilliance as a financier. The stock value of the Burke Corporation had swollen enormously from the profits from war contracts and from the beginnings of the North American boom that was to continue to expand until its bursting at the close of the decade. Randall, the inheritor of the sixty per cent of the stock retained by Black Dick when the Burke enterprises had been incorporated, reduced his holding to ten per cent. The remainder he sold at a vast return. The return constituted the capital for the Foundation, aside from a small proportion, unspecified, that was to stay as Burke family property but was in some way, also unspecified, linked to the financial arrangements of the Foundation.

The advantage of this stroke was that Randall, no longer the majority shareholder, could divest himself of the day-to-day direction of the affairs of the Corporation while still continuing to profit from his ten-per-cent holding. He was thus free to apply all his huge energy to the running of the Foundation, to which his crusading Christian commitment called him.

A further bonus was that, although the Foundation was immensely rich, and its aims were international-political, it was in essence a family business. It was subject to no legal obligation to publish either audited annual accounts or a comprehensive list of its activities.

Alice reread the whole passage several times, thought that she had mastered it, and went for a walk in the garden. She said, 'My God,' as she went.

When, after a pensive ten minutes, she returned to her armchair she wrote on her notepad:

The sincerity of Randall Burke's philosophical Christian opposition to communism is not in question. The possibility that his motives in mounting his crusade might include an element of vengeance for the murder of his wife's family, and of his business partner, her father, is. So is the failure to mention the clear connection between his new obsession and the Russian destruction of a profitable venture in which he had invested tremendous amounts of money, thought and ambition.

The enormous power held by a rich body accountable to nobody was focused in the hands of one man, hereditary, the current Burke. Now Sepelov, brother of Tanya Burke, uncle of Hugo, great-uncle of Ulick. How did that happen?

This was getting interesting. She reopened the Report.

*

Hugo Sepelov Burke, the son of Randall and Tanya, was born in Ottawa in 1921, the year before the Foundation went into operation. His father had planned the boy's education very carefully. The Burkes as a family had by now been away from Ireland for the fifty-odd years since Black Dick had emigrated, and were fully integrated Canadians with Canadian loyalties, but they had always kept alive their Irish connection by providing financial help to their less fortunate relatives, and through frequent visits. Hugo, when he was sixteen and had completed Grade Thirteen at Lisgar Collegiate in Ottawa, was sent for two years to Clongoweswood College, a Jesuit boarding school in County Kildare, and subsequently to read economics at Trinity College, Dublin. Aside from fostering the Irish link, Randall's calculation was that Irish Jesuits in the overwhelmingly Catholic atmosphere of the contemporary Irish Free State would inculcate in his son a purer understanding of Catholic teaching and values than was available in religiously multi-confessional Canada; and that Trinity, one of the oldest universities in the British Isles, would give him a polish unobtainable in North America.

Hugo S. Burke, the Report went on, did not complete his degree at Trinity. He enlisted in the Royal Marines in early 1942, was commissioned at the end of the year, and was killed in action in Italy in 1945. A brilliant and attractive young man of enormous promise, his loss had been felt grievously by his distressed parents and by the whole Foundation. Great things had been expected of Hugo Burke. Had he lived, he would have returned to TCD to finish his degree, would have gone on to Oxford to read politics, philosophy and economics, and after a period of on-the-job training and further grooming by his father would have inherited his mantle as Director of the Burke Foundation.

Randall Burke was in failing health, a process accelerated by his grief, and that of his wife, at the premature death of his only son. He had determined to retire from his task whilst still capable of discharging it efficiently, and he had already made provisional arrangements for any gap between his departure and the delayed accession of Hugo to be covered by his adopted son, Andrei Sepelov. Randall now brought forward the date of this planned interim handover. Colonel Andrei Sepelov, DSO, MC, CD, was demobilised from the Canadian Army in 1946 and immediately took up his duties with the Foundation.

What had initially been designed as a temporary measure to fill in for Hugo grew, *faute de mieux*, into something much more lasting. Shortly before his death in Italy, Hugo Burke had married Helen Grant of Grantsbridge, County Monaghan, Irish Free State, who was with the British Red Cross Society. Helen Grant Burke had been pregnant when Hugo Burke was killed, and there was uncertainty about the line of succession until it became known whether the child would be a son or a daughter. A son, Ulick Maurice, had been born 'in 1946'. In accordance with his mother's wishes Ulick Burke had been brought up in Ireland. During the years of Ulick's legal minority, Andrei Sepelov had continued at the helm of the Foundation. When, in 1967, Ulick had attained his majority, he had, for private reasons, decided not to play an active role in the Foundation's affairs. He had voluntarily delegated his entitlement to the Directorship-General to Andrei Sepelov for the duration of Andrei Sepelov's life or, alternatively, until such time as Andrei Sepelov became incapacitated by age or infirmity from discharging his duties. By this generous act of self-abnegation, in particular, by his agreement to transfer his authority for the full period of Andrei Sepelov's working life, Ulick Burke had ensured that vital ingredient, continuity, without which any great enterprise would be hamstrung. The Foundation owed a deep debt of gratitude to Ulick Burke.

'Jasus, Ulick,' said Alice aloud. 'How do you *do* it?'

She went to the garden for another think. She was still thinking when she heard a developing drumming sound, the gate burst open, and Ulick, ruddy-faced with health and panting slightly, sprinted to a halt beside her.

'One hour, forty-two minutes,' he puffed proudly, looking at his watch.

'Well done,' said Alice.

When Ulick had showered and changed, and had had a drink, and had chewed voraciously at bits and pieces of leftover food that he found in the fridge, Alice joined him with the report and with her notes.

'Anything interesting in that stuff?' he asked.

'Indeed there is. When did you, in a heroic spirit of self-abnegation, earn the gratitude of all sufferers under Marxist oppression by handing over control of the Burke Foundation to Andrei Sepelov. Voluntarily?'

'Did I do that?'

'So it says here.'

'Must have been one of those pieces of paper the lawyers got me to sign.'

'Voluntarily.'

'I suppose it counts as voluntarily. The solicitors didn't connect up my goolies to the electric light system, if that's what you're getting at.'

'I think you were conned.'

'Conned out of what?'

'Conned out of being the Director-General Designate of the Foundation. It seems to be a hereditary appointment, like a dukedom. Only better-paid.'

'It takes two to make a conning. If that's what you say the old bastard did, I'm sure he did it, congratulating himself on the clever way he outwitted his dumb nephew. What he didn't realise was that the dumb nephew wouldn't have been a blind bit interested in the job even if he knew it was rightly his, which I suppose I should have but didn't. . . . I'll start again. The grammar got a bit mixed up there. What that thieving old bandit didn't—'

'OK. Message received and understood. The first part anyway. Are you sure that you wouldn't have liked it?'

'*Me?* Don't be bloody ridiculous. All those Yanks and jetlag and ulcers and oil-wells and double-crossing your friends for a fast buck and—'

'The television'll be the death of you. It's not that kind of foundation. This one combats communism. In the name of God and the Goodies.'

'Well, I suppose that God and the Goodies know what they're doing in investing their reputations in a shifty sod like Uncle Andy, although I think that they might have slipped up somewhere. Let 'em all get on with it. Me, I have you and the girls and all these other interesting things I do. I wouldn't know where to begin if I had to keep arguing with Stalin and—'

'He's dead.'

'All right, the other fellow. The one after Stalin.'

'He's dead, too.'

'Well, if they're all bloody dead what does Sepelov do all day?'

'Ulick, you're right. I don't think that you're really cut out for the job.'

'That's what I've been trying to tell you. I admire your intelligence, but sometimes you're very slow on the uptake.'

Alice returned to her researches. She stared again at a passage that she had underlined in the last paragraph that she had read: '. . . there was uncertainty about the line of succession until it became known whether the child would be a son or a daughter. A son, Ulick Maurice, was born in 1946.'

Well, now, if you, Alice Burke, weren't Alice Burke in this present year, but were Andrei Sepelov in 1946, and you were as tough and singleminded as your war decorations suggested that you were, and you had the best possible reason to hate all things communist, in that your father and mother and three sisters had been murdered by Bolshevik revolutionaries, and you yourself had spent two terrifying and miserable years of your childhood hiding and running from them, and because of that, or perhaps because it was just a natural part of your make-up, you were not conspicuously scrupulous. . . . And if, as the Cold War was in its early stages, you had, almost within your grasp, a richly endowed instrument, the Burke Foundation, that would give you the fullest possible scope to do what above all else you wanted to do, which was to help to clobber the commies. . . . And if, a few months before your agreed taking over of control of that instrument in trust for the training to maturity of Hugo Burke, Hugo Burke was killed. . . . And if. . . .

Uncertain line of succession 'until it became known whether the child would be a son or a daughter' only made sense if it meant that in the Burke family scheme of things daughters, in so far as the real, solid, serious business of life was concerned, didn't count. It was a view that would have come automatically to old Black Dick, the Victorian Catholic Irishman from County Mayo. The notion that a *woman* could be trusted to have any part in the control of anything of fundamental importance would have been to him as absurd as it would have been to press whiskey upon the navigator of one of his ships just as the man was about to take a starsight.

If this deep-lying Male Chauvinist Piggery had been enshrined in the Burke ethos, either by legal deed or by passed-down attitudes from father to son, a very interesting layout would begin to unfold. Shorn of its niceties and courtesies it would go like this: Randall Burke's son is dead. Randall Burke's widowed daughter-in-law is pregnant. Randall says to Sepelov: 'Andrei, there's hope yet. I thought when Hugo was killed that I'd go on for a few years and then close the whole thing down. I love you as a son, but you're not a real son, only an adopted one, and this is strictly Burke of-the-blood stuff. With no Burke heir I'd have paid everyone off handsomely, dispersed the assets and formed a trust for my wife, you and my distant dependants in Ireland. If Helen has a daughter, I'll do that anyway. If it's a boy, we're back in business and you can run the show until he's of age.'

Andrei hopes to God that it's a boy, finds that whether it is or not its father can't be Hugo Burke, but decides what the hell, any boy child born by Helen will do. He connives with, or bullies, Helen into representing the child to be Hugo's, probably by pointing out that if Helen discloses that she's been sleeping around since Hugo's death not a penny of Burke money will go either to Helen, who may be too proud to care, or to the child, about whom she is certain to care.

Child turns out to be a boy, Sepelov and Helen fudge the date of birth between them, concealing it from Randall and Tanya Burke. How? Difficult, but not impossible. Parents wrapped up in their own sorrow, particularly Tanya who had already lost her father and mother and sisters violently. Sepelov says that Helen, also distracted by grief at the loss of her husband, wants to have the baby in total seclusion at her mother's home in Ireland. When Ulick finally arrives everyone is so confused with new joy and constant mourning that they don't bother to do any sums or look at a calendar.

What about that for a plot? Far-fetched? Certainly. But no more far-fetched than thirteen-month pregnancies, Immaculate Conceptions, or any other possible explanation that she could imagine. It had also the merit that small, otherwise inexplicable things fell into place. How could an organisation with the resources of the Burke Foundation fail to take notice of something so elementary as the date on a birth certificate? Why did the Report say merely that Ulick had been born in 1946, instead, as would have been more normal, of specifying the date? Why did Helen detest Andrei Sepelov? There might be all sorts of reasons, but few better than this hypothesis.

Alice began to feel rather pleased with herself.

She put the Report on the short length of shelf that she had cleared for the folder, loose notes, books on the Italian Campaign, and anything else useful that might come up as raw material for what in her mind she was beginning to think of as The Book and Hugo. Plot mixed inextricably with sub-plot; one, with parts of the other, for publication. The other parts of the other emphatically not for publication.

There was an immediate decision to be made. Should she tell Ulick of the conclusion that she had reached about the Foundation's acceptance of him as Hugo Burke's son? Reasons in favour: He was the central party to the issue and had an absolute right to know. He had complete faith in her, and she unquestioningly honoured her obligation inherent in that faith. His future life (and her own, and that of the girls until they were grown up) would be conditioned by the knowledge that she thought she now held.

Reasons against: The Sepelov–Helen collusion theory was a possible explanation, perhaps the only possible explanation, but its status was still that of a plausible hypothesis. There would have to be confirmation, from Helen, or from Andrei Sepelov, or from some so far unthought-of source, before the hypothesis could be translated into acceptable fact.

The problems of seeking the confirmation were identical to those already faced in the search for basic information. Something, somehow, would have to be gleaned from Helen Burke, from Hugo Burke's old soldiering companions, or from both. It would still be necessary for Ulick to try to persuade his mother to talk about his conception and birth. This last consideration narrowed the question down to: Would Ulick be more effective as an interrogator of his mother if he knew in advance what he wanted to be told? Some of the answer, already accepted, was that he probably wouldn't be effective at all. The rest of the answer was that if he started with a set objective, instead of with a general disposition to discover what he could, the chances of his finding out anything of use would be diminished, and the chances of his missing something essential would be enhanced. So would be the chances of his generating some chaotic shambles by behaving like an American district attorney in one of the television films that he was so fond of.

There was another valid reason for postponement. Ulick and nuances were incompatible. Conjecture and proof were all the same to him. Let

him once get it into his head that Andrei Sepelov and his mother had
conspired to use him to further their differing financial interests and he
would be off like a rocket, proclaiming that that was that, then. His
mother was free of the risk of being charged by the Foundation with
embezzlement. It was only fear of that that had so far held him back.
Nothing more to be said. If his mother wished to continue to profit from
the deal, that was her affair and OK by him. As for himself, he wanted no
further part of it. He would cut the painter, refuse any more Burke
money, and reorganise his life on his own. Et cetera.

Which was entirely admirable. And which was what would doubtless
happen in the long run anyway. But it shouldn't happen before suppo-
sitions had been turned into certainties, before everything that needed to
be known was known, and before all the implications of whatever it was
decided to do had been considered.

Postpone.

Ulick was in the sitting-room, making pencil marks against the names of
horses in the racing pages of the *Irish Times*.

'Anything more in that sludge?' he asked.

'Some of it's interesting. Useful background for you to put questions
to your mother about.'

'Oh Christ,' said Ulick.

CHAPTER TWENTY-THREE

JOHNNY LAING sank his putt, replaced his putter in his golf-bag, thanked his partner, changed his shoes in the carpark and drove straight home. The partner had been a reformed tosspot who made clear his intention of not going near the bar. Laing, who usually followed a round of golf with a relaxed tot or two, was glad to be freed of any obligation to do so on this evening. He had his mind to clear and a long-neglected collection of memorabilia to sort. The woman historian, Helen Burke's daughter-in-law, would be with him the day after the following one. Laing had neither seen nor heard of Helen for more than thirty years. The break in communication had been at her instance, not his. He still regretted it.

The woman historian sounded nice on the telephone and wrote civilised letters. Laing had never heard before of a woman *military* historian, but an enquiry to a golfing friend of his who lectured at the Royal Military Academy at Sandhurst brought the reply that Laing had better catch up with the last quarter of the twentieth century. There was a Queen on the throne, and a woman Prime Minister in Downing Street, and women soccer correspondents, all-in wrestlers, Grand National riders, single-handed round-the-world-sailors, television newsreaders, airline pilots. . . . Laing said yes, but surely a woman military historian would be handicapped by her lack of experience of what she wrote about. The lecturer said that very few historians had any experience of what they wrote about. How many had been politicians, or industrialists, or social workers, or revolutionaries? Historians were recorders and analysts and commentators. Women were as good at the job as were men. Better in some ways. More intuitive. Laing didn't have to believe all this bullshit any more than he believed it himself, but his wife was a female historian and he was quoting her. Which particular woman had Laing in mind?

Laing said that she was Irish. Name of Burke. The lecturer said that, if that was Dr Alice Burke of TCD, Laing had picked one of the good ones. Very balanced. Growing reputation. The three books that she had so far published hadn't sold all that well, but were admired among the academics.

That conversation had been reassuring. So had the testimonial passed on by Paddy Madden. Laing, satisfied that the Burke woman was a genuine seeker of information and not a prober into Burke matters that could best lie unprobed, was prepared to be as helpful as she could wish for. If she asked for the whole truth, warts and all, she would get almost the whole truth with plenty of warts attached. What she wouldn't get was a wart or two that would add nothing to an understanding of the events in which she was professionally interested. They might titillate some, but they could damage others, including the husband of the historian herself.

He kept his souvenir oddments in an old box-file. He hadn't opened it for years. He did so when he got home, after first pouring himself a whisky and water. He went slowly through the contents of the box, reading reminiscently, mostly to refresh his memory for the benefit of Dr Alice Burke, partly to remove anything, if there was anything, that he didn't want Dr Burke to see.

There was a cyclostyled 'History of the Operations of No. 49 Royal Marine Commando in the Mediterranean, 1943–5', printed on low-quality wartime paper, by now yellowed. It was a bland and factual account of what had happened, where, when and at what cost, in which triumphs were modestly exaggerated and disasters underplayed. It had been written in a hurry by the Intelligence Officer shortly after the war ended. At the time it had served its purpose, which was to provide everyone with a record of shared experience. Now its style read strangely, an incongruous parody of a school magazine covering sum-marily the fixtures of the First XI. For 'After a lively knock that included seven fours and a towering six over the pavilion boundary, Simkins fell to a yorker in the last over before tea', substitute 'X Troop, led by Captain J. D. Laing, MC, RM, put in a spirited attack on Pod Vlake (621372), and with the loss of one killed and three wounded, one seriously, took the hill'.

A page cut from the *Illustrated London News* was headlined 'Comman-dos in Action in Italy'. The captions to the pictures had been censored into meaninglessness. One showed Richard, looking dramatic in his cap-comforter and jumping-jacket, standing beside a Buffalo and gazing steadfastly along the beach at Commachio. 'Royal Marine Business', classified 'Restricted', gave short accounts of commando operations at Walcheren, at the Rhine Crossing and in the Dalmatian islands.

Jottings in a frayed field-service pocket-book, stiff brown cover and held together by what looked like knicker elastic, reflected such long-forgotten preoccupations as replacement Bren-barrel, boots O'Driscoll, NAAFI ration 'Q' sub-section, and Tpt 3-tonner and 15 cwt Trebinje, 0800 hrs, 25 Oct 44. A mysterious indecipherable entry seemed to be the name of a VD sufferer, recorded in a personal code in case Laing got shot and a third party read his notes.

In a large buff envelope were some Allied Military Government lira (now worthless), some hundred-dinar notes issued by the Independent Kingdom of Croatia (Pavelic's Ustachi crowd – notes intrinsically worthless, but possibly of some scarcity value), a receipted bill from the Imperiale hotel in Bari, two more from the Club Ravenna, and a cardboard label. On the label was written in indelible pencil: 'Capt. Laing. 49 Cdo. Gunshot wounds, left thigh, left forearm, scalp. AT, 18.4.45.' That must have been pinned to him in the dressing-station at Argenta and have accompanied him to hospital, Helen's hospital, in Bari. Whether 'AT' meant that he had been given an anti-tetanus injection, or that the 88 that had hit him had been an anti-tank gun, or that the orderly who had written the label had had some name like Arthur Tomlinson, he no longer knew. Not much in the envelope to excite the historical researcher, and nothing to be hidden from her.

In another buff envelope were a few photographs, faded snapshots, taken in Montenegro by that nice gunner major. Chester? Chichester? Chisholm? Chisholm, that was it. They showed groups of marines, grinning self-consciously against backgrounds of limestone rocks. One picture, postcard size, was of a field firing exercise near Bileca, held in the lull after the Germans had been chased out of Risan. Snow on the ground, ragged hills ahead, and there was X Troop, advancing in extended order close up behind an artillery barrage, he himself in the front centre, Hugo front right, Silent Mott front left.

Held together by a staple that had rusted, and that left a brown mark when he removed it, were half a dozen snaps of Helen Burke looking extraordinarily, devastatingly lovely. She was wearing her navy-blue Red Cross winter uniform, beret lodged rakishly on her short fine fair hair. The snaps had all been taken in Bari over a spread of time. In the first five she was with Hugo, both laughing, variously holding hands, with their arms around one another's waist, with his arm around her shoulder. In the last she was not laughing. She looked sad and brave, and the man whose hand she was holding was himself. He removed that picture and returned the rest to the envelope.

There was nothing else that should be abstracted. He put back the papers in the box-file, closed it, and tied it with tape to the bundle of maps that he kept in a separate folder.

The other skeleton in the cupboard, first rattled during a chance meeting in Zagreb fourteen years previously, had neither been recorded by him nor disclosed orally to another living soul. Not even to Gert, his wife. That skeleton, after all, was unconnected with the events that followed Helen Burke's miscarriage in Bari in the late spring of 1945, of which Gert knew everything that he did.

Aer Lingus Flight No. E164 met the runway at Heathrow with a discreet bump and decelerated with a lot of noisy reverse thrust from its engines and showers of spray from undispersed rainwater. Customs were grimly indifferent, security must have existed but wasn't seen to do so, and Immigration didn't apply to travellers from Ireland. Alice reread Laing's travel directions and caught a coach to Staines station and a train from there to Camberley. Laing was awaiting her at the ticket-barrier, easily identifiable because he was the only man there on a Saturday and matched roughly the description that he had given her of a sort of red-faced chap with a bent nose and glasses and a roll-neck sweater.

'Mr Laing? I'm Alice Burke.'

He grinned. 'I hope my description of me was better than your description of you. I was expecting some fearsome tough woman with muscles and a moustache.'

'I was expecting a human horse with a gundog at his heels.'

He had booked her into a hotel. He drove her there, helped her with her baggage and said that he'd meet her in the bar when she had sorted herself out in her room. What could he line up for her?

'Gin and tonic, please.'

She laughed at the expression of relief on his face. He decided that he was going to enjoy their collaboration better than he had thought he would.

In the bar he asked her how she wanted to set about her task. She had no firm ideas. Why not play it by ear? Perhaps she could start with the papers that he had mentioned, and then ask questions and just talk? Her earlier work had been about concepts, and the relationship between strategy and political manoeuvring, and broad sweeps illustrated by arrows on maps. That sort of thing. This was the first time that she would be writing about living people, the ones who were represented by the arrows and had had their lives affected by the concepts. She was anxious to get it right. Would he agree to go through her notes after she had written them up, and be ruthless in correcting solecisms and the silly mistakes that somebody with no personal knowledge of what it had been like was liable to?

Laing was much cheered. 'I raise my glass to you,' he said, raising his glass to her. 'I didn't know what you were going to be like. On your basis this'll go fine. I'm sure that there won't be any silly mistakes. There are certain to be some plain mistakes. I'll help in any way I can.'

An hour later she was sitting in an armchair in front of a log fire in a comfortably furnished house on Yateley Common. Laing had gone shopping. His wife, he explained, was visiting her sister in Scotland. His son and daughter were grown up and away. The house was at her disposal. He didn't know what to recommend if she felt that her virtue was imperilled, but he supposed that she could scream or dial 999. Something like that.

She had a cup of coffee on a low table beside her, Laing's folder of old maps on a Persian rug at her feet, and his box-file open on her lap. She read first the sepia-coloured cyclostyled unit history. She had been through it once, and was dipping into it for a second glance when he came back. She was frowning, and looked to him to be very serious.

'Can I clear my mind on something that's already beginning to bother me?' she said.

'Clear away.'

'I'm an academic and a woman. I told you in that pub that so far I've dealt only with trends, and decisions by the Top Brass, and so on. Chessboard stuff. I've never before met and talked to and tried to write about real people who were the raw material. The ones to whom phrases like "the objective was taken after prolonged hard fighting" meant a personal experience that someone of my generation, let alone of my sex, can't begin to imagine. I've just been reading in this things like Lieutenant Burke and Lieutenant Mott were both killed in this attack. Troop Sergeant-Major Mayne, who had earlier been wounded, was later killed by shelling while he was being evacuated. Total casualties were. . . . Et cetera. What I'm trying to say is – and I'm saying it very badly – does this probing into the past by a stranger stir up too many sad memories for you and people like you? Because, if it does, I'll abandon the whole. . . .'

Laing decided that Alice Burke was a very nice young woman.

'No, you go ahead,' he said. 'Most of us like it, within reason. Gives us a chance to be boastful and reminiscent, and pretend that we used to be rather more dashing than we actually were. Anyway, we tend to forget the bad bits. We remember the good times and the funny ones. There's only one thing that I for one can't stand about outsiders who write about it, and that's when some supercilious young know-all passes scathing judgements on people who were operating under pressures that the know-all knows nothing about.'

'I'm not a—'

'I know you're not. You wouldn't have asked me to vet your stuff if you were. Mind cleared?'

'Mind cleared,' said Alice. 'And thank you.'

'What's this about O'Driscoll's boots?' asked Alice.

'God knows. He must have worn them out and needed a new pair.'

'You mean you even had to pay attention to things like boots?'

'Why not? O'Driscoll didn't march on his stomach. He did his best to, sometimes, mind you. He was an Irishman. One of yours. Very good he was. He had some mysterious Christian name he wouldn't tell anyone about. Even in his paybook it said F. Something O'Driscoll.'

'You still remember details like that?'

'Some of them. Forgot about most of it for years, but I went through that stuff before you came. Brought a lot of it back.'

'Pleasurably?'

'Mostly. They were good people.'

Good people, Alice realised, was a Laing synonym for OK chaps.

'This is Helen, isn't it?' she said. She had come to the photographs. 'She was lovely. She's still beautiful.'

Laing was wary. It would have been impossible to go through several days of question and answer with Helen's daughter-in-law without some discussion of Helen, which was why he had left the snaps in the box-file. He wanted to provoke talk, not have it thrown at him suddenly. In that way he had some control over it.

'Yes,' he said, 'she was a honey. Do you see much of her?'

'Every year. We go over to see her in Canada. She moved there shortly after Ulick and I were married. She inherited a house when her mother-in-law died. Hugo Burke's mother.'

'That's Hugo with her in those pictures, of course.'

'I recognise him from the one she keeps of him.'

'Still?'

'Still. She must have been devoted to him. She never remarried. It's slow-witted of me, but I'd totally forgotten that you must have known her.'

'I was Hugo's best man at their wedding,' said Laing, and she knew at once from the way that he said it that here was one aspect of his part in the Italian Campaign that he preferred not to say too much about.

'Is this picture of a genuine battle? The explosions and the line of—'

'No. A field firing exercise. Live ammunition, but all going the right way. Nobody shooting back. A practice.'

'Did you do a lot of practices?'

'We never seemed to stop.'

'I've a terrible lot to learn.'

'You're asking all the right questions.'

He ran her back to her hotel, and after dinner she wrote up her notes. She showed them to him on the Sunday morning, and he read through them while she studied his maps. He was impressed by the scope and grasp of the notes. She had missed very little. Her interpretations were sensible and imaginative. He suggested a few minor alterations, which she accepted with gratitude and without argument. He invited her to lunch at the Ely Inn.

Over the coffee she said: 'Am I allowed to ask you about when you were wounded? I've never before met anyone who was.'

'Why not? But a strictly anonymous contribution. Background information of general application. I don't want to be laughed off the stage when I meet old chums.'

'All I've seen about it is in that stiff-upper-lip unit history. "Captain Laing was wounded early in this attack." Plus that label thing about gunshot wounds. How long were you in hospital?'

'It ended up as about three months. It became something of a holiday. I was out of bed in ten days or so, but there was some complication – about a tendon, I think it was – that might have gone wrong. It had to be checked every week. I just hung around, doing damn all.'

'Boring?'

'Not really. By damn all I mean damn all of what we'd all become used to. There were plenty of our wounded in the hospital. I used to go and see them. Talk to them, write letters for the ones with bandaged hands, do a bit of shopping for them. That sort of stuff. Then of course there was Helen. She was there in the same hospital. The Welfare girl. Hugo had been killed only a few weeks before, and she was badly shaken, but she was damned good. Just got on with her work.'

Alice decided not to ask any more about Helen. Laing calculated that he'd said just enough to dissuade her from asking any more about Helen.

'What I'd really like to know about the wounded', said Alice, 'is what happened to them *after* they were hit. This book of mine's supposed to be about people. When somebody was shot what were his reactions? I don't just mean pain and shock and so on. What did he think? What did he feel? What happened to him? Who attended to him? How was he taken away? Who . . .?'

'Alice,' said Laing, 'you'd better come to the reunion. A lot of us get together once a year. It's in two weeks' time. I'll get an invitation sent to you. Then instead of just listening to my tall stories you can try your luck on whoever you like, and collect addresses for future questioning. If you think that a good idea.'

'I think it's a marvellous idea. But won't they mind? A woman. . . .'

'Wives come. Some sons and daughters. After all, you are Hugo Burke's daughter-in-law. We'll ask Ulick, too. Everyone'll be delighted to see you both.'

'Thanks, Johnny,' said Alice, 'I'd like that.'

Alice stayed for two more days in Camberley, writing by day, passing her work to Laing for scrutiny in the evenings, when he came back from his work in London. He continued to be impressed by its quality, and told her so.

★

Ulick met her at Dublin Airport.

'What's he like?' said Ulick.

'Charming.'

'Oh,' said Ulick.

'His wife wasn't there.'

'Oh.'

'I wish you'd stop saying "Oh". He was very helpful and very kind and he's asking us both to the reunion they hold every year.'

'Ah.'

'I suppose "Ah" is a bit of an improvement on "Oh". But there's something he's hiding. He's pretty slick at heading off a line of questioning that he doesn't want followed.'

'Those sorts of chaps always are,' said Ulick.

'What sorts of chaps?'

'Charming chaps,' said Ulick darkly.

Laing met his wife at King's Cross Station.

'What's she like?' asked Gert.

'Charming. Sensible. I think she'll do a good job with her book.'

'Was there much talk about Helen?'

'Not much. There had to be some. Helen's her mother-in-law, after all. But I diverted it pretty fast.'

'Is she developing any unfortunate ideas?'

Laing thought carefully. 'I rather think she is,' he said. 'But what they are, and how far she's got, I don't know.'

CHAPTER TWENTY-FOUR

ULICK left for Ottawa full of briefing from Alice, good intentions of his own, and Irish coffee downed at the airport bar after a delay in his connecting flight to Shannon was announced over the Tannoy. The Irish coffee made him overconfident.

'Shouldn't be too hard to get it out of her,' he said easily to Alice. 'Just a matter of playing my cards cleverly.'

'I hope you're right. Your cards are about a pair of tens.'

'High straight at least.'

'If you say so. She holds four aces.'

'Which four?'

'There *are* only four aces. Hers add up to her only having to keep her mouth shut and she wins the hand.'

'I can't follow all these card-sharping allusions of yours. I'm confused.'

'Yes,' said Alice.

'PASSENGERS FOR FLIGHT NUMBGRRHHAAAAGHTRR-RKARRRSSSGHB-annon PLEASE REPORT TO GATE. . . .'

'That's me,' said Ulick.

They hugged each other goodbye. Ulick waved again from the gate. Alice waved back and drove home. She wondered what he'd come back with.

As she expected, what he came back with a week later was unexpected. He was in high good-humour and smelling of whiskey when he kissed her, and he nursed his good news chucklingly as he loaded his baggage into the boot of her car. He started to tell her the moment that she let in the clutch.

'I was on the telly,' he said. He beamed, awaiting congratulations.

'Good for you.'

'I was interviewed on the steps of the Burke Foundation Building. By CBC. The interviewer was called Harry something. Great guy. I said that I'd never been on the box before and felt a bit shy, so he gave me a tumbler of whiskey. Said it would relax me. He was right.'

'You drank it in front of the *cameras*?'

'Not all of it. Only the bit that I hadn't finished before the thing started. About two-thirds of it. Harry said that I could hide it when the cameras rolled, but I thought: What the hell? Everyone knows that these television people have a few scoops to start them off, so why not be honest about it?'

'I see,' said Alice. 'So there you were, drinking whiskey and talking outside the Burke Foundation to the whole population of Ottawa. . . .'

'Not only Ottawa. The whole of Canada. It's what they call a coast-to-coast hook-up. I was talking about international politics and the Burke Foundation. Harry loved some of the stuff you told me about the Foundation. He said that it was one of the—'

'You *broadcast* live to the whole of Canada what I told—'

'Not live. It was recorded. This morning. I didn't see it myself. Goes out tonight. Prime Time they call it. . . .'

'Suffering Jesus,' said Alice. 'You'd better save it till we get home. Otherwise I might wreck the car.'

'I knew you'd be excited,' said Ulick, gratified, squeezing her knee, 'but I hadn't thought that you'd be this much excited.'

She poured herself a stiff drink when they reached home, and a less stiff one for Ulick.

'Let's hear now about the big broadcasting sensation,' she said.

'Well, this guy Smithy—'

'I thought he was called Harry.'

'That was the other one. He appeared later. Smithy—'

'Ulick. Start at the beginning. If Smithy *was* the beginning. How did you meet Smithy?'

'The British High Commissioner introduced us.'

Alice drained half her glass in one hefty swallow. After two refills and nearly an hour of patient cross-examination she thought that she had the story assembled in more or less of a coherent sequence.

Ulick's mother ('No, we didn't talk about my birth or anything like that. Never seemed to get round to it') had been invited to a drinks party by the British High Commissioner at his house, Earnscliffe, 'a Presbyterian-looking joint like those things you see in the posher parts of Belfast'. The party was something to do with voluntary organisations. Helen was an obvious candidate for the guest-list because of her former service with the Red Cross. She had asked Ulick if he would like to come along, too. Ulick, who loathed diplomatic receptions, had agreed in a spirit of filial dutifulness. He had stood about feeling bored, making polite conversation to a lot of people he didn't know, and thinking of golf.

His host, not a bad, bald old bugger who roamed about chatting everybody up, had told him that he must meet Smithy, and led him over to him. Smithy was the Public Relations Director of the Burke Foundation. The High Commissioner was sure that Smithy would be only too glad to have a word with the last surviving male Burke, who so seldom set foot in Canada.

Smithy was. He was also, according to Ulick, a bit pissed. He was a short, fat, cheerful little fellow, who endeared himself at once to Ulick by some trenchant comments about the habits of the original owner of the house and their relevance to the state of the modern world.

'He was called Sir John A. Macdonald,' said Smithy, 'and he was the Prime Minister of Canada at the time when the Canadian Pacific Railway was being built. The one on which your great-grandfather Black Dick made his pile. The Macdonald reaction to national crises was to take to the bottle. Not just take to it, but take it with him and bugger off. They never knew where to find him, and they couldn't settle anything without him. We've been one of the most peaceable, prosperous countries in the world ever since. If all these whizzkid international statesmen we now have threatening to fry us to a cinder because they can't find a better solution were automatically issued with a case of hooch when they assumed office, and took off with it for an unknown destination when the going got rough, we'd all be guaranteed a happy old age.'

Ulick was impressed by this analysis and said so. Smithy's next offering was to point out that as a matter of fact he himself was supposed to be on the wagon. It was an entirely personal piece of self-discipline, adopted by him because he had a funny metabolism. It might be due to when he was a kid and was hit over the head with a baseball bat. Strong drink had a strange effect on him. He got soused after about four and stayed so for two days. This had led to some interesting disagreements with various of his former employers. He'd have been on the tomato juice tonight but for the fact that his present employer was in Calgary quoting the Apocalypse of the Blessed Apostle John to a bunch of Albertan Tar Sand Oil millionaires who agreed with him that socialism was morally defective. Without the old bugger's eye on him – he only had one eye, but it always seemed to be on him – he had let things go loose a little and was now on his fifth Scotch. Well, sixth, counting the one he'd just taken from the tray of this good-hearted waiter chap here.

What Smithy was privileged to be able to say to Oolick was that, although he'd been directing Public Relations at the Burke Foundation for the past two years, he'd never been able to get the publicity mileage he really wanted out of a real live Burke. Sepelov was a sort of Burke, but not a real one. Mrs Helen Burke was a dear, dear lady, but she wasn't a proper Burke Burke, either, and anyway he could never get her anywhere near the goddam Foundation. Maybe it brought her out in hives or something.

Well, there he was, stuck ass-down in this adman's dilemma, when Sir

Whatsisname who now lived in Sir John A's apartment had brought over his buddy Oolick and opened up a whole new ballgame. Why didn't Oolick come round to the Foundation at about nine-thirty the next morning? Smithy would show him round the building, introduce him to a few people and afterwards hold a news conference. Most of the kids around the place had been in their diapers when old Randall Burke died, and a few words from his grandson would do the world for staff morale. If Oolick was stuck for the words, Smithy would provide them. That was his job. Oolick would be on his own when he dealt with the media, but by that time he should have got the hang of the thing. The media would lap him up. The Burke Foundation *meant* something in Canada. There would be wide public interest in whatever a direct descendant of Black Dick and Randall Burke had to say. Old Cyclops Sepelov would be tickled pink when he got back from the Prairies and heard about the PR *coup* that Smithy had pulled off for the Foundation.

It was this last consideration that clinched Ulick's willingness to co-operate. ('I don't like public speaking, but Smithy was a nice guy and I wanted to help him in his career.') Ulick presented himself to the Foundation's security guards in the front lobby promptly at nine-thirty on the next morning – *this* morning – and found that elaborate arrangements had been made for his reception. There was a lot of hand-shaking, and there was the popping of photographers' flash-bulbs, and there was Smithy, flushed and euphoric, walking evidence that his curious metabolism was meeting its specifications. Smithy suggested that a background briefing in his office over a couple of snorts would be the best way to get the show on the road. Ulick concurred. Smithy gave a short run-down on the Foundation's activities, drawing as necessary from a copy of the same Annual Report that Alice had been studying recently. As he tossed it into his out-tray he remarked: 'To think I actually wrote that crap.'

The tour of the offices had been very interesting. Smithy oiled the wheels with plenty of joshing and back-slapping. Ulick, furnished by Smithy with a list of suitable phrases, had said in rotation: 'Keep up the good work', 'My father, grandfather and great-grandfather would have been proud of you' and 'Unless we get the Reds by the throat, they'll get us by the throat'. There had been some extemporisation in a typing pool where Ulick had addressed some rather good-looking girls on the subject of Stalin. ('He thought he could take over the world, but look what happened to him. He's *dead*.')

Smithy then led Ulick from the typing pool to a pre-news-conference gathering. Believe you him, he knew, he said, there was no better way to get a news conference off on the right foot than to have the boys and girls in for a quiet jar beforehand so that everyone knew everyone else. It took the starchiness out of things. Ulick admired Smithy's professionalism.

The familiarisation process lasted a little longer than Ulick had thought that it would, but it relaxed everybody satisfactorily, and he made a number of new friends. The nicest of a nice crowd was this guy Harry, the television interviewer from CBC. He was a dreamy-looking chap with thick glasses and wispy hair, and he held strong views on hypocrisy. He told Ulick that in fifteen years of television interviewing he had rarely come across anyone who had spoken frankly, really frankly. Too many of his subjects had held something back or played to the gallery. Ulick thought that deplorable. He would, he hoped, be the exception that proved the rule. This pleased Harry.

Ulick couldn't remember much of what he had said to the press when the formal questioning started. His mind was on the television interview that would come afterwards, outside on the steps. He did recall a naïve question from the man from the *Toronto Globe and Mail* to which he had replied that once the Pope got married he would change his mind about contraception. There was also one from a girl on the *Ottawa Citizen* about the nuclear threat; he silenced her by telling her that multilateral disarmament wouldn't work unless both sides did it at the same time.

He'd been a bit nervous when he'd faced the television cameras on the steps, with a piercing blue sky above, but he'd got back his old form after a few swallows from that tumbler of whiskey that Harry had given him. The one he'd mentioned in the car.

Smithy would be sending over a full transcript of the interview. As reconstructed by Alice from what Ulick could recall, the more arresting parts of the dialogue were:

Q. Mr Burke, you're the son of Hugo Burke, the grandson of Randall Burke, and the great-grandson of Richard Manus 'Black Dick' Burke. Why is it that you yourself are not at the head of this great Foundation?

A. I gave it to my Uncle Andrei in a spirit of heroic self-abnegation. Voluntarily. My solicitors in Bachelor's Walk, Dublin, can verify this. They were there when I did it.

Q. Do you regret your decision?

A. I do not. It would have meant that I'd have missed the Dublin Marathon. Last year I came 429th out of a field of 12,641, in a time of 2 hours, 51 minutes, 18 seconds. I hope to improve on that this year.

Q. What do you think of the way in which the Foundation is carrying out its work?

A. Admirable. It's a pity that they have to continue to support fascists and neo-fascists like General Franco, but I suppose that it's inevitable in the circumstances. If you don't get the Reds by the throat, they'll get you by the throat.

Q. Continue to support General Franco? He's dead.

A. Christ, is he? So's Stalin.

198

Q. What principles do you think should guide world statesmen in their search for peace in this thermonuclear age?

A. They don't have to look farther than this country. Your man Sir Jock A. MacGregor, I think his name was, the one whose house you flogged to the Brits, had the answer. Buy a case of this stuff (holds up glass to camera), drive off to the bondooks, and hide.

Q. Do you share the view of the Foundation that international communism remains the greatest single threat to Christian civilisation?

A. Of course it does. It has to be hit hard, where it hurts. None of this namby-pamby Queensberry Rules stuff. Go for the groin. That's why the Foundation is so valuable. It's not accountable to anyone. If you've read its latest Annual Report, you'll have seen that there's any amount of underground carry-on that's been covered up by a load of sleuthering balderdash.

Q. You mean it's a sort of privately funded mini-CIA?

A. (Winks at camera.) There are some things best left unsaid.

During the next few days there was a large volume of mail from Canada for Ulick, most of which he was unable to understand and all of which he gave to Alice. The bulk of it was forwarded by Harry of the Canadian Broadcasting Corporation. Ulick lost interest in it after three letters opened by him successively expressed irreconcilable points of view. The first congratulated him upon a fearlessly chilling exposé of a right-wing politico-religious conspiracy to reimpose reactionary domination over the freedom-loving democratic peoples of the world. The second called him a traitorous fink intent upon the destruction of Christian morality. The last described him as the greatest deadpan comic since W. C. Fields. Ulick said that this sort of thing made him despair of the sterility of the teaching methods in use in the North American educational system.

There were two letters to which both Alice and he paid close attention. The first was from Ulick's mother. She was coldly angry, not with Ulick. Andrei Sepelov, to whom she had refused to speak for years, had insisted on calling at her house. He had accused her of deliberately inciting Ulick to sabotage the work of the Foundation. Andrei had been almost out of control with rage, and he had made threats about both herself and Ulick.

For reasons that she wouldn't go into, she had at her disposal resources that made her more than capable of calling the Sepelov bluff. But she was concerned about Ulick. Andrei did not take his enmities lightly. She was writing simply to warn Ulick of this development and to urge him to take care.

She did not specify what she thought Sepelov might try to do, or what sort of care she thought Ulick should take.

The threat to his mother drove Ulick to a black fury. He talked of taking the next plane back to Ottawa and breaking Sepelov's neck. Alice soothed him by pointing to the passage about Helen's bluff-calling resources. Helen seemed confident enough of her ability to look after herself. Did Ulick know what she meant? Ulick cheered up and said no, he didn't know what his mother meant, but if she said she had resources she had them. She was a tough cookie. So was he. If Uncle Andrei wanted to start any rough stuff. . . .

'This one's from your chum Smithy,' said Alice.

Smithy's letter began 'Old Pal', and said that he was out of work. Ulick's bloody uncle had thought Smithy's PR initiative to be less of a *tour de force* than Smithy had intended it to be. Smithy had been in a sick-bed suffering from amnesia when Sepelov returned from Calgary, but this indisposition had not inhibited Sepelov from disregarding accepted conventions of humanitarian behaviour and from firing Smithy by telephone.

Smithy was not altogether sorry about this. He had been becoming fed up at having to put out all that tendentious gunge about the Burke Foundation, which undoubtedly did a lot of good but had its seamier aspects. In his spare time, while still employed by Sepelov, he had privately assembled some interesting info.

Now that he had been given the bum's rush, he had more time to dig deeper yet. When his diggings had yielded enough for a reasonably comprehensive dossier to be put together, he'd show it to Ulick. Ulick was the last of the real Burke Burkes, and had a right to know of some of the not altogether savoury things that had been done in the Burke name.

He wished Ulick the best of luck, and sent his compliments to that lovely wife of his.

'How does he know that you've a lovely wife?' asked Alice. 'He's quite right, of course, but how does he *know*?'

'I told him.'

'Thank you.'

'What do you think this dirt is that he's digging up?'

Alice laced her arms around his neck and kissed him with enthusiasm. 'I don't know what it is,' she said, 'but I do know this. I've been beavering about in my methodical historiographic way for weeks to get to the bottom of this thing about your father, and I've made a certain amount of progress. You've done more in ten minutes with a glass of whiskey and a television camera than I've even approached. You've smoked out Andrei Sepelov into going around uttering threats, which shows that he's worried about something. Your mate Smithy seems to have become a full-time volunteer snooper, which can only be helpful. And I'm proud of you.'

'Did I do all that?'

'You did indeed. It's not the only thing you've done.'

'Christ. What else?'

'You've made me pregnant again,' said Alice, tightening the hug with delight, and applying herself to intensifying the kiss.

It was by now late September. Some fresh information of relevance was contributed by Oliver Grant when, as was his custom, he invited them to his club for lunch on his birthday.

CHAPTER TWENTY-FIVE

BRIGID AND ORLA, assessed as old enough to put in a first appearance at the club without inconveniencing the other guests and embarrassing their Uncle Oliver, followed their father and mother up the staircase in search of their host.

They found him in the bar. He had clearly been there for some time. He was making a point to a bishop of the Church of Ireland, who wasn't enjoying it very much.

'Just because you wear your collars back to front,' Oliver was saying, 'you people seem to think that you've a prescriptive right to pretend that the satisfaction of carnal lust isn't a healthy recreational activity. Oh. Hallo, lovelies.'

He bent his knees to kiss the girls. He straightened them again to kiss Alice. He welcomed Ulick hospitably. His birthday was a time for family solidarity, insults to be eschewed unless, seemingly, you were a bishop. The bishop left.

Oliver ordered drinks, hugged the girls again, and said that the thing to do about birthdays was to take them seriously. He put this doctrine into practice in the dining-room by advising the girls to work through the menu in reverse order. Start with the pud, he said. Bit of roast beef after that, and end with the soup. The world was full of ridiculous conventions that should be challenged. The girls must grow up to think for them-selves, not let themselves be boxed in by—

'Oliver, you're ruining a life's work of dedicated child-upbringing.'

'Upbringing for what? You and Ulick between you have given these two an appalling genetic burden to carry. They'll be passing scholarship exams and playing hockey for Ireland all at the same time. Bulging brains and bulging calf-muscles. They've got it coming to them. Give 'em a break. Let them gather their rosebuds while—'

'My hamster's called Rosebud,' said Orla.

'Exactly what I mean,' said Oliver obscurely. 'Are these girls allowed a glass of wine, Alice?'

'No,' said Alice.

Over coffee and liqueurs in the upstairs drawing-room Oliver gave the girls a box of chocolates. Ulick took them to look at the waterfowl in St Stephen's Green. Oliver asked Alice how the book was going.

'Not bad. Coming along. I can't thank you enough for introducing me to Paddy Madden. He's put me on to a man in England named Johnny Laing, who's helpfulness itself. I went over a few days ago and he let me grill him. *And* checked my notes for accuracy. He's invited Ulick and me to a commando reunion dinner, where there should be any number of other sources.'

'Did this fellow Laing give you much on Hugo?'

'Quite a bit. Enough to make it clear that he'd had an enormous regard for him. Paddy Madden was the same. Neither had a hard word to say against him.'

'I heard a hard word said against his uncle,' said Oliver. 'Last week.'

'Which uncle?'

'Man named Sepelov. He was supposed to have been some sort of war hero. Covered in decorations. He was crooked.'

Crooked to Oliver was the direct antithesis of OK chap. Alice tried to look as if she had never heard of Andrei Sepelov. Oliver looked at her and laughed.

'You look as if you're trying to look as if you've never heard of Sepelov,' said Oliver.

Alice laughed, too. One of the coincidental things that they had in common was that their minds worked on almost identical lines. Sometimes they spoke in a sort of shorthand, finishing off each other's sentences. Sometimes it fascinated her. It could be disconcerting. Now it was disconcerting.

'You can leave out the mind-reading, Oliver,' she said. 'And yes, I've heard of him.'

'You must have. He runs this Burke extravaganza that pays for Ulick's jockstraps. Even your bird-brained Mr Universe – sorry, it's my birthday – even Ulick must have mentioned his name.'

'He has. What's crooked about Sepelov?'

Oliver sipped at his brandy. 'Well, you see what you make of it,' he said.

Oliver was on the committee of an association that looked after the interests of former prisoners of war of the Japanese, many of whom had never recovered in health, physical and mental, from the near-starvation and casual brutality that they had experienced. At a recent committee meeting in London he had been deputed to get in touch with similar bodies that dealt with prisoners from other theatres of war, to find out if they did anything for their members that his own organisation didn't do for theirs. In the course of this liaison he had met a man named Jock Wemyss, with whom he established the sort of friendly rapport that leads to the conduct of business in pubs.

In one pub, in which they stayed longer than was prudent, they fell to talking about the quirks of human behaviour stimulated by the strains of imprisonment. Conditions in German and Italian POW camps had been vastly better than had those in Asia, but Oliver had been interested to hear that the most unexpected people went wrong in European camps as well as in places like Changi and on the Burma–Siam railway. Wemyss quoted as an example a Canadian with whom he had once escaped. Wemyss was still bitter about him. He supposed, he said, that after all this time he should have forgiven and forgotten, and until he had started to talk to Oliver he more or less had, but the conversation and the booze had revived old resentments which he now proposed to pander to with no regard to the legislation about slander. ('That's the way he talks,' said Oliver.)

This Canadian, whose surname was Sepelov, had been captured in the Dieppe Raid in the summer of 1942, which according to Wemyss, also captured there, had been a cock-up of truly spectacular dimensions. Wemyss, a Royal Naval Volunteer Reserve sub-lieutenant, had been left behind after his landing-craft had been disabled on the beach. Sepelov, a captain in 2 Canadian Division that provided the main part of the force put ashore and was pretty well written off, had lost an eye in an unequal fight near the Dieppe Casino. Fellow Canadian witnesses whom Wemyss later met in the Bag said that Sepelov on this occasion had behaved with a wild, inspiring bravery. Sepelov, after a long stretch in German military hospitals and several painful operations, had eventually come to the camp in which Wemyss was locked up, and from which he was thinking hard about how to get out.

They teamed up. Sepelov was a dour, tough character, of impressive strength and determination. He was a careful and thorough planner. He contributed most of the detail to the scheme that they put forward to the camp escape committee, and he did more than his fair share of the physical work after it was approved. They tunnelled patiently towards the wire from under the floorboards of a hut, with volunteer helpers to dispose of the spoil, others to keep watch, and others, controlled by the committee, to provide forged papers, rudimentary maps, iron rations and adequately convincing-looking civilian-type clothes retailored from uniforms and dyed.

Sepelov was a tireless and fearless tunneller. From the night on which they broke to the surface into the fresh, free air, hid the rough-and-ready overalls that had protected their imitation civilian clothes, and started hopefully on an 800-mile journey towards the Pyrenees, Sepelov showed himself to be equally tireless, fearless and resourceful. The first part of their journey was a complicated saga of bluffing their way through controls on a local passenger-train, cross-country night-marches, jumped rides on goods-trains, thefts of food, frequent evasion, much hunger, and stowing away for three days in a Rhine barge captained by a friendly Dutchman.

In northern France they struck luck. A suspicious-looking farm-worker whom they couldn't avoid on a narrow country road was insistent on walking a few kilometres with them, and badgered them with too many questions for their peace of mind. Sepelov, one of whose assets for this sort of enterprise was a fluent colloquial mastery of European languages, modified the impact of the questioning by interrupting it unexpectedly by a series of irrelevancies, grunts and filthy comments, but the farmworker demonstrated how wasted this effort had been by saying: 'All right. You've passed. You're prisoners on the run. I'll help.' There was nothing that they could do about it. They accepted his help and hoped for the best.

They got it. He put them up in the loft of a barn, and fed them mightily for two days. He brought them to an *estaminet* in Lille, where the food was nourishing and the accommodation cramped but better than any-thing that they had known since their capture, and where an efficient, neat, grey-haired man with pleasant manners told them what he had in mind for them. He was sensibly reticent about the organisation of which he was a member, but it was clearly extensive. After five days of recovering their strength and eating everything that they could lay their hands on, they travelled elegantly to Paris by train, equipped with authentic foreign workers' papers authentically stamped by a French girl secretary who worked in the German Control Office and with authentic railway tickets supplied by a *résistant* employee of the national railway system.

Their instructions for their reception at the Gare du Nord were of schoolboy simplicity and of total effectiveness. At the nearest newspaper-kiosk to the ticket-barrier they would see a fat, middle-aged woman identifiable by a clutched parasol, a flowered dress and an expression of sweet, maternal welcome. They were to address her as Tante Marie. They did. She embraced them emotionally and led them, gossiping noisily about grandchildren, past Gendarme and Feldgendarmerie checks, to the street, to a short walk, to a small, sordid hotel of the type that let rooms by the hour as well as by the night and by the week.

It was while they were sharing one tiny room in this establishment that Sepelov, who until now had inspired Wemyss only with admiration and confidence, began to deteriorate.

The root of the trouble in that squalid Parisian Left Bank hotel was, in its early manifestations, simple boredom and ignorance of what would happen next. The two of them had come a long way together, dangerously and in hardship. While they were working on the tunnel, and during the first part of their journey, they had calculated odds together, shared decisions, in moments of crisis reacted instinctively with a mutual trust in each other's judgement and capacity. The trust had been complete, and always justified. A central element in all this was now, however, absent. Then, whatever the narrow constrictions faced by men on the run in hostile country, they had controlled their own activities. Now, as beneficiaries of an escape organisation that for sound reasons of security was scrupulous in telling them no more than was basically necessary about its ramifications and intentions, they had become passive pieces on the board, to be shifted arbitrarily for reasons that were not explained to them. Tante Marie visited them at irregular times to bring them food. She said little, other than that they would be told when the time came.

Two energetic, ardent individualists, under strain, cooped up together all day in a small space with nothing to do, soon irritated each other. They fell to bickering. It began over small matters like tidiness and disturbing restlessness in sleeping, and personal hygiene. It soon led to vicious diagnoses of alleged character shortcomings, and the resuscitation of past, half-forgotten slights and annoyances, magnified in retrospect. There were long hating silences. On the fifth day Sepelov, after two hours of one of these silences, and in defiance of rules laid down unambiguously by Tante Marie, walked out of the room.

He did not come back. Tante Marie called on the following day and became almost insane with rage. She raved of irresponsibility, ingratitude and the selfish prejudicing of the lives of dedicated volunteers. She took her fury out on Wemyss, which added to his misery and bitterness.

He was lying listlessly on his bed two afternoons later, hands linked behind his head on a pillow that smelt of old sweat and scent, when Tante Marie returned, no longer passionate with anger. This time she was urgent, and coldly practical. There had been a betrayal. There were contingency plans to meet it, and they were in operation. A planning assumption had always been that any member of the escape organisation cell who was arrested by the Gestapo would sooner or later talk under torture. The only possible foolproof counter was the immediate dissolution and dispersal of the cell. It had already dispersed. Wemyss was their last responsibility. She gave him money and a railway ticket to the Unoccupied Zone and instructions on how to get to the Gare de Lyons, and told him the times of the trains. She was sorry to have to leave him on his own, but there was no alternative. She wished him Bonne chance.

She added a bitter warning. Normally, she said, she would not have disclosed details of what had gone wrong, but she would this time because his safety might depend upon it. One of the organisation's unsung contacts, a provider of useful background information, was a waiter in the Abwehr's officers' mess. On the previous evening a dinner guest had been a one-eyed man in a badly fitting new suit who spoke Russian for most of the meal to the local Abwehr specialist on *Ostpolitik* and exchanged a few remarks in French with other officers. They were deferential and addressed him as *Herr* Sepelov.

'Pause for breath', said Oliver.

Alice stared at him.

'You're supposed to ask intelligent questions now,' said Oliver. 'Keep up the dramatic impact.'

'OK. What happened to your chum Jock Wemyss?'

He got through the controls at the station all right, and on to the train. He was picked up by the first bunch of military police or whatever they were who came round checking tickets and papers and asking questions. He ended up in the cooler. After another try or two, in Colditz.'

'And Sepelov? Did he stay long with the Abwehr?'

'Can't have done. He turned up in Spain a few weeks later, and was interned by Franco's people. Short stretch only. He was sprung by the Brits in the embassy in Madrid and delivered to Gibraltar. Trip to England in a convoy, reunion with the Canadians, local hero. Awarded the MC.'

'How do you know all that?'

'Partly from what I recall Helen telling me years ago. She went to some trouble to find out about him. Partly from Jock Wemyss. When he was released in 1945 he went to some trouble, too. He went to see MI something or other – 9 I think he said it was. They dealt with escapers and evaders. He told them that Sepelov was a crook. They listened courteously and said that Sepelov must have been a pretty odd sort of traitor. He'd later lost a hand and won the DSO in Sicily, and finished up as something grand on the Staff. They hinted that Jock had become unbalanced mentally. Been locked up too long, they said. Not uncommon phenomenon. They offered him the use of a psychiatrist they kept on tap to deal with cases like his. Finally they called in a military lawyer who gave him a run-down on the law of libel and advised him to keep his mouth shut. Even if Jock's story were true, said the lawyer, and no one was accepting that it was, the evidence he offered was unsustainable in a court. All hearsay. If Wemyss made the story public, he'd be stuck with truly enormous damages. Particularly since Sepelov was something of a Canadian national hero and was about to become a big wheel in Canadian political life. Try defaming someone with that sort of reputation at stake and Wemyss would be ground to powder.'

'What did Wemyss do?'

'Not much. Went off to celebrate being free. Got a job. Got married.

Raised a family. He'd more to think about than Sepelov. Used to brood about him occasionally, but otherwise wrote him off as one of life's injustices. Shortly before he was married he went to Paris to look for Tante Marie, but that led nowhere.'

'He couldn't find her? Poor soul. Did the Germans kill her?'

'Not at all. Wemyss found her all right. Through some ex-Resistance set-up. She was OK and so, she said, were the rest of her escape-line friends. The Germans hadn't come near any of them. When Wemyss pressed about Sepelov she wouldn't hear a word against him. Let bygones be bygones. She may have had harsh things to say about him in the old days but that was all water under the bridge. She had misjudged him. He hadn't betrayed her and her chums, and he hadn't betrayed Wemyss, either. If he had, she'd have ended up in a concentration-camp and Wemyss would never have got past the controls at the Gare de Lyons. Sepelov was *très gentil*.'

'She'd hardly known him. How did she decide that he was *très gentil*?'

'You're right on the ball, Mrs Burke. She must have seen him again. Wemyss was certain about it. Sepelov must have been back and bribed every bugger in sight.'

Alice pondered and said: 'Two questions. Devil's advocacy.'

'Only two? I'm more convincing than I thought.'

'Two's enough. First one. Are you sure that it's the same Sepelov?'

'How many Canadian Sepelovs do you think there were who lost an eye at Dieppe, were captured, escaped, were decorated, lost a hand in Sicily, got decorated again . . .?'

'OK. Same Sepelov. Second question. Could it not have been a brilliant bluff? Sepelov goes to the Abwehr, spins them some persuasive story, offers to do whatever you like for them, cons them into helping him on his way to England, and goes back to war again. After all, he didn't shop Wemyss or Tante Marie's crowd, he was wounded and bemedalled again in Sicily, he ended the war in some senior job. . . .'

'I thought of that, too, and put it to Jock Wemyss. And he said that *he'd* thought of it also, and rejected it. His argument was that, if that was what had happened, Sepelov would have got in touch with him when he was released, and would have told him. After all, Sepelov had quite a bit of explaining to do. Wemyss never heard another word from him. Wemyss's other point was that if Sepelov had done that, and had got away with it, it would have been one of the outstanding escape stories of the war. Sepelov would have publicised it, and there'd have been books and a film and probably a television serial about it. There hasn't been a cheep.'

'Oliver, you brought this up. What's your explanation?'

'I haven't one. I always try to save up a good story for you on my birthday. Especially a true one with family connotations. After all, this is close to home. The man's Ulick's great-uncle. Helen's uncle-in-law. I suppose the bastard's even some connection by marriage of yours and mine. Just shows how careful you have to be about who you marry.'

Ulick and the girls, flushed and happy, came back from the Green. There were thank-yous, and avuncular hugs by Oliver of Brigid and Orla, and an unabashedly non-avuncular hug for Alice, and a friendly handshake for Ulick, and a tuneful drive home with the girls singing in the back seat of the car and with Alice and Ulick joining in the refrains.

CHAPTER TWENTY-SIX

THE WRITING-PAPER was engraved stylishly '49 Royal Marine Commando Reunion', below what Alice took to be a regimental badge: a globe of the world surrounded by a laurel wreath and surmounted by a crown. Underneath was 'Gibraltar', presumably a battle honour of special significance, and 'Per Mare Per Terram', which she translated for Ulick as 'By Sea, By Land'. The names, addresses and telephone numbers of the executive of the association were listed below the letterhead. The president, a knighted general with many letters after his name; the chairman, an un-knighted major with fewer letters; and the secretary and treasurer, Christian and surnames only with no following letters at all and not a Mr in front. To Alice it all looked very formally British and rather dauntingly hierarchical. There was nothing daunting about the style of the letter. The message was as friendly as could be.

Bob Hart, Hon. Sec., wrote that Johnny Laing had passed the Burkes' address to the committee. They would be delighted to have Hugo Burke's son and daughter-in-law as guests at their next annual dinner, to be held at a motel in Oxford. Dress would be informal, and so would the evening, aside from brief toasts and a couple of speeches to which a closely applied time-limit was enforced. In case they were worried about being marooned for the evening among a lot of boring old men talking about the war, they should know that several sons and daughters of members usually attended. A map with arrowed directions to the motel was efficiently attached, along with a booking-form for a room at a reduced, block-booked price.

'Well, that's warm and welcoming,' said Alice. 'I hope that all these decorated generals and majors aren't too pompous.'

'They'll eat out of your hand. Like Oliver and Paddy Madden.'

'What about your hand?'

'I'm not going.'

'Why not?'

'I'd be cheating. I'm not Hugo Burke's son. You're OK. You're writing your book. Makes an honest woman of you.'

'You're right, I suppose,' said Alice.

'You're dead right I'm right,' said Ulick.

He was, too, thought Alice. This was one of the occasions when he got straight to the core of an issue, unlike others when he was unable to recognise the issue at all.

She would miss his support in strange company. But his absence would hold one compensation: conversations carefully steered by her to where she wanted them to go would not be wrenched off course by Ulick's fastening on to some muscular old marine and diverting him to interminable discussion about the selection of a scrum-half for the next Lions tour, or whether euthanasia was the best cure for young louts who argued with umpires at Wimbledon.

She stayed with an academic friend at Somerville. When she reached the motel Laing was waiting to greet her in the foyer. He helped Alice off with her coat and checked it into the cloakroom. She looked around while she was waiting, and had no difficulty in identifying among the normal traffic of a big motel some gatherings of her hosts. Groups of middle-aged men, mostly of above-average size and with unusually straight backs, wearing identical striped ties with upthrust daggers sprinkled among the stripes, chatted comfortably with glasses in their hands, breaking off at intervals to shake hands cheerfully with new arrivals. Affable insult seemed to be in fashion.

'Hallo, Ron. They suspended your sentence, then?'

'Good to see you, Lofty. Herpes still troublesome?'

'You managed to wake up in time, Paddy?'

Laing took her by the elbow and led her to one of the downstairs bars. It was deserted. He ordered drinks and said: 'We're all meeting upstairs. I'm probably being unnecessarily solicitous, and wasting your time, but I brought you in here first because it occurred to me that you might feel slightly apprehensive, if that's the right word – thrown in among a lot of plummy-voiced old Brits, all stamping about and standing to attention, and calling each other 'sir' and 'Corporal'. Well, if you are, don't be. It's not like that. It's first names all round, and thoroughly relaxed. You won't be deafened by war-talk, either. It's just old friends with a shared past, meeting and enjoying themselves.'

Alice *had* been apprehensive. She was grateful to Laing, and she grinned, and raised her glass and said: 'Kind Johnny. Thank you.'

The upstairs bar was thronged, and buzzing with friendly chatter and calls of recognition. There was much laughter, and many a 'Hallo, Johnny' and 'This is Alice Burke, Hugo's daughter-in-law' and 'What will you have'. Laing introduced her to the knighted general and explained that he used to be their Colonel, 'who buggered us all about'. The General who used to be the Colonel said that he still would if he had half a chance, asked about Alice's book and told her not to pay too much attention to the lies that Laing would tell her. His own lies were much better than Johnny's lies, and if she wanted any help from him he would gladly give it.

'Thanks. I'll take you up on that. The Ministry of Defence in fact sent your name to me, but I'd already got on to Johnny through Paddy Madden.'

'Right. It's a deal. I'll give you my addr—'

'I have it, thanks. Bob Hart gave me the complete list.'

'You don't seem to have wasted any time. Any news of Helen? Hard to believe that you're married to her son. She was younger than you are now when I last saw her.'

'She was fine when I last saw her. In the spring in Ottawa. She lives there now.'

'The heart of the Hugo country. There was an uncle of Hugo's who came to see me once in Italy. A Canadian colonel. Some Russian-sounding name. Is he still around near Helen? I suppose Canada's so big that—'

'Andrei Sepelov?'

'That's him. You know him, do you?'

'Heard of him only.'

'Well, he's probably mellowed like the rest of us,' said the General ex-Colonel. He laughed. 'But, unless he's changed a great deal, he's one of the ones who're better heard of than met.'

'Why d'you say that?'

'I'll need notice of that question. I'm a sensitive man at heart. I might tell you when you come to see me. Also I might not. I'll think it over. That bunch lining up behind you were in Hugo's old section. Crowd of rogues. You'd better say hallo before they steal your money.'

Alice turned. Laing made the introductions.

'This is Busty Hankins, and Paddy O'Driscoll, Bob Hart you've met: Alice Burke, Hugo's daughter-in-law. The one who's writing that book that was mentioned in the newsletter. You'd better watch out what you say. It'll be immortalised in print. . . .'

The head waiter, an apprehensive-looking short fat man who had newly shaved, announced to the ladies and gentlemen that dinner was served.

O'Driscoll summed him up. 'The trouble with these young buggers', he said, 'is that they're thirty years behind the times. They think we're going to wreck the place.'

'Don't do it, Paddy,' said Hankins warningly.

There were no set places for dinner. The X Troop old-timers drifted towards a table set for eight, glittering with silver and glass, and with a red carnation in a vase in its middle. It matched the ones worn by all the womenfolk, presented to them, Alice included, by a burly, jovial, grey-haired man with a Yorkshire accent who kissed them benignly on the cheek as he made his offering.

'Don't let him try to pin it on,' said Hart. 'He'll do anything for a feel.'

They stood behind their chairs, chatting, the wives of Hart and Hankins with them, pleasant middle-aged women who volunteered their Christian names smilingly and were soon engrossed with concerned questioning with Laing about the state of his wife's flu. There was the sound of a spoon tinkling on glass, and then instant silence. A voice at a table at the far end of the room, behind Alice's back, said a one-sentence Grace. They sat down noisily. Menus were consulted, the wine-waiter instructed.

Talk was relaxed and comfortable. Of a group tour some of them had been on to Dalmatia, where the hospitality of former Partisans had been as dangerous as the war had ever been. Of grown-up children and new grandchildren and of what a bunch of layabouts the younger generation were. ('Not you, of course, Alice. You should have been born twenty years earlier. We'd have been queuing up for you'). Of two old friends who had died recently, one of drink, one from the delayed effects of wounds. Of what a pity it was that Hugo's son couldn't be there ('If he's anything like what his father was, you must have a lively life'). Of friendly, inconsequential everythings, almost none of which were about what she would write about. She wasn't worried. She liked these people. She was enjoying herself. She could grill them later, Laing had recommended, or could at any rate get their agreement to future visits.

Jack Ingram, a tall, lean, hoarse-voiced man at the far end of the table, turned to Hankins and said: 'Time to have another go at cracking the Mick code, Busty?'

'Be careful. He's brought reinforcements. Alice.'

'We'll get her on our side. Paddy O'Driscoll has a guilty secret,' Ingram explained to Alice. 'While we all have decent simple names and aren't ashamed of them, he's always hidden his. Calls himself F. James O'Driscoll. There's an annual bet on it. Drinks on him if we find out what the F's for. Drinks on us if we don't. We've tried 'em all. Fred and Frank and Ferdinand and anything else we can think of. The great lump gets his tank filled free every year at our expense. What's an Irish name beginning with F?'

'Fintan,' said Alice.

'No,' said O'Driscoll smugly.

'Fergus.'

'No.'

'Finbarr.'

'No.'

'That's three we never thought of,' said Hankins. 'I don't think he's got a name. He's just F. Like the S in Harry S. Truman.'

'It's a name right enough,' said O'Driscoll. 'A saint. Which is more than can be said of yours. Saint Busty, how are you? I suppose you're aiming for canonisation yourself.'

'Fechin,' said Alice.

O'Driscoll reddened. There was a roar of laughter.

'Would you mind saying that again?' said Ingram.

'Fechin,' said Alice firmly. 'He was an Irish saint.'

'Yes,' said O'Driscoll defiantly. There was more laughter, and delighted applause.

'Drinks on Fechin O'Driscoll,' said Hart. 'And about fechin time, too. That's what we used to call him anyway. "Fechin O'Driscoll's fechin fallen asleep again!" "Where's Fechin O'Driscoll got to now?" "What's the silly fecher . . .?"'

O'Driscoll grinned, winked at Alice and said: 'I must apologise for these crude English yobbos. Brishin an dhuacais tré shúile an chait!'

'Gan dabth ar bith,' said Alice, and winked back. O'Driscoll chuckled happily. So did Alice.

'God, she's broken the code and then betrayed us,' said Hankins. 'Conspiring with Fechin in fechin Erse.'

'*Erse*' said O'Driscoll. 'An 'earse is what they'll take 'Ankins's corpse to the graveyard in. 'Art's, too. The language is known as Irish.'

'OK, then, Irish. What does it mean?'

'You'd better tell them, Alice,' said O'Driscoll. 'They'll take it better from you. I've been persecuted by these people all my life. I don't want any more of it.'

'They won't banish me?'

'We might banish him,' said Hankins, 'but not you. Free pardon guaranteed.'

'Well, what he said was: "The breeding breaks through the eyes of the cat!"'

'He did, did he?'

'And what I said was: "Without a doubt in the world."'

'That leaves you in the clear. I don't see what else you could have said after that offensive nonsense of his. If this goes on, we'll need a simultaneous translation system at these dinners in future.'

'What we need at these dinners in future is more daughters-in-law,' said Ingram. 'About two to a table. . . .'

They don't have to do it, thought Alice, and they're going a long way round to do it, but they're doing it very nicely, and they're making me feel at home, and it's a pleasant, comfortable feeling.

She picked up a menu, folded, stiff, with a high gloss, a programme as much as a menu, with a globe and laurel embossed on its front and an elegant thin cord woven of navy blue, scarlet, yellow and green strands at its fold, the list of courses printed on one of its interior sides, the list of toasts on the other.

'This is a work of art,' she said to Johnny Laing.

'Louder,' said Laing. 'So that Bob Hart can hear. He prints them.'

'I heard her,' said Hart. 'Jack's wrong. We don't want two daughters-in-law a table in future. At least three.'

'What's the Silent Toast?' Alice asked.

'We stand in silence for a minute and think of dead friends.'

The spoon tinkled on the glass again. Conversation halted.

The General stood up, raised his glass and said: 'The Queen.'

Everybody else stood up, too, raised their glasses and said: 'The Queen.' Alice had never toasted the Queen before. In this company she found it no problem to do so.

The loyal toast over, cigarettes and here and there a cigar were lit. There was an appealing well-mannered discipline about these proceedings that she liked. The wine-waiters resumed business, with pints of bitter, and brandy for some. Chit-chat became less parochial. Chairs were turned to start discussions with neighbours at adjacent tables. The noise grew. Again the tinkling spoon, and quiet.

A bishop, wearing a dark suit and a mauve dicky beneath his clerical collar ('Used to be our padre,' Laing had said. 'We called him Bish then. He's a proper one now') proposed The Silent Toast in those three words. They all stood again.

For the first time during the evening Alice felt an outsider. These men, suddenly serious, were thinking of a past that she would try her best to represent on paper. She would never, she knew, be entirely successful. Their minds were on events that occurred before she was born, in circumstances that only they could truly remember. They were commemorating the short lives of people whom she had never known, whom they had lived and worked with side by side for months, years on end, who had died violently and who but for fate or chance might instead have been here tonight, thinking of them. She supposed that some of the people around her were simply thinking affectionate thoughts, and that some were praying, but there was no way of telling and it would be an unforgivable intrusion even to try to calculate what was behind the quiet, impassive faces. She herself said a little prayer for all these friendly men who had been kind to her, and another for all the unknown absent ones who hadn't survived, and a special one for Hugo Burke, who was responsible for her being here.

The speeches, as forecast in Bob Hart's letter of invitation, were few and short. They were also presumably witty, because they generated much laughter, but were so rich in allusion to bygone happenings as to be largely incomprehensible to Alice and to the rest of the female laity. Ron

Oakes, the carnation-presenter, ran a raffle for bottles of whisky and boxes of chocolates amidst a general sardonic commentary about the system he operated to corner the prizes for himself. There was a gradual shift from the tables to the bar, kept open especially late for the occasion.

There Paddy Madden, whose aircraft had been delayed and whose late arrival at the dinner had prompted an ironic outbreak of cheering, came to say hallo to her, asked her if she found the frigid formality of the occasion to be too much for her, and bought her a drink. Laing, Hankins, O'Driscoll, Ingram and Hart treated her like a baton in a relay race, ensuring that one of them was always with her, relinquishing her to the next with flattering reluctance, introducing her to everyone that they thought she should meet. She absorbed a great deal of information, and of knowledge about how to get further information, of value to her book and of interest about Hugo Burke. She pressed no particular line of enquiry. She simply listened to volunteered recollections, unsentimental, some doubtless distorted by time. She shamelessly wrote down names and key phrases to jog her memory. She asked permission to get in touch later with some, and was given an enthusiastic assent.

At midnight she decided that it was time to leave. This was their own evening, and it only came up once a year, and it was right that they should have what was left of it entirely to themselves. She bade her goodbyes. Laing collected her coat from the cloakroom and saw her to her taxi. As he held open the door for her she said: 'I'd no idea you'd spent your youth with such delightful people.'

Laing laughed. 'They didn't look all that delightful at the time,' he said. 'I don't suppose I did, either.'

He thought for a little and then laughed again. 'You should know', he said, 'that you've attracted the highest possible praise. "Smashing bint, that Alice" was what Reg Skinner called you.'

Alice chuckled, and waved goodbye as the taxi drove off. Later, she fell into a deep sleep, feeling flattered and contented.

Ulick was awaiting her at Dublin Airport. He kissed her and took her bag.

'How were the brutal British soldiery?' he asked once the car was under way.

'They couldn't have been more welcoming. I don't think that I'd have wanted to get on the wrong side of any of them when they were young, but they looked after me marvellously.'

'Get much for the book?'

'A lot of useful background stuff. Nothing dramatic. It wasn't that sort of evening. Mostly funny bits, and things that went wrong. Like how they got accidentally gassed in some vehicles with the exhausts in the wrong place and ended up staggering drunk. But I've a whole list of names and addresses, and invitations to come and see them or write to them. And stop looking jealous. They're all old enough to be your father.'

'One of them probably is,' said Ulick gloomily.

'There were several who knew your mother.'

'I bet there were,' said Ulick. 'Any of them look like me?'

'Not that I noticed. There was a nice old general who used to be their colonel who was asking after her. Said she used to be beautiful. I said that she still was. And a whole lot more who'd been wounded – they *all* seem to have been wounded, some of them two or three times – who ended up in the hospital where she was working. There was one named Busty Hankins who was Hugo's sergeant. He was badly hurt at the same time as Hugo was killed. He was full of admiration for Helen and the way she continued to help people after she'd been told that Hugo was dead. She must have been in a terrible state, he said, but she just got on with it. You know, I hadn't realised any of this before, hadn't known of it, but your mother must have—'

'Yes,' said Ulick, 'she must have. I hadn't realised it, either. It's good to hear of it. She's never spoken about that side of things, and I've never really given it any thought. I can imagine how bad it was for any woman to be at home and to be sent a telegram to say that her husband was dead. It must have been a damned sight worse to be told that you're a widow while you were looking after people who knew your husband, and then have to go on looking after them, pretending to be cheerful.'

Alice was silent for a moment, thinking of what it was like all those years before for the mother of this live husband sitting beside her, driving skilfully through chaotic traffic, thinking the same thoughts that she was thinking.

'I'd squeeze your hand if you weren't driving,' she said at last.

'Squeeze my leg instead,' said Ulick.

'Why's this fellow Busty Hankins called Busty?' asked Ulick, braking reflexively to save the life of a dome-helmeted motorcyclist, who acknowledged his endowed survival with a fierce two-finger signal and a roar of 'Fukkya'.

'I asked about that. He was a physical-fitness freak when he was young. Like you. He had a big busty chest.'

'Like me? I thought you said that none of them looked like me. Are you seriously trying to tell me that I've a father with a name like Busty Hankins. God Almighty. . . .'

'Like you as a fitness fanatic. Not like you in appearance. He's a short, dark man, about as wide as he's tall.'

'Sounds deformed,' said Ulick.

'He was nice,' said Alice.

'Are you sure it was his own big, busty chest he was concentrating on? Not my mother's? Or yours for that matter?'

'Fairly sure,' said Alice.

After supper that evening Alice went through her notes. She was by now keeping them in two separate cross-referenced folders. One, growing satisfyingly thicker, held material for the book – a historian's material, as accurate as she could establish it, sources carefully recorded, differing versions of the same event checked one against the other, reconciled or, where they were irreconcilable, discrepancies analysed dispassionately. The other folder, marked *Hugo* on its cover, was more diffuse. Its contents were unhampered by professional constraints. She put into it a summary of everything that she had heard or read about him, and added without inhibition comment and conjecture as they occurred to her.

When she had added her Oxford gleanings to each collection she reread the *Hugo* folder several times. There was something in it that puzzled her. Everyone whom she had met who had known Hugo Burke had spoken well of him. They would. He was long since dead, and they knew that they were talking to his daughter-in-law, although the praise had been so unanimous and unequivocal as to be altogether convincing. That was Hugo as a man. Hugo as a resourceful soldier had been even more highly talked of: reliable and quick-thinking, always several moves ahead of the game, adding an entertaining seasoning of eccentricity to his activities. But when you studied one thread that ran through the eccentricities they began to seem like near-irresponsibilities.

He had wandered off on his own at Risan and had got himself captured. Johnny Laing had described this as 'plain bloody silly', but had laughed when he said it, and had offset the criticism by remarking that Hugo's performance on that occasion had been all of a piece with some of his previous unorthodoxies on his island reconnaissances. Then he had got away with it, and it had paid military dividends. At Risan his luck had run out.

Inexperienced, unqualified Alice would accept that judgement from experienced, qualified Johnny Laing. But it was a judgement made in isolation. What did it look like when set beside some of Busty Hankins's cheerfully fond recollections? Alice was totally ignorant of the tactics of patrolling, but it seemed to her that for a man commanding a patrol simply to get up without explanation and roam away from it for long periods, and to do it not on one patrol but repeatedly on a series of them, was inefficient. Hankins had spoken of it as the quirk of an individualist, a man who liked to hunt alone, a matter for irritation and worry at the time, a matter now for wry retrospective amusement.

But would it have been so funny if something had gone seriously wrong? If Hugo himself had stumbled into something that he was unable to deal with, as he had once before at Risan? There *had* been an incident, smoothly summarised in that cyclostyled unit history, more earthily told by two of the participants, Hankins and O'Driscoll, when a fight had developed with Hugo not present at its initial stages. That had been the one on the beach, a few days before Commachio, controlled by Hankins until Hugo had suddenly reappeared and by all accounts had extricated the patrol brilliantly.

What if he hadn't reappeared in time? He would presumably have stood – and rightly, so far as Alice could see – convicted of negligence or worse. He had got out of that one because, aside from rather tardily applied skill, he clearly had the quality most valued by Napoleon in his marshals: luck. Or had had it, with the one aberration at Risan, until he was killed. But – and it nagged at her – was there not a flaw in the pattern of Hugo Burke *beau sabreur*?

She leafed through the rest of the file and glanced again at one of the earlier entries, photocopies that she had made from the folder about Hugo that Ulick had brought back from his mother in Ottawa. There were three printed articles dating from 1940, one from the *Irish Times*, two from a now-dead College magazine, *TCD*. There was nothing to indicate where Helen had got them from. The first said that Hugo had been an accomplished actor. The second that he was an outstanding Rugby-player with an exceptional sense of anticipation. The third that he had made a memorable speech to the College Historical Society about the communist threat to Christian civilisation, on entirely defensible premises that none the less bore the inherited imprint of the philosophy of the Burke Foundation.

A flair for acting, she supposed, must have a part in military or any other sort of leadership. Athleticism and an anticipatory gift would have been assets in a junior officer. Political polemics would have been irrelevant. The articles were touching memorabilia preserved by a widow, but had no particular bearing on Alice's present purposes.

Ulick's television débâcle had enraged Sepelov, but it also led to the concentration of his mind upon thoughts that had simmered for some time. He was now into his seventies. He was active, healthy and shrewd, but he could not go on for much longer. He continued to work efficiently to the achievement of the objectives that he had set for the Burke Foundation. He also began a long, leisurely self-questioning examination of its future. His conclusion was that it hadn't one. It had, in a changed world, outlived its original purpose.

Modern Western governments needed no persuasion of the existence of a communist military threat, as had their predecessors in the twenties and thirties, the halcyon days of Foundation activity. The armed forces of modern Western governments were in NATO, lined up against those of the Warsaw Pact. The dangers of communist subversion might still be ignored by the gullible, but they were recognised and attended to by national intelligence services with resources and of a sophistication that even a wealthy private organisation like the Burke Foundation could not match. The Foundation's anti-communist propaganda output was becoming redundant. The independent media, and government information services, needed no prodding from a body that a sceptical younger generation was coming to regard as reactionary, fuddy-duddy and suspect. The supply of dissidents and refugees to be rescued had diminished almost to nothing. The old ones had been got out, had died in their gaols or had compromised with their consciences.

Sepelov had always been unsentimental in his professional assessments. He now reduced the number of available courses of action open to him to two. He could either devise a modified charter for a redesigned Foundation that would use the acquired experience and skills of the old one to complement the efforts of governmental bodies now doing what the Foundation had once done; or, more drastically, he could simply close down, make adequate financial provision for loyal former employees, disentangle the Burke family funds from the capital assets, and distribute the huge remaining balance among those who would use it to do the most of what Sepelov saw as good.

He had a slight preference for the first alternative. He chose the second. He had, he told himself, achieved enough to afford a pleasurable vengeance upon several people who had thwarted him.

He went into long and discreet discussion with his confidential legal and financial advisers. The processes of orderly, publicly imperceptible dismantlement were set in train. Sepelov turned his mind to other matters, suppressed for years by a steely self-discipline.

CHAPTER TWENTY-SEVEN

'ARE YOU the beautiful Mrs Burke?' asked the voice, a North American one.

'I am indeed the beautiful Mrs Burke,' said Alice. 'How did you *know?*'

'Well, since you answered on the number Oolick gave me, and he told me that Mrs Burke was beautiful, I strung the facts together and made an educated guess.'

'I can't keep up with this,' said Alice. 'You sound as if you must be Smithy. From Ottawa.'

'The very same,' said the voice. 'I'm in Dublin.'

'Come round for a drink,' said Alice. 'Ulick will be back in ten minutes or so. He's gone out for a run.'

'The spirit of Black Dick Burke, our hyper-active Founder, lingers on,' said Smithy. 'How do I get there?'

Alice told him.

Smithy was a good guest. He touched briefly upon his metabolic disabilities and drank orange juice, thus putting himself in step with Alice, who was scrupulously evading Foetal Alcohol Syndrome. He talked amusingly of this and that, reminisced with Ulick about what he called Canadian Television's Greatest Day, offered some scurrilous comment upon Andrei Sepelov and stayed to supper. A few neatly worded phrases of culinary appreciation further endeared him to Alice, as did his offer to do the washing-up. He was sipping a cup of coffee when he said suddenly: 'I'm enjoying myself so much I almost forgot why I came. To see you again, Oolick, and to meet the lovely Alice, but also to report progress.'

'Progress?' said Ulick.

'Yep. The digging into the foundations of the Foundation. I've found a few constructional flaws. I'm still working on it, and there's plenty more to come, but there are two bits of dirt that I think'll interest you. I've written them up for you. They're still raw, and I'll have to do a lot more refining before I let them loose publicly, but I think you should take a look at them. Specifically the second one. It's a little – er – delicate.

Can I get my briefcase from that chair in the hallway?'

'Please do,' said Alice.

'What's the delicate one about?' said Ulick.

'Your father,' said Smithy as he rose to his feet.

What Smithy had to say was embodied in about thirty pages of double-spaced typescript, clipped into two separate sections and enclosed in a brown folder. He brought the folder into the room, sat down and said: 'Who will I give it to?'

'Alice,' said Ulick promptly, mercifully. 'She looks after these matters for me,' he added grandly, equally mercifully, and entirely infuriatingly.

'Before I give them to anyone,' said Smithy, 'there's something I want to say. About both these pieces really, but particularly about the second one. The delicate one. Oolick, I don't know what age you are but, whatever it is, you can't have remembered much about your father Hugo.'

'He wasn't. . . .'

'Ulick never met him at all,' said Alice. 'I'm sorry to interrupt but, as he so rightly said, I look after these matters for him. We might as well be consistent.'

'Well, that simplifies things a bit. There's some stuff in this that puts Hugo Burke in a fairly – ah – ambiguous light. It could shift his image a bit. I'm gunning for Sepelov, but I don't want to hurt anyone unnecessarily. If you want Hugo Burke left out of it, I'll leave him out. You don't even have to read it if you don't want to. There's plenty more I can draw on. You just tell me to forget about it, and I'll take it away and destroy it.'

'Let's read it first,' said Alice. 'Then we can make up our minds. Is that OK?'

'OK. Part Two of the proposition. I'm having a go at Sepelov, and when this gets published it won't do him much good. It won't do the Burke Foundation much good, either. I don't mean it'll destroy it. I'd like to make clear here my view that the Foundation does a lot of good. But there have been abuses. By Sepelov. Some of the mud I'll fire at Sepelov will stick, for a time at least, to the Foundation. Does that upset anyone?'

Alice thought fast. It certainly wouldn't upset her. Or Ulick, who wouldn't recognise it as upsetting. Helen? She didn't know. The Hugo element very probably would. The Foundation element was less certain. 'Same answer as before,' said Alice. 'Read it first. Comment later.'

'Sure. I'm off to Munich and thereabouts to do some more muck-raking first thing in the morning. I'll be back in a few days. Tell me then.'

He gave the folder to Alice. If she were to make sense of what was in it, he said, she'd need to know something of the background. The two pieces were distilled from long talks that he had had with two people. He'd better explain how he found the people. And, for that matter, why he'd started looking for them in the first place. Which would mean that he'd have to give Oolick and Alice a run-through of an autobiographical fragment that would flow a little more smoothly if he first had a proper drink – on the strict understanding that if he asked for more than two Alice would guarantee to hit him over the head and throw him out of the house.

Ulick gave him the drink. Alice gave him the guarantee.

When Smithy had first gone to the Burke Foundation as its Public Relations Director he had been received warmly by Sepelov, given a free hand and a handsome budget, and told simply to get on with it. He attended Sepelov's short morning meetings of heads of department, so as to keep himself abreast of current developments. Once a week he reported orally to Sepelov on what he was doing, what he intended to do, and was told what in addition Sepelov wanted him to do. Sepelov ran a tight ship, and an efficient one. He believed in delegating responsibility. Thereafter he backed or sacked, depending upon performance.

Smithy found the work to be enjoyable and satisfying. His own thinking was in rough accord with the objectives of the Foundation. He was by no means a doctrinaire commie-basher. He conceded that in some societies – mostly ones in which he himself would hate to live – communist regimes were an improvement upon the entrenched, stratified injustice and exploitation that had preceded them. Sepelov would not have shared this view, but Smithy was at one with Sepelov on a broader, essential issue. Smithy objected to the attempt to export and impose communism universally and indiscriminately through violence and guile.

Smithy's first few months in the job thus passed happily and smoothly. He began to be troubled when, because of the nature of his work, he had looked closely into what everyone in the place was doing, and it became clear that information was being withheld from him. He went to see Sepelov about this. Smithy argued that if he were to operate with full effectiveness he must have access to knowledge of everything that was being done. Unless he knew the background to what was in progress he would be handicapped in tailoring his propaganda output to its full potential. He would be in danger of including things that would be better omitted, of being too cautious about other things that would benefit from a public airing, of misjudging emphases.

Sepelov was abrupt and dismissive. Smithy, he said, was being told everything that he needed to know for the effective discharge of his responsibilities. There were some matters that were no concern of his, or of anyone other than those dealing with them. End of interview.

Smithy's next discovery was of who some of 'those dealing with them' were. They had no offices in the Foundation building, and they seemed to drop in as necessary, or be summoned by Sepelov as necessary, to *ad hoc* discussions, individually, sometimes in groups, that were given an exclusive, overriding priority above all Sepelov's other activities. What they talked about nobody knew. Sepelov's door was locked on these occasions, with a 'Do not disturb' notice attached to it. Discreet questioning of colleagues about these people drew obliquely humorous references to 'Spooks' and a gently worded private hint that the last man to show overmuch zeal in trying to find out about them was still out of work.

No form of human activity that required continuity could, however, be conducted without some system of records. It did not take Smithy long to find out that the records of this Spook inner ring were maintained in a room shielded by an innocuous-seeming green-baize door that stood behind Sepelov's desk. Sepelov was closing the door one day when Smithy walked into his room. The door was sufficiently far open for Smithy to see behind it a steel grille like the ones in a police lock-up, backed by a heavy steel door guarded by combination locks. The whole set-up looked to Smithy 'like the security zone in a goddamned embassy'. Two otherwise inexplicably placed employees, who at erratic intervals sat at desks in the private secretary's office adjoining Sepelov's, presumably serviced the contents of this fastness. One of the two was a large silent man with a crewcut who looked like an ex-Mountie. The other was a middle-aged stringbag of a woman who looked like nothing on earth. Both were as impermeable as sources of information as the strongroom was impenetrable. Smithy wasted time on neither.

Smithy had complete latitude to divide his day up as he found fit. He had become curious. He spent an increasing amount of time in the Foundation's unclassified registry and its adjacent storeroom, which between them held the uncontroversial files on every activity in which the organisation had been engaged since its inception. Smithy said – and it was true – that he was preparing a series of press releases on the more outstanding of the Foundation's earlier achievements. At the same time – and he did not say it to anyone – he was seeking signs of a phenomenon that he had first come across as a young trainee reporter.

He had then been given the joyless task of sifting through huge quantities of government records recently released for public scrutiny. Smithy had been instructed to find snippets around which a story or two that might interest his newspaper's readers could be written. Many of the classified files in the collection, and all the ones that could shed light on bygone scandals, incompetences, maladministration and internal bickering, had been carefully weeded of sensitive papers. Smithy's discovery, one that, although he did not know it at the time, had been made by many a researcher before him, was that, however ruthlessly conscientious the weeders were in removing the more obvious evidence from the main files, a remarkable amount of revealingly indicative matter could be unearthed by casual devilling in routine papers to do with innocent-seeming subjects grouped under such headings as Welfare, Finance and the archivist's despairing last resort, Miscellaneous Correspondence.

From these fringe sources Smithy began to assemble an engrossing but formless list of unexplained references to payments for unexplained services, the meeting of hospital bills and funeral expenses, the funding of complicated journeys to unspecified destinations, and *ex gratia* lump-sum grants. There were solicitous enquiries about whether someone or other had yet recovered from the hardships of his last job, and there were offers of further employment to people who had given satisfaction in the past. In some cases names, mostly Slavic, were named. In a few there were addresses. All these letters had been filed haphazardly among others that dealt with the identifiably legitimate business of the Founda-tion. Smithy, a frequent patron of the registry's photocopying machine, photocopied all that interested him for his private purposes. When Sepelov sacked him after Ulick's television débâcle, Smithy took his purloined collection of papers with him.

It was from the nuggets spread sparsely and at random among this previously unmapped vein that he had ultimately identified, located and interviewed the sources of the information that was in the folder that he had given to Alice. There had been a mass of frustrations met with, and blind alleys entered, in the course of his search, which had also demanded persistence, patience, ingenuity and a natural flair for detec-tive work of such a high order that he felt no embarrassment in asking Oolick to top his glass up, provided that Alice would confirm his own impression that he had so far had only one of the covenanted two. Alice did.

Smithy bade a grateful goodbye and left for his hotel and an early-morning flight to Munich. Ulick went early to bed to fit himself for his next day's exertions. Alice sat up until one o'clock in the morning, reading Smithy's folder, reading some bits of it again and again, checking it against material in her Hugo file, and against remembered fragments of past conversations. By the time that she went to bed she had, she was sure, assembled almost the entire jigsaw puzzle. The few missing pieces were with Oliver. She hadn't quite made up her mind whether or not to compare notes with Oliver, but she thought that she probably would. Before she fell asleep she said a special prayer for poor Hugo Burke.

CHAPTER TWENTY-EIGHT

THE FIRST of Smithy's two bits of dirt had come from an old Croat named Stanko Mikic, who lived in Regina, Saskatchewan. He would not live there for much longer. He was suffering from terminal cancer. He was also suffering from an unsettled resentment to do with the inflated public regard in which a man known to Mikic to be a liar and a consorter with his country's wartime enemies had continued to be held in that country, now also Mikic's. Mikic had been one of the country's enemies with whom Andrei Sepelov had consorted, in his case in the Vatican.

Smithy had traced him through the beneficiary of a lump-sum payment who featured in one of the Foundation's welfare files, who had a grievance, who passed Smithy on to a friend, who in turn pointed him to Stanko Mikic.

Mikic as a young man in Zagreb had been a political activist of versatility, an unstable romantic concerned with being politically active for its own sake. In the early 1930s he joined assiduously in ill-understood protests, and fought in street fights, and was beaten up by the Royal Yugoslav Police, and kept getting put into gaol and let out again. He was an articulate polemicist with a developed hatred for Serbs, and he drifted naturally into the wilder reaches of extreme Croatian nationalism. His status on the police Wanted List rose from minor nuisance to dangerous menace. He escaped to exile in Italy, where he helped Ante Pavelic to polish his scheme for an independent State of Croatia.

Mikic was a languages graduate of Zagreb University. When not carried away by an urge towards melodrama and martyrdom, he was a cultured sophisticate entirely at home among concert halls, art galleries, theatres, in the drawing-rooms and at the dinner-tables of the influential and wealthy.

He became an unofficial Ustacha diplomatic agent. His task was to seek the support of bodies that could reasonably be assumed to be predisposed in favour of the ideal of the setting up of a Catholic Croatian State, committed to traditional values, heirs to all that had been best in a historic and heroic people who for centuries had defended the marches of Christendom against the Islamic inroads of the Ottoman Empire and against the schismatic followers of the Christian Eastern Orthodox churches.

Mikic did his job very well. Surprisingly, he did it with discretion. One of his earlier contacts, met in Naples through the agency of a sympathetic Croatian monsignor in the Vatican Secretariat, was with Andrei Sepelov of the Burke Foundation, an embittered young Russian refugee who had been brought up in Canada.

It soon became clear to Mikic that if Sepelov's objectives were broadly compatible with the aims set out in the Foundation's publicity-sheets the methods that he was prepared to use to achieve them went considerably further. Sepelov was an extremist and an intriguer. So, at that time, was Mikic. They found much in common.

Sepelov spoke with candour. The Foundation's prime concern was with frustrating communism. The current absolute priority was to the backing of General Franco in the Spanish Civil War. There were sinister manifestations of communist advancement in most Western European countries, notably France. The future establishment of a Croatian Catholic bastion had its attractions, and the concept fitted in with a pessimistic, and on the whole accurate, analysis of the short-term prospects that Sepelov offered on the European future. But at the moment there was nothing that the Foundation could, or should, do about it. The kingdom of the Serbs, Croats and Slovenes had its imperfections, but it was a kingdom, it was Christian, and it was ruthless in eliminating communism.

The existing regime was one that the Foundation wished to sustain, not to subvert. In any case, added Sepelov sardonically, Mikic had picked the wrong man to talk about all this with. Sepelov himself was of the Russian Orthodox faith, with an affinity for Serbs, not Croats. He certainly had no intention of recommending that the Foundation should involve itself in a late instalment of a longstanding traditional Balkan race-war.

But what he would like to do, he said, was to keep in contact with Mikic. Informally, sporadically, nothing systematic about it. A time, unforeseeable, might come when the association could be of mutual value. They kept in touch. The frequency of the contacts diminished when Sepelov joined the Canadian Army on the outbreak of war in 1939, and ceased altogether when Germany invaded Yugoslavia in 1941.

The value of the contact was put to the test with the occupation of Rome in June 1944 by troops of the United States Fifth Army. Mikic, still in Italy, still a Ustacha diplomatic envoy, by now of a functioning puppet government of a ramshackle Independent State of Croatia, was left behind when the Germans withdrew northwards. He prudently removed himself to the sanctuary provided in the Vatican by his friend the Croatian monsignor. The monsignor, like Stanko Mikic, was gravely concerned by the turn that events were taking in his native land.

The dominant domestic military force in Yugoslavia was now the communist-led Partisan movement. When the Germans lost the war, as they would, a post-war communist Yugoslav government was inevitable. Croatia would cease to be either independent or a state, and there would be pitiless reprisals upon those who had temporarily made it both.

There was little to be saved from the forthcoming wreckage except people, and not very many people. The monsignor and Mikic settled down to the preparation of a shortlist of those who would be most worth saving: the exemplars and practitioners of everything good in an ancient heritage. It was a wholly unemotional compilation. Only those who demonstrably possessed a physical and mental stamina that matched their intellectual and moral gifts were included.

After deciding upon who should be rescued, which was relatively easy, the monsignor and Mikic went on to consider how to rescue them, which wasn't easy at all. Clearly there must be outside help. The victorious Allies would have little sympathy for the vicissitudes of people whom they would see as traitorous collaborators, not as guardians of Christian spiritual values. Mikic was the one who suggested that they might try their luck with the Burke Foundation.

Ten days later, a one-eyed, one-handed Canadian lieutenant-colonel from the intelligence staff at Allied Forces Headquarters at Caserta called upon the monsignor. Later, Mikic was invited to the meeting. His reunion with Andrei Sepelov was warm.

Sepelov studied the list jointly prepared by the monsignor and Mikic. He was brisk and incisive.

Yes, said Sepelov, if at all possible these people must be got out.

When? Not yet. It would be cowardly for them to run away while fellow-Croats were still fighting. It would destroy their later credibility. Their recovery was in any case physically impossible at the moment. It would have to await the confusion that followed the end of any war.

How? The first leg of their individual departures would be up to them. They would have to make their own way to the Yugoslav frontiers with Italy or Austria, the other side of which would by then be controlled by the British Eighth Army. The legitimate British would doubtless refuse them entry. Sepelov was confident that he could arrange secure alternative crossing-points. He could only decide where they should be and how they would operate in the light of the conditions that would prevail at the time.

Once, or if, the refugees were safely over the frontier, where would they go, and how would they go there? Perhaps the monsignor could help? The monsignor said that he had already made useful progress on a scheme for the succouring, provision of passports, and onward transmission to Latin America of selected leading Germans who came into much the same category as the Croats they were discussing. Mikic was surprised. He was more surprised when Sepelov smiled broadly and said that he was glad that that was coming along well. He himself had made some of the tentative preliminary arrangements during talks that he had had in Paris with the Abwehr. He did not elaborate. Mikic wasn't sure if it were true. He did not understand how it could have been.

One problem left in abeyance was that of how to pass information and instructions to the Ustachi escapers. The only channel available to the monsignor was through the Spanish ambassador, who could transmit messages to his colleague in Berlin, who could ask the Germans to send them onwards through their people in Zagreb. It would be potentially lethal. If the Germans and Pavelic found out that leading Croatian nationalists were involved in contingency planning for escape after defeat, they would soon be dead Croatian nationalists. Fanatics, Nazi or Ustachi, would make short shrift of renegade despairers of victory.

Sepelov said offhandedly that he would go away and think about it. He did. It was some weeks, and several more visits, before he said that he might have found a solution. It wasn't a very satisfactory one, and he hoped to be able to devise something better, but it could work.

A young British officer whom he had known since he was a child, and who was imbued with the principles that guided the monsignor, Mikic and Sepelov himself, had for the past few months been operating with the British force based upon the Dalmatian island of Vis. The force was due to be withdrawn shortly to Italy, after which some of it, including the young officer, would go to Montenegro. He had all the singleminded impetuosity of youth, and was totally dedicated to the soldiers he worked with and to the job that he was doing, but Sepelov was in no doubt that if he were worked upon skilfully he could be persuaded to subordinate his present narrow loyalties to those of a more universally applicable set of philosophical and ethical values. Sepelov would personally put the indoctrination process in train as soon as the young man returned from Vis. What Sepelov had in mind for him would be dangerous, and would require a high level of resourcefulness and ingenuity, but fortunately the boy was exceptionally brave, resourceful and ingenious.

The indoctrination would be unnecessarily complicated, added Sepelov with a laugh, by the fact that the fellow had recently fallen in love. Sepelov was confident that he would be able to overcome that obstacle, too.

Mikic's account ended in simple bathos. He slipped on some wet stone steps and broke his leg. While in hospital he pondered deeply upon his political philosophy, decided that he had been wrong about Fascism, and became an enthusiast for parliamentary democracy. The monsignor looked after him during his convalescence, excluded him from his councils, shielded him until well after the war was over, and equipped him when the time came with suitable documentation for emigration to the parliamentary democracy of his choice, Canada. Mikic never met Sepelov in Canada. It was the sight of him on television screens, being deferred to while he pontificated about liberty and loyalty, that had been at the root of Mikic's wrath.

The subject of Smithy's second summary was a man named Achmet Rashidov, who lived in Winnipeg. Smithy had picked his name and address from a Finance file. Rashidov was unusual in that he had returned uncashed a cheque for five thousand dollars sent to him by the Foundation. His short accompanying letter read in its entirety: 'You will not buy my silence.' Smithy went to see him.

He was a short, voluble, sallow man with high cheekbones and almost imperceptible eyes, who owned a small and clearly lucrative supermarket. Rashidov had met Sepelov after Sepelov had addressed a Kiwani's lunch about the evils of communism. Rashidov had gone up to him afterwards and had said that he himself had personal experience of the evils of communism. He had also experience of the evils of fascism, and of the evils of British democratic, bureaucratic callousness. Would Sepelov like a written account? Sepelov said: Yes, please. Send it to the Foundation. Rashidov had done so, and had received an enthusiastic reply. Sepelov proposed to publicise it in the Foundation's next broadsheet and would leave out all the stuff about fascist brutality and British callousness. That would only diminish the force of its impact. His interest was solely with an indictment of communism.

Rashidov wrote back to say that he had more cause than most to loathe communism, but that he didn't want the thing to be out of balance. The point of Rashidov's story was to emphasise that human viciousness was a widespread malaise, not confined to any one people or political theory. Sepelov could publish all of it, or none of it.

There followed much blustering by Sepelov and stonewalling by Rashidov. Eventually Sepelov, with the confidence of a rich man who had rarely failed to buy anything or anyone that he wanted, had sent the cheque 'to cover Rashidov's expenses', and had said that he would go ahead with publication on the lines that he favoured. Rashidov's reply ended the argument.

Smithy would probably have abandoned the interview at that point if he had been able with reasonable courtesy to stop Rashidov from talking.

By origin Rashidov was a Tatar, born in the Caucasus in the early 1920s in a nomadic society whose ways had stayed fundamentally unchanged for centuries. Their incorporation into the Tsarist Empire during the period of major Russian expansionism in the nineteenth century had meant little to them, and the ideological pedantry to which they had been exposed after the Revolution, an upheaval that had passed largely unnoticed by them, had meant less. They continued in their immemorial cycle of lonely migration from one exhausted grazing-land to another that had been given time to recover. That there might be other peoples in other parts of creation who lived differently was beyond either their understanding or their interest.

Towards the end of 1941, Achmet Rashidov was conscripted into the Red Army. The recruitment was conducted in much the manner and spirit in which cattle are collected for market. He and his companions were given rudimentary training and primitive weapons, and were put – driven – into battle against German Panzer divisions. Rashidov was one of the hundreds of thousands of Red Army soldiers to be taken into captivity during the Wehrmacht's early deep penetration into Russia.

Conditions for the prisoners were abominable. The Soviet Government was not a signatory to the Geneva Conventions, and disdained German attempts to negotiate *ad hoc* arrangements by which the prisoner-of-war camps of both sides would have been opened to inspection and supervision by the International Red Cross. The Soviet attitude was a simple one. Red Army soldiers did not surrender. They were too exalted by their faith in their cause to do so. The claim that huge numbers of them had was mendacious German propaganda. There was no point in setting up machinery to protect the interests of non-existent captives.

The Germans had no difficulty in substantiating their propaganda. Newsreel pictures and conducted tours by the neutral press followed. The Soviet line changed. The prisoners were transformed from publicity myths into traitors marked down for future punishment. Soldiers who had been overrun while incapacitated by wounds, or who had been rounded up without food, ammunition and water after Russian generals had been out-manoeuvred and out-gunned by German ones, or who had otherwise become victims of the misfortunes of war, were disowned, denigrated and condemned *in absentia*.

Few of them knew it. Their German captors, unaffected because of the Soviet's abandonment of the interests of their citizens by inhibitions that indifferent treatment of Russian prisoners in their hands could lead to the reciprocal mishandling of German prisoners in Russian hands, behaved towards these *untermenschen* as they customarily behaved towards *untermenschen*. The prisoners, starving, rotting and dying by the thousand in crowded, insanitary cages, some of them taking to cannibalism to stay alive, were given hope by General Vlassov.

Vlassov was an able young Red Army general who had been captured early on by the Germans and had changed sides. His proclaimed motives were disillusionment and disgust at Stalinist hypocrisy, corruption, cynicism and incompetence. Stalin, said Vlassov, had betrayed the principles of the Revolution. There might, of course, have been more behind Vlassov's defection than that, but it was enough for him to be commissioned to raise an army recruited from Russian prisoners to fight alongside the Germans.

Rashidov was one of Vlassov's early recruits. He was sent to the Turcoman Division that was forming at Neuhammer in Silesia. For the first time in his brief soldiering experience he was properly housed, fed, clothed, administered, equipped and trained. Chance, and ethnic origin, had brought him to the only one of Vlassov's formations that was to see any serious fighting.

162 Turcoman Division went to Italy in the middle of 1944. It operated throughout the winter and spring. Its survivors once again became captives, this time of the British, when the Division laid down its arms near Padua at the time of the German surrender in May 1945. Rashidov was not with it. He had been taken prisoner in April, at Argenta.

From the day of his capture he had been beset by two worries. The first was a shared one. For the past few years his thoughts and longings, like those of many.another soldier in every army, had centred upon an end to the war and a return home. He was a simple man, and the idea had never entered into his mind that he might be less than welcome when he got there. He now had alarming evidence of what would await him.

A fellow-soldier, a Talmuk, had been captured by the American Fifth Army during mountain fighting in the previous autumn. The Talmuk had been repatriated through Odessa, under an inter-Allied agreement. The Talmuk, illiterate, naïve, had looked forward with enthusiasm to the end of his misadventures.

He had been sent to a forced-labour camp in Siberia, and then transferred to a penal battalion committed to lifting mines on the German front. The mine-clearance technique in use had been to cover the clearers with machine-guns and to order them to tramp through the minefields. Those still on their feet after the first sanitising excursion were taken to the next minefield. There were any number of minefields, and progressively fewer numbers of clearers. The Talmuk was durable, lucky and tough. He ran away during the bangings, hid, crossed to the German lines, and soon found himself back among the Turcoman Division in Italy. He became a persuasive advertisement about the unwisdom of a return to the Soviet Union by soldiers of the Division.

It soon became clear after the war ended that, however reluctant the soldiers were to go home, the British Government was determined to send them there. The bulk of the surrendered division was sent under escort by sea to the Crimea. A regimental mullah ritually burnt himself to death in protest. There were mass suicides by jumping over the sides of ships in the Black Sea. Years later, Rashidov heard of what had happened to those of them who were landed. The standard sentence was to twenty years' forced labour. Most were put to the fatal task of bringing back into production the flooded coal-mines of the Donetz basin. Rashidov's luck held. He did not return to the Soviet Union.

Rashidov owed his exemption to a British gunner colonel in charge of a Turcoman party of eight hundred Muslims, held in a camp at Aversa, near Naples. The Colonel had heard reports of what had happened to earlier drafts of Turcoman prisoners when they had reached Odessa. He was revolted by his orders to send more. He saw off the eight hundred on a train consigned to the Soviet Repatriation Commission in Leghorn and then had the train diverted back to Naples, where its passengers were rapidly embarked for Egypt, to the Islamic protection of King Farouk. From Egypt the group was dispersed to other Muslim countries. Rashidov ended in Damascus.

He was an adaptable man. He learnt Arabic. A trader employed him first as an odd-job helper; then, when he had shown a flair for accounts, as a clerk. He learnt English. He was given more responsibility, well rewarded. But he had seen enough of war, and if he stayed in the Middle East it was clear to him that he would see much more, endless war. In the early 1950s he was accepted on the Canadian immigration quota. In Winnipeg he prospered.

The second worry to afflict Rashidov at the time of his capture was a personal one. He had taken part, unwillingly, in an atrocity, and he was afraid that he would be found out and punished.

The atrocity had been recent. Rashidov had been bullied into complicity by an SS officer, who threatened him convincingly with immediate death if he failed either to co-operate or to keep his mouth shut afterwards. Rashidov, sentenced by his Company Commander to additional fatigues for some venial military offence, a dirty rifle-barrel or some such, had been lent to the SS captain to do any tedious jobs that needed to be done. He was put to cleaning vehicles and sweeping billets and helping in the cookhouse. One night he was kicked awake and taken, without explanation, to what had been the local *carabinieri* station, now in temporary use as a German Military Police lock-up.

In the cells was a German soldier, presumably there for doing something serious like striking an officer or appearing drunk on parade. The spring fighting had already started, and a man fit to take part in it would not be diverted to sterile imprisonment for a trivial misdemeanour. Rashidov, who had been given a kitbag to carry, accompanied the SS captain and two equally frightening-looking SS men to the soldier's cell. The captain ordered the soldier to stand to attention, checked his height and build carefully, and told him to strip. Rashidov was told to unpack the kitbag. Its contents were British uniform clothing, showing signs of heavy wear. The soldier was instructed to put the clothing on. He did so, from cellular underwear to khaki shirt, short jacket and trousers, a camouflage netting neck-scarf and a camouflage smock.

The SS officer took from his pocket a pair of asbestos discs fastened to a leather cord and hung them around the prisoner's neck. There was a further appraisal of the prisoner's appearance by the three SS men, who agreed that it was satisfactory. A relaxed discussion about boots followed. Would it, or would it not, look better if the man wore boots? If his body had been recovered by Turcoman barbarians, would they not be likely to steal his boots, especially if they were the exceptionally fancy ones that went with the rest of the ensemble? It was agreed that the absence of boots would add plausibility. For the first time Rashidov suspected that something terrible would happen. So did the prisoner, who asked an anxious question. One of the SS men punched him in the mouth and told him to shut up.

'Give the boots to the monkey, then,' said the captain. The SS men laughed, and threw the boots at Rashidov. They *were* unusually good boots of an uncommon pattern, calf-length, with leather flaps secured by buckles. 'Keep them as a souvenir, monkey,' said the SS captain, and they laughed again.

They all went out to the captain's Volkswagen staff car. The prisoner started to struggle. He was knocked senseless and bundled into the back seat, with the two SS men on either side of him. Rashidov was told to get into the front. The captain drove.

After four or five kilometres the Volkswagen stopped at an abandoned smallholding, where other SS men were waiting. These were armed with Schmeissers and a Spandau. The prisoner, once more conscious, became frantic. He was bashed into insensibility and roped to a tree. The car's headlights were focused upon him. The Spandau was set up fifty metres from the tree, and was fired under precise directions from the captain. 'Three in his right thigh.' 'Two in his chest.' 'Now smash his face, but not too badly.'

Rashidov vomited. They laughed at him, and gave him a pick and a spade. He was made to dig a shallow grave. They inspected it and said that it would do. While they smoked and chatted, he put the body into the grave and covered it up. When he was done they hit him, just once, hard, painfully, in the stomach. As a further warning to keep his mouth shut, they said. They drove him back to his battalion in the Volkswagen. They pushed him out of the car and threw something after him. 'At least, monkey,' said the captain, 'you've got a pair of boots out of it.' Then they all laughed, and the car went away. Rashidov was too frightened to tell anyone of what he had been forced to do, at an isolated place that he recognised only on his way back from it. It was just outside Porto Garibaldi, where he had recently been in action.

He was even more frightened two weeks later. He had kept the unusually designed boots, on a soldier's realistic assessment that their original owner, whoever he had been, had no further use for them. He was wearing his new pair when he was captured by British troops near Argenta, and he at once realised that he had made a serious mistake. The boots provoked an extravagant wrath among his captors, who clearly recognised them as having belonged to a friend of theirs. He couldn't understand a word of their language, but for a brief period he thought that he was in danger of being shot on the spot.

Then they regained control of themselves and took him grimly to an officer who was sitting with a sergeant and a signaller at a crossroads, looking at a map and drinking tea from a tin mug. The officer made him take off the boots and examined them carefully. The officer behaved very correctly, and must have given firm orders that his men were to behave correctly, too, because although Rashidov was separated from his fellow-prisoners and escorted away no harm of any sort was done to him. But the fact that he had been singled out upset him. It was obvious that the boots had stimulated the trouble, although he was unsure why. The British couldn't possibly know of his passive part in the killing of the prisoner by the SS. And, even if they did, the prisoner had been a German, so why should they worry? But the prisoner had been dressed in a British uniform, and if they found out about that they certainly would worry.

Rashidov was too experienced in the inconsequential illogicalities of both Russian and German army disciplinary procedures to take any chances. He thought up a story, embellished it with accurate references to the recent fight that he had been in at Porto Garibaldi, and held to it when he was questioned closely by a Russian-speaking British interrogator. The story held up. The interrogator could not shake him from an account of how the boots had been given to him by an NCO of the SS after a pile of bodies, including a British one, had been stripped of their equipment.

Rashidov was soon back with his comrades, and was sent to the camp at Aversa. He was still concerned about whether some chance investigation might expose him in his lying, but that concern was outweighed by the larger one of fear of compulsory repatriation to Russia. And then both worries had disappeared with his safe arrival in Egypt.

Smithy had appended numbered notes.

1. Rashidov's purpose in talking to me was (*a*) to point out how unscrupulously selective Sepelov could be in the use of propaganda material, (*b*) to illustrate from personal knowledge that Russian communists had been barbaric, German Nazis brutal, and the British official insistence on the forcible return of Russian prisoners callous. He modified the last by the respect he showed for the humanity of individual Brits – the correct captain, the colonel who

switched the trains and got the prisoners to Egypt.

2. The shooting of the German by the SS was an integral part of this pitch. The boots affair was ancillary and not particularly relevant, but had clearly been on his mind for years. Once he started talking there was no stopping him.

3. I have seen only the Burke Foundation account of the death of Hugo Burke. It was at Porto Garibaldi. His body was recovered from a shallow grave some weeks after the war ended. Rashidov's unfortunate German was dressed in British uniform, including a camouflage smock which sounds as if it might be commando clothing, and buried in a shallow grave near Porto Garibaldi. It might be coincidence. It might not. Further information needed from eye-witnesses of circumstances of H.B.'s death; particularly, if anyone can remember after all this time, about what sort of boots he was wearing.

4. If the body found wasn't Hugo's, what happened to Hugo?

CHAPTER TWENTY-NINE

AFTER the Oxford reunion Alice wrote many letters that asked detailed questions, and took her notebook with her on a round-trip visit that brought her to Leeds, Glasgow, Liverpool, and Budleigh Salterton in Devon, trying, while she did so, to keep the Rashidov story in a mental compartment separated from that in which her historian's curiosity operated. Her Devon host was the General, the one-time Colonel, a rich vein of knowledge, reminiscence and relaxed professionalism, who had preserved his battle-maps and liked talking about them, 'particularly to someone genuinely interested like you, who doesn't put on an expression of frozen enthusiasm while calculating how soon you can decently get the hell out'.

She left the General's presentation happy that she had now a clear idea of the higher thinking and control of the Commachio battle, and happier that he had agreed to check a draft of how she would write it up. 'I'll be delighted to mark your card for you. Might try to slip in a few bits to show what a genius I actually was, but I suppose you'll only take them out again. It's all this damned integrity that gets me down.' He drove her to Exeter and put her on the train for Paddington. In London she called on two more sources and had lunch with Johnny Laing.

It was very much a working meal. She summarised how far she had got. She sought advice on some points, clarification on others. He was as helpful as ever. And at last she touched upon the subject of boots.

'Yes,' said Johnny Laing, 'they were a wedding present. From me. I bought them in the officers' shop in Rome. They were like a Canadian lumberjack's. I remember them very well because a few weeks after Hugo was killed we took a prisoner who was wearing them. Paddy O'Driscoll was so hopping mad that I thought he'd try to kill him. I had to smarten things up a bit.'

'Thanks,' said Alice.

'You do come up with amazing details. Why do you want to know?'

'It all adds colour to the background,' said Alice.

'I suppose it does,' said Laing.

*

In his commuter train that evening he wondered how far she had really got. That night he discussed one aspect of it – the Hugo Burke aspect – with his wife Gert. After she had fallen asleep he ran through in his mind the segment of the Hugo Burke aspect that he had mentioned to no one, not even to Gert.

In the spring of 1968, Laing, five years after a premature retirement, product of Nigerian independence, from the Colonial Service, was a conscientious but less than ambitiously dedicated principal at the Board of Trade. It was a living, and he earned his pay. He had recently been transferred to a job that carried responsibility for helping to promote British exports to Eastern Europe, and he was disproportionately pleased at the chance it gave him to expel the air of Whitehall from his lungs on an annual tour of the commercial sections of the embassies to the client countries with which he dealt. His first journey took him to Prague, Bucharest, Budapest and Belgrade. From Belgrade he went to the consulate-general in Zagreb, which covered Croatia and Slovenia, the two republics in which the bulk of Yugoslav industrial and commercial activity was concentrated.

He arrived on a Friday, and finished what he had to finish in the morning. The consul-general took him to lunch, reintroduced him to *slievovica* and black Dalmatian wine, introduced him to bear's brains as a course not customarily listed on the menus of London SW1, questioned him with interest about his impressions of wartime Yugoslavia, and made a suggestion. Since, said the consul-general, this was Laing's first return visit to the country, why not make the most of it and stay for the weekend? The Monday morning JAT flight would get him to Heathrow in time to be in Whitehall by noon. The Board of Trade would doubtless be thrown into panic-stricken despair by his absence from his desk for two or three hours, but with luck should regain their equanimity at some time in the afternoon. Laing accepted without hesitation.

To the traditional charms of Zagreb, said the consul-general, he could add a further attraction. Laing, if he so wished, could come out with the Hash House Harriers. He explained who these were over Turkish coffee and *Vignac*.

The Hash House Harriers, it seemed, were a sporting organisation, a branch of a loosely connected (very loosely connected) worldwide body of vaguely disreputable origin. They had been founded as a hangover cure in Kuala Lumpur in the 1930s by an Australian misogynist with faith in the therapeutic advantages of working up a good sweat on the morning after. The proceedings had much in common with those of a paper-chase. Two hares left in advance and laid a cross-country trail with flour. To add mental stimulus to the pursuit, and to accommodate those who were relatively infirm as a consequence of advancing years or of too powerful an attack on the bottle during the previous evening's relaxations, the hares were sparse with their distribution of clues. They further slowed things down at intervals by marking what was known as a check, a circle of flour. The restart of the trail from each check was deliberately designed to mystify. The result of few clues and baffling checks was that, while the young and fit scented vigorously around to find out where everyone had to go, the geriatrics and the alcoholic battle-casualties had time to catch up. The standard length of the course was about seven miles. Ample refreshments, capable of destroying whatever good the exercise had done to the participants, were provided at the finish.

Laing said that he'd enjoy that very much.

On the following morning Laing, fixed up by his host with a pair of old tennis-shoes and some spare sweaters – 'It can get damned cold at a long check on Sljeme' – was driven to the meet at a quarry on the lower slopes of the beech-covered mountain that dominated Zagreb. Cars were parked haphazardly around the floor of the quarry. The hounds, from the consular corps, from airline offices and from Western businesses, with a few English-speaking Yugoslavs among them, stood chatting affably in groups. They were dressed variously in windcheaters, sweaters, tracksuits, jeans, slacks with the bottoms tucked into woollen socks, and a colourful range of ski-caps, beach-hats, and miscellaneous headgear of cricketing and baseball derivation.

They were sheltering beneath dripping beeches and gazing critically at an overcast sky when the consul-general led Laing round to be introduced. They all shook hands with great friendliness, but he remembered few of their names. There was one other guest starter – 'new boot' in the Australian–Malayan's handed-down jargon – a tall, straight-backed German a few years older than Laing. The German, who was a house guest of the local Lufthansa manager, stared hard at Laing as they exchanged greetings. Laing was used to Germans who stared hard at people they shook hands with. He smiled genially and moved on.

The Master, the British Airways ground engineer, a cheerful burly man in a tracksuit and a long-peaked maroon cricket-cap, said that two of the young keenies, the British vice-consul and an American language student at Zagreb University, had been sniffing around and had picked up flour at the start of the trail. The Master cupped his hands and shouted: 'On, on.' The others, led by the two young keenies, headed for an uphill zig-zag path through the towering beech-trees, and shouted 'On, on,' as well. So did Laing, feeling rather foolish.

Twenty minutes of climbing a steep, slippery clay path in a pervasive drizzle reminded Laing that he wasn't as young as some. The wisdom of the choose-your-own-pace convention early became apparent. From far ahead, high among the trees, came a shout of 'Check' from youthful voices. The consul-general, plodding along behind Laing, said: 'Thank Christ for that.' In front of Laing the tall German strode stolidly along the path with long, economical paces. From far back came the sound of a thumping crash and a stream of sobbed Mediterranean cursing.

'The Italian cultural chap,' said the consul-general, 'he does it every time.'

They panted up to the site of the first check, a narrow clearing on a ridge with intermittent views through the mist of the smog-ridden city far below, and of the River Sava winding through a vast plain, fields newly planted with Indian corn. Laing was just getting his breath back when there was a further cry of 'On, on'.

'They've found the next trail,' said the consul-general gloomily. 'Dammit.'

'Aw, *shit*,' said the American information officer.

'Captain Laing, sir,' said the tall German, smiling, 'I renew my thanks for your Christmas present. We last met near Ledenice twenty-four years ago. I and my friends were in a cage on a hillside. Sergeant-Major Schneider.'

Laing stared at him and said: 'Well, bugger me. I thought you were dead.'

'I think we might talk together,' said Schneider.

'I think we might, too,' said Laing.

'But perhaps not here? It is becoming cold, and the young gentlemen athletes are calling "On, on".'

'At the finish,' said Laing.

'At the finish,' said Schneider, still smiling. 'You lead the way, Captain Laing.'

And then the smile grew into a huge happy grin. He threw his head back like a yodeller.

'On, on,' bawled Schneider.

The next leg of the route was steeply downhill, to a valley with an overfull stream foaming through it. Laing slipped twice on the innocent-looking clay, and glissaded along on his bottom. He stopped himself each time by thrusting his feet against a trackside tree. Schneider, beaming, helped him up after both falls, remarking: 'One good turn deserves another, even if the opportunity for the other took too long to arrive.' Laing, sweaty and muddy and puffing, was grateful, but began to develop a slight feeling of resentment at Schneider's still immaculate appearance. The Italian cultural chap put this right.

There was a familiar crash from behind, and some noisily voiced self-pity, growing rapidly louder. Laing jumped to one side and hugged a tree. Schneider was slower. The Italian cultural chap whizzed, whimpering, around the bend in the track like a Cresta Run competitor who had fallen off his toboggan, caught Schneider a fierce blow behind the knees and brought him down on top of him. The two disappeared around the next curve, locked together, gathering speed.

'The fucking Axis rides again,' said the United States information officer. 'Some of these bastards just can't let it alone.'

The trail became easier after the next check. There were gravelled paths, not slippery, and a tarmacked road that brought them past high-gabled cottages with intricately carved wooden beams at their fronts and yellowed cobs of dried corn hanging from their eaves. Laing and Schneider could have talked then, had not Schneider taken on another responsibility. He was encouraging the Italian cultural chap to be of courage and to complete the course. He did it gently. Laing liked him for that.

'It's like Rommel in the Western Desert,' said the United States information officer.

The flour led to a track over a grass field. A pensive Friesian bull stood in it. Schneider put himself between his protégé and the bull, masking it from view. The information officer said: 'For Chrissakes claim it's a cow, or we'll have to send out a search party with a goddam ladder to retrieve him from a goddam tree.' Schneider looked benevolent and said nothing. Laing plugged on, feeling thirsty. The consul-general said that all that mucking about on mountain ridges was absurd, but that he enjoyed the home straight. Laing said that so did he. A large flour arrow pointed to a dilapidated hut. Inside was a blazing wood fire, crates of bottled beer, and supplies of *slievovica*, *travarica*, whisky and gin, the last two courtesy of the consular corps.

Laing, muscles stiffening, sweat drying, filthy, clutching a glass of beer, contemplated the gang of similarly decrepit international companions of his morning's exertions. They were laughing and drinking and comparing notes, and criticising the swinish ingenuity of the hares, who were cynically unrepentant. Laing decided that it was the best morning that he had had for years. And a live Schneider, too!

Schneider, having seen to the resuscitation of his Italian mate with a dose of *travarica*, came over grinning to Laing with a bottle of beer in his large hand. He clinked the bottle against Laing's glass. 'Zivilje,' he said.

'Zivilje. Am I glad to see you! I was thinking of you, coming over that field with the bull in it. The last time I saw you, you were conducting a choir in the snow on a hillside. Singing "Stille Nacht".'

'And the last time I saw you, you brought us those Christmas presents and gave us hope. I haven't forgotten. I never will. I think it will be hard to talk here. We have our social obligations. Captain Laing, the least of my debts to you is a meal. Will you dine with me at Okrugliak tonight?'

'I'd love to. Thank you.'

'And now, with your permission, I'll rejoin our Italian friend. I still have some way to go to compensate him emotionally for unfriendly remarks I addressed to him when he knocked me over.'

'*My* permission?' said Laing. He put on a cold, remote, deadpan expression. Schneider recognised it at once. His own face became sterner, more formal than Laing's.

'Carry on, please, Sarnt-Major,' snapped Laing.

'Sir!' barked Schneider, crashing his heels together.

They both laughed.

'I answer to Johnny,' said Laing.

'Kurt,' said Schneider.

They went their separate ways among the recovering cross-country enthusiasts.

Okrugliak was warm and Slavic, with a strong element of the Imperial Austro-Hungarian legacy in its ambience. Carved woodwork, log fires, a whole lamb and a whole sucking pig turning on spits over red-hot banked charcoal. Ceramic beer-steins hanging from hooks. Friendly, efficient waiters. Much cheerful noise, and much smell of tobacco among the more succulent garlic, and wine, and roasting meat. It was a prosperous, well-stocked Yugoslavia unknown to either of them when they had first met, trying to kill one another at Ledenice. Schneider seemed to be more familiar with it than was Laing. Laing left the ordering to him and was glad. Waiters produced mussels, and charcoal-grilled duck, and tomato salad, and *palacinka*, preceded by an aperitif of *travarica*, washed down by endless bottles of *Kastelet*, the heavy dark wine from the vineyards above Split.

Laing insisted that Schneider should be the first to talk.

'They shot our officers.'

'That was before we left. We thought that they'd shoot you, too, when we'd gone.'

'So did we. Instead we were tried by a People's Court. There was a lot of baying for blood and vengeance, but fortunately the president of the court took his regard for the rule of law as seriously as he took his Marxism. He was a law student from Belgrade University. He had rimless glasses and he looked about fifteen years of age. I was our spokesman.'

Laing smiled. 'Who else?'

'I said that we'd come up from Greece and hadn't had time to do anything bad in Yugoslavia, even if we had wanted to, which we didn't. We were simply trying to fight our way home. We lost. Soldiers often do. The blood-bayers said that that was irrelevant. We shouldn't have been there in the first place. Death to the lot of us. *Smrt Fascismu*. The president came down on our side. Guilty, with mitigating circumstances. Five years' forced labour to help build the new socialist society.'

'Rough?'

'Rough. It got better as time went on. The food was always bad, but so was everyone else's. A few local people who'd lost families tried to harm us, but there'd been so much killing of and by Ustachi and Chetniks, not to speak of the Partisans, that German killings were more or less forgotten. We were all pretty weak, mind you. There were several deaths from hunger and exhaustion. And one man was shot and one strangled.'

'What for?'

'The first idiot nearly landed us all in the shit by deciding to defend the honour of the Fatherland. He gave the Nazi salute and shouted "Heil Hitler" at the guards. They shot him.'

'Who strangled the other one?'

'I did. He wanted to copy the first idiot.'

'What was the work?'

'Road-making, bridge-building mostly. Some mine-clearance. We lost a few on that.'

'When did you get out?'

'Early '51. Those of us who were left were suddenly released, put on slow trains and sent back to Germany. I hadn't much to come home to. My wife and little boy were killed by the RAF. In Cologne.'

'I'm sorry.'

'It's OK. A long time ago. I now have another wife and two little girls. Big girls.'

'What did you do when you were put back as a civilian?'

'There were welfare schemes for released POWs. They got me a job as a clerk with the Americans. I learnt English properly – well, by your version not properly – from them. Then I did a lot of study. Then I became a clerk with Lufthansa. Then I got promoted with Lufthansa. Then I kept on being promoted with Lufthansa. Now I'm quite a big wheel with Lufthansa, who inspects the European offices and goes out running with the Hash House Harriers of Zagreb, and meets an old enemy soldier whose decency I've never forgotten. Also I get tripped up by fat Italian culture vultures on Croatian hill tracks and try to make up for being rude to them.'

Schneider laughed a deep belly-laugh, raised his glass. 'Prosit, Johnny.'

'Prosit.'

'What about you, Johnny? What happened in your life?'

'Nothing much. We went to Italy after we left you. When the war was over I joined the Colonial Service. I was in Nigeria. Administering, and advising, and coaching them on how to run a free, independent, democratic country. When they became one we all got sacked. Now they're a military dictatorship and I'm a Whitehall bureaucrat. Grey-faced commuter. I promote British exports to Eastern Europe. Try to persuade communist bureaucrats that British Airways is superior to Lufthansa. That kind of thing. Also I have dinner with an old enemy in a country where we once fought against one another.'

'Have you a family?'

'Yes. I married a nurse I first met in Italy. Boy and a girl. Eleven and nine.'

'What happened to that nice, smart corporal who helped you with the Christmas presents in Montenegro?'

'Smithwick. Yes, he was a good one. He was killed in Italy.'

'I'm sorry. And the dashing young Lieutenant Burke? Our guest in Ledenice.'

'He was killed in Italy, too. You've a very good memory for names.'

'I had a little to do with Lieutenant Burke.'

'When he was captured? Or later?'

'He wasn't captured,' said Schneider. 'He gave himself up.'

Laing stared at him. Schneider continued to masticate a mouthful of duck, washed it down with wine. He looked unblinkingly into Laing's eyes.

'If', said Schneider with formality, 'I have distressed you, I apologise. Lieutenant Burke must have been your friend. I am not suggesting that he was a coward.'

'I know bloody well that he wasn't a coward.'

'I suppose that technically he was a traitor, and I don't like traitors, but I liked Lieutenant Burke. He thought much more deeply than simple soldiers like you and me. We saw it as our duty to obey orders and get on with it. He looked behind the orders and he didn't like what he saw. He had the courage and the self-confidence to try to do something about it.'

'To do what about it?'

'I've often wondered what he was trying to do. I only know what I saw him do. My company's positions were in that big hospital in Risan, and in some houses and slit-trenches around it. All overlooked by that high escarpment that you Tommis and your Partisan friends were sitting on. . . .'

Before he fell asleep that night in the consul-general's guest-bedroom, Laing thought back over and over again to the distant time at Risan. He made allowances for distortions in his memory brought about by the passing of the years, but he thought that his reconstruction was about right. First there had been the march to the Observation Post with the Force Commander. That singleminded and insouciant young Gunner

Forward Observation Officer, concentrating upon his job of calling down fire on all moving Germans, indifferent to tourists of whatever rank. Laing's muted angry exchange with Hankins:

'Where's Mr Burke?'

'I think he'll be along in a minute, sir.'

'Well, why isn't he here . . .?' And the sudden realisation that Hugo had drifted off somewhere, that Hankins was covering up, that Hankins was right to cover up, that it was unfair to take out on Hankins anger properly directed at Hugo. There was nothing that Hankins could have done to stop an officer from doing anything he chose to do.

The later call from Hankins above on the hillcrest, interrupting the Force Commander and himself in their slightly ridiculous conversation about something that he had forgotten. Hankins, clear-headed and well trained, giving a precise target indication of the little house with Hugo in front of it, and cursing when Hugo, hands in the air, disappeared into it.

And days later, in that filthy monsoon-like weather, when Laing had splashed his way to the Observation Post again with the Colonel, and the Observation Officer had for the first time said that Hugo had told him that he had lost patience with high-level inertia and had gone off to do unilaterally a recce for a commando attack on Risan. And Hugo's reiteration of the story, after he had been sprung. It had been in character, persuasive, and until now Laing had been persuaded. It had never occurred to him to be anything else. He thought that he probably still was persuaded.

But Schneider had been persuasive, too. The persuasiveness of Schneider lay in three things. First, Schneider and he had met today by blind chance. Second, Schneider was a common-sense, balanced man, as he had demonstrated by the way in which he had led and controlled and encouraged his fellow-captives, both as Laing remembered them and during their later trial and forced labour. Third, Schneider had no imaginable reason to invent his story. He had every reason not to pass it to Laing as a calumny, because his gratitude to Laing was clearly genuine and he would not wish to cause hurt to a man to whom he was grateful. He had passed it on not as a calumny, but because he thought that it did Hugo credit. As Schneider saw it, Hugo had had the brains and the nerve to examine what he was being ordered to do by higher military commanders and political leaders, had disliked his findings, and had put his concept of duty to humanity above loyalty to a cause, and above military discipline.

Well, had he?

Schneider's post in the Risan hospital had been in a small first-floor room that had once been a dispensary. The glass had been knocked out of the windows to pre-empt its being blown lethally about by shellfire, and

Schneider conducted his affairs from a sandbagged enclosure set up against the inside wall. He had heard a lot of ill-disciplined shouting from a Ustacha position in and around a small house in front of the hospital. Schneider the Sergeant-Major was not a man to overlook that sort of lapse, even from allies. He was in any case fed to the teeth with the Ustachi. He went down to sort them out. (Laing, when told this, thought briefly and fondly of his dead friend Sergeant-Major Mayne, whose reaction would have been identical. Mayne and Schneider would have got on remarkably well together, had they been on the same side.)

Schneider at the time spoke no Croatian, but some of the Ustachi spoke German. One of the German-speakers, an NCO, in a slit-trench in the side-garden of the house, was in shouted conversation with a German-speaking voice coming from a shallow gulley about sixty metres ahead. The owner of the voice was calling that he was a British officer, that he wished to surrender, and that he had a personal message for *Pukovnik* Bilic.

Schneider knew Bilic by sight. He was a big noise on the staff of Ante Pavelic, the Head of Government in Zagreb of the Independent Kingdom of Croatia. Bilic, an elegant colonel, had earlier offended Schneider's sense of what was militarily fitting by carrying a briefcase with him wherever he went, and clutching it grimly even when being shelled or mortared. He had recently got rid of it somewhere, and in Schneider's view now looked more like a soldier should. What Bilic was doing in Risan, Schneider never knew, and wasn't particularly interested in. In Schneider's experience, staff colonels appeared inexplicably and left abruptly.

The use by the disembodied voice of the name Bilic deterred some of the more bloodthirsty Ustachi from going ahead with a plan that they were discussing. Schneider found both the nature of the plan, and the fact that these self-styled soldiers were actually *discussing* a plan – any plan – to be equally disturbing. The idea had been to assure the surrenderer that he would be safe, to invite him to walk forward with his hands up, and then to butcher him. Schneider added reinforcement to the second thoughts induced by the naming of Bilic by booting a few Ustachi backsides, and shouting to the owner of the voice to stay where he was, and not to try any tricks. Then Schneider sent one of the more reliable Ustachi to work his way through cover to the gulley, collect the prisoner, and bring him in, taking care over the last part of the journey to keep the prisoner at gunpoint firmly between the escort and the enemy – the Tommis on the escarpment and Partisans closer by.

The prisoner had come along cheerfully enough, hands in the air, and had said coolly in German: 'Good morning. My name's Burke. Take me to Colonel Bilic, please.' Schneider had sent him off in the company of one German and one Ustacha soldier, the German's role being to keep the

Ustacha 'from doing anything stupid'. Schneider, for the moment, had promptly forgotten about it. It was a strange incident, but Schneider's war had been full of strange incident.

A few days later Schneider had been sent by his Company Commander, Hauptmann Goertz, to the Risan Garrison Headquarters to kick up a row about what the fire-eating Goertz considered to be the tardy and inequitable distribution of ammunition. Goertz was the sort of fighting soldier who in no circumstances would leave his company position when his troops were under fire. Schneider had followed his orders to the letter, and had successfully raised merry hell, respectfully expressed. On his way out he had passed a room without a door. Inside, Bilic and Burke were sitting at a table, drinking coffee and *rakija*, and chatting away like old friends. Schneider promptly forgot about that, too. It was nothing to do with him.

The next thing that happened was that Goertz, Schneider and their company were sent up the hill to the old barracks at Ledenice. Burke, under escort, came in with the last mule convoy before the Partisans cut the route. He was lodged in a guardroom in conditions of reasonable comfort and minimum restraint. Schneider was too busy to wonder much about this, but later it occurred to him that it was probably a prelude to a connived-at escape.

'But then', Schneider had said to Laing smilingly, 'your damned guns interfered with that and everything else, and I met you for the first time.'

'How long was he at Ledenice?' asked Laing.

'About three days.'

'You said that you were too busy to wonder about him.'

'To wonder about what he was doing there. But I got some idea of how his thoughts were running. I spoke to him in the evenings, when I was on my inspection rounds.'

'You asked him?'

'He told me. Johnny, he was an officer. I was a Wehrmacht sergeant-major, remember. German sergeant-majors didn't ask officers, even foreign officers in some vague form of captivity, what they were thinking. Or what they were going to do next. We listened, and commented when invited to. It was a matter of disciplined habit. Probably quite unnecessary in dealing with him. I think that Lieutenant Burke would have been happy to have had what the international politicians now call a frank and friendly exchange of views. But, as it was, I listened.'

'What did he have to say?'

'It always came back to the same thing. War was horrible, but the passive acceptance of evil was worse. That was why he had volunteered to fight us Germans. Nazism was evil. But there was another evil now. Russian communism and its stooges, supported by the Western democracies who thought it realistic common sense to encourage the forces of one evil to destroy the forces of another. Lieutenant Burke thought it neither realism nor common sense. To him it was immoral. He couldn't fight the whole huge apparatus on his own, but in a small way he could do something to mitigate the damage. I remember him laughing, and saying: "But I won't get down to it seriously until we finish off you bloody Germans first."'

'Kurt, you may have been a reflex-conditioned German sergeant-major, but were you prepared to take that kind of talk from him?'

Schneider grinned. 'My problem was that I agreed with him,' he said. 'I intended to fight as hard as I could for as long as I could, because I couldn't think of anything else to do. But I was delighted to meet an idealist. I hadn't come across many during the past few years.'

Just before he switched off the bedside light Laing subjected the whole of Schneider's account to a last ruthless, critical analysis. He could find no flaw in it. Schneider was straight and had no reason to lie. Schneider's version of events in Risan as seen from the inside tallied precisely with Laing's observation of some of the same events as seen from the outside. Schneider's story fitted too well, or too badly, with other, almost forgotten things. Hugo's refusal to join Laing and Smithwick on that long-ago Christmas delivery of presents to the German prisoners – in case some of them, especially Schneider, struck up embarrassingly reminiscent conversations about what Hugo had been doing during his captivity? Hugo moody, and drinking about twice as much as was usual after his release. Hugo defiantly inviting in that unfortunate doomed Chetnik major for a drink on Christmas morning. . . .

And, if all this was true – and, however hard he tried, Laing could not think of a way to make it not true – poor bloody Hugo. Passionately loyal to the troops he soldiered with. Passionately conscientious about his job of leading them effectively and economically in action. Passionately convinced that one of the consequences of the winning of the war that in a small way he was helping to win would be the emergence and domination over a large part of Europe of a form of Godless totalitarianism that he abhorred. Passionately in love with Helen Grant.

Was it surprising that, with all that to contend with, he hit the bottle and hit Silent Mott and had to be sent on compulsory leave to Italy? And how on earth had he managed to dam it all up, to hide it from someone as close to him in friendship and daily propinquity as Laing had been? Laing switched off the light and fell asleep wondering wryly if Hugo had ever tried his hand as an actor.

CHAPTER THIRTY

THE VOICE on the telephone was faintly Scottish and very firm, that of a woman who has reached a decision and intends to implement it, all obstacles to be disregarded.

'Mrs Burke? I'm Gert Laing. Johnny's wife. I've always been away, or sick, when you've been in England. I think that it's time we met. There's something that I want to say to you.'

Alice felt irrationally guilty, a schoolgirl summoned to the Headmistress's study, an aspirant novice adultress detected in what she had imagined to be a skilfully concealed enthusiasm for someone else's husband. The voice's timbre, and that 'something that I want to say', not 'something that we might talk about', carried a touch of menace. There were none of the soft Irish circumlocutions that Alice was used to about this approach.

'I'd love to meet you,' said Alice. 'I'll be over in England again in—'

'I'm in Dublin. In Donnybrook. Staying with friends. Can we have coffee together? Or a drink?'

'You have a drink and I'll have coffee,' said Alice. 'I'm pregnant.'

She told Gert Laing how to find her way to Madigan's in Morehampton Road. She felt some unkind feminine pleasure when they exchanged identifying descriptions. It was nice to be able to tell an intimidating faceless voice whose defined specifications included 'large', 'grey-haired' and 'late fifties' that you were five feet four, fair and in your early thirties.

The only large grey-haired woman in her late fifties when Alice arrived at the upstairs lounge in Madigan's was dressed in a polo-necked lambswool sweater and a tweed skirt, and was drinking gin and tonic. She had a weather-reddened face and a humorous mouth, which helped to offset her no-nonsense manner. Introductions completed and coffee ordered, she wasted no time over social small change.

'The thing about men', she said, 'is that they're too damned impressionable. You've got Johnny wrapped around your little finger.'

'Oh,' said Alice. There were times when Ulick's vocabulary was serviceable as well as infectious.

'Not only Johnny,' said Gert genially. 'Busty Hankins and Bob Hart and the rest.'

'I'm unsure what. . . .'

'I'll tell you exactly what. This book that you're writing. I've no doubt it's a genuine book and will get written. I've equally no doubt that any woman married to a man who thought he was the son of somebody who's bound to figure in the book, and who also knows her husband's mother, would start getting very inquisitive indeed when she compared the date of her husband's birth with the date of his alleged father's death.'

'Yes,' said Alice.

'After Johnny showed you those papers with the date of that battle I take it that you started speculating about the longest gestation period in human history.'

She laughed. Alice laughed, too. She began to feel a liking towards this forthright woman.

'I'll come clean,' said Alice.

'I was hoping you would. And let's get one thing clear. I'm not trying to catch you out for the sake of catching you out. I'm here to try to protect an old friend who a long time ago had a personal tragedy – a series of personal tragedies. It's a private little story of private sorrow, and it'll do no good to anybody if you stir it all up accidentally. Note the "accidentally". Johnny reckoned that you'd never do it deliberately, and I trust his judgement on that – even if he is wrapped around your little finger. But let's hear first what you know about your husband's conception. Then I'll work out what else to tell you.'

'I knew about the discrepancy in the dates before I ever met Johnny,' said Alice. 'Ulick went to see his father's grave in Italy. He found out that Hugo Burke wasn't his father.'

'Ah. So that's how it started. What happened then?'

'Well, Ulick wasn't all that worried about illegitimacy. He was more concerned about the money complications. Hugo Burke left a lot of it. When Ulick discovered that he wasn't entitled to it he wanted to say so openly. That would have caused difficulties for – er – a third party.'

'I admire your reticence, but it's unnecessary. You mean that you were afraid that Helen would have ended in the dock on a fraud rap.'

'I hadn't realised that—'

'Inspired guesswork,' said Gert. 'I was in on the early stages of all this. I must confess that the fraud side of it hadn't occurred to me before, but it makes sense. So what did you decide?'

'We decided that we couldn't make up our minds on what to do until we'd found out who Ulick's father was. Even that wouldn't necessarily have settled anything, but we thought that it would give us a line to go on. The person of course who knew the answer was Helen, but we felt that we couldn't ask her.'

'Why not?'

'It was a question that only Ulick could have put to her. He couldn't bring himself to do it. Call it shyness, if you like. Or delicacy. Or sparing her hurt. There was also the point that Helen's always been a sexual puritan. That added further difficulty to what was already difficult.'

'I see. So you cooked up this story about research for a book?'

Alice thought carefully. 'I think that's a little harsh. I suppose that cooked up is a fair description of how it started, but I've become genuinely absorbed in the book. I'll soon have enough—'

'My apologies. So far I've found what you've said to be very reassuring. May I ask you two questions?'

'Two more won't overload the total,' said Alice, and grinned.

Gert grinned, too. 'Touché,' she said. 'First one. You keep saying we and us when you talk about all this. Am I right in thinking that we and us is primarily you, with husband Ulick trailing somewhere along at the heel of the hunt? And don't be misguidedly loyal. Or misguidedly modest. I'd a drink last night with Paddy Madden. I've known him for years. He said that he liked Ulick very much, but that he wasn't exactly Nobel Prize-winning material. Paddy liked you very much, too. He'd no doubt who the brains of the outfit was.'

Alice tried to look neither misguidedly loyal nor misguidedly modest. 'All right,' she said. 'We and us is mostly me.'

'Well, that's straight,' said Gert cheerfully. 'Second question. I don't know how far you've got, but you must have reached some provisional conclusions. Who do you think Ulick's father is?'

Alice sipped at her coffee, looked Gert carefully in the eye and said: 'I don't think that you'll like this very much. My guess is Johnny.'

Gert gazed straight back at her, smiled, raised her glass sardonically and said: 'A very good guess, too. And it could have been the right one. Only it isn't. I stayed with Helen shortly after she last slept with Johnny. She had the curse.'

'A few minutes ago,' said Gert reflectively, jiggling the ice and the half-slice of lemon in her glass, 'I said that I was reassured by what you'd told me. What I had in mind was that I liked the sound of some of what you've done. You wouldn't let Ulick say publicly that he wasn't Hugo Burke's son, because you feared that if he did he'd land his mother in legal trouble. You wouldn't press Helen for information because it might hurt her. I'm now satisfied that whatever you might have found out about Ulick's birth would have been used solely to help resolve Ulick's problems. Not broadcast about as prurient gossip, which is what I was afraid of. Johnny said that he considered you to be thoroughly responsible, but I wanted to see for myself. I have. Johnny and I also agreed that, if my impressions were the same as his, I should tell you the whole story. On the grounds that if you knew it all you'd be less likely to blunder into doing something ill-judged and accidentally cause a lot of damage.'

Alice interrupted. She felt a sudden fondness for down-to-earth, no-frills-on-her Gert, who had taken the trouble to come all this way to make sure that no harm came to an old friend as a result of the disclosure of events that had taken place many a long year ago. 'Could we not do this better over an omelette in my kitchen?' said Alice.

'We could indeed do it better over an omelette in your kitchen,' said Gert.

'Also, there's gin in the house,' said Alice.

'Better still,' said Gert.

They had the house to themselves. The girls were at school. The cleaning woman had finished her morning's work and had gone home. Ulick was in Edinburgh prior to watching Ireland playing Scotland at Murrayfield. Alice did some delicate magic with mushrooms and beaten eggs at the cooker. Gert sipped at her gin, and busied herself with the electric toaster and the coffee-grinder. It was a companionable meal. Alice wasted no time on an attempted analysis of how it was that two women, of different generations, of different nationalities, of different experience, of different attitudes, had come to achieve a sympathetic understanding of one another so quickly. They had, and they were both content.

They talked about children and pregnancies whilst they ate – their own children and Alice's pregnancy. 'We'll deal with the other one after lunch,' Gert said. Then Alice put the dishes in the dishwasher, and Gert poured each of them more coffee, and Gert said: 'I suppose that the best point to start is at a remark you made earlier in that pub about Helen. You said that she was sexually prudish, or puritanical, or some such expression.'

'Yes. She never in her life mentioned sex to Ulick. Or to me. Occasionally, when one or other of us has made some slightly off-colour wisecrack in her presence she's looked so upset and embarrassed that we fall over ourselves to try not to slip up again. Ulick once described her as the sort of woman who if she'd been alive in Victorian times would have covered table-legs with drapery to douse impure thoughts in men.'

Gert laughed. 'Well,' she said, 'when I first knew her she wasn't like that at all. Not in the slightest, she wasn't. You could say that in one sense she was ahead of her time. She made love with men who made war. She wasn't totally indiscriminate, mind you. But any man who was reasonably attractive, and was available, was liable to wake up between the sheets with her. A lot of it was simple, generous kindness of heart. She wanted to give comfort in the best way she knew to young men who mightn't have much more of their lives left to them. But that wasn't the whole story. She frankly enjoyed it. She enjoyed it most of all when she married Hugo. She was fiercely faithful to him. As for her and Johnny after Hugo was killed, that was a little more complicated.'

Like most abnormal situations, Gert said, the one in the hospital in Bari had seemed entirely normal to the people who were experiencing it at the time. In essence, the patients were mostly battle casualties who, wounds aside, were healthy young men conditioned to a peak of physical fitness. The nurses were healthy young women selected for their resilience and resourcefulness. The men, and the women who tended them, were in a closed national community far from their homes. It was a medical truism that doctors or nurses who became emotionally enmeshed with the plight of their patients would find the job of caring for them almost unbearable. But any realistic look at what was likely to happen in the circumstances would have to include an acceptance of the fact that the burgeoning of some physical and emotional attachments was inevitable. The men had recently faced death, and once they were healed would face it again. To some of the women the hint of hovering death gave the patients an aura that stimulated feelings of mixed pity, pride, sympathy and gratitude. There were passionate affairs, simplified, added the practical Gert, by the local bonus that a well-found hospital was equipped to prevent or deal with unwelcome consequences.

Helen, the Red Cross welfare officer, was affected more than most by the prevailing highly charged atmosphere. She had early formed a friendship with Gert, a nursing sister, with whom she exchanged views and confidences about sex, God, war, men, the future of the human race, and everything else under the sun. The two of them enjoyed each other's company, and found much the same things to be admirable or funny or irritating. Gert at one time had given her a serious talking to, an affectionate warning. Gert was worried that if Helen continued to fall so easily into masculine beds ('or, for that matter, into the backs of jeeps or up against trees') she was in danger of suffering real psychological damage, of destroying her capacity for genuine love.

And then Hugo Burke had appeared upon the scene and everything had begun to change. Initially the change was gradual. Helen was attracted to Hugo, but Hugo was soon back in Yugoslavia, was for a time reported as Missing, believed Prisoner of War. Helen had a few more experimental flings, notably with a rather dumb naval officer whom Gert disliked, and with a convalescent New Zealander after a hospital Christmas Eve party that got out of hand. Then Hugo came back to Bari on some sort of post-prisoner leave, and that was that. Helen became a devoted, besotted, one-man woman.

Helen had always been a naturally happy person. Marriage to Hugo had made her happier than Gert had ever known her to be. Pregnancy had brought her to a level of contented joy that was delightful to see. But of course there was the damned war and—

'Pregnancy?' said Alice. 'You mean that Helen *was* pregnant by Hugo Burke?'

'Oh, yes,' said Gert.

'That's a thing I didn't know. Listen, Gert, I'm finding it hard to take all this in. The Helen you're describing is very different from the Helen I know – or that Ulick knows.'

'You're not morally outraged, I hope?'

'Not at all. Just amazed. And enormously grateful that you're telling me all this. When I think of what I might have stirred up inadvertently by getting Ulick to ask Helen. . . .'

'There's much more to come. You haven't heard the half of it yet.'

'Sorry. You go on.'

And there was the damned war, Gert said. And there was Hugo fighting in it. And there was Helen looking superficially calm, and underneath being permanently terrified, and praying to a God in whom she'd only recently come to believe to spare Hugo, and confiding fearfully in Gert, and getting on with her job with smiling, compassionate efficiency. And then had come word of the disaster of Hugo's death.

'The effect was dreadful,' said Gert simply. 'She just froze up emotionally. Completely. She cried a little when she was first told, and I did what I could to comfort her, but I was useless. I think that anyone else would have been useless, too. She put on a tremendous act by day of looking cheerful while she was working, and she used to sit for hours at night with a couple of patients who were dying. And then she'd lock herself in her room and sob in solitude. Her room was next to mine. I could hear her. I tried knocking on her door, but she'd never let me in. Said that she'd rather be alone. She was very polite about it. Too damned polite. I'd have been happier if she'd started ranting and screaming. Then she'd start the next day off looking bright and brassy and red-eyed. I was worried that she'd have a total breakdown. So were the doctors. But she refused, all very quiet and courteous, any attempts to give her sedatives at night or offers of leave to take her mind off it. She didn't even respond to normal friendly little things from me, like a hug or an arm around her shoulders. Then Johnny got wounded, and was brought down to Bari. He did something that none of the rest of us had been able to do. He started to pull her out of it.'

'How?'

'By accident. He made her cry. In company. Not just lonely crying.'

'Oh, Gert.'

'He did it twice, actually. Once when she first saw him in the ward.

And once when he was up and she insisted on his telling her about Hugo's last couple of days, and how he was killed. That was therapeutically good in the long run. It had sad immediate consequences. She had a miscarriage.'

'Look, Gert, I. . . .'

'There's more. Let me get on to Johnny for a moment. I'd met him before a couple of times, at Helen and Hugo's wedding, and once when he took me to dinner, but I didn't know him all that well then. I liked him, but at the time no more than that. It's almost impossible to project yourself into another person's mind, however close to them you think you are, but I'll try. Here were the two of them, Helen and Johnny. Helen destroyed with grief about a dead husband she'd loved and a lost baby. Johnny, the husband's closest friend, with him when he was killed, missing him in a different way.

'Johnny was kindly, sympathetic, attractive. Remember also that, although the war in Europe was over, the war in the Far East wasn't. Johnny was due to go and fight Japs. He'd been in and out of action for the best part of two years, and he'd been wounded twice, and I don't think he rated his chances of survival all that highly. Too many of his friends had been killed during the past few years. He wouldn't show it, of course, any more than Helen had been prepared to parade her sorrows about Hugo. But it was there. So there you had a situation with the two of them naturally spending more and more time with each other, with the common tie of a dead husband of one who was the dead friend of the other. One despairing attractive female drawing solace from an attractive male with a short life-expectancy, and who wasn't willing to admit it but was in need of solace himself. It's an explosive mixture. The consoling hugs progressed to something more serious. Both sides of the transaction conducted with a sort of physical and spiritual desperation. Both sides drawing and giving comfort. Helen told me about it at the time. Johnny told me about it later. Much later.'

'Gert,' said Alice, 'if you don't want to, please, please don't say any more. You've told me more than enough to keep me from making a fool of myself with Helen. Poor Helen. If I'd had the slightest. . . .'

'I think that you *should* know it all. It'll help you to understand her. Now that I've got this far I'll finish it off. That's if it isn't upsetting you too much. You're looking a bit distressed.'

'I was just thinking of what it would have been like if I'd had to spend the first months of my marriage and pregnancy wondering every day whether Ulick had been killed. And then being told that he had.'

'I know,' said Gert. 'I often thought that, a few years later when I married Johnny. You and I were lucky. Let's have some more coffee.'

The staff of the Bari hospital began to be dispersed, said Gert. The fighting was over. There were no more customers. Patients were sent home as they recovered, some of them, including Johnny, 'to be fattened up for the next piece of human lunacy, against the Japanese'. Helen didn't particularly want to go anywhere. No husband, no foetus to take home to Ireland. They were kind to her. They arranged a special posting to a small military hospital in Graz in Austria. Alpine air and edelweiss and walking trips in the mountains, and rough red wine and steins of beer, and jolly, red-faced singing people in fancy dress who 'thought that Nazism was abominable, after deciding that it was about three weeks before they lost the war'.

Gert, who was standing by for a temporary posting to Egypt, went up to Graz on a few days' leave to stay with Helen. Helen was very grave, and very calm. One night, in tears this time, unusually, she told Gert that she'd never get over Hugo. She supposed that from time to time she'd end up copulating with some man, but it would be as a physical release. There could be no repeat of the almost mystical dimension it had reached with Hugo, or of the anguished search for consolation that it had been briefly with Johnny. She felt badly about the way she'd behaved with Johnny, but it had helped her and she thought that it had helped him. She was relieved that she had the curse. She and Johnny had taken no precautions. In her present state she couldn't have dealt with a child by him.

Gert and Helen put in a lot of walking, and gathered wild flowers, and twice Helen took her to the local Catholic church, where Helen with concentrated composure prayed for Hugo's soul, and unbelieving Gert thought generally benevolent thoughts and was glad that Helen had this source of comfort. When Gert left she was happier about Helen than she had been since Hugo was killed.

Three months later, when Gert was in the Canal Zone, a badly delayed letter arrived from Helen. She was pregnant again, she wrote.

Alice, who had been trying to associate in her mind the young victim of this personal purgatory with the elegant, aloof, generous Helen that she knew, blurted out a question that she at once felt could have been phrased more carefully and put less precipitately.

'Who was the father?'

'I don't know,' said Gert levelly. 'Nor does she. She was knocked unconscious and raped, while picking spring gentians in a beech-wood. To put as a little memory to Hugo in the church.'

CHAPTER THIRTY-ONE

ALICE sat in frowning silence for a while. Then she stood up and turned on lamps, and with preoccupied precision moved them an inch or two. Then she moved them back again. She shifted ornaments, adjusted the hang of pictures and drew the curtains, with an absorbed interest in the way in which the runners worked. She stared critically at the pictures that she had squared off, and tinkered about with the ornaments that she had displaced. She put them back where they had been. She returned to her armchair, sat down and contemplated Gert.

'Fuck it,' said Alice.

'Yes,' said Gert.

'Why didn't someone tell me earlier? Before I started behaving like an eejit.'

'What someone? Helen? How could she? Why should she? Ulick? He didn't know. Still doesn't. One of the things you'll have to work out is whether to tell him. And, if so, how? Johnny and me? We both loved her, in our separate ways. All we wanted for her was that she would get over it. Platitudes about letting time cure all. It sounds unimaginative, but time *does* cure most.'

'I've never had to put it to the test,' said Alice, 'but I'm sure you're right.'

'Are you being cynical, Alice?'

'No. Grateful. To you. There are still some unanswered questions.'

'There usually are. Ask 'em.'

'OK,' said Alice, 'suppose we take the simple human mechanics of the thing. Helen gets raped and made pregnant in Austria. Ulick gets born in Dublin. What happens in between? There's nine months and a bit to be accounted for.'

'I wasn't around for the first part of it, and Helen never spoke of it. It must have been routine. Harrowing routine, but still routine. Initial medical treatment, statement to the Military Police, pregnancy later suspected, pregnancy confirmed. Somebody presumably suggested an abortion, and Helen presumably rejected it. Repatriation to Ireland. The military come in for a lot of criticism nowadays, but they do run a very big machine with big resources, and they do it efficiently. They'd have looked after her very well. And discreetly. I hadn't thought of it before, but I suppose that if you must get raped it's best to have it done to you when you're working in a military hospital.'

'I'd prefer to pass the opportunity by,' said Alice.

'Me, too. Anyway, my secondment in Egypt was a short one and I came home. I'd a lot of leave due. I went to stay with Helen at Grantsbridge. She was about six months gone. Very silent, but controlled. Determined to do all she could to prepare sensibly for the birth. Ate the right food and did exercises and walked a lot and swam in the lake. I was very glad that I went. Her mother was there, and was a nice woman, but she was getting on and the whole thing was beyond her. She wasn't much help. She was preoccupied with poets and playwrights and musicians and the like, and seemed to find it difficult to focus on Helen. Fortunately, Helen's brother had been present for most of the time. He was recovering from having been a prisoner of the Japanese, but Helen said that he'd been an enormous support. He'd gone back to Malaya just before I arrived. So I got there just at the right time.'

'That's Oliver. He's still around. Did you ever meet him? Later?'

'No. I'll come to that. It soon became pretty clear to me that, although Helen was tightly under control, she was dangerously close to the edge. She hardly spoke. A thing that sticks in my mind is how agitated she used to get when the mail came in, particularly letters she got from Canada and from her brother in Malaya. She'd take them to her room, and come down hours later, looking confused and flushed, a strange mixture of bitterness and triumph showing in her expression. But she'd never talk about that, either, any more than she'd talk about anything else other than practical ante-natal preparations. I eventually decided that unless I stuck around there might be another tragedy. I was going to resign from the nursing service anyway. I brought it forward and stayed with Helen.'

'Until Ulick was born?'

'And afterwards. She was OK until he was born. Just. Then she fell into a post-natal depression. Not unusual, but it was too much for her. For several weeks – months – she was what the undiscriminating would describe as mad. She developed delusions. She was convinced that the man who'd raped her was Hugo. I got her fixed up in a psychiatric nursing home here in Dublin. It was all done very discreetly. It had to be in those days. Mental illness still carried something of a stigma. People tapped their heads and talked about loonies.'

'*Jesus*, Gert. . . . Who looked after the baby?'

'I did. Ulick was a lovely baby.'

'A thing that I can't understand', said Alice, 'is that. . . .'

'I suspect that it's the same thing that Johnny and I have never really understood. We both helped her at times when she was terribly troubled. Johnny, and to a lesser extent me, after Hugo was killed. Me, before and after Ulick was born. Why had Ulick and you never heard of us until you started digging into all this? Why aren't we honorary aunts and uncles? Or at least close friends, regularly in touch, visiting each other?'

'That's it,' said Alice.

'I can tell you what happened. I can't tell you why it did. But I can make a sympathetic guess. Helen came out of the nursing home completely recovered. I was at Grantsbridge with Ulick and her mother. I handed back Ulick to her, and she was marvellous with him. It was lovely to see. I left after a few days, and a very warm parting, and went off first to Edinburgh and then to London, looking vaguely for a civilian nursing job. Johnny'd kept in touch and was in London. He'd been demobbed and had just had an interview with the Colonial Office. They accepted him, posted him to Nigeria and put him on a year's course at the School of Oriental and African Studies. I saw a lot of him. We decided to get married. We'd both of us written frequently to Helen, and she'd written back – happy, cheerful letters, full of news about the baby. Then one day we each got almost identical letters. They were full of warmth and love and kindness, but they said that she'd had an appallingly difficult decision to make and she'd made it. There were two reasons for it. The first concerned herself. Thoughts of the past made her so sad and miserable and desperate that she'd decided that the only hope for her was to put it behind her, to forget it. We were parts of her past – good parts, the best parts, but still parts. The second reason was to do with Ulick. It would be hard enough to tell him when he was older that he was a bastard. To have to tell him that his father was an unknown rapist would be unthinkable. She and her brother had therefore worked out a scheme, agreed to by some member of the Burke family in Canada whom she didn't seem to like very much, by which Ulick would be passed off as Hugo's son. There was one essential corollary both to wiping out the past and to safeguarding the truth of Ulick's paternity. She would have to cut all connections with anyone she had known who had had anything to do with either. It was a dreadful thing to have to do, but she had made up her mind to do it. So she was doing it. For the rest of her life she would think of us with love and thankfulness, and she would always pray for us. This was goodbye, and all God's blessings upon us.'

'And that', said Gert, 'was that.'

'Suffering Christ,' said Alice.

'You're in danger of running out of deplorable language,' said Gert.

'I already have,' said Alice. 'What did you do?'

'Nothing. We talked about it a lot of course. We both felt rather hurt.'

'*Rather* hurt?'

'All right, *very* hurt. But then, the more we thought about it, the more it made some sort of sense. After all, I'd spent months going on and on to her about Time, the infallible healer – the sort of stuff I mentioned to you just now. If she'd worked out that the best way to give Time a helping hand was to cut the painter with her entire past, including us, there was an ironic logic to the whole thing. There were other ways that she might have done it, but it was her choice and she'd picked this one. Sad for us, but perfectly defensible. So we went to a lot of care in writing and rewriting and re-rewriting a letter to her, in which we said that we understood and would honour her decision. And sent her all our love. And meant it. And after we'd posted it we talked about her a lot, and I got a bit tearful, and Johnny comforted me, and we agreed never to say a word about what had happened to her to a living soul. Which we didn't. Until you, Alice bloody Burke, hove into view, waving your inquisitiveness about like a banner and getting too damned close to the truth for comfort.'

Gert smiled. 'And remember,' she said. 'You've run out of improper expressions.'

Alice stood up silently. She walked over to Gert's chair and sat on the arm. She put her own arm around Gert's shoulders and hugged, hard. 'Not an improper expression,' she said at last. 'Just a genuinely meant one. Thank you.'

'I've thought of a postscript,' said Gert as she got out of Alice's Mini in Donnybrook. 'I think you now know why Helen seems a prude about sex.'

'Yes,' said Alice, 'I do. Among many other things I now know.'

They kissed each other goodbye affectionately.

Alice put the Mini back in the garage, locked the doors and wandered about the house thinking, not coherently, glimpses of the previously masked parts of the lives of people she knew and had thought that she knew about. Bereaved Helen, raped Helen, mad Helen, recovered, determined, calm Helen. Matter-of-fact Johnny Laing, helpful, constructive adviser on a book about the war, who'd been drawn inexorably into a complex emotional ferment compounded of sympathetic love for a dead friend's widow and his own suppressed fears about his survival. Alice's new acquaintance, the formidably voiced and formidable-looking Gert, who with a consistent and loving practicality had cherished and nursed a badly hurt friend through a succession of sorrows, and had met the rebuff at the end of it with a saintly acceptance. . . . Alice began to be touched by an unusual feeling. She identified it as humility.

Humble Alice answered a noisily rung doorbell and hugged Brigid and Orla, who showed no sign of noticing a difference in their mother's philosophical outlook. They hugged her back, and hung up their attractively ridiculous school berets, and their coats and satchels, and chattered away over glasses of milk and baked beans on toast about their day's doings at school. They considered and agreed between them, on grounds that Alice thought privately to be insubstantial, that they would watch that boring international Rugby match on the television on the following afternoon in the hope of the cameras picking out Daddy in the crowd. When they had cleared the table and had settled down to their homework, Alice went to her writing-room and took down the *Hugo* file from its shelf.

It no longer had a purpose. She had established what she had set out to establish. She knew the facts of Ulick's conception, and the reason for their concealment by his mother. She knew that, however the transaction between Helen and the Burke Foundation had been arranged, and whatever its details were, and whatever had been the motives of Andrei Sepelov – clearly the member of the Burke family in Canada whom Helen didn't seem to like very much – in agreeing to it, it had been agreed to and was watertight. Helen was not vulnerable to legal reprisals. Ulick had a continuing entitlement to the income he drew from the Foundation.

At the end of her quest, now, Alice also knew a few other things. About herself. About people, who on the surface could seem to be alarming, or stuffily conventional, or cynical, and who would go to enormous unobtrusive trouble to protect and look after those whom they loved. And that brought her to cynical Oliver, and that made her grin.

So, as Gert had now told her, Oliver had been involved in the negotiations with Sepelov that had led to the endowment upon Ulick of the identity and privileges of Hugo Burke's son. Crafty old Oliver, with his courteous enquiries about the progress of her book, and his helpful introduction of her to Paddy Madden and all that followed from it, and his casually introduced birthday gossipy tale about Sepelov the untrustworthy holder of ambivalent loyalties, had been up to something all along. He had presumably divined that sooner or later she would uncover – or get near to – the truth, and he had been playing some genially devious hand that it would be intriguing to find out more about. Only she wouldn't. It was all over. Or at any rate the Ulick-paternity side of it was all over.

Her future researches would be rigorously professional, confined to the production of as good an account as she could write of the last phase of the campaign in Italy, with the Commando Brigade fight at Commachio as its centrepiece. The production of the book would be complementary to, and take second place to, the production of the developed version of the little life that was nestling so satisfyingly within her. Now, wasn't that a nice immediate programme for any woman to have ahead of her?

There remained one outstanding problem. Ulick. Gert, in her downright way, had summarised it as 'One of the things you'll have to work out is whether to tell him. And, if so, how?' It didn't take Alice long to decide that it would be wrong for her to tell him anything. It was a confidence that rested with Helen, and one that only she had a right to choose to share with her son or not share with her son. She had kept her silence for all these years, and her silence must be respected. There was still the complication that Ulick relied upon Alice to furnish him with a solution to the questions of what his origin was, and of how he and his mother stood in relation to the Foundation's wealth, but that could be dealt with. She would defer it until later. Much later. She should be able to come up with something plausible, as close as possible to the truth, not so close to it as to expose all of it. It was a comforting ingredient in her life with Ulick, and one that in her judgement brought no discredit upon either of them, that when in his own interests Ulick had to be bamboozled he was easy meat for bamboozlement.

What, of course, Alice had overlooked was that when a series of interrelated actions by several different people is set in train by the initiative of one of them the actions, like a body subject to the force of gravity, acquire a gathering momentum of their own. The initiator may decide to stop, and may have the capability of doing so. The rest go plunging on.

The prime plunger was Andrei Sepelov. In a mood of what Helen Burke in Ottawa interpreted as alcoholically supported recklessness, he telephoned Helen one evening and made silky, unspecified threats. Helen was unworried, but again warned Ulick to be careful. This time pregnant Alice became worried about her children.

She telephoned Oliver. The call was routed in its devious country way through chatty and helpful operators in Clones and Newbliss. Oliver answered after a short delay. He'd been in the garden, he explained. The peacock was there. It had dropped in for a short stroll. The peacock had escaped from some private aviary two years before, and had won the admiration of Oliver by living rough, adapting to changed conditions and surviving two winters through its initiative in exploiting available resources. Oliver was fond of self-reliant birds, he said.

'Are you trying to seduce me again, Oliver?'

'Yes.'

'It's very flattering when I'm in the pudding club. Can I come to see you?'

'To be seduced?'

'No. Something I'd like to talk about. What about this afternoon? I've a lecture in the morning, but I can leave after lunch.'

'This afternoon'll be fine. Happy surprises is what life's full of.'

CHAPTER THIRTY-TWO

OLIVER had a log fire glowing in the grate in the sitting-room of his gate-lodge, and tea and soda-bread and honey waiting on a tray. Shelves of books covered completely one side of the room. A rack of fishing-rods was on one of the others. There were some Chinese prints, a Kazakhstan rug, and some pieces of Kelantan silver that he had brought back from Malaya. Two chintz-covered armchairs, a record-player and a television set completed the inventory. Oliver disliked overencumbrance with possessions, but made the most of those he had kept. He and the peacock had at least one characteristic in common.

He kissed her, and took her coat, and said that she knew where the loo was, and poured the tea when she came back. There was some preliminary verbal fencing that amused them both. Then Alice got down to specifics.

'I think', she said, 'that it's time that we both showed our hands. Starting with me. And I hope to God that you don't raise your eyebrows and look enigmatic.'

Oliver raised his eyebrows and looked enigmatic.

'All right,' said Alice, 'why don't you read this?'

She gave him Smithy's notes about Stanko Mikic and Achmet Rashidov. She explained who Smithy was, what he was doing, and why. Oliver read expressionlessly.

'I see,' he said when he had finished.

'Is that as far as you'll go?'

'As far as I'll go at the moment. I'll await the next instalment before I decide.'

'How d'you know there'll be one?'

Oliver laughed. 'There is one,' he said.

She laughed, too. The identical-twin-like mind-reading process was at work again.

'There is,' she said. She gave him a full version of Gert Laing's account of Helen's first pregnancy, her miscarriage, the rape, the birth of Ulick, and of what had followed.

Oliver listened carefully, without interruption. He stayed silent, thinking, when she had finished.

'Still nothing to offer?' said Alice at last.

'One preliminary contribution.' Oliver stood up. 'Let's have a drink.'

'You go ahead. Not for me, thanks. I have to be wary of FAS.'

'What's that? The Fenian SAS?'

'Foetal Alcohol Syndrome,' said Alice.

'Good God,' said Oliver.

He brought over a bottle of Bushmills and glasses, and orange juice for Alice. He poured the drinks, raised his glass to her and swallowed extensively. He stayed in silent concentration, and then said: 'OK. I think I have it now. A long time ago I was told a number of things in confidence. I also did some things in confidence. I've honoured the confidences ever since. I've been trying to work out during the past few minutes whether a confidence should remain a confidence if it ceases to be confidential because someone else finds out what most of it's about. I've concluded that it depends upon who does the finding out. The best answer to some could be deadpan evasion. In your case, because I trust you, and because you've been sniffing around only to clear matters up about Ulick, and because if you know it all you'll be able to safeguard it all, I'll tell you it all. And then we can exchange ideas on some of the gaps. Not that I've much to tell you that you don't know already. You've dug up most of it. I was pretty sure that you would, from the moment that you told me that you were beginning that book and started asking me innocent questions about Hugo Burke.'

'You mean that you *guessed*? *Then*?'

'Alice,' said Oliver, 'don't be silly.'

'The reasoning behind my birthday-party story for grown-ups', said Oliver, taking another slug from his drink, 'was to try to warn you obliquely that Sepelov could be more dangerous than either you or Ulick seemed to have hoisted in. Helen wrote to me about Ulick's television message to the people of Canada. By God, I'd go a long way to see that. If you ever get hold of a video copy, let me know. Helen said that she'd written to Ulick that he might have to watch out, but that she'd been deliberately vague about it. I thought that she might have been a little too vague. So I thought it wise to use a true story to try to underline the message. I doubt if I was very successful.'

'Not very. We put our money on something she said about having a hold over him of some sort. We thought that it should keep him quiet. Do you know what the hold is?'

'Yes. She's been blackmailing the bastard for years.'

'*Helen*'s been—?'

'Certainly. With my advice and help. I set it up in the first place. Now I've modestly stepped down in rank. I'm only the Assistant Chief Blackmailer at present. Unpaid. Never was, mind you. Paid, I mean.'

'Oliver. . . .'

'I'll tell you,' said Oliver.
'I'd be interested,' said Alice.

When Oliver, all the five and a half stone left of him after nearly four years as a Japanese prisoner, newly told that he was a childless widower, had been flown back from Singapore in the autumn of 1945, he had arrived home in County Monaghan in a condition of what he described as self-centred self-pity. The best cure for self-pity, he said, was to be confronted with someone – preferably someone whom you loved – who was in a worse state than you were. Helen, whom he loved, was in a worse state than he was.

She was in a shocking amalgam of grief, mental confusion, shame and despair. In trying to restore her, Oliver restored himself 'rather faster than I did her'. They talked for hours, partly about his dead wife, partly about her dead husband. They went for long walks amongst the drumlins and around the lake. He sat in a chair beside the fire in her room after she had gone to bed, and they talked more and more and more. All her early talk was of her life and hopes with Hugo. The story of her desperate, comfort-seeking liaison with Johnny Laing came out slowly, and the story of the rape more slowly still, both of them choked out in guilt and in spasms of sobs. He had no experience of insanity to guide him, but he became convinced that there were periods during which she was insane. The wild belief that the man who had raped her was Hugo, related by Gert Laing to Alice, dated from long before the birth of Ulick. Oliver had been told it several times in those early, tormented days at Grantsbridge.

Aside from his therapeutic role, Oliver took over the handling of practical matters that had been neglected. Their mother had been so distressed by the state of the two of them that she had withdrawn into a self-protective cocoon from which she sidetracked her anxieties into a fierce preoccupation with the furthering of the interests of her poets and painters and pianists, 'the predecessors of the crowd who are in the house now'. Oliver thought the withdrawal to have been just as well. 'Two wrecks of adult children were two more than any mother in late middle-age should have to deal with.'

Oliver began, with no conspicuous interest shown by Helen, to busy himself about her financial future. He helped her to fill in forms and he made her sign them, thereby getting for her a derisory widow's pension from the Royal Marines. He learnt from her, for the first time, that Hugo Burke, without being either specific or boastful, had told her that he was 'fairly rich'. She said listlessly that Hugo had mentioned something about the Burke Foundation to her. He looked it up in the reference library of the Royal Dublin Society when he was in the city for a medical check-up, and concluded that Hugo Burke must have been very rich indeed. Oliver said to her that surely, after Hugo was killed, there must have been an exchange of letters between herself and Hugo's parents. His mother had written, said Helen. It had been a distraught, almost unintelligible letter. Helen, equally distraught, had replied. There had been no further correspondence.

Oliver, without telling Helen, wrote on her behalf to the Foundation. The reply was signed by Andrei Sepelov, the first sight that Oliver had had of the name. It said that Hugo's father, distressed by his son's death, absorbed in the care of his wife who was even more distressed, now had little to do with the running of the Foundation. Sepelov was managing it. Sepelov would not further upset Hugo's father by showing him Oliver's letter. It would have been different had Hugo had a son, but sadly Hugo had not been spared long enough to father one. There was no question, therefore, of inheritance. Sepelov did not want to sound uncompassion-ate, but he was bound by strictly laid-down legal rules that governed the administration of the Foundation and of the Burke family fortune. Childless widows were not catered for in these arrangements. Sepelov was prepared to offer, without prejudice, *ex gratia* and to Oliver's mind every other cliché in a lawyer's book, a monthly payment that Sepelov trusted would help her. It would be discontinued were she to remarry. The sum was little more than the pittance provided by the Royal Marines. Oliver became angry.

He replied that he considered the offer to be insulting, the tone of Sepelov's letter to be disgusting, and the conduct of the Foundation's business to be inept. If they had shown the least interest in Hugo Burke's widow and if they were serious about their hopes for a Burke heir, they would have discovered that Helen Burke was pregnant. ('I was chancing my arm a bit there, but I was bloody cross.')

Sepelov replied by return of post. Oliver's latest information, he wrote, put an altogether different complexion on the matter. A Burke heir on the way was a subject that needed to be discussed in depth. Would Helen please come to Ottawa as soon as possible to discuss it? This suggestion infuriated Oliver even more. How the hell, he said, could Helen be expected to go anywhere to discuss anything?

At this point there was a diversion, 'which like all the best diversions wasn't as divergent as it originally seemed to be'. Oliver's medical tests in Dublin had been satisfactory. He was gaining in weight, strength and health. He was summoned to London for a further medical examination, to be followed by a visit to the Colonial Office and a talk about his return to Malaya and his next posting there. He was told that the medicos had stipulated two more months of recuperation. After that he would go back as Commissioner of Labour in Johore. Johore was in an even bigger mess than was the rest of Malaya.

Communist anti-Japanese guerrillas, sustained by the British during the war, no longer had the Japanese to be anti about. They were now anti everything else. They were determined upon a communist takeover of the entire country. Negotiations were under way for the turning in of their arms, but if they did turn them in it would be a partial and tactical move. In the meantime they were stimulating and organising sabotage, arson, labour unrest, and the widespread murder of political opponents. Oliver was given a room, a massive pile of files, an assured supply of tea, and instructions to read himself into his new job.

He enjoyed the getting together with his profession again. On the second day he was invited to a confidential talk with the Assistant Secretary in charge of the Department, who said that there was a potential embarrassment that Oliver should know of.

'There's an anti-communist outfit in Canada called the Burke Foundation,' said the Assistant Secretary. 'They're loaded with money. They've offered to help in Malaya.'

'I've heard of them,' said Oliver.

'There's a difficulty. Their help could be very useful. Clinics and schools and rural roads and such. Unfortunately, they're suspect. More than suspect. Conclusive evidence against, but it's unusable.'

'Evidence of what?'

'It's from secret sources,' said the Assistant Secretary carefully. 'The Foundation got up to some pretty strange things during the war. Some of it treasonable.' ('I didn't know it then,' Oliver explained to Alice, 'and I only found out very recently when it was made public, that secret sources referred to in that sort of context were code-breaking intercepts of diplomatic and military radio traffic. Ultra.')

Oliver asked how treasonable was treasonable.

'The Burkes kept in touch with the Germans, and some of their friends, through the Spanish. Most of their dealings were on abstruse philosophical stuff about preserving the values of Western European Christian civilisation against communist inroads, and so on. The Burkes were anti-Nazi, but even more anti-communist. There's a tremendous intelligence row going on about them at the moment. The hardliners, the purists, want to clobber the Burke people. The argument is that, whatever the Burke motives were, they treated with an enemy and should be smacked down. There's a pragmatist opposition, supported by the Dominions Office and us, who say why not forget it? It's old-hat, no real harm was done, the war's over. There's a strong practical argument against, too. The clinching evidence can't be used because it would compromise the source, and the residual evidence probably isn't strong enough to stand up in court against a slick counsel. If the prosecution went ahead, we could end up with an appalling uproar in Canada, an acquittal, and accusations of irresponsible and vicious mud-slinging at a respected Canadian institution. At a time when we want all the Canadian economic help that we can get.'

'I don't know enough about it to comment usefully,' said Oliver, 'but from what you've so far told me the pragmatists seem to make the more sense.'

'Unfortunately, it's not as easy as that. The new boss of the Foundation is a man named Sepelov. He sounds a very odd character. A sort of schizophrenic crusader who seems to have done rather well by both opposing sides simultaneously. Impressive fighting record. Wounded and captured at Dieppe, escaped and was decorated. Later lost a hand and won the DSO in Sicily. In between all that there's convincing evidence coming in from returned POWs – one in particular – that during his escape after Dieppe he collaborated with the German Security Intelligence people. There's also firm evidence that he was up to something similar, repeatedly, when he was in Italy. A lot of that's from unquotable secret sources, too, as it happens.'

'And he's the joker in the pack?'

'More or less. If he wasn't in it, we'd have won the argument by now. We almost certainly still will. But some of our harder-nosed intelligence friends want to see him in the dock. They say that since they're initiating prosecutions against defectors like Joyce and Amery, and POWs who misbehaved – mostly of junior rank – it's intolerable that a man who ended up as a colonel should be let off the hook. The internal battle rages on. I can frankly only see it going one way. Ministers will jump on any attempt to prosecute unless success is as good as certain. Which it can't be because the best evidence can't be used.'

'You fellows in Whitehall do have some interesting balancing acts to perform,' said Oliver.

'This one's more like a conjuring trick. But why I'm telling you this is that we'll have to head off the Burke Foundation from Malaya. We'd end up as propaganda mincemeat if it suddenly came out that we'd accepted help in our efforts to bring about an independent democracy from an organisation that went to bed with Nazis.'

'I entirely agree,' said Oliver.

'Good. I didn't want you to start complaining that offers of help from a perfectly good and wealthy Canadian Foundation were being frustrated by we stuffy troglodytes in the Colonial Office.'

'I won't,' said Oliver.

'It was after that', said Oliver to Alice, 'that I went to Ottawa and blackmailed the bastard.'

'How did you set about it?'

'It was easier than I thought it would be. The first problem was getting there. Civilian shipping and air services were only just starting up properly again after the war. But I looked up a chum in the RAF who'd been in Changi with me. He'd just gone back to duty. He fixed me up with a ride to Canada. Nobody had ever got around to sending me a piece of paper releasing me from the Straits Settlements Volunteers, so according to him I was still Lance-Corporal Grant, travelling on service business. The RAF put me down in Montreal, and I took a train to Ottawa. Then I rang up Sepelov's secretary.'

'Weren't there all sorts of security precautions? Identification checks and the like?'

'My generation', said Oliver with dignity, 'may have bumped off a large proportion of the world's population, but we did it wholesale, in style. Casual assassinations and car bombs and the rest of it only caught on to any great extent much later. With your lot. In those days, unless you were an obvious raving nutter, you simply went to see whoever you wanted to see. The secretary suggested a time, and I went to see him.'

'Was he surprised?'

'Rather pleased. At first he thought I'd come like the angel Gabriel, bringing good tidings of a Burke heir who'd keep him drawing his pay for at least twenty-one years. He looked a bit thoughtful when I explained that that was only part of it. I had to be careful of the Official Secrets Act, but I was able to skate over where my information came from. I said that I knew bloody well what he'd been up to, hobnobbing with people he shouldn't have been hobnobbing with, and I'd blow it all wide open if he didn't give Helen a fair deal – with particular reference to what was expected of him if the child turned out to be what he would doubtless call "only a daughter". I'd also taken the precaution, I said, of writing the whole thing down and lodging it with a solicitor. Hollywood movie stuff. To be opened in the event of my death or that of Mrs Helen Burke.'

'Had you? Lodged it with a solicitor?'

'No. I only thought of it on my way up in the lift.'

'How did he react?'

'Surprisingly. Full of joviality. What he liked, he said, was a real tough cookie. He knew where he stood, made him feel at home. I had him by the short hairs, and I was doing to him exactly what he would have done to me if the situation had been reversed. He didn't quibble at all. He proposed a huge bloody great settlement for Helen, to be doubled if she produced a boy and not a girl. I didn't quibble, either. I accepted. Then he wrote it all down in longhand, signed it, wrote a copy, signed that, too, asked me to sign both and gave me the original. I was rather impressed. Then he spoiled the impression by suddenly looking smarmy, and produced his chequebook. He asked me what I wanted for my services.'

'What did you suggest?'

'I told him to fuck off,' said Oliver with satisfaction.

'I see,' said Alice.

'When I said I see earlier you went all petulant and obstreperous.'

'That was a different kind of I see. What I think I see now is that

269

there's a neat simplicity to Ulick's being taken up as a Burke of the one true succession. I'd worked out earlier that Sepelov needed a Hugo son to meet the medieval dynastic requirements of the set-up, but I hadn't dreamt that Sepelov had been squeezed first. What did he do when he found that Hugo couldn't have been the father?'

'What he did when I first put the bite on him. It was complicated by the fact that I was back in Malaya by then, and it all had to be done by post, but the reaction was identical. Practical, businesslike, man-of-the-world stuff. Genuine admiration from one skilled conman to another. We both had to be careful about the wording, of course. It was going through the open mail. But he made it clear that so far as he was concerned he was stuck with our written agreement. He'd abide by it if it was a girl. Nothing would suit him better than if it was a boy. Indeed, he went further. He hinted that if it was a girl he'd be prepared to organise the adoption and substitution of a boy of suitable age, if Helen would come in on the scheme. She'd keep the girl, of course, as well as bring up the boy. She'd have to lie low somewhere until they were both old enough not to provoke questions, but Sepelov would have no trouble in arranging that. She'd get a handsome extra bonus. I forget the rest of it. I think they were to end up as twins.'

'It's as well it didn't arise.'

'It is. It all became much simpler when a boy was born.'

'You said earlier that Helen *is* blackmailing Sepelov. Continuing?'

'Passively, most of the time. He's a foul-tempered lout, and every so often shows it. That's when she gets tough. I had to wait until she was recovered until she could really join in the spirit of the thing. Then on my next leave from Malaya I gave her a full briefing and *really* lodged the hard word on Sepelov with a solicitor. Hers. To be opened, et cetera.'

'Was she pleased?'

'Delighted. I hadn't known until then that she'd met him in Italy with Hugo. She hated Sepelov. Every time that Hugo met him, Hugo'd end up desperately upset. To the point of nightmares. Totally uncharacteristic. She didn't know what Sepelov said or did, but she detested him for it.'

'What do you call passive blackmail?'

'That's the annual row when we negotiate the cost-of-living adjustment.'

'You're an *index-linked* blackmail team?'

'That's us,' said Oliver complacently.

Oliver put more logs on the fire, gave Alice another glass of orange juice, and poured himself another whiskey. Alice settled back in her armchair, adjusted herself comfortably, and stretched her legs to toast her feet at the fire.

'What', she said, 'do you make of the notion that the body buried as Hugo Burke's wasn't Hugo's at all? That poor German dressed up in British uniform and shot by the SS. Rashidov's story.'

'There are two separate things,' said Oliver. 'Hugo's body dug up from a shallow grave. Rashidov's German, dressed roughly like Hugo, buried in a shallow grave near the same place. It might be the same body. Might be two entirely different bodies. On the evidence available, who knows?'

'Have you thought about it?'

'I've done a lot of thinking about it. Before ever I'd seen Rashidov's contribution. I played about with a hypothesis. Or a set of hypotheses. What's more, I did something about it. I made enquiries about theoretical possibilities. From your chum Johnny Laing. I was over in London about ten days ago, so I rang him up and asked him to lunch. He thinks very highly of you, by the way. So does his wife.'

'What made you get in touch with him?'

'Intelligent anticipation. I bumped into Paddy Madden in the Club in Dublin. He said that Gert Laing had been over, and had had a drink with him and had been on her way to see you. I've never met Gert Laing, but I'd only heard good things of her from Helen. Since Gert was in on Ulick's birth from start to finish, and after, I assumed that, as a result of your poking your nose in, Gert had felt a need to do some explaining. To keep you from inadvertently blowing the whole works into the open. And since it was inevitable that you'd end up spilling your beans to me I thought it as well to take a pre-harvest look at the crop.'

A log spurted into sudden flame. Alice wiggled her toes in front of it. Then she looked up and grinned at Oliver.

'Oliver,' she said fondly, 'you're a self-satisfied, devious old scoundrel.'

'Nothing so enviable,' said Oliver. 'Just a prudent planner.'

'One of the remarkable things about this whole carry-on', said Oliver, 'is that almost everyone involved in it has been hiding something from somebody else. With the best of intentions. Laing had hidden something from his wife. He told her about it when she reported back after her talk with you. He told me about it when I floated this hypothesis of mine. I don't doubt that you've a similar one of your own. What Laing said was that some time after the war he'd met a German whom he'd fought against in Yugoslavia. The German was present when Hugo Burke was captured. Only, according to the German, Hugo wasn't captured at all. He gave himself up. Said he wanted to talk to some Ustacha colonel. The German never fully understood why, except that there was some highfalutin talk about Hugo having loyalties of greater significance than the accepted run-of-the-mill ones to democratic ideals and national causes and so on. Laing disliked the story intensely. He questioned the German closely. He reached the conclusion, partly from what he himself had seen of the other end of the performance, that the story was true. But it would do Hugo's memory, and Helen's restored peace of mind, no good. So Laing kept it to himself.'

'I guessed that there was something he was keeping to himself. After Gert's visit I assumed that it had been his affair with Helen.'

'You reckon he's another devious old scoundrel?'

'Not in your class.'

'I'll let that go for the moment. Your turn to talk. You've the look of a woman who's distended by more than a baby. A rival hypothesis bursting to get out.'

'It may be a rival to the baby, but I don't think it is to what I think you're getting at. We seem to be pointing broadly in the same direction. Has the patrolling conundrum come your way?'

'No.'

'In essence, everyone I've met who was around at the time agrees that Hugo Burke was a first-class soldier. I know nothing about soldiering, but what I couldn't understand was that he seemed to have a persistent habit on night patrols of leaving them somewhere and wandering off on his own. As good as abandoning them for long periods. The people who'd been with him laughed it off. Old Hugo was an individualist. Had his eccentricities, which were irritating at times, but good for morale. And so on. But I began to wonder if. . . .'

'I can see what you began to wonder. I should think that you're wondering even more since you've heard the latest Laing tale from Yugoslavia.'

'Yes. Was he trying to find a way over to the other side again? And did he actually do it when he was supposed to have been killed? I thought that perhaps he tried, and failed. By getting killed. It was only after Rashidov's stuff that I started to speculate on whether there was a chance that he hadn't been killed at all. But from what I've read and have heard from people who saw it happen there was no chance at all. So. . . .'

'I've news for you. You've reached the theoretical possibilities I asked Johnny Laing about.'

'Take it in two parts?' said Oliver. 'First, could he have done it? Second, why?'

'OK. But it's the third that worries me.'

'Me, too. We'll deal with that when we come to it. With luck, we won't come to it. Part One. My question to Laing. I asked it because until he and I had talked earlier on about the general circumstances of Hugo's death I hadn't taken in fully an important point. That was that although

Hugo was seen to be shot, and to go down, no one from Laing's troop actually saw the body afterwards. All of them, Laing included, were certain that Hugo was dead. He'd run into an enormous volume of short-range machine-gun fire. Nobody, Laing said, could have survived it. Well, I've no more fighting experience than you have, and I wouldn't argue with the experts, but I asked Laing this question. In his experience, I said, had he come across instances in which people had come out unharmed from what had seemed to be a totally lethal volume of shot? He had, he said. Not very often, but he'd known it happen. All this shooting stuff wasn't as conclusive as chaps firing off guns in television serials made it seem. In real life there were all sorts of random effects, brought about by poor or excited marksmen, worn gun-barrels, defective ammunition or badly zero'd weapons, whatever that means. And so on. Sheer luck could come into it. An inch either way could mean life or death. So, I said, is it, then, theoretically possible that Hugo Burke could have been knocked unconscious by a glancing bullet on the skull, have gone down, and have been missed by everything else? He thought hard, and said yes, it was theoretically possible. But, before I drew any conclusions, I should ponder on one thing. It had happened years ago, and neither he nor anyone else could remember the details. But at the time it had been the unanimous opinion of experienced witnesses that Hugo, beyond all doubt, had died.'

'End of hypothesis?' said Alice.

'Almost certainly. But not one hundred per cent. Expert witnesses, even in bulk, have been wrong before now.'

'One stage further?'

'Yes. I think so.'

'Before we go there, what about Hugo's boots?'

'You're losing your grip. They don't affect the issue one way or another. They ended up on Rashidov's feet. They'd have ended up on somebody's feet if Hugo was dead. If he was alive, they could have been given away casually.'

'All right. Next stage. Hypothetical live Hugo. He's picked up by the Germans, given medical treatment if he needs it, and is passed on to whoever he wants to get to. What happens then?'

'You've left out a thing or two that knocks further holes in the theory. I take it that we're both assuming that he was carrying out some scheme of Sepelov's?'

'Yes.'

'He'd need three things. The first is astonishing luck. To survive. We're assuming that he had it. The second is an extraordinarily efficient organisation on the other side. We'll assume that it existed. The third is one I can't see a way round. Sepelov would have needed secure and effective means of communication with his mates. He could have used

Spanish diplomatic channels through Mikic's monsignor, but there'd have been the same difficulty that Mikic mentioned about communications to Zagreb. The people that he was trying to make plans with would have been dead ducks. Their own side would have shot them, or worse, for even thinking about defeat.'

'I've thought of one channel that Sepelov could have used,' said Alice. 'I came across it during my researches for the book. While the fighting in Italy was still going on there were secret negotiations in Switzerland between the Americans and a German general named Wolff. Wolff was the SS commander in Italy. He wanted to arrange a separate surrender. To that extent he was as much compromised as were Sepelov's survival candidates. The chief American negotiator was Allen Dulles of OSS, but the Intelligence Staff at Allied Force HQ in Italy were brought into it from time to time. Sepelov was on the Intelligence Staff. I don't know if he ever went to Berne but, if he did, he could have made the Hugo reception arrangements with Wolff. Or with an understrapper.'

'Ah,' said Oliver.

'And if Wolff told his SS units, even without saying why, to look out for someone like Hugo they would have been effective. Another thing I'd never heard of until I started my researches was that there was a German order, signed personally by Hitler, that all commando prisoners were to be shot. A lot of German officers couldn't stomach it, and it was often ignored, or obeyed erratically. What could be more natural than for Wolff's confidants in the SS to decree that all commando prisoners were to be handed over to them? And it wouldn't be as if the whole Italian Front would have to be covered. German military intelligence would have logged in the Commando Brigade on their Enemy Order of Battle. It was the only one in Italy. All that the SS would have needed to do was to instruct the limited number of German units opposite the commandos to hand over prisoners.'

Oliver sipped his whiskey. He looked depressed.

'OK,' said Alice. 'We have our hypothetical live Hugo. . . . Oliver, can you think of a synonym for hypothetical? We're overdoing it.'

'No. We're stuck with it.'

'We have our hypothetical live Hugo successfully ensconced with the SS. They give him a new identity and documentation. Whatever help he needs. Discreet use of transport and communications. His clothes have been taken away from him. They dress that luckless poor prisoner up in them, and shoot him. And bury him in the hope that he'll be dug up as Hugo. Oliver, from all I've heard of Hugo I can't imagine him co-operating in a dreadful thing like that. . . .'

'He needn't have known about it. They'd just have taken his clothes away and given him new ones. He wouldn't have bothered a damn about what happened to the old ones.'

'All right. Hugo gets on with passing on his messages. Either personally or through safe contacts. How he did it, or what they were about, or who they were for, doesn't matter very much. Or does it?'

'It doesn't.'

'He's achieved what he set out to do,' said Alice, 'and I wish he hadn't.'

'I don't think he has. We've demonstrated that, if a chain of things that could theoretically – just – have fallen into place had actually fallen into place, Hugo Burke could have been where we've now put him on the board. On the German side of the line, sponsored by a powerful faction of the SS, adequate logistic support if that's the right military jargon, and doing what it is that he's persuaded himself he has to do. We could also demonstrate, with equal ingenuity, that Hugo could have fathered Ulick. He didn't, but we could show that he might have.'

'How? The chances of his finding Helen would have been non-existent.'

'The chances of his being alive were almost non-existent. Demonstrate that he *could* was the governing phrase.'

'Try me.'

'We start with the proposition that Hugo's roaming about in Austria dressed up as a displaced person, or a refugee, or whatever you like. The SS, or Sepelov, have left him with identity documents, resources to keep himself alive. And reasonably mobile. His job for Sepelov is taking much longer than he thought it would. He's going quietly crazy about Helen. He doesn't know how she is or where she is. He's pretty close to breaking-point, but his sense of commitment to his ideals is still just winning over his love and duty to Helen. Then he finds out that she's in Austria, too.'

'How?'

'God alone knows. Keeps an eye in hope on military hospitals. Or tactfully questions off-duty medical orderlies in pubs. Or even sees her in the distance by chance. Take your pick.'

'All equally unlikely.'

'But *possible*. Horrible Scenario One. Hugo somehow manages to make contact with her. They meet in private. In secrecy. He explains what he's been up to, and why. He tells her that it'll soon sort itself out, and they'll be together again. They make love. Then he goes off, saying that he'll be back. He doesn't come back. He's killed, or locked up, in the Russian Zone or by the Yugoslavs. Or killed when failing to stop at a British or American roadblock, and buried under his false identity. She goes mad. She finds that she's pregnant again. She fakes the rape story.'

'There are weaknesses.'

'It's riddled with them.'

'Remember that she's just lost a child. Through grief. Grief at Hugo's supposed death. He suddenly reappears in her life, but his reappearance won't bring back the baby. She won't be able to forgive him for that. Not at once, anyway. She might become reconciled in time, but she'll hardly forgive him immediately. Or get straight into bed with him.'

'There could have been more than one meeting.'

'There could. But what woman would agree to them in those conditions? She'd say: "Damn you, Hugo. You've betrayed me. I was in agonies of sorrow about you. I lost a baby because of you. Now you want me to connive at your part in some ridiculous, traitorous charade that further imperils whatever prospects there are for our future. And to make love with you as if nothing out of the ordinary had happened. The first thing you do is get yourself out of this mess you're in. Once you're out of it, if you can ever get out of it, we might talk it over. But there's only one move you can make now, and until you make it I don't want to see you."'

'That's roughly what I think,' said Oliver.

He sank his whiskey, refilled his glass, and stood with his back to the fire.

'Scenario Two', said Oliver, 'is that Helen has done what she told Gert Laing that she might sooner or later do. She hasn't got over Hugo, but she feels the need for plain, unloving physical satisfaction. She picks on some man and hops into his bed – or his car, or jeep, or whatever or wherever. Displaced person Hugo, who's tracked her down but is still unable to break his cover and reveal himself to her, follows her around from a distance and sees what's happening. Again, let's not be specific about how. Let's just assume that he does. He goes berserk with jealousy. Illogical, unreasonable, but jealousy is illogical and unreasonable. All that he understands is that the wife he's pining for, and who he has thought has been pining for him, is being unfaithful. Never mind that she thinks he's dead. That's irrelevant to him in his state.'

'You don't have to go on,' said Alice quietly.

'No point in being mealy-mouthed,' said Oliver. 'He waits for an opportunity, knocks her out and rapes her. And disappears. He might mean to come back later when he's cooled down, but he doesn't. The Russians, or the Yugoslavs, or an Allied checkpoint get him. Same end to him as in Scenario One.'

The fire was burning low. Oliver didn't replenish it. He and Alice stared gloomily into the red embers.

'I wish we hadn't started this,' said Alice miserably.

'We're playing theoretical games, dammit. Instead of deducing the conclusion from the evidence, we've used the evidence to substantiate a pre-selected conclusion. If you genuinely believe what you're trying to prove, you can make evidence confirm almost anything. You just take bits of it and hang them round the edges. There's no doubt in my mind about what happened. Hugo was killed. Helen lost her baby. Helen was raped by an unknown man. Ulick was born. There's no controversy about what happened after he was born. Or after he was conceived, for that matter. A lot of it was kept quiet by different people for a long time, but it's all straightforward.'

'Sad. But better than what we've been talking about,' said Alice.

'I should have been more sensitive to your delicate condition, Mrs Burke. Come and expose it to further peril at Annie McGinn's.'

They stood up and stretched comfortably.

'I'll drive,' said Alice.

'I think you should,' said Oliver, draining the last of the Bushmills.

Alice came down early to her breakfast in the guest-house. She had slept dreamlessly. She felt well and happy. She doubted that Oliver would feel equally well. In McGinn's he had built extravagantly on his handsome base of Bushmills with a serious succession of pints of Guinness. He and Alice had been joined by two likeable men and two likeable women, who had a guitar with them and were described generically by Oliver as 'poets'. There were songs in Irish and songs in English, and more pints, and more orange juice for Alice. Oliver's rendering of 'Come Home, Paddy Reilly, to Ballyjamesduff' had drawn much applause. So had a composition of her own about unrequited love, involving blackthorns and hawthorns and the sweet little song of the lark. She had delivered Oliver home by way of his old house, where there had been more music and more Bushmills for Oliver.

She wondered whether to telephone to thank him and to say goodbye before she left, or to postpone it until she was back in Dublin. Human kindness suggested postponement. She paid her bill and took her bag out to her Mini. Oliver's scarf and cap were on the back seat. A six-pack of Guinness was on the floor below the front passenger-seat. A leather glove lay behind the gear lever. She returned to the guest-house and telephoned.

He sounded quite brisk, but as if he hadn't the full use of himself.

'Oliver,' she said, 'I'd meant to call you later to thank you. But I've had to do it now. There's a certain amount of stuff of yours in my car.'

'Stuff?'

'Well, a six-pack of Guinness—'

'Christ.'

'And a glove. And your scarf. And—'

'Don't go on,' said Oliver. He paused for a moment, thinking. 'Just checking,' he said. 'About the only thing I don't seem to have left in your car is my virginity.'

'You mean you don't *remember*?' said Alice. 'Oh, of course. I'd forgotten. You were asleep at the time.'

CHAPTER THIRTY-THREE

ANDREI SEPELOV patiently, almost leisurely, developed his reprisal plans. Although one of the cornerstones of the Foundation had been its dedication to the preservation of Christian values, there was one Christian value by which Sepelov set little store. He did not believe in forgiving his enemies. He preferred to kick their teeth in. He had down the years put this policy into effect on a large scale, with almost invariable success, usually vicariously, often after such a long interval between offence and retribution that the victim was hard put to it to recognise the connection between the two. Sepelov's memory was tenacious. High on his shortlist of people to be dealt with were Helen Burke, Oliver Grant and Ulick.

Helen had treated him with a contemptuous disdain almost from the time when he had first met her, and had blackmailed him successfully for more than thirty years. Sepelov had felt a distorted admiration for Oliver, the brains behind the blackmail and to Sepelov's mind the sort of cheerfully unscrupulous rogue that Sepelov liked to deal with, but Oliver had once told Sepelov to fuck off. Oliver would pay for that. Ulick had given that disgraceful television interview. His number was due to come up, too.

On one reading, indeed, the television interview could be said to link all three in an anti-Sepelov conspiracy. The Foundation's staff of analysts had made a detailed study of the transcript, and had reached a disturbing divergence of opinion. The majority view was that Ulick's answers added up to the sort of incoherent gibberish to be expected from an alcoholically excited moron. The minority, and they were the ones who upset Sepelov, argued that it was something of greater subtlety. Ulick's pronouncements may have seemed inconsequential to the point of near-idiocy, but if you examined their effect in isolation from the manner in which it had been reached you could interpret them as a sophisticated attack, shrouded in pretended buffoonery, upon the way in which Sepelov had taken control of the Foundation and upon what he had done with it.

But that, by now, was irrelevant, except in so far as it required punishment. Sepelov sent for one of his lawyers and put to him a simply worded question. If Helen and Oliver were provoked into making public their knowledge of Sepelov's wartime dealings with his country's enemies, what damage could be done and how could it best be obviated or mitigated?

The lawyer went away and wrote a detailed opinion. To this he appended a summary, the only part read by Sepelov. It was cheering.

Since the British Government, and possibly the Canadian Government, too, had years ago decided not to prosecute and in the meanwhile had not changed their decision, they were hardly likely to be stimulated into doing so by the presentation to them by a private citizen of evidence that could only be a fraction of what they themselves already held. (Sepelov, the one-time Colonel on the Intelligence Staff, had never been in doubt that Ultra had recorded at least some of his less reputable messages. He had relied at the time on delay in their unbuttoning, caused by the higher priority given to signals of more pressing moment.) The only recourse that would be open to Helen Burke, therefore, would be to pass her information to the press, radio and television.

If – when – she did so, Sepelov's lawyers would issue a writ for libel. There could be no comment or speculation by the media whilst the case was *sub judice*. The lawyers would engineer legal delay after legal delay. With luck they could keep the process going for years. Parallel to the stonewalling in the courts, a publicity campaign would be mounted to emphasise Sepelov's outstanding record of gallantry as a wartime soldier, the accuracy of the Foundation's assessments of communist intentions, and the consistent value of its work as a guardian of Western democratic institutions. Further, less overtly expressed thoughts would also be fed to the media. Was it not strange, the word would be put about, how often it was that middle-aged women, particularly those like Helen Burke who had suffered early bereavements and who had lived alone for too long, threw themselves hysterically into embittered family vendettas against benefactors who had provided for them with outstanding generosity since their husbands' deaths? Despite her manifest malevolence the poor creature inspired pity more than she deserved condemnation. . . .

Sooner or later, wrote the lawyer, all opportunities for legal procrastination would have been exhausted. But before then there were two possibilities, perhaps a combination of both, to be considered: (1) Sepelov might have died; (2) Helen Burke, intimidated by the rumours being spread about her, plus whatever else Sepelov had in mind for her, might have lost her resolution, withdrawn her allegations and agreed to an out-of-court settlement.

If neither (1) nor (2) happened, and the case went ahead, the chances of Sepelov winning it were high to the point of near-certainty. Probably the conclusive argument would be that she had tried to blackmail him. The fact that she had done so with success would be glossed over by counsel for both parties. Hers, because a self-confessed blackmailer would lose both sympathy and credibility. His, because it would be maintained that he had provided for her handsomely despite, not because of, her mentally unbalanced resort to threats.

'Green Light' were the last two words above the lawyer's signature. Sepelov, who liked succinct colloquialisms as much as he relished the frank brutality of '(1) You might be dead', congratulated himself yet again on his talent for picking the right men for the right jobs. He passed the next few evenings in the pleasurable planning of retributive hurt. He would, he decided, start in a moderately small way. He would see how things went and would then, if necessary, increase the pressure. He didn't yet know how far he was prepared to go, but that was part of the charm of the game. You never knew where it might lead. You might ultimately think it worthwhile to go the whole way, so long as your cover was fireproof. Which until now, on similar occasions, it always had been.

On an October afternoon in Ottawa, with the fall at its most beautiful, the sky an unflawed blue, the air with an invigorating bite, and the leaves on the trees a flaming mass of golds and scarlets, Sepelov summoned two people to see him separately in his office. The 'Do not disturb' notice was on the door for both meetings. The first was with the Foundation's accountant, and was short. The second, with a well-barbered man in a well-cut suit, who looked like a moderately prosperous businessman, took longer. Sepelov was satisfied with both meetings. The subordinates he spoke to had been as carefully chosen as had been the lawyer who wrote the opinion that had earlier brought him pleasure.

Ten days later the tyres of Oliver's car were slashed while it was parked outside a pub in Cootehill, County Cavan. The entire vegetable crop in his gate-lodge garden was uprooted and scattered by night, to the last cabbage, Brussels sprout, head of broccoli, cauliflower and spinach plant. Stones were thrown through his cottage windows on a day when he was buying Bushmills whiskey at Northern Ireland prices in Lisnaskea, County Fermanagh. Oliver attributed these incivilities to extremist Republican supporters, disapproving of his earlier colonial career as a hired dupe of a foreign queen. He reported them, crossly, as such to the sympathetic local sergeant of the Gardai Siocchana, who said that this class of vandalism was mercifully rare in the area but, regrettably, was not unique.

In Dublin the stone garden wall of Ulick's house in Ballsbridge was daubed with tall-lettered slogans, applied with white paint, that argued unconvincingly that an Armalite rifle was a necessary and logical adjunct to a parliamentary vote. Ulick's car, too, suffered damage. He left it in the driveway of a friend's unoccupied house while watching a Rugby match at Lansdowne Road. When he got back to it its windscreen-wipers had been torn off, its headlights kicked in, and its paintwork scored systematically by what appeared to have been flintstones. The Gardai sergeant at Irishtown was sympathetic, and said that such vandalism was, regrettably, becoming commonplace in modern Dublin. It was the unemployment and the hard drugs.

On the following afternoon Oliver telephoned Alice to ask her opinion about a book that he was thinking of buying. She gave it. She added that Ulick, put out by the paint on his walls and the damage to his car, was irritable. She provided some descriptive detail of both Ulick and of the vandalism. Oliver said that he, too, was feeling irritable, for similar reasons. He told Alice of what had been done to *his* car, his vegetables and his windows. They commiserated with one another. Neither thought of a connection between two isolated instances of varied hooliganism that had taken place sixty miles apart from one another.

Later still on that afternoon, Oliver was telephoned from Canada. Helen, angry but calm, reported that her monthly cheque from the Burke Foundation had not been paid into her bank account. Her bank manager had told her about it as a matter of courtesy, the drawing of attention to what he, and, at first, she, thought to be an administrative hiccup or computer error. She put through a casual enquiry to the Foundation's finance section. An embarrassed accountant said that payment had been stopped, permanently stopped, not deferred, he added, on the personal instructions of Mr Sepelov. She telephoned Sepelov and demanded to see him.

'What about?' asked Sepelov, clearly enjoying it.

'I don't have to tell you.'

'Well, you've consistently refused to see *me*,' said Sepelov, 'and I've no wish to see you. We'll keep it like that.' And he rang off.

Helen told Oliver that it was being hung up on by a lout like Sepelov that enraged her more than what she still seemed to think of as a suspension, not a severance, of payments to her account. She appeared confident that Sepelov would soon be brought back to heel by a further application of the familiar squeeze. Oliver, who at once recognised that a new, unidentified element had been introduced into the piece, was less sanguine, but did not say so. He knew that Helen, aside from smarting under insult, was worried, for a reason known only otherwise to himself and to a small number of bank officials bound to discretion. Helen lived comfortably but, given her means, modestly. Most of her Burke income went to the support in Canada and in Ireland of voluntary organisations who looked after unmarried mothers-to-be and mothers-that-were, and to volunteers who manned rape centres.

Oliver soothed her, advised her to do nothing precipitate and said that he would sleep on it. He would get in touch with her when his thoughts were in order. They could then discuss further action. Helen thanked him and said that she would await word from him before she did anything.

At much the same time as Helen and Oliver were talking, the first of five telephone calls to Ulick's house was answered by Alice. The caller said nothing and breathed pantingly. Alice rang off. Alice answered a second call, a repeat of the first. She rang off again. The next two were explicitly, vehemently obscene. Alice crashed down the receiver on its cradle and went furiously to report to Ulick, who was in the garden, putting the final touches to his idiosyncratic training programme for the Marathon. He was vigorously hacking a wind-fallen tree to pieces with an axe. He listened with growing rage. During this conversation there was the fifth call, more obscene than the last two. It was answered by Brigid, just home from school. She ran into the garden, sobbing. Ulick went berserk.

'You sound upset,' bawled Oliver into the telephone. It was a confused connection. There were sporadic deafening, crackling bursts from what sounded like a firing squad at work in one of the rural exchanges.

Alice's voice came faintly, against a background of pop music and masculine laughter. A man named Ciaran, on a crossed line, was deep in lamentation to a sympathiser in Athlone about the social penalties attached to sex in a country in which contraception was a late starter, bureaucratically supervised.

'I am,' shouted Alice through the static.

'Where are you?'

'In a pub. I didn't want to speak from home in case Ulick came in and heard me. The phone boxes are all wrecked as usual. So I. . . .' Her voice was lost in a swelling chorus about the Old Triangle going Jingle Jangle. 'All You Need Is Love' competed forlornly from a jukebox. Alice had picked her pub badly.

'. . . and de old bastard says: "Bejay, if you've put her up the spout I'll fuckin' kill ya",' said Ciaran.

'Get off the bloody line,' roared Oliver.

'Jasus. Her da's tracked us down.'

'I'm not her bloody da.'

'Oliver. Can you hear me?'

'Just. Start again.'

'Ulick's gone crazy with anger. Unless I can calm him down I'm afraid he'll kill somebody.'

'Kill who?'

'De old bugger's enlistin' the heavies. I don't know dis Ulick, but dere's a coupla fellas out there in Finglas. . . .'

282

'I'll come down tonight,' shouted Oliver.

'Thank you,' shouted Alice back. She rang off.

'Well, dat's one less on the line,' said Ciaran to his friend, 'and the National Concert Hall's faded out, too.'

'It's called withdrawal,' said Oliver. 'You want to try it sometime.'

He went to pack an overnight bag.

It was nearly ten o'clock when he reached his club. He booked a room and dialled Alice's number. Ulick answered, in a creaking soprano.

'Hallo,' he said seductively. 'Please speak clearly. For as long as you like. I love it.'

'Ulick,' said Oliver, 'stop buggering about.'

'Oh. It's you. I thought it was that fellow again. I'm trying to get him on tape. For the voice-prints. There was this programme on the telly and they–'

'Where's Alice?'

'Here,' said Alice's voice. 'Beside him. Can you come out?' She sounded subdued.

'Not if I have to spend the rest of the night listening to Ulick's impersonations. What's he doing?'

'I'll tell you later. I'll collect you.'

'OK. Thanks. I'll be in the drawing-room.'

He went to the bar to order a pint of Guinness for himself and an orange juice for Alice.

He kissed her on the cheek, handed her her drink, watched her sit down on a sofa and gulp down half of it, and said: 'I think you'd better tell me about it.'

She told him of the telephone calls. 'It was bad enough for me. But *Brigid*.' She shuddered.

He stood up, squeezed her shoulder, and ordered replacement drinks. 'What did Ulick do?'

'He comforted Brigid, and then he handed her over to me. Then he went wild. I thought he'd lost his reason. He ran into the house and told Orla not to answer the telephone until he said that she could. Then he got on the phone himself and started talking to the Gardai. Talking is not the right word for it. It was a strange rasping, frightening monotone. I came in halfway through it. I think he put the fear of God into them. He certainly did into me. When he'd finished with the Gardai he just stared at me, not seeing anything, and said in a murderous sort of voice: "I'll crucify that bastard." What worried me was that he meant it, literally. Then he went back to the garden and picked up the axe and set about the tree he'd been chopping. He was like a maniac. He broke it into little chips. After that he came back to the house, hugged the girls without a word, special hug for Brigid, hugged me, poured himself a huge whiskey, and went and sat by himself in the garden. Brooding.' Alice shuddered again.

'It was terrifying,' she said. 'When he's like that he really *will* kill somebody.'

Oliver looked at her sympathetically, clinically. 'You sound as if you've seen him like that before.'

'I have. Two or three times. He's the gentlest man I know. It's one of the reasons that I love him. But if ever he thinks that there's a threat to me, or to the girls, or to his mother. . . .'

'His mother?'

'Any of his womenfolk. I suppose most men feel an urge to protect their womenfolk. Most men who are worth a damn, anyway. With Ulick the instinct's exaggerated to the point of pure blind savagery. Until he cools down he's not responsible for his actions.'

Oliver looked at her carefully. 'I don't like to say it, but I must,' he said at last. 'You'll have to get used for a time to Ulick running amok. There's a threat developing to his mother. She phoned this afternoon. Sepelov's cut loose.'

Alice burst into tears. Oliver moved fast to her side. He sat down on the sofa and put his arm around her. She turned her head against his chest and sobbed in great spasms. When she tried to bring herself under control he said: 'Relax. Have a few more.' She took his advice gratefully.

'I'll drive,' said Oliver.

'I think you should,' said Alice. She gave him her car keys. He gave her eyes a final wipe with his handkerchief, took her by the elbow and led her down the stairs. They both said goodnight to the porter, who held open the front door for them and recommended that they should mind themselves, now.

Alice's Mini was parked immediately opposite, on the north side of Stephen's Green. Oliver threaded it through the narrows of Merrion Row.

'All right?'

Alice sniffled, blew her nose violently and grinned. 'Thanks, Oliver. Yes.'

'Stop and talk?'

'Yes. But very briefly. I must get back to Brigid. And I've calmed Ulick down, but if that man gets on the phone again I don't know what'll happen.'

'Raglan Road should be quiet. Five minutes.'

Oliver took them through Baggot Street and along Pembroke Road, turned right into the peace of Raglan Road and pulled up against the kerb under a tree, midway between two pools of light from lamp-posts. Large early-Victorian houses lay well back from the roadway behind railings and hedges and shrub-broken lawns. He switched off the engine.

'Let's start with Ulick,' he said. 'How did you smooth him down? Mind you, if it had been me I'd have taken some smoothing, too.'

'He mostly did it himself. A combination of things. Thumping that tree into little pieces took a lot of the steam out of him. I think that he genuinely imagined that the tree was that awful man. The whiskey helped. It never makes him aggressive, only better disposed to the world than he usually is – and that's saying something. I gave him ten minutes on the first glass, and then brought him out another. Real killer dose, same as the first. That was when I sneaked out to that pub to telephone you. When I came back Ulick was helping Orla to cook the supper, and after that I knew it'd be OK.'

'Knew it *would be*? Not *was*?'

'*Would be*. I still had to work on him. I said that it had been revolting and horrible, and I knew how he felt, and I felt the same. But blind hate would get none of us anywhere. The only way to deal with these twisted people, I said, was by guile. And if they were caught they needed psychiatric treatment, not assassination. I—'

'You suggested that Ulick should use *guile*?'

'I did. And, Oliver, don't laugh at Ulick now, because if you do I don't think I can. . . .'

Oliver put his left arm around her shoulder and hugged. 'I'm sorry,' he said. 'I wasn't sneering. Just impressed by your tactics. I take it that that female-impersonator caper was something to do with them?'

'Yes. I jockeyed him into thinking that he'd thought of it himself. Reminded him of some abysmal television programme I'd watched with him. He took to it at once. He started playing about with the tape-recorder and the telephone, and became so immersed in it all that I knew we were all right. He's something to concentrate upon. It won't last. Fortunately, he's his final Marathon training to keep him occupied for the next few days. After that, God knows.'

'When is it? The Marathon.'

'Next Monday. The thirty-first. Hallowe'en. We're going to a fancy-dress dance in the evening.'

'After Ulick's run a *Marathon*?'

'Ulick', said Alice the academic with pride, 'is *tough*.'

'Do you want Sepelov and Helen now, or wait until you're more ready for it?'

'Now, please. I must know everything that's likely to set Ulick off again.'

Oliver told her of Helen's telephone call. He related it to what had happened to his car and to his vegetable garden and to his windows, and to the daubed slogans on Alice's garden wall, to the damage to Ulick's car, to the telephoned obscenities. It all seemed to be of a piece, he said, explicable only in terms of Sepelov's having decided for reasons so far unclear that he no longer gave a damn whether the shady side of his record became public knowledge or not. The blackmail that had preserved the balance of power successfully for so long had lost its bite. A war, its nature and extent so far indicated only by the tactics of one side in preliminary skirmishing, had been declared.

'Broken out. Not been declared,' said Alice.

'All modern wars break out without being declared. Just starting the bloody things counts as a declaration.'

'You need at least two sides to make a war.'

'This one has two sides. Sepelov on one. Versus the Allies. Helen, Ulick and me. You're cast in the role of the luckless civilian population. The ones the overshots fall on, or who come in handy for a little secondhand arm-twisting.'

Alice thought about it, and said that she didn't think much of Oliver's metaphors. And anyway, she said, there was another essential component of warfare that Oliver had overlooked. It wasn't much of a war if all the fighting were done by one side only.

'Our lot haven't started yet.'

'What'll you do when you do start?'

'The High Command hasn't worked it out, or even got together to discuss strategy, but I'll tell you a thing. If Sepelov gets genuinely rough, don't underestimate our best asset. As Sepelov probably does.'

'What asset?'

'Ulick,' said Oliver simply.

Alice was touched.

She was also frightened. For the girls more than for herself. For her pregnant self, too, of course. Of what might be done to the girls and to herself. Of what Ulick might do to somebody trying, or threatening, or pretending to threaten the girls and herself. Of the seriousness that Oliver attached to the threat, demonstrated by the clearness of the warning that he was issuing and wrapping it up in a confidently delivered set of cheerful generalities. She understood, none better, the operating mechanism of the Oliver brain function. He dealt seriously with serious matters with a surface lightness of heart. She did the same herself, which was why. . . . Time to damp all this down, or she would be in tears again.

'Oliver.'

'I'm listening.'

'Can we agree on one thing? Ulick mustn't know of any of this until it affects him personally. I know it affected him personally tonight, but that's not what I mean. He thought tonight was the work of some spare nutcase.'

'Point taken,' said Oliver. 'I was about to suggest the same myself.'

'Time to go home.'

Oliver drove the remaining half a mile. Alice brought out her keys and opened the front door. Watching a boxing match on the television, smoking a cigar and holding a glass of whiskey, was the largest nun Oliver had ever seen.

'Nearly took him in the second,' said the nun, 'but he hung on and coasted through the third. Then, Christ, in the fourth, *wham*. Never seen anything like it.'

Protestant Oliver stared. Alice giggled, and then blushed.

'Just trying on my togs', explained Ulick, 'for the Hallowe'en fancy dress. It's always sound practice to test things in advance. I forgot last year, and do you know what happened? I was bloody nearly crippled. I went as a Harlequin and the tights caught under my crotch.'

Oliver continued to stare at his side's best asset, and at last said: 'Jesus.'

Alice giggled again, and brought drinks.

CHAPTER THIRTY-FOUR

TEN THOUSAND MEN and one thousand women in houses and flats and bedsitters and university rooms and low-priced hotels throughout the city and its suburbs ate their breakfasts on the morning of the Dublin Marathon in privately adjusted individual moods. These embraced confidence, apprehension, irritability, preoccupied concentration, nervous brashness, and masochistic self-exasperation, the last expressed gloomily in such statements as 'Why the hell do we *do* it?' Consorts who didn't know why the hell they did it, either, and who hoped to God that they wouldn't do it again, stayed silent if they were sensible. Training schedules for the past few months had made a terrible mess of social lives, family lives, sex lives, and the orderly preparation and serving of meals. A return to normality, possibly by gentle stages, lay one day ahead. It would be the height of unwisdom to prejudice it by provocative comment at the eleventh hour.

Most of the weight of these domestic disabilities had fallen upon Dubliners, but many others endured elsewhere. There were entries from all over Ireland, and from twenty-three foreign countries. Only a few of the runners were potential Olympic material. Five hundred were under twenty years of age and four were over seventy. The majority, of whom Ulick was one, were between twenty and forty. They came in all shapes and in all sizes. Some of the more lighthearted were in such guises as Charlie Chaplin and Batman. One, seemingly indifferent to exercise-generated heat, was in a gorilla suit. Slogans on T-shirts advertised a range of sponsorship from cancer research to cat lovers. A few competitors, the bravest, came in wheelchairs.

Oliver went with Alice and the girls to watch the start. There was no point in trying to get into Hatch Street, where eleven thousand more or less philosophical athletes were compressed into a cheerful mass between the high façades of Georgian houses. Oliver and his women friends stood amidst a three-deep throng of well-wishers who lined either side of the road near Leeson Street bridge. Oliver was querulous. He hadn't forgiven himself for being conned by Ulick, the whiskey-drinking nun, into sponsoring him for twenty pounds, payable for the successful completion of the course to the charity that Ulick had chosen to represent. It was the combined unnerving effect of the sight of Sister Ulick and of the strength of the drink that Alice had poured that had promoted this indiscretion.

'Who gets Ulick's money?' asked Oliver. 'Save the Chimpanzee Fund?'

'The Samaritans.'

'He should cut out the exertion and become one himself. The suicide candidates who rang him up would change their minds out of pure curiosity.'

'That's enough of that, Oliver. Relax and kiss your twenty quid goodbye.'

'Set some sort of record, will he?'

'No. No records. Just finish up with the first couple of hundred or so behind the leaders.'

Alice was wrong on both counts. Ulick did not finish, and he did set a record. He was the first runner in the brief history of the Dublin Marathon to be arrested by the Gardai Siochanna in the Phoenix Park, charged with making an affray, causing grievous bodily harm, wrecking a wheelchair, property of a paraplegic, and destroying a statue of Our Lady of Lourdes.

The start-time was at eleven o'clock. Everything was in place. Crash-barriers blocked access roads to the route. Volunteer stewards, feeding-stations, St John's Ambulance teams, static television cameras, radio commentators, and foot patrols of the Gardai were where they should have been. Mobile television teams and Gardai squad cars moved about on the course. Temporary lavatories and politicians keen to be seen in the camera's eye were correctly positioned. Hospital emergency services were on standby. The Lord Mayor, wearing his gold chain, emitted an incomprehensible rasping noise into the loudspeakers and, to a happy cheer, competitors in singlets and shorts, or tracksuits, or sweaters, surged forward in a colourful torrent. Most took careful note of the time registered on a large digital clock. Ulick was indistinguishable in the throng. Alice drove Oliver and the girls home to watch progress on television.

The front runners had covered three miles before the field thinned sufficiently, between Kilmainham and Inchicore, for the spectators to be able to pick out with no difficulty the features of individual runners and the numbers fastened to their chests. By then number 5321 had found the working-room he needed to operate in a comfortable rhythm. The two spotters, one with a walkie-talkie radio, on the Ballyfermot Road identified him efficiently. The number matched the one that they had ticked off on the list that they held. The features and build coincided with the photograph they had been given.

The walkie-talkie man passed a message to his link in the Phoenix Park. The link, who was seated in a wheelchair sited among dense shrubs, ran a finger along the inside of his soft clerical collar, scratched his stomach below the number pinned to his crimson tracksuit, and said: 'Roger. Out.' He disliked having to say things like 'Roger. Out', as much as he was embarrassed by the secreting of his radio in a hollowed-out two-foot-high religious statue; but both requirements had been specified in the briefing and training session, the cash deposit had been handsome, and the fee for successful completion was more handsome still. With that sort of paymaster, no sane man would quibble about his instructions, however absurd. The link switched off his set, tucked the statue beside him on his seat, and called in a muted voice: 'Stand by, lads. He won't be long. Warn the others.' A large man in a blue tracksuit, also with a number on it, slipped away to pass word to colleagues at the side of the road a quarter of a mile closer to the oncoming runners.

Ulick had shaken himself clear of the congealed main body of runners. He was breathing well, moving easily within his capacity and within his planned timings. He was enjoying himself. It was a crisp late-autumn morning with an unsullied blue sky and just enough of a nip in the air to stimulate energy. A wind gusted from the north-east, and would doubt-less be troublesome towards the end when the route through Fairview and along the Howth Road lay close to the shore of Dublin Bay, but that was a long way ahead. He consulted his watch at intervals. From time to time he grinned and waved in acknowledgement of some of the more inspired commentaries from the wayside spectators. Number 5321 approached the scene of the planned damage that was to be done to him, described as 'anything leaving visible marks, the more the better, injuries not to exceed one, repeat one, broken leg', in a spirit of relaxed contentment.

Ulick ran comfortably into the Phoenix Park. There was an immediate change in the ambience. The earlier part of the course had been through streets thick with houses and shops and offices, the pavements packed with cheerful, encouraging, applauding onlookers. The park was different. There were three miles of road to be covered through the uninhabited expanse of the largest parkland attached to any city in Europe. There were scattered well-wishers in small bunches. The psychological lift from a friendly crowd was absent. Ulick felt a mild let-down, but no more. His preparations had been thorough. He was confident that he would beat his previous year's time.

The planner and paymaster had chosen his ambush-site well. The road here, bordered by high evergreens, wound gently. Ulick's running tactics helped the opposition that he didn't know existed. He had left a gap of sixty yards between himself and the man ahead of him, and was about the same distance in front of a loosely strung-out agglomeration behind. From these last came the sound of voices raised in outrage. Five broad, appropriately dressed and excruciatingly slow-moving competitors materialised from the roadside shrubbery and plodded along in line abreast, blocking the entire road, spoiling the concentration and rhythm of a steadily accumulating, bitterly complaining mass behind.

Ulick, on his own in a short straight channel between the evergreens, ignored the noises at the rear. They were nothing to do with him. He was interested only in whatever relevant happened ahead. He saw no relevance in the sudden appearance of a bearded priest, clutching a two-foot-high statue of the Blessed Virgin Mary, who careered on to the road in a wheelchair from behind a bush, braked, spun around expertly and faced him.

Ulick admired handicapped people who fought their disablement. He waved, shouted, 'Good luck, Father,' and altered course slightly to pass to one side. He was forced back to his earlier line when four exceptionally muscular, tracksuited runners appeared from nowhere that he could imagine and took up station around him, keeping in step. There was one on each side, one close behind, and one immediately in front, running backwards. Ulick felt annoyance at what he thought of as a lack of consideration, but became absorbed in the technique of the man who ran backwards. Ulick had never seen this done over any distance before. He started to ask if the fellow intended to do the whole 26 miles, 385 yards backwards and, if so, why?

The man behind Ulick timed his stroke well. He bent forward as he ran, studied closely the movement of Ulick's feet, waited until the rear one came up again to four inches behind the front one, and slapped Ulick's ankle hard with an open palm. Ulick's right toes locked behind his left ankle. The top part of his body continued on its way, in a developing downward arc. This descent had barely begun when his instincts, which were lightning fast, took over from his thought processes, which weren't.

The major ingredients of Ulick's reaction to being tripped were an immediate flaming resentment and the fact that his left knee was bent and his left foot about to touch the ground. The foot met the ground as his momentum carried him to his front. He thrust hard from the ball of his foot, used the frontward speed behind fifteen and a half stone to assist his take-off, and took off, parallel to the road. His head arrived with the impact of an unexploded shell in the stomach of the man who was running backwards. The man doubled up from the middle like the handles of a pair of nutcrackers. There was a noise like the brief climax of a gale of about Force 10 on the Beaufort Scale. He went down, retching.

Ulick disentangled himself from this sad human wreckage and rose to his feet, feeling angry. The other three were coming at him. The two flankers were slowed by the need to run round the extremities of their prostrate, vomiting friend. They were a yard behind the tripper. The tripper hurdled straight at Ulick over the body. Ulick hit him in mid-hurdle. He stayed suspended for a moment, reminding Ulick of a shot wood-pigeon, and then crashed down soundlessly on top of his mate.

Until this point, as Ulick explained later to a bemused detective inspector of the Gardai, the contest in Ulick's opinion had been rough but clean. It deteriorated into squalor when the left flanker skidded to a stop and drew a knife from the waistband of his tracksuit trousers. Ulick, a keen student of the techniques in vogue in simulated bar-brawls in Western movies shown on television, and a rehearser who practised in private in case Alice complained, knew two counters to knifers. One involved kicking the knife out of an attacker's hand if he came in low. The other was violently destructive if he came in high. The left flanker came in high. He rushed Ulick with an up-stretched right arm, ready to stab downwards.

Ulick stepped inside him as he stabbed. Ulick blocked the stabbing arm with his own left forearm, pushed his right hand under the man's upper arm, clutched his own left wrist and pushed, hard. There was a brittle crack, a tearing noise and a scream. The knife dropped. The knifer stumbled back. Ulick clouted his jaw. He went down in a collapsed heap.

Number Four wasn't difficult. He ran to hide behind the crippled priest in the wheelchair. Ulick took off after him. It was about then that external happenings began to exert an influence.

Well to the front of the congested blockage caused by the five wide dawdlers whose task was to seal off Ulick for a working-over was a television van with a camera mounted upon its platform and a commentator attached. The camera and the commentator had been tracking the progress of the front woman runner in the contest, Ms Claudine Comisky of Clonmel, an attractive, lithe girl, who enjoyed the publicity but was beginning to feel the effects of overexposure to exhaust fumes. The van had added to the irritation felt by frustrated, slowed runners when it had been driven insensitively through the mêlée with the arrogance that afflicts a profession that cherishes an illusory belief in the sacred importance of its role. The commentator gibbered the all-purpose platitudes that he had first used successfully when describing ballroom dancing. The cameraman ranged in search of something sensational. Claudine Comisky took in a few more lungfuls of carbon monoxide. The leading section of runners lost patience and burst by force through the cordon. The rest followed on in a crowded, jostling, petulant column. The television van, with Claudine Comisky hard on its heels, pushed ruthlessly to the fore. The leading elements pounded around a shallow bend that gave them a clear view of a straight stretch ahead, and saw a sight that gave them double cause for renewed fury.

Something was happening that would impose more delay. They could not, in conscience, ignore it. The nature of the event reinforced their rage. A big, well-constructed man, who seemed from the bodies lying about to have already killed three rival competitors with whom he had been in disagreement, was well on his way to dispatching two more, one of them a crippled priest. He had just thrown his surviving non-clerical adversary at the priest seated in his wheelchair, and was now attacking the two of them with a statue of Our Lady of Lourdes, held by the head. The runners broke into a sprint, intent upon the prevention of further mass murder, assault on the helpless, blasphemy and iconoclasm. They were beaten to the scene of the crime by two Gardai motorcyclists, who roared up from the other direction to investigate an extraordinarily large gap that had developed in the field, and who accelerated sharply when they saw what was going on. Before they could brake and dismount the crippled priest sprang from his wheelchair and ran away into the park with smooth-moving agility. He was pursued by the other assault victim, who went more slowly, because of a noticeable limp.

The two Gardai propped their motorcycles on their stands, walked towards Ulick and stood warily in front of him. Ulick, clutching what was left of the shattered blue and white statue, looked pleased to see them. The Marathon runners, surprised and relieved that responsibility for the righting of an injustice was now out of their hands, slowed to a realistic pace and surged past on either side of Ulick and the Gardai, like a river dividing at an obtrusive rock. The television camera, which had been focused on Ulick from the time that the van had first rounded the corner, continued to keep its sights on him.

Alice, the girls and Oliver were among the estimated 800,000 viewers who saw these occurrences. They were in the sitting-room, Oliver in an armchair nursing a pink gin, with Brigid and Orla on the carpet on either side of his legs, and protrusive Alice on a sofa.

The girls said simultaneously: 'Look. It's Daddy.'

Alice said: 'Oh my God.'

Oliver took a draught of his gin, studied the screen closely, counted the casualties and said that it was like the last scene in *Hamlet*. It was good to see, he added, that Ulick had diverted the attentions of the camera from that good-looking girl Claudine whoever-it-was, who would now be able to get on with some constructive, unimpeded roadwork.

*

The two Gardai, still regarding Ulick with caution, poised to put an armlock on him if he tried any funny stuff, allowed themselves a conversational exchange that puzzled him.

'Recognise him?' said the first.

'I do.'

'Recognise who?' asked Ulick.

'Bad news.'

'The spoiled priest,' said the second Garda.

'Is he really a priest?' asked Ulick.

'No. But you did a great job with the spoiling.'

They both laughed. They gave him friendly pats on the back.

'Good man yourself,' said the first.

'You're under arrest,' said the second.

The first Garda threaded his way through the unending tide of runners to his motorcycle. He unclipped his radio and reported to Headquarters. The second Garda advised his prisoner not to wander, and wandered himself to Ulick's three supine victims, now regaining consciousness with varying evidence of pain and discomfort. The Garda inspected them, named names, made clucking noises, and looked at Ulick with respect.

The television commentator bustled over, and asked for and was given Gardai permission to interview Ulick. The commentator addressed the Irish nation and told them that they had been witnesses to the unusual. A fight of this scope and complexity during a sporting event had never been recorded on film before, not even during the All-Ireland Football Final at Croke Park or at a Rugby International against Wales at Lansdowne Road. They would now, he said plummily, see an exclusive interview with a participant.

The camera turned upon Ulick, who looked modest. The commentator spoke into his microphone.

'Can you say', he said, 'what happened? Briefly.' He thrust the microphone under Ulick's nose. Ulick looked the Irish nation in the eye and told them, sucking his knuckles.

'I did the first six miles', he said, 'in thirty-three minutes, twenty-eight seconds. This was within forty seconds of my race-plan, which made allowance for contingencies. But not this class of one.'

The Garda who had been at his motorcycle radio, a kindly man who was worried that the evaporating sweat on Ulick might cause a chill, arrived in front of the camera with improvised ameliorative protection. He had cut a semi-circular hole in the sealed end of a black plastic garbage-bag. He stepped behind Ulick and fitted him into it. Two hands the size of dessert plates, and of the texture of corned beef, appeared in the picture, below a large, preoccupied red face. The hands clutched the garbage-bag, inside which Ulick disappeared momentarily until his head peered out through the freshly cut aperture.

''Tis a fierce cold day,' said the Garda solicitously to Ulick and to the people of Ireland, 'and with the lather you have on you you could do with a piece of a windbreak.'

The commentator, up-staged, came back into the act. 'You've not answered my question,' he said accusingly. 'I'll repeat it. What *happened*?'

'What happened', said Ulick over the rim of his garbage-bag, 'is *sub judice*, I think it's called. I'm not sure of its exact meaning, but its general drift is that it's illegal for me to talk in public to self-important fat men who drive about in vans getting in the way of Marathon-runners.'

Two squad cars had arrived. The Gardai in them loaded up the people flattened by Ulick. Ulick was led away in his plastic garbage-bag, an armless wobbly-dolly in a mini-length black sheath dress.

Oliver passed the evening in walking and in thinking. He felt lonely. His natural ally, Alice, was still an ally, but she was a vulnerable mother of young children. She could still be consulted, but it would be unfair to treat her as a collaborator. Her contributions would be to the thinking. What was now needed was some kind of action, but Oliver had yet to work out what kind of action. Ulick, if his eccentric energies could be controlled, would be the man to implement it, but the implementation would inevitably shift into strange, unpredictable confusion, unrelated to the intentions with which he was pointed in the right direction.

The morning's mayhem in the Phoenix Park had entertained Oliver immoderately, and he was proud of Ulick's performance, but stepped-up reprisals were inevitable. Sepelov would not stay inactive in the face of the destruction by what he would doubtless consider to be the luck that attended an amateurish, muscular cretin of what was obviously a delegated planned object-lesson. Sepelov would want to know what had gone wrong, and would devise something that would compensate for the fiasco, and with interest. Oliver found himself almost sympathising with Sepelov. Anyone who had dedicated a lifetime to conflict must be accustomed to dealing with opponents whose behaviour was susceptible to logical analysis. Ulick's wasn't.

Ulick's morning local success had brought an unexpected and welcome bonus. He had been delivered home in the late afternoon, still dressed in his garbage-bag, by now modified to include armholes. He was in genial mood, and was accompanied by two affable detective Gardai, for whom he expressed affection. They were considerate chaps, he said, who had recognised the danger of his catching cold on the journey home and had stopped their squad car successively at Searson's, Crowe's and, by way of a dog-leg, O'Reilly's in Sandymount to help him withstand the chill. The three of them had parted on the doorstep in a cloud of camaraderie and whiskey fumes. The senior of the detectives, after offering what was clearly a reiterated thank-you to Ulick for doing to those gougers what the detective had wanted to do for years, had also confirmed what equally clearly had been an earlier commitment. Ulick need not worry, he said, about any attempts by the friends of his foes to get their own back. His house and his family were now under round-the-clock Gardai protection. Alice had been much comforted. So had Oliver.

Ulick's simple pleasure in being something of a celebrity had been infectious. All charges had been withdrawn, he explained, after he had made a bloody great statement taken down in longhand. He had been fed well, and taken to a back room to see himself on the lunchtime television news. Since he was nearly twenty miles short of the exercise he had thought that he would get, he intended to use up the saved energy at the fancy-dress dance that night. Meanwhile he proposed to take a glass of whiskey to his bath.

When he left for it, Alice and Oliver had a brief, inconclusive discussion. They agreed that they would have to tell Ulick all that they had discovered about Hugo Burke and Helen, and that the recent violence was a product of a Sepelov vendetta and not of casual crime. They could not decide on when to tell him. He was a force not to be unleashed too soon.

CHAPTER THIRTY-FIVE

SMITHY, by introducing some unexpected new food for thought into their calculations, postponed the reaching of a decision to tell Ulick by a few days more. Smithy, aside from a postcard from Munich thanking Alice and Ulick for a delightful evening, had been out of touch. He telephoned Alice, and sounded mysterious.

'Is Oolick there?'

'No. He's playing golf. He'll be back at—'

'Good. I don't think he should know about this. Not yet, anyway. Not until you've had time to consider it.'

'Consider what?'

'Something I've dug up. It's weird.'

'Smithy, come to the point.'

'Does Oolick read your mail?'

'Of course he doesn't read my mail.'

'Sorry. But I had to check. I know he's a man of principle, but I wanted it confirmed.'

'He doesn't even read his own mail.'

'Ah. I hadn't thought of that. I'll post it to you, recorded delivery.'

'Post *what*?'

'You'll have to wait until you get it,' said Smithy enigmatically. 'But broadly speaking it takes over from where Mikic left off.'

It arrived in a heavily sticky-taped foolscap-sized envelope. It carried a heading: 'Not to be used unless specifically authorised by Ulick Burke or his appointed agent Alice Burke.' Smithy's ethical standards were still in good working order. So was his nose for the pursuit of almost-dead scents.

In a covering letter he said that he was having an interesting time in Munich, a city in which a profusion of ageing dissident exiles were disposed to be talkative. ('One leg in the grave loosens the tongue.') Enough material had come his way to keep him working to capacity on his major enterprise, the uncovering of abuses by Sepelov of legitimate Burke Foundation projects, and Smithy was thinking of turning what had been planned as a series of articles into a book. But he held to his guiding principle that kicking Sepelov in the teeth was one thing, and flinging muck about that would distress unnecessarily the Burke family was another. He had now been told something that he put entirely at the disposal of Alice and Ulick. Digest attached.

The teller had been a Croatian poet, who had worked in an organisation that once helped to get refugees out of Yugoslavia. As a young man he had been got out himself, with a party of cultural *Eminente* whose attitudes and wartime behaviour had made them anathema to the communists. Milan Jovanovic had not been eminent, but his father had – a painter of distinction whose political astigmatism was such that he had seriously thought it possible in wartime Croatia to be associated openly with Ustachi leaders without being listed for vengeance by their successors. Milan's role in the escape had been that of shepherd and watchdog. His father was too old to attempt the crossing of the Yugoslav–Italian frontier by way of the Triglav, 2,800 metres at its highest, without help. Milan had been recruited for the task of helper, in Zagreb in the late winter of 1944, by a Ustacha colonel named Vladimir Bilic.

Preparations were made in secrecy throughout the winter. They were based on arrangements made earlier by Bilic in Montenegro in a manner that was never disclosed to the travellers.

The party left Zagreb in the late spring of 1945. By then the advancing Partisans were at the periphery of the city, Ante Pavelic, the *Poglavnik*, had made an emotional appeal on the radio to all patriotic Croatian men and women to fight it out to the last drop of their blood and had himself run away, and inhabitants with a sense of self-preservation had locked themselves into their houses.

Vlado Bilic's plans were thoroughgoing, his procedures simple. He was dressed smartly in his black uniform, peaked cap, colonel's insignia, with a Luger in a polished black holster on his waistbelt. Less elegant, similarly competent-looking, and more menacing were the five men in field equipment, carrying Schmeissers, who were the escort. Each had stepped down several Ustachi ranks. All knew what to expect if they fell into Partisan hands. They also knew that they would have deserved it. They had a Volkswagen open staff car and a canopied truck, both provisioned with spare petrol, food and sleeping-bags. The assembly of the party offered no problems. Vlado Bilic simply made a round tour with his vehicles of flats and houses, and arrested the travellers one by one. They had been prepared for him. Rucksacks were packed with a specified range of contents to a specified maximum weight. Strong boots and clothing warm enough to withstand the cold of spring mountain nights were worn.

All twelve musicians, scientists, painters, sculptors and a philosopher were packed into the truck in less than a minute a head. Vlado leading in the Volkswagen, they wound their way out of the falling city, past rubble and jettisoned transport and equipment, and occasional dead bodies, and roadblocks set up by military policemen who were no match for Vlado's authentic papers and arrogant manner. They fitted themselves into the jumble of wheeled vehicles, horsed transport, infantry marchers and limping civilian walkers who were making their chaotic way along the road to Ljubljana and the north-west.

The journey in the back of that truck had its moments, said Milan wryly to Smithy, but he wouldn't bore Smithy with them. He would say only that there was tedium, discomfort and fear; that bickering broke out early amongst the intelligentsia and never altogether ceased; and that in one particularly bad episode in the middle of Ljubljana, when a German Feldgendarmerie Hauptmann was intent upon the summary confiscation of a truck carrying civilians and its diversion to a more worthwhile load of artillery ammunition, Vlado Bilic shouted him down with a magnificent hauteur that made them all proud for once, and once only, to be of the same race as the Ustachi.

Before dawn, when they were just short of Kranjska Gora, Vlado led them south along a bumpy track away from the main road. There were further, increasingly bumpy tracks that greatly discommoded the by now unitedly petulant passengers. They halted in front of a roofless, burnt-out farmhouse, visible in the light of a three-quarter moon. It was there that Vlado Bilic showed his real worth as a leader. He made it plain that he had no intention of launching a shapeless collection of unfit, middle-aged, untrained, argumentative individualists at a mountain barrier that would have strained the stamina of practised young enthusiasts. Vlado destroyed the transport, enforced a ruthless lightening of all rucksacks, and marched the complaining intellectual cream of his country to an isolated upland valley. There, he told them, they would stay until he had licked them into the shape that they would need to be in for the journey ahead.

He imposed an iron discipline. ('If you don't do what you're told to do, you're no use to me or to anyone else. If you don't like it, you can get out and die by yourselves.') He put them through over a month of hard training, in progressively longer hill-treks carrying progressively heavier weights. He taught them elementary navigation, and how to move cohesively in a group through rough country by night. Initial resentments abated as the days passed and the good sense of what was being done became apparent. By the end of the period they were lean, fit, hard, dirty, bearded and self-confident. They were ready. Late one afternoon two of the Ustacha escort slipped away up the mountain, heading west. They were back three days later. Vlado, who no longer needed to bully, and who wanted his pilgrims to know everything possible of what was in store for them, debriefed the reconnaissance pair in public, at a general meeting on the bank of a stream.

The approach route, said the reconnoitrers, was hard but negotiable. The frontier was difficult. The more obvious crossing-points, and the crests around them, were swarming with Partisans. Even the more inaccessible upland track routes were picqueted and patrolled. The two had been puzzled by what seemed to be a disproportionately extravagant misuse of troops, until they had found a temporarily unguarded gap and had wriggled through. They had made contact with 'Reception'. Reception had explained the reason for this concentration of force. While Vlado's party had been isolated from the outside world, the war, as expected, had ended in German surrender; the Partisans, as expected, had taken over Yugoslavia and were hunting down their enemies; and the Yugoslav communist government had laid claim to the old Italian port of Trieste. British and New Zealand troops were in position to frustrate the claim. Partisans were in position all along the Italian frontier as an earnest of their hope to enforce it.

Vlado ran a last exercise on silent, disciplined movement by night. Late in the afternoon, with blocks of deep shadow developing on rock-faces shielded by the higher peaks from the descending sun, they set out. The going was rough, dangerously so at times. But a full moon rose in a clear, starry sky, Vlado's navigation was faultlessly accurate, and no sweat was wasted demoralisingly on false trails. And of course the thought of escape was a powerful stimulant.

An hour before dawn they reached a high ridge half a kilometre from the frontier. Vlado, in the bright moonlight, gestured to them to get down in the shadow of a tall rock buttress. He signalled to Milan and to one of the Ustachi to go with him. Vlado led them down to a narrow, enclosed, shallow valley, across its floor and, cautiously, up a thin, winding goat-track that brought them to a saddle. At each end of the saddle, about two hundred metres apart, were two rocky knobs. The recce party had reported that, when they came through three days before, the knobs had been occupied by Partisan picquets. They still were. Low voices carried from them. There was muted laughter, a raucous cough, the flare of a match, the glow of cigarettes. Bored lookouts, expecting nothing, impatiently passing the time until their reliefs took over.

Vlado pointed forward and began to crawl. Milan and the Ustacha followed suit. From the far side of the brief flatness of the top of the saddle they peered down a reverse slope that fell as steeply as the approach slope had risen. There was a similar zig-zag track going downwards. At its bottom was a small rock platform, nearly horizontal. Beyond the slab was an unseen drop to a stream that tumbled through rocks. Beyond the stream was Italy.

Vlado kept Milan with him and sent the Ustacha to collect the others.
They arrived, demonstrating from the way in which they did so that they
had profited from Vlado's lessons in night movement. He paused to
count heads, and then took them down the almost vertical track of the
reverse slope. It was, so far, the worst part of their journey. The moon
was masked by the hillside behind them, an advantage to concealment, a
handicap to vision. There were slitherings and falls and a quickly
choked-off cry of pain. Stones rattled in small cascades. The Partisan
picquets stayed undisturbed.

The group assembled on the slab of the rock platform, most of them
breathless, some grazed and bruised. Vlado kept them closed up in a
tight bunch. Dispersal, according to the textbooks, was safer. He wanted
immediate, absolute control. He sent Milan and the Ustacha who had
been with him from the beginning over the stream. The password, said
Vlado, was 'Nikola Tesla'. The man who was organising the reception
was to be called 'Reception'.

Below the rock platform was another that sloped gently downwards to
a jumble of boulders, to the water. Milan stepped in. It was cripplingly
cold, shelved until it was chest-deep, and faster flowing than he had
thought it would be. He lost his footing and was carried downstream
until he was brought up short by a thin lateral obstruction. A rope, taut,
half a metre or so beneath the bubbling surface of the water, had been
fastened from bank to bank, part guideline, part safety device. Reception, decided Milan, knew what he was about.

There was immediate confirmation of this assessment when saturated
Milan and his saturated mate scrambled up on the far bank. A calm voice
said in Croatian from the darkness: 'Stand still. Raise your arms. Be very
quiet.'

They raised their arms. There was a hint of movement, hands frisked
them.

'Anything to say?' whispered a voice in Milan's ear.

'Nikola Tesla.'

'Follow me.'

They followed. Behind a large potato-shaped rock, in a short defile
scattered with pebbles, they met Reception. He was a casually competent-looking youngish man, dressed in Italian mountain-peasant
clothes and bare-headed. A Sten gun was slung over his right shoulder.
His Italian was halting, his Croatian more so. Milan was unable at first to
place his nationality, and didn't mind. Whatever it was, it didn't affect
the impression the man left. He looked completely at home in what to
Milan was a bizarre situation, and he dealt with matters as they arose with
an easy confidence that suggested an experienced familiarity with this

sort of thing. He smiled hospitably at Milan and spoke in English. The Croatian frisker interpreted.

'You up to a return trip?'

'Yes.'

'Find the rope?'

'Yes.'

'Good. Well, off you go, then. Tell Vlado to send them over one at a time.'

'OK,' said Milan before the sentence could be translated.

Reception laughed. 'I suppose that it would be more secure if I did this stuff in Esperanto,' he said, 'but who bloody cares?'

Milan, shivering in his wet clothes, returned to the stream. The prospect of moving forward, while paralysingly cold rushing water crept up his calves, his thighs, his genitals and his waist to his chest, was charmless. He splashed his way out until he was knee-deep, and then ducked himself under, wallowing for a moment on the stony bottom and then standing up and shaking himself like a dog. That, he felt illogically, left him committed without reservation to a series of yesses in answer to what he had no doubt would be a repeated 'You up to another trip?' from Reception. Milan crossed, and spoke to Vlado. Vlado pushed forward the first client, who to Milan's disappointment wasn't his father. Milan guided the philosopher's hand to the rope and brought him over. Milan went back for another, and was midway across with him when Vlado made the first tactical error – more a drift into ill-luck than an error – that he had made since the departure from Zagreb. Vlado told his closely grouped followers to spread out. They did. One trod on a mine and one set off a trip-flare.

CHAPTER THIRTY-SIX

THE MINE EXPLODED startlingly with a yellow-bluish flash and a bang that was acoustically amplified by enclosing cliffs. The echoes reverberated among the peaks. The trip-wire released the firing mechanism of a parachute flare that hissed vertically upwards, hovered, and burst into a blue-white light that illuminated the entire area with a clarity emphasised by the sharpness of the boundaries of shadows. The man who had trodden on the mine screamed, and continued to do so. There was shouting from the Partisan picquet above. The shouting abruptly stopped. Aside from the screaming of the mine victim, and the light, nothing new happened.

Milan never remembered who it was that he was helping over the stream at the time. The two of them clung to the rope, unmoving, mesmerised by fright. Milan was jerked from his stillness by a friendly hand that shook him by the shoulder and a cheerful voice that offered advice.

'The pause won't last,' said Reception, as soaked as was Milan and with his hand, too, holding the rope. 'They'll start up with mortars. They'll have this bit ranged. All sorts of shit's going to come down here in a moment. You'd better get that fellow across. You up to coming back?'

'Yes,' said Milan.

There was a distant pop-pop-popping from beyond the saddle. It was followed by a high whispering and growing shriekings. The shriekings came to a climax with a patterned set of deafening, echoing bangs, momentary gusts of flame, and succeeding whining, zinging noises. Most of the delivery was on the Yugoslav bank. Two mortar-bombs landed in the stream and sent up tall plumes of water.

'Time you were on your way,' said Reception.

Milan went, dragging his companion with him.

The next concentration of mortar-bombs came down as he reached the Italian bank. Milan tripped up his companion and threw himself flat on his front, covering his ears with his open hands. A tangy pungency lingered in the air. When the last zipping whine of bomb fragment and rock splinter had ceased, he stared upwards. The bluish-white flare had been supplemented by two more. It was as light as day. On the far bank

Reception was standing up, hands in his pockets, saying something to Vlado, who was crouched on his hunkers. Everyone else was prostrate, immobilised by terror as Milan himself had been a few moments earlier. He waded into the water again, pulled himself along the rope and stood in the centre of the stream, white water breaking about his shoulder and splashing into his face.

Reception had somebody in a grip by the scruff of his neck and was forcing him to the bank. The man tumbled in in a jerking flurry of arms and legs. Milan caught him by the jacket and heaved. Milan reached the rope. The man struggled, all reasoning power gone. Reception spoke.

'If any of the bastards gets too obstreperous,' he advised, 'thump 'em. Then haul 'em across.'

Milan, his mouth full of water, followed the recommendation but did not acknowledge the message. He dumped his cargo and went back for more. The next delivery was easier. Two men, shocked, gibbering, but with residual self-control, came along the rope to where he had moored himself in mid-stream. He gave each of them an encouraging pat on the back as they pulled themselves past him, and continued to watch Reception at work on the Yugoslav bank. The pop-pop-popping began again. Another salvo of mortar-bombs howled down. Milan ducked his head under the water as they exploded, and felt a painful, thrusting pressure on his eardrums as one bomb detonated on a sub-merged rock.

He had time for a very brief moment of reflection after he surfaced. He found that he no longer felt either fear or cold. He was dominated by worry. His father still hadn't come over. Exhaustion was closing upon worry. Both were at once buried by responsibility. Reception had another customer for him. Reception was holding someone by the collar and by the seat of the pants, and was running him at the bank in a classic bum's rush. Reception shouted, 'Catch,' and threw the man forward. He landed with a disorganised splash, sank and came again to the top. Milan grabbed a handful of hair and walked backwards, step by step. The man wriggled violently and bit Milan's wrist. Milan hit him. ('The only full member of the Yugoslav Academy I ever punched in the teeth,' Milan said reminiscently to Smithy.) Milan left him thrashing about in the shallows like a salmon in a landing-net, and made his way wetly, wearily to his mid-stream post.

Two other travellers, cajoled into calmness, were already on their way. One was bleeding from a head wound. One was hampered by a shattered arm. Neither was Milan's father. Milan pulled himself to the other side and scrambled ashore. Reception and Vlado were arguing. A body, distorted in death, lay behind them. Milan's father, his leg broken, lay beside them. A thin whimpering came from the direction of where the mine had gone off. From the hillside above came the rattle of tumbling displaced stones, a Partisan party on its way down.

Milan listened to terse disagreement. Vlado, a pistol in his hand, was for shooting the mine casualty and Milan's father. His advocacy was convincing, and when later – much later – Milan was able to weigh it dispassionately it seemed to be logically unflawed. Vlado's argument was that losses in this sort of operation were inevitable and should be accepted as such. There were a great many other people on the waiting-list for extrication from Yugoslavia. Their chances depended upon the skilled help of the likes of Reception and himself, who were irreplaceable. To hazard their lives, and prejudice the prospects for survival of future refugees, in a death-or-glory attempt to save two wounded old men who would probably die anyway, was absurd and irresponsible. The sensible course was to kill them cleanly now, so that the Partisans couldn't interrogate them, and to get out.

'OK, Vlado. You go,' said Reception. 'You're the king-pin we mounted all this for. We'd look pretty silly if we lost you now.' He laughed.

'What about you?'

'I'll have a go at getting the last two out.'

'No, you won't. You're needed,' said Vlado. He raised his pistol and pointed it at Milan's father's head.

Milan lunged at Vlado. Reception was quicker. He chopped down hard on Vlado's forearm with the edge of his right hand, fingers extended and together as in a military salute. The pistol clattered to the rocks. Vlado, in pain, stumbled backwards. The Partisan patrol on the hillside above sounded much closer. Reception leapt after Vlado, picked him up, held him on high like a weightlifter with barbells, and tossed him into the water.

'After him. Fast,' said Reception to Milan.

'This one's my father,' Milan said, pointing.

'That's different. Shift him now. It'll hurt him, but do it. I'll go for the other fellow.'

More mortar-bombs, a smaller concentration this time, howled down. A machine-gun – a Spandau, said Reception – opened up in ripping bursts. Reception was informative about the reason for this fire, too. The rock shelf was on ground out of view of the summit, mortarable on pre-set ranges, inaccessible to aimed shots. The patrol must now have a clear view.

Milan crouched over his father, caught him under the armpits, lifted and pulled. The broken leg bumped along the ground. His father grunted in agony, clenched his teeth and fainted. Milan stumbled backwards towards the bank. Chips of stone scattered from a sustained ripple from the Spandau. Milan bundled his father into the stream, jumped after him, held him by his collar with one hand, pulled himself jerkily along the rope with the other. A further burst of shot splashed beside them. Vlado, with helpers, was waiting on the other side. They dragged first Milan's father, then the exhausted Milan, from the water and hurried them to cover, roughly, no concessions for pain. Milan, gasping, cut and bruised, sat up and said: 'Where is he?'

'Just reached the far bank. With the last one.'

Milan scrambled to his feet and walked, staggered, to where he could get a sight of the stream. Reception, holding in his arms a man with a missing foot, blood gushing from the stump, was poised to jump. Further flares had been put up. The leading men of the Partisan patrol were clattering down the steepness of the background slope, bounding recklessly across the zigs and zags of the track, mountaineers born.

Reception jumped, clumsily, still cradling his burden, the two of them looking like small children showing off at the deep end of a swimming-pool. Milan forced himself back into the stream to help. They met at mid-rope, in mid-stream. Two Partisans with Schmeissers ran up to the far bank and began to fire from the hip, hosing the surface of the water. Milan clutched the mine victim's hair and began to tow him.

Reception, tired now, said, 'Thanks,' and reached his hand beneath the water for the rope. The mine victim's head, clear of the water, suddenly started to disintegrate. The bubbling surface of the stream changed colour, red fading to pink. Milan let go of the hair. The body floated swiftly down-current. Both Schmeissers stopped shooting almost simultaneously. Milan felt relief.

'Changing magazines,' said Reception chattily. He was moving strongly, both hands freed for the rope.

The next burst hit him in the neck, the shoulder and the side of the head. He collapsed under the water, spreading a stain as red and as extensive as the mine victim's. Continued shooting gave an illusion of boiling to the water around Milan. He inhaled hugely, ducked below the surface, felt about until he touched a part of Reception that seemed to be an ankle, fastened on to it, put up a hand to the rope to guide him, and moved, submerged, Reception in tow, towards Italy. When his lungs could stand no more, and he was faced with the alternatives of drowning or of getting shot, he chose the risk of getting shot. He broke to the surface and met total darkness. The Partisans had run out of flares and the moon had set.

'You were very brave,' said Vlado.

'Not so brave as he was,' said Milan.

They were standing, blankets around their shoulders, drinking grappa in front of a hot stove in an Italian farmhouse kitchen. Milan's father, unconscious, sedated, was lying between other blankets spread on the stone flags, his leg splinted, his wet clothing changed. Reception, beside him, also unconscious, heavily bandaged head and neck visible above *his* blankets, had an unhealthy waxy-green look to his complexion.

An unshaven Italian doctor, plump and with a cigarette between his lips, stood judiciously between them, spilling ash upon the front of his jacket, writing something in a small black-covered notebook. The rest of the survivors of the crossing party, also swaddled in blankets, also drinking grappa, stood about in listless cohesion, one with his arm in a sling, one with a dressing on his skull. They were suffering from shock, yet to grasp that they were free of the threat of death in their homeland. They reminded Milan of pictures that he had seen of shipwrecked travellers rescued by lifeboats.

The doctor put his notebook into his breast pocket, stubbed out his cigarette on the floor and lit another.

'What's the prognosis?' said Vlado.

'This one,' said the doctor, pointing to Milan's father, 'is too old for this sort of thing and he'll mend slowly. But he'll be all right. The other one? I don't know. He's young and built like a bullock. The neck and the shoulder will heal without trouble. It's the head wound that's worrying. There are complications.'

'How soon will you know?'

'*I* won't know. I'm a simple country quack with simple country qualifications. I've been doing a sort of first aid because I was roused from my bed, with my beautiful new wife in it, by a very rude, very persuasive man. He was very persuasive because he paid me about twenty times my usual fee and then doubled it if I swore to keep my mouth shut. I've now earned my fee. I shall keep my mouth shut. I shall also now go back to my bed, with my beautiful new wife in it.'

He picked up an old-fashioned Gladstone bag, nodded and said offhandedly: 'The only guaranteed way to save that man's sanity, and probably his life, is to get him to a specialist brain surgeon. The nearest one's in Venice. You can't play about with head wounds. I wish you all good fortune.'

A bulky man in civilian clothes, bearing a slung Sten gun, opened the farmhouse door to let him out.

'Can he be got to a proper surgeon?' asked Milan bleakly.

'I doubt it,' said Vlado.

'I hope he lives. His courage was inspiring.'

'Hugo has a reputation for that,' said Vlado. 'He showed tonight that it's a deserved one. Like you, I hope he lives. I'm not sure that he himself hopes he does, though. He was only put on this job for recognition purposes. He knew me personally. I'm always cautious about using clichés like death wish, but he didn't go to conspicuous lengths to stay alive, did he?'

*

Half a lifetime later Smithy, in Munich, asked Milan a question.

'Did he get to a surgeon?'

'Not in Italy. The top man of the Italian side of the operation saw to that. He had to be brought into it personally because with Reception hurt and casualties to be dealt with there was no one on the spot to take major decisions. He must have been kept in close touch. He arrived early on the following morning. He was careful not to show himself to too many people. Vlado Bilic took me to see him in an old barn some way from the farmhouse, because I'd been more with Reception than anybody else in our party and Vlado thought that the top man might want a first-hand description of what had happened. He didn't seem all that interested. He listened politely, but he was more concerned about what to do next. He was insistent that there was no question of Reception or my father or anyone else going to an Italian hospital. His reasoning was much the same as Vlado's earlier at the stream. Future operations mustn't be prejudiced for the sake of the minority. If the British or the Americans tracked back from unexplained casualties treated by Italian medicos, the whole network could be exposed. The one doctor used already, and bribed to keep quiet, was one too many.'

'What happened?'

'It was all very simple. We were given new clothes and convincing-looking passports, correctly stamped. Courtesy, I heard much later, of a Croatian monsignor in the Vatican Secretariat who was in co-operation with a well-disposed alcoholic in the Italian Foreign Ministry. There was a convoy of three surrendered German army ambulances, manned by medical assistants who seemed to be genuinely qualified. The convoy was led by a British army captain in a jeep. At any rate, he was dressed like a British army captain. The stretcher cases went in one ambulance, and the rest of us sat in the backs of the others. So far as I understood it, we were supposed to be a group of refugees who had suffered in Nazi concentration-camps and were sponsored by the Pope, with Allied approval, on a journey to a new life overseas. It didn't really much matter what we were supposed to be. Nobody asked us. The captain in the jeep dealt with the few questions there were. Almost all at the docks in Genoa. We embarked in a very comfortable Spanish ship and left the next day for the Argentine.'

'And what happened to Reception? Or do you think of him as Hugo?'

'No. I still think of him as Reception. Vlado was usually very strict about security and the use of these slightly ridiculous code-names. He only let slip the Hugo once. By mistake, when he was tired. There was a good doctor in the ship, but he wasn't a specialist, either. I asked him every day for progress reports. He wasn't optimistic. Reception was in a coma all through the voyage, and was still in one when he was taken off in an ambulance to a hospital in Buenos Aires. I never heard of him again. I don't know if he lived or died. I found that I'd got myself undeserved regard as a sort of Scarlet Pimpernel. I was asked to help in getting more people out of Yugoslavia. Nothing dangerous this time. I was sent almost immediately to Mexico City. Organising onward transport and raising funds. That kind of thing.'

'But surely you asked about him?'

'Oh, I asked all right. But I've mentioned Vlado Bilic's preoccupation with security. He wasn't the only one. My new bosses made a fetish of it. The less anyone knew about what he didn't have to know the better, in their view. What happened to Reception was one of the things I didn't have to know.'

'What happened to Vlado?'

'He left us in Genoa for Rome. I think he had some business to do in the Vatican. I never saw him again, either.'

'And your father?'

'He got better. Limped a bit, but lived to a good age. Painting until nearly the end.'

'I liked the poem you wrote about it,' said Smithy.

'I'm glad you did. It's part of a collection. I must show you the rest. Their theme is a celebration of a special kind of love. The self-sacrifice of men and women to the benefit of strangers with whom they have no ties of blood or previous affection.'

'You couldn't have found a much better example.'

'That's why I showed it to you. And told you the story behind it. I've also told you that Vlado Bilic said that I was very brave. I mentioned that because I'm old enough to confirm without embarrassment that it was true. I'm also old enough to recognise a flaw in my bravery. If I'd been on my own, with no responsibilities, I'd have hidden myself the moment I was safely over that stream. But I had to go back, several times over, because my father still hadn't crossed.'

'But you went to help Hugo with the guy who'd gone up on the mine. *After* your father was safe home.'

'As I've told you, that's what the poem's about. I was shamed into it by a man who loved people as people. Nothing selective about sons and fathers.'

'What do you think about Vlado's death-wish theory?'

'I'm sceptical about it. I've no true basis for judgement because I'd never met Reception before. But my interpretation of his actions at the time was that he was just a man getting on with an unpleasant job that he was good at, and who felt a commitment to try to save people in danger.'

'You don't sound as if you were too fond of the top man in the Italian side of the transaction. The one who wouldn't get Hugo to a surgeon.'

'I had the highest respect for him. He made the right decision. I just disliked him intensely. He was too clinical about it.'

'Did you ever find out who he was?'

Milan smiled, and swirled his drink around in his glass. 'Mr Smith,' he said, 'that is a very indiscreet question, and you know it. But I'll tell you something. Because of my earlier activities, on the Italian–Yugoslav border, in Mexico, and later still here in Munich, I make a point of checking independently on the credentials of agreeable North American freelance journalists who cultivate my company and induce me to become reminiscent. I'll name no names. But, if I say that he had a patch over one eye and a missing hand, you might wonder if he bore a resemblance to a former employer of yours.'

Smithy had added two notes to his précis of this conversation:

1. I have no reason to doubt any of the story told to me by Milan Jovanovic. Where I think that he may have been less than frank is in omissions. I suspect that he had dealings with Andrei Sepelov subsequent to the episode on the Italian frontier, probably to do with help sought from the Burke Foundation by his (unnamed) organisation; and that, like Mikic and Rashidov before him, he became seriously disillusioned. For all his references to discretion and security, he showed neither in naming Vlado Bilic, describing his activities in detail, and in pointing the finger clearly at Sepelov as the senior operator in Italy. Jovanovic would not, I am convinced, be sorry if any of this were to be made public, so long as his own role as the source remains protected.

2. It's easy to underestimate coincidence. But the resemblances between Reception/Hugo and what I know of Hugo Burke are too close to be dismissed. Only one discrepancy puzzles me. Why would Hugo Burke have been picked for the job because of his ability to recognise Vlado Bilic, whom he can't have met before?

CHAPTER THIRTY-SEVEN

ALICE made another urgent telephone call to Oliver when she finished reading Smithy's piece on Milan Jovanovic. Something had arrived, she told Oliver, that was of interest and might be of tactical value in the counter-Sepelov campaign, although she herself was unable to work out how. She was too distracted by thoughts of danger to the girls to be able to concentrate properly. Would Oliver come down? She was glad that there had been a respite in aggression since Ulick had won within the distance in the Phoenix Park, but even with Gardai protection of the house she was feeling uneasy. She was developing a feeling that the respite wouldn't last much longer.

Oliver replied grimly that the respite hadn't lasted as long as she thought it had. He had just been telephoned again by Helen from Ottawa. Her cottage on the shore of Lake Mahon, left to her as a legacy along with the Rockcliffe Park house by Hugo's mother, had been destroyed that morning by what the Ontario Provincial Police had described as a time-bomb. Helen was unhurt. She hadn't been in the cottage at the time. Oliver would leave straightaway for Dublin and would tell Alice more when he arrived.

Oliver thought that Alice looked worn and wan when he saw her. Alice thought that Oliver looked plain ferocious. She was glad that Ulick was out of the house. She couldn't at the moment deal with two ferocious men.

Helen, said Oliver, had closed the cottage for the coming winter, but had driven out that morning to bring back a chair in need of repair and curtains that had to be cleaned. The explosion, heard and reported by the storekeeper in Rupert, had been twenty minutes after her departure. No, she had told the police, nobody had known that she intended to go there. She hadn't known herself until the last minute. She had gone on impulse, after the sudden cancellation of an earlier commitment. No, she had also told the police, still plausibly but less accurately, she knew of no personal enemies who would wish her that degree of harm. The police said that she had been very, very lucky. Nobody who had been in the cottage at the time could have survived.

Helen had told Oliver that she had booked a flight on the following day from Dorval to Shannon. Would he meet the link flight in Dublin? It would be nice if they could talk things over, she said calmly. Oliver admired the calm, and agreed that it would be nice to talk things over.

'There'll have to be some straight talk with Helen,' said Oliver to Alice. 'We've agreed until now that we should keep what we know and what we've guessed to ourselves. Things are different. She'll have to be told what we know. It's necessary for her protection.'

'I agree,' said Alice. 'Also Ulick. He'll have to know, too.'

'Why? There'll be hellish complications if he starts jumping into the mess with both feet.'

'There are hellish complications already. It can't get much worse. He'll jump anyway. If he knows the whole story, there's a chance at least that he'll jump in the right place.'

'All right. Have you any new ideas?'

'Not many. Have you?'

'None at all. Except that if we go through the thing piece by piece we might get it into some sort of shape. God alone knows what shape.'

'OK,' said Alice. 'You do the talking. I'm sorry, Oliver, I'm not much good at this at the moment. I'm run ragged about the girls.'

'It could help them if we get it right.'

'Well, you try to get it right. I'll add what I can.'

Oliver looked at the ally he admired, noted her despond, and felt momentarily even more ferocious. Then he established control of himself. 'We'll start with the Sepelov programme of harassment, minor violence – whatever we call it – designed to worry us, frighten us, short of actually killing someone.'

'That bomb might have killed Helen.'

'Probably a miscalculation. It was pure chance that she went to the cottage when she did.'

'He might miscalculate again.'

'He might. But let's take the reasoning behind the whole thing. Something's clearly happened to make Sepelov no longer care whether or not his wartime dirty linen goes on public display. He's confident that although we know, as he intends us to know, who's responsible for what's happening, he's leaving no evidence that would stand half a chance of being believed in a court. Taking the two together, and aside from Ulick in the Park, he's so far got away with everything he wants to get away with. It's hard to understand his change in thinking. After all, Helen and I did effectively shut him up for over thirty years.'

'Perhaps he's gone mad. Or senile.'

'The less said about senility in my presence the better. But you might have a point. Suppose that he calculates that he hasn't long to go, and he doesn't give a damn so long as he can pay off a few old scores?'

'He wouldn't want to expose the Foundation to damage. It's been his whole life.'

'Well, modify it. Suppose that he calculates, or has been advised, that if we blow it we haven't enough material to make it stick.'

'It was enough to frighten him before. What's changed?'

'Times. He was setting himself up then. Couldn't risk even a ripple in the pool. By now it may not matter. He must be personally on the way out, and his operations are either over or so well developed that they're impossible to upset. And, anyway, what I tried on him was largely bluff. I had no hard evidence to put forward.'

Alice stirred her coffee, frowned, pondered. 'Give this a thought,' she said at last. 'If you're right, and Sepelov really thinks that you've nothing to scare the pants off him with, then Sepelov's wrong. There's a lot of unused stuff lying about. There's your chum Jock Wemyss and your birthday story for a start. Sepelov and the Abwehr in Paris would make a good read. An experienced journalist should be able to dress it up enough to keep clear of the libel. . . .'

'I don't know any journalists. Experienced or otherwise.'

'I do. There's one well into the act already. Smithy. He could throw in bits of Mikic and Jovanovic to add to the weight. Leaving out all references to Hugo Burke.'

'Is that possible? To be selective without bringing Hugo into it?'

'I don't see why not. I'll have to take another look at the stuff first, though.'

'Your idea is to leak all this to the press and. . . .'

'Or threaten to. Your old vague blackmail, but this time with real teeth to it.'

'You're a devious young scoundrel, Alice Burke,' said Oliver in admiration.

'I'm a mother protecting her young,' said Alice, patting her tummy.

Oliver watched her as she left the sitting-room, and thought thoughts about the female of the species being more deadly than the male. Some of Kipling was insufferable. Some was timelessly apt. He heard the sound of her on the telephone. Most of it filtered through the door as murmurs, but she raised her voice in a farewell. 'Thanks, Smithy,' she said. 'Tomorrow, then.' She returned looking pleased with herself. She looked him in the eye and said: 'You're looking pleased with yourself.'

'I was thinking of a bit of Kipling. You reminded me of it.'

'You and your reactionary Imperialist mates. I can't imagine a thing he could have said that applies to me.'

'A woman is only a woman,' said Oliver, 'but a good cigar is a smoke.'
'We'd better concentrate on making sure that when it comes to
slaughter, Smithy does his work on water,' said Alice. 'He's flying over
tomorrow.'

Oliver kissed his sister when she was through Customs at the airport and
thought, as he always did when they met, what a remarkably attractive
woman she still was. She was into her sixties, but it gave him a silly,
irrational pride to be seen with her, to be identified with her, just as it had
over forty years before when he had been in his last year at Trinity, and
she had been a lovely and lively young girl just out of school, up from the
country to join his party at some dance or celebration, with him cast by
their mother in the hopeless role of the male equivalent of a chaperone.
He had been magnanimously inefficient at the task, and Helen had been
grateful.

Helen, elegant and composed, walked beside him to the carpark, no
surface indication that she had missed being blown to pieces less than
forty-eight hours previously. He explained Ulick's absence while he put
her bags into the boot of his car.

'Ulick's apologies. I wanted to speak to you alone, and Alice wants to
speak to Ulick alone, so I volunteered as taxi-driver. There's a lot of
breast-baring to be done before we all get together to try to work
something out. Unless we all know the same things there'll be
confusion.'

She seemed to be mildly amused, but raised no disagreement.

'We'll have tea at the Club,' said Oliver. 'I hope you're not too jet-
lagged. What I have to tell you is complicated, and some of it could be
pretty harrowing for you.'

Helen smiled, a tranquil smile. 'I know a thing or two about being
harrowed,' she said. There was neither pomposity nor self-pity in the
comment.

At that time in the afternoon they had the drawing-room, high ceiling,
prints, chintz, shining silver and polished dark wood, to themselves.
They sat side by side in front of the fire, with a pot of tea and buttered
toast. Oliver talked. It was a very long talk.

With one exception, he told her everything, in the order in which it
had happened or had been discovered. The finding by Ulick of the date
on Hugo's headstone. Alice's investigations. All the evidence collected or
chanced upon. The statements of Mikic and Rashidov recorded by
Smithy. He reserved Milan Jovanovic and the frontier crossing for later
use or, possibly, suppression, depending upon her reaction to the rest of
it.

Helen sipped at her tea, looking absorbed but unflustered. When

314

Oliver had finished she stared silently at the fire for a while. Then she said: 'I assumed that she'd found out most of it. I wasn't sure how much.'

He wasn't really surprised. 'How did you guess?'

Helen laughed, an affectionate, indulgent, motherly laugh. 'When Ulick was last in Ottawa, the time he put on that television turn of his, he was like a cat on hot bricks. He obviously wanted to ask me something, and I was pretty sure what it was and gave him plenty of openings. But he always backed out at the last moment. With relief. He'd fall back on talking skiing. Or golf.'

'Why didn't you just tell him?'

'I nearly did. Or, at least, about the basic fact of the rape. But I couldn't bring myself to do it, either. Whether because of maternal concern or pure cowardice I still don't know. I knew it had to be done, but I postponed it.'

She gazed at the fire again, and then poured herself another cup of tea, slowly, thoughtfully.

'As you know as well as I do,' she said at last, 'one of the advantages of growing older is that you can look back with detachment on earlier events that practically devastated you at the time. The hurt gets dulled by forgetfulness, and overlaid by the preoccupations of daily living. I can now talk with detachment about what nearly destroyed me. Talk to you, at any rate. You already knew most of it, from the early days. You and Alice worked out the rest, and discarded it as too improbable. You may have got a few details wrong, but your central finding was right. Hugo wasn't killed in Italy.'

Oliver felt a pang of distress. It apparently showed.

'Don't be upset on my behalf,' said Helen evenly, 'not any longer. I'm beyond it myself. The strange thing is that when I was far from detached, and tried to tell people about Hugo, no one believed me. None of you. You, that marvellous Gert Laing who I treated so appallingly, the doctors in that loony-bin in Dublin. When I said that the man who raped me was Hugo, you all dismissed it as deluded wishful thinking by a half-mad young widow who'd been through too much. I don't blame you. The fact of the matter is that it *was* Hugo. I've never mentioned the details before, but I'll tell you now. I was knocked out by someone I didn't see. I recovered consciousness towards the end of it. A woman who's loved a man, and has loved making love with him, *knows* that man's body. The knowing was emphasised on this occasion because I'd recently been making love with a body I didn't love. And since we're being frank I'll tell you that I responded to Hugo, almost like in a dream. Only it wasn't a dream, because when he was finished he spoke to me.'

'*Spoke* to you?'

'Yes,' said Helen. 'He said, "You faithless bitch," and gave me a backhander around the face. And then he said: "I might be back at some time in the future, but don't bet on it." And then he disappeared.'

Helen took a handkerchief from her handbag. She dabbed at her eyes. 'I'm sorry,' she said. 'I was overconfident about the detachment. It was all a long time ago. But it still hurts.'

Oliver, wordless, took her hand and held it. Later she did skilful things with a powder puff and examined the results in a small mirror. She seemed to find them satisfactory. She put the compact back in her handbag.

'Since we've at last got down to all this,' she said with composure, 'I'd better give you a definitive postscript. There's a point to be cleared up. There may be some doubt in your mind about whether Hugo or the other man I'd slept with was Ulick's father. Well, I took precautions with the other one, and made sure that he took them, too. And, what's more, unlike some precautions these worked. I'd just finished my period when Hugo attacked me. Hugo was Ulick's father.'

The hall porter came into the room and removed the tray, remarking critically upon the weather while he did so. Helen endorsed his opinion.

Oliver fastened his gaze on the fire again, and then looked up. 'Can you take any more?' he asked. It was time to quote from Jovanovic, and he hated the thought.

'Oh, yes. I've had my little weep,' said Helen. She achieved a smile.

He told her of Hugo's wound at the frontier mountain stream, of Sepelov's insistence that survival for the majority must take precedence over essential surgery for Hugo, of the comatose Hugo's journey to Buenos Aires, of his admission to the hospital there.

She listened gravely, no interruption. At the end of it she was silent once more for a long time. Then she said: 'I thought it probably finished in some way like that.'

'Finished? He might have recovered.'

'He didn't,' said Helen with finality. 'If he had, he'd have forgiven me. And, somehow, we'd have been reunited.' And this time she really broke down, into tearing, racking sobs.

'Alice is breaking things gently to Ulick,' said Oliver, as he drove them through the mass of traffic in Pembroke Road.

'I wish her luck,' said Helen with a mother's objectivity. 'I've never been able to break anything gently to Ulick in his life. He misunderstands most of it, and gets his teeth into one bit that's maybe important, but it's a different bit from the one you're trying to tell him about.'

'I recognise the symptoms,' said Oliver, an uncle, less objective.

'How much is she telling him?'

'As much as he can take in at one go. She was hoping that you'd do some of the difficult bits.'

'I'll do my share,' said Helen. 'I've ducked it for too long. I'll consult Alice. I'm very fond of Alice.'

'So am I,' said Oliver.

Helen chuckled.

Helen, with a smile of happiness, kissed Ulick and hugged Alice, and hugged Brigid and Orla. There were drinks and family chat, and no mention of malevolent intimidation and decisions to be taken. Smithy arrived by taxi and was introduced by Alice to Oliver and Helen. He shook hands formally with Oliver and said: 'Hi, Mrs Burke.'

'Hi, Smithy.'

'Didn't know you two knew one another,' said Alice.

'He was always trying to con me into becoming a stooge for Burke Foundation publicity. He was unsuccessful.'

'I've given that up now,' said Smithy.

'I heard,' said Helen, and began to laugh.

Alice looked worriedly at Ulick. He had not said a word throughout these affable proceedings.

After the girls had said goodnight and had gone up to bed Helen took Ulick to a corner and attempted to break the news of his origins as gently as she could. From his continued silence it was impossible to tell whether he had understood or not. Alice took Smithy into another corner and had a long talk with him. Smithy looked respectfully at Oliver. Oliver called the meeting to order.

'We've a lot to discuss,' he said in his best chairman's manner, 'and unless we do it in a logical sequence we'll be here all night.'

He took an envelope from his pocket. 'I've jotted down some headings,' he said. 'I'll read them out. If anyone else wants to suggest a few more, just say so and we'll see where they fit in. If we start. . . .'

'Sir. There's probably a shorter way,' said Smithy.

Oliver, a chairman interrupted before he had reached Item One, looked insulted. 'What shorter way?'

'If what you want to do is fix Sepelov,' said Smithy, 'I've fixed him.'

Nobody said anything. Ulick seemed to have given up saying things for the time being, and the rest of them couldn't think of anything to say.

Smithy courteously started the conversational ball rolling again.

'Alice, can I have a drink?' he asked. 'Standard conditions. First of an upper limit of two.'

'I'll get it,' said Ulick. It was his first remark for two hours.

Oliver put his envelope back in his pocket without regret and said: 'OK, Smithy. You tell us.'

Smithy sank a large slug of his drink, nodded appreciatively and told them. 'Well, a week ago,' he said, 'I went back on a quick trip to Ottawa.

To check the background on some leads I'd picked up in Munich and Rome. I ran into a couple of guys who'd been in my PR outfit in the Foundation. We went off for a few drinks.' He grinned at Alice.

'I didn't have Alice to keep me in order, so it all went on for a bit. We were in one of those gloomy, bare boozing-factories that pass for pubs in Ottawa, and in came another guy I recognised. He'd obviously been at the sauce seriously, and he got straight back to it, still seriously. Alone. His name was Charbonneau. He was in the Foundation, too. He was the fellow I once mentioned to Alice and Oolick, who worked with a desiccated old bag looking after Sepelov's classified registry.'

'The one with a crewcut who looked like an ex-Mountie?'

'Gee, Alice, what a memory. That's him. Well, in view of the way in which I'd left the Sepelov employment the guys I was with didn't want to be seen by Charbonneau in my company, so they sensibly said goodnight and went. And since, unrestrained by Alice, I was feeling alcoholically intrepid, I went over to Charbonneau's table and slapped him on the back. I expected a pretty chilly reception from him. He was, after all, a leading loyalist in the Sepelov Supporters Club, and I was ready with a rather good comeback I'd thought of if he said something nasty. It wasn't like that at all. He asked me to sit down and join him. He was even farther on than I'd thought he'd been. It seemed he was having trouble with his conscience. So I ordered a couple more to help his conscience along a little, and kept 'em coming.'

Smithy took another swig from his glass, measuring his intake with care and checking the residual level against the time shown on his watch.

'Charbonneau became more and more chatty about his conscience. His problem turned out to be over a conflict of loyalties. He had to tell someone about it, he said, and he was glad to have me to do it to because, although we'd hardly exchanged a word in the old days, he'd always thought of me as a straight guy. Unlike some. There was a lot of confused stuff like that. It seemed that the introduction to his problem had been by way of his teenaged daughter. Sweet kid, he said, but unluckily she got herself in the family way. While still in Grade Twelve at High School. She got pretty desperate about it, but had the sense to tell him. He was upset, but he was a proper sort of father. He started working on ways to help her. Unfortunately, there was a hitch. His wife was one of those old-style French-Canadian Catholics who treat virginity like the Holy Grail. There was a lot of ranting and screaming and tears, and eventually Ma Charbonneau socked the poor kid in the face and threw her out. Said she wouldn't have a slut like that befouling a Christian home. So old Charbonneau calmed the kid down and took her to a motel for a few nights, and asked around a bit and turned up some organisation run by rather more Christian Christians than Madame Charbonneau, who cared for unmarried pregnant Catholic girls who didn't believe in abortion.

318

This lot. . . . Mrs Burke, how far can I go?'

Helen was looking uneasy. She stayed quietly in thought for a while and said: 'Is it essential?'

'Afraid so,' said Smithy, 'if this is to make sense.'

'All right,' said Helen reluctantly, 'but not to be mentioned outside this room. By anybody.'

She looked at each of them in turn, embarrassed, pleading almost.

'It won't be mentioned outside this room,' said Chairman Oliver firmly, 'whatever the hell it is. By anyone. Go on, Smithy.'

'To cut it short, this organisation lined up one of its members and she took the kid in. Into her own home. Treated her like she'd treat her own daughter. No condemnation, but friendly talk, advice, medical care arranged, schooling attended to, and old Papa Charbonneau welcome to drop in whenever he liked. Which was often. Charbonneau reckoned you were the nearest thing to perfection he'd ever met, Mrs Burke. He still prays for you every day. So does Celestine. . . .'

'Smithy, please don't. . . .'

'Sorry. But I had to say enough to register one half of Charbonneau's dilemma. The other half of it came out much later in a blurred sort of manner when I was beginning to feel fairly blurred myself. The essence of the Charbonneau Morton's Fork was that in the course of his duties as the trusted confidential archivist to a man he revered as the greatest commie-bashing hero of all time he found himself filing away papers about a scheme to terrify the wits out of a person he grades in precedence a short head behind the Mother of God. Enough to drive anyone to the bottle. Talking about which, Alice, can I have my second scoop now?'

'Not until you tell us what happened next,' said Alice.

'I gave him some advice,' said Smithy, 'and also a couple more shots of Bourbon. He took the advice after he'd taken the Bourbon. He went off to the Foundation offices and made photocopies of a random selection of entries in the file and gave them to me. In private. In the dark part of the carpark. The deal was that I'd use them to stop Sepelov from harming Mrs Burke, on the strict condition that I wouldn't risk compromising Charbonneau as the source. It all seemed easy after about half a bottle of Bourbon. It looked much trickier on the following day.'

'It must have looked bloody impossible on the following day,' said Oliver.

'I suppose it did,' said Smithy. 'And I was pretty slow on the uptake, too. There was material in the file about how the cover-up would operate and a list of all your names as nominees for unpleasant things to be done to you. But no details of what form the unpleasantness would take. And no indication of when it was due to start. So I kept an eye open for signs or reports of visible damage to Mrs Burke, and when there seemed to be none assumed that there was time in hand. For me to work out how to settle Sepelov without landing poor old Charbonneau up the creek. I didn't realise that things had already started off here in Ireland. I was back in Munich, still trying to puzzle it out, when I heard that Mrs Burke's cottage had gone off bang. So I became active, before it got worse. Now, Alice, can I . . .?'

'For God's sake give the man a drink,' said Oliver. 'And don't restrict it to him. A few more of us could do with one, too.'

Ulick, still silent, again went to get them. He passed them around, stood briefly near the door and went out. Oliver sipped reflectively at his whiskey.

'Smithy at the beginning said that he'd fixed Sepelov,' said Oliver. 'I've no doubt he has. He's a very enterprising chap. What intrigues me is the technical side of the thing. We old coal-fired blackmailers from the Dark Ages like to know how the nuclear-powered lot set about the job. How *do* you put on pressure when you can't quote what the reason for the pressure is?'

'You don't,' said Smithy. 'You rely on something else. You trust your luck. Mikic died. He left no family. Once he was dead there was no chance of reprisals. I cut out a few bits from my note of what he'd said to me that might stimulate a question or two about Hugo Burke, and posted the rest of it to Sepelov. I typed a covering letter on headed paper I'd pinched from a hotel in Paris. I didn't sign it. It said that, unless Sepelov laid off from a few unnamed people he seemed to have it in for, copies of Mikic's memoirs would go by the next post to every newspaper in North America and Europe. I asked for an acknowledgement that he'd got and understood the message, and would comply.'

'Acknowledge how?' asked Oliver, interested.

'In the personal column of every damned paper I could think of,' said Smithy. 'I spent some time devising a suitable reply for him. In the end I picked: "Andy's contrite."'

'Is Andy contrite?'

'That's what it said in the classified ads.'

'We'd have made a great partnership, Smithy,' said Oliver.

'You pioneered the genre, sir,' said Smithy respectfully.

Oliver said, 'H'm,' and looked self-satisfied.

Everybody else looked self-satisfied, too, until Ulick put a stop to it. He returned to the room holding a hand-grip and wearing an anorak, and he made a statement that was impressive.

'I was told a lot of stuff earlier this afternoon by Alice,' Ulick said slowly, 'and I can't say that I understood all of it. And I've listened to a lot of talk this evening and I've probably missed the point of some of that, too. But there's one point that I haven't missed that it seems to me the rest of you have. Sepelov, aside from scaring one of my daughters, and worrying my pregnant wife, and taking a chance that might have killed my mother, actually *did* kill my father. Sepelov refused him the medical treatment that was his only hope.'

Ulick paused and glanced around him, seemingly not quite in focus. Alice at once felt very frightened. The last time that she had seen that expression on Ulick's face had been a few weeks before, after those telephone calls, when Ulick had said, and meant it, that if he laid hands on the caller he'd crucify the bastard.

'I've been looking up timetables while you were talking,' said Ulick. It was a flat, murderous monotone. 'There's a flight to Montreal from London at two in the morning. I'm off to see Sepelov.'

He did not say goodbye. He closed the door gently. Half a minute later they heard his car starting.

EPILOGUE

I

HELEN, after an unusually protracted holiday with Oliver in his gate-lodge, had once given him a thank-you present of a portable radio. It was an expensive and elaborate apparatus, capable of picking up transmissions from almost anywhere in the world. Oliver had rarely used it. After Ulick's sudden departure for Canada, Oliver listened to it twice a day, tuned in to the wavelength of CBC Ottawa.

On the fourth day he heard the news that he had hoped not to hear. Word was just coming in, said the newsreader, of a shoot-out at the Rockcliffe Park home of Andrei Sepelov, the Director-General of the prestigious Burke Foundation. Sepelov himself was dead, and so was a man assumed by the police to have been his assailant. The second body had yet to be identified conclusively, but papers found in his pocket indicated that his name was Burke.

Oliver switched off miserably and prepared himself for the breaking of unbearable news.

II

The Coroner's summing-up reduced the evidence presented in the course of a complete morning's hearings to a brief chronological reconstruction of events, followed by speculation about what had motivated the late assailant, Burke.

Evidence from Mrs Dudgeon, the daily cleaner, had established that the late Mr Sepelov lived alone in his house in Mariposa Avenue, Rockcliffe Park. She prepared his breakfast, and he habitually ate lunch and dinner out. On the night of his death he had dined at the Cercle Universitaire. He had said goodnight to friends there at about 10.45 p.m., and had presumably driven straight home. At any rate, the police investigating on the following day had found his car in his garage, the block-heater plugged in, the garage door locked and the lights switched off, all factors suggesting a routine and unexceptional return.

Mrs Dudgeon had let herself into the house at about 7.30 on the next morning. Despite her shock at what she saw, she behaved with praise-worthy good sense and self-control. She telephoned first Mr Sepelov's doctor and then the police. She then returned to both bodies, one in a chair behind the desk in the study, one on the floor in the doorway between the study and the hall, and concluded that her earlier impression that both men were dead was correct.

Dr Maxwell, when he arrived, gave professional confirmation of this. Both men, he had said in evidence, had died of gunshot wounds. Mr Sepelov, at the desk, had been hit in the throat, the right side of the chest, and the thigh. Dr Maxwell had elaborated upon the medical significance of each wound, but in the present summary it was sufficient to say only that Mr Sepelov had not died instantly. He had lived for anything up to twenty minutes, immobilised in his chair by the thigh wound. The proximate cause of death was analogous to drowning, caused by the ingestion of blood to his lungs from the chest injury.

The man lying in the doorway, who was not known to Dr Maxwell, had been shot in the head, by one round only, and must have died instantly. From the medical testimony alone it was possible to deduce that Burke, the man found in the doorway, had fired first, and that Mr Sepelov, although severely injured, had been able to get in a single, fatal shot.

Police evidence gave credence to this deduction. Sergeant Greer had testified that the bottom right-hand drawer of Mr Sepelov's desk was lying open. Technical analysts at the police laboratory had examined the drawer and had found in it traces of oil that matched that with which Mr Sepelov's Colt .45 pistol had been cleaned. It was a reasonable assump-tion that Mr Sepelov, after being attacked by Burke, had pulled open the drawer, taken out the pistol and fired back. Mr Sepelov's war record demonstrated his courage and resourcefulness. It was not as incongruous as it might seem that even when desperately wounded he should fight back instinctively and effectively against an attacker.

One of the matters that remained unresolved, and in the absence of witnesses would doubtless remain unresolved, was that of Burke's admittance to the house. The police had inspected all windows and both outside doors. There was no sign of forcible entry. Burke could only have been let in by Mr Sepelov. It was a well-known fact, substantiated in police evidence, that Mr Sepelov's political activities had made him enemies, some of whom had threatened violence. Mr Sepelov had scrupulously reported all these threats to the police, but he was a brave and strong-willed man who had declined resolutely all offers of police protection. It was for this reason that he had been licensed to hold a gun. He had also acted on police advice on precautions that he should take against intruders. There were security locks on all his doors and windows, and his house was wired with an alarm system that activated a light and a buzzer in the police station. His front door was reinforced with concealed steel plating. There was a bullet-proof glass peephole in it through which he could identify all callers, and a two-way communication system by which he could talk to them. It must be accepted that Mr Sepelov had recognised Burke and had admitted him to the house voluntarily.

The Coroner, who for the past few minutes had been glancing at his watch with increasing frequency, here recessed the Court for lunch.

III

When the Court resumed, the Coroner proceeded to another unresolved aspect of the case: the relationship between Mr Sepelov and Burke. Nothing brought forward in evidence had established, or even hinted at, how, when or where they had previously known one another, said the Coroner. This gap in the Court's knowledge led in turn to a further puzzle. Who was Burke? He had been described throughout the hearing, and in press reports based on publicity releases from the police before the hearing, as 'Burke' because the only identifiable content of what he brought with him had been a piece of paper recovered from his inside pocket upon which was written: 'I am Burke.' His clothing had been commonplace, labelled with the labels that were attached to standardised garments on sale in every store in Canada. The police, said the Coroner censoriously, had been remiss in their willingness to placate the media. The piece of paper had carried the claim that the man was Burke, but was it not conceivable that a mentally disturbed, aggrieved fanatic, with a grudge against Mr Sepelov and the Foundation of which he had been the head, might have written the name in the expectation that if he were killed on a suicidal mission the use of the name would leave confused doubt in the public mind? It would certainly further the purposes of left-wing opponents of all that the Burke Foundation stood for.

This, however, said the Coroner after he had speculated, was speculation. Their Public Relations lapse aside, the Ontario Provincial Police had behaved with admirable professionalism. They had photographed and fingerprinted the dead man, and had circulated the pictures and prints to every police force in Canada and in the northern United States. The surprising result had been the entry into the story of somebody previously using the name of Slansky. For the bulk of the evidence about Slansky, the Court was indebted to Mr Fraser, the Ground Facilities Superintendent of Vancouver Airport, and to Dr Sweeney, one of the more eminent psychiatrists in practice in British Columbia.

Mr Fraser had read in the newspapers and seen on television accounts of the killings. The description in these reports of the alleged killer of Mr Sepelov had tallied with that of Slansky, a janitor employed by Mr Fraser. Slansky, who held an unbroken attendance record until then, had failed to appear for work for the previous ten days. Mr Fraser, clearly an exemplary employer, had been worried by Slansky's absence, and had tried without success to telephone him at the rooming-house where he lodged. The housekeeper, who described Slansky as quiet, clean, tidy, and a careful payer of rent on time, had said that he had come downstairs one morning with a packed bag and had told her that he would be away 'for about a week'.

The reason for Mr Fraser's concern was an unusual one, and did him credit. He was an active member of a voluntary organisation for the promotion of mental health. One of his contributions to the organisation's aims was to give jobs on the airport staff to former mental patients guaranteed by a panel of consultant psychiatrists to be capable of doing a normal day's work. Slansky had been one of those so recommended, and had worked at the airport for eight years. Mr Fraser had described him as, within the limits of a not too demanding job, something of a star turn, conscientious, helpful and uncomplaining, a walking refutation of the prejudice that held former mental patients to be unreliable and unstable.

Mr Fraser, after rereading several times the newspaper description of the dead man found in Mr Sepelov's house, had telephoned the police. The police had examined Slansky's room at the lodging-house, where they took fingerprints that were later found to match those circulated by the Ontario Provincial Police. They also found there a copy of the *Ottawa Citizen* dated the day before Slansky had packed his bag and left. The main front-page story was of the bomb explosion at Mrs Helen Burke's cottage on Lake Mahon. There were three accompanying photographs: one of the cottage as it had been before the explosion, one of the damage that had been done, and one of Mrs Burke.

Each photograph had been ringed by a ballpoint pen. The name Burke, wherever it appeared in the text of the story and in the captions to the pictures, was underlined. Police forensic tests had established that the pen used was the same as that with which 'I am Burke' was written on the piece of paper found in the pocket of the deceased. It was, of course, unusual for a copy of the *Ottawa Citizen*, the circulation of which was largely local, to have found its way so soon to Vancouver. It needed no great stretch of imagination to conclude that an airport employee could have picked it up after it had been discarded by a passenger on the daily Air Canada flight.

The description, the fingerprinting and the ballpoint pen proved beyond doubt that Burke and Slansky were the same man. What had not been established was whether the man was really called either Burke or Slansky, and what his motive was in attacking Mr Sepelov. The evidence of Dr Sweeney, the psychiatrist, was relevant.

Dr Sweeney had testified that Slansky had been referred to him as a patient in circumstances that were, to say the least, out of the ordinary. A man who declined to give his name had telephoned Dr Sweeney at his clinic and had asked if the doctor would treat a friend of his who had incurred serious head injuries, had undergone extensive surgery, and who was suffering from regressive amnesia. Dr Sweeney had said that he would accept the patient and had asked for further information. The caller had rung off. On the next day three thousand dollars in twenty-dollar bills arrived by registered post, with a typed note attached that read simply: 'Reference our conversation'. On the day after that Slansky presented himself.

Dr Sweeney in his evidence had very properly gone into considerable medical technical detail about Slansky's condition. Reduced to layman's terms, the injuries to Slansky's brain had been caused by what could only have been gunfire, either bullets from small arms or fragments from a shell or mortar-bomb. Dr Sweeney assumed from the condition of the injuries that they dated from the Second World War. It was an assumption, and not transmitted information, because the patient had no recollection of what had happened to him. The doctor had been restrained by the ethics of his profession from being too critical of the quality of the surgery performed, and of the competence of the surgeon who had performed it, but it was clear that he regarded both as unsatisfactory.

The severity of the injuries and the inadequacy of their early treatment had combined to produce in the patient a condition that could best be described as an almost total forgetfulness of everything that preceded the infliction of the damage. He retained the acquired skills possessed by the uninjured. He could, for example, speak, read, write, keep himself clean, drive a car, accept the responsibility of working, tell the time, and so on. But he did not know how he had acquired them. In short, he was an otherwise normal man who did not know who he was, and whose life, in so far as he could remember it, had begun when he was already fully mature. He had one physical disability. He was subject to sudden crippling headaches, usually brought on by periods of mental concentration. It was for this reason that Dr Sweeney had recommended that he should be employed on manual work.

A central part of Dr Sweeney's treatment had been attempts to stimulate the patient's memory by exposing him to contact with what could be guessed to have been facets of his earlier life. These, as Dr Sweeney had put it frankly, had been pretty hit-or-miss ventures. Slansky was clearly an educated man. A tour of Simon Fraser University had evoked in him no response whatsoever. His wounds suggested that he had once been a soldier. Dr Sweeney had taken him to see several movies about the war. These visits had been partially successful. Slansky had shown a familiarity with the weapons portrayed, and had made remarks like 'The noises weren't like that at all', but he was unable to account for his possession of this background knowledge. Several other experiments had been entirely fruitless. One, an attempt to trace Slansky's origins from his speech and accent patterns, had met with some success, but was too broad-based to be of specific use. The doctor had taped a recording of Slansky reading a passage from a book and had given it to a friend who taught speech and drama and was an amateur specialist in the analysis of accents. The findings were that Slansky was from eastern Canada, but had spent some of his early life abroad, probably in Scotland or Ireland. The tantalising thing about these experiments was that, although none of them led very far, and most of them led nowhere, there were enough favourable indications to suggest that if Dr Sweeney could hit on the right stimuli the patient might react to them positively.

The Coroner had rehearsed these experiments at some length because Dr Sweeney had put forward the view that the article and the photographs in the *Ottawa Citizen* had indeed provided the right stimuli. In what way remained obscure. The doctor's guess, and he had stressed that it was no more than a guess, was that Slansky had in fact been named Burke, that the repetition of the name in the article had in some way excited his memory, that mention of Mrs Burke as being a member of the family that had formed the Burke Foundation had caused him to think about the purposes of the Foundation, and that in his mental confusion he had taken the Foundation to be a repository of genealogical information about all Burkes. He had then gone to Ottawa on impulse to try to find out more about himself. He would have had no difficulty in Ottawa in either locating the Foundation's office or in establishing that its Director-General was Mr Sepelov. It would have been equally easy to have looked up Mr Sepelov's address in the telephone directory.

The circumstances that led to the meeting between Burke and Mr Sepelov, and to the resultant tragedy, were incapable of reconstruction. It was not known how Slansky, or Burke, had come into possession of the pistol that he had used, but the slack gun-control legislation in the United States made it notoriously easy to buy hand-guns there. Slansky, or Burke, could have brought one over the Canadian border at any time with little risk of detection.

To sum up, the evidence was regrettably incomplete but it all pointed in one direction. Slansky/Burke, probably but not certainly of unsound mind at the time, had fired the three shots that fatally wounded Mr Sepelov. Mr Sepelov had killed Slansky/Burke in self-defence.

The Coroner would like to convey his sympathy to the relatives of the deceased.

★

327

He was a kindly Coroner, who always made it a practice to convey his sympathies to the relatives of the deceased. On this occasion he did it with more feeling than was his habit because one of the relatives, who had been sitting in the Court throughout the hearing, was plainly in deep distress. His feeling of sympathy was tempered by some puzzlement. He had for years heard gossip about the ill-feeling between Helen Burke and Andrei Sepelov. It was strange to see her weeping silently about his death.

During the evening of the day of the inquest, Helen went to the church in which Hugo's mother, long ago, had prayed first for her son's safety, had later given thanks for his survival, and had later still prayed for his soul. Helen prayed for Hugo's soul.

She also gave thanks for the safety of Ulick. She acknowledged apologetically to God that she had sometimes been troubled by the peculiarities of the son with whom she had been blessed. She now had a better understanding of the intricacies of divine wisdom. A son who habitually lost concentration after reading the first syllable of most words, who set out for Montreal in a mood that was at once murderous and implicitly suicidal, and who arrived in Montevideo after leaving his chequebook and credit cards in the bar at Heathrow Airport, London, might give rise to concern. But he was *alive*.